PRAISE FOR LEE GOLDBERG

PRAISE FOR *GATED PREY*

"The seamy side of California dreaming . . . Goldberg not only ties up . . . but links some of Eve's investigations in ways as disturbing as they are surprising."

—*Kirkus Reviews*

"Lively descriptive prose enhances the tight plot of this episodic crime novel, which reads like a TV show in narrative form. Columbo fans will have fun."

—*Publishers Weekly*

"A great series . . . Eve Ronin continues to dazzle and show her gritty side as she progresses in the Los Angeles Sheriff's Department."

—*Mystery and Suspense Magazine*

"Goldberg finds the perfect balance of treachery and resolve in the strong female character of Eve Ronin. She is a force to be reckoned with that all criminals will hate to come face-to-face with and one that is deserving of the big screen."

—Chris Miller, Best Thriller Books

"Violent crimes and desperate criminals and homicide detectives, oh my! Lee Goldberg delivers an intriguing, fast-paced, satisfying novel in *Gated Prey*."

—Steve Netter, Best Thriller Books

"This is going to be a must-read series for me year after year. Eve is such a badass character who will stop at nothing to see that justice is done."

—Todd Wilkins, Best Thriller Books

PRAISE FOR *LOST HILLS*

"A cop novel so good it makes much of the old guard read like they're going through the motions until they can retire . . . The real appeal here is Goldberg's lean prose, which imbues just-the-facts procedure with remarkable tension and cranks up to a stunning description of a fire that was like 'Christmas in hell.'"

—*Booklist*

"[The] suspense and drama are guaranteed to keep a reader spellbound."

—Authorlink

"An energetic, resourceful procedural starring a heroine who deserves a series of her own."

—*Kirkus Reviews*

"This nimble, sure-footed series launch from bestseller Goldberg . . . builds to a thrilling, visually striking climax. Readers will cheer Ronin every step of the way."

—*Publishers Weekly*

"The first book in what promises to be a superb series—it's also that rare novel in which the formulaic elements of mainstream police procedurals share narrative space with a unique female protagonist. All that, and it's also a love letter to the chaos and diversity of California. There are a lot of series out there, but Eve Ronin and Goldberg's fast-paced prose should put this one on the radar of every crime-fiction fan."

—National Public Radio

"This sterling thriller is carved straight out of the world of Harlan Coben and Lisa Gardner . . . *Lost Hills* is a book to be found and savored."

—BookTrib

"*Lost Hills* is Lee Goldberg at his best. Inspired by the real-world grit and glitz of LA County crime, this book takes no prisoners. And neither does Eve Ronin. Take a ride with her and you'll find yourself with a heroine for the ages. And you'll be left hoping for more."

—Michael Connelly, #1 *New York Times* bestselling author

"*Lost Hills* is what you get when you polish the police procedural to a shine: a gripping premise, a great twist, fresh spins and knowing winks to the genre conventions, and all the smart, snappy ease of an expert at work."

—Tana French, *New York Times* bestselling author

"Thrills and chills! *Lost Hills* is the perfect combination of action and suspense, not to mention Eve Ronin is one of the best new female characters in ages. You will race through the pages!"

—Lisa Gardner, #1 *New York Times* bestselling author

"Twenty-four-karat Goldberg—a top-notch procedural that shines like a true gem."

—Craig Johnson, *New York Times* bestselling author of the Longmire series

"A winner. Packed with procedure, forensics, vivid descriptions, and the right amount of humor. Fervent fans of Connelly and Crais, this is your next read."

—Kendra Elliot, *Wall Street Journal* and Amazon Charts bestselling author

"Brilliant! Eve Ronin rocks! With a baffling and brutal case, tight plotting, and a fascinating look at police procedure, *Lost Hills* is a stunning start to a new detective series. A must-read for crime-fiction fans."

—Melinda Leigh, *Wall Street Journal*
and #1 Amazon Charts bestselling author

"A tense, pacy read from one of America's greatest crime and thriller writers."

—Garry Disher, international bestselling author
and Ned Kelly Award winner

MOVIE
LAND

The Diagnosis Murder Series

The Silent Partner
The Death Merchant
The Shooting Script
The Waking Nightmare
The Past Tense
The Dead Letter
The Double Life
The Last Word

The Monk Series

Mr. Monk Goes to the Firehouse
Mr. Monk Goes to Hawaii
Mr. Monk and the Blue Flu
Mr. Monk and the Two Assistants
Mr. Monk in Outer Space
Mr. Monk Goes to Germany
Mr. Monk Is Miserable
Mr. Monk and the Dirty Cop
Mr. Monk in Trouble
Mr. Monk Is Cleaned Out
Mr. Monk on the Road
Mr. Monk on the Couch
Mr. Monk on Patrol
Mr. Monk Is a Mess
Mr. Monk Gets Even

The Charlie Willis Series

My Gun Has Bullets
Dead Space

The Dead Man Series
(coauthored with William Rabkin)

Face of Evil

Ring of Knives (with James Daniels)

Hell in Heaven

The Dead Woman (with David McAfee)

The Blood Mesa (with James Reasoner)

Kill Them All (with Harry Shannon)

The Beast Within (with James Daniels)

Fire & Ice (with Jude Hardin)

Carnival of Death (with Bill Crider)

Freaks Must Die (with Joel Goldman)

Slaves to Evil (with Lisa Klink)

The Midnight Special (with Phoef Sutton)

The Death March (with Christa Faust)

The Black Death (with Aric Davis)

The Killing Floor (with David Tully)

Colder Than Hell (with Anthony Neil Smith)

Evil to Burn (with Lisa Klink)

Streets of Blood (with Barry Napier)

Crucible of Fire (with Mel Odom)

The Dark Need (with Stant Litore)

The Rising Dead (with Stella Green)

Reborn (with Kate Danley, Phoef Sutton, and Lisa Klink)

The Jury Series

Judgment

Adjourned

Payback

Guilty

Nonfiction

The Best TV Shows You Never Saw
Unsold Television Pilots 1955–1989
Television Fast Forward
Science Fiction Filmmaking in the 1980s
(cowritten with William Rabkin, Randy Lofficier,
and Jean-Marc Lofficier)
The Dreamweavers: Interviews with Fantasy Filmmakers of
the 1980s (cowritten with William Rabkin, Randy Lofficier, and
Jean-Marc Lofficier)
Successful Television Writing (cowritten with William Rabkin)

MOVIE LAND

LEE GOLDBERG

THOMAS & MERCER

Text copyright © 2022 by Adventures in Television, Inc.
All rights reserved.

Published by Thomas & Mercer, Seattle

www.apub.com

Amazon, the Amazon logo, and Thomas & Mercer are trademarks of Amazon.com, Inc., or its affiliates.

ISBN-13: 9781662500657 (hardcover)
ISBN-10: 1662500653 (hardcover)

ISBN-13: 9781662500664 (paperback)
ISBN-10: 1662500661 (paperback)

Cover design by Shasti O'Leary Soudant

Printed in the United States of America

First edition

To Valerie & Maddie

CHAPTER ONE

The most valuable commodity at the Las Virgenes Municipal Water District was the water it piped into the homes and businesses in Calabasas, California, a small city in the southwest end of the San Fernando Valley. But nobody needed to rob the two-story office building to steal those riches. They just had to open a faucet and hold a bucket underneath it. That's what made the break-in so perplexing to Los Angeles County Sheriff's Department detectives Eve Ronin and Duncan "Donuts" Pavone on that unseasonably warm Tuesday morning in April.

They'd been dispatched from the Lost Hills sheriff's station to investigate the crime, which had been phoned in by Wallace Ewell, a water district bureaucrat. He met the detectives in the parking lot beside the broken ground-floor window where the burglar had gained entry to the building. Ewell was in his forties with a meticulously groomed mustache, round-rimmed glasses, and bright-red polish on his manicured fingernails.

"What did the intruder take?" Eve asked, while Duncan, who was nearly two times older and three times heavier than her, shifted his considerable weight impatiently from side to side on his shiny Florsheims.

Ewell cleared his throat and consulted a list on his phone. "Two bags of Doritos, two cartons of Jimmy Dean frozen sausage, a bag of carrots, and a package of Oreos."

Duncan narrowed his eyes at him. "Were the Oreos regular or Double Stuf?"

"I believe it was Double Stuf," Ewell said.

"That makes it a felony."

Ewell didn't seem sure how to take that comment, so he turned to Eve. "This is the second time in three months that he's broken into our break room."

The dull square office building faced Las Virgenes Road, which ran along Malibu Canyon, through the Santa Monica Mountains, and to the Pacific Coast Highway. The back of the building was tucked against rolling hills carpeted with dry mustard grass and dotted with fire-scorched oaks that looked to Eve like blackened crucified skeletons. The hills buttressed a ridge topped by a gated community of multimillion-dollar tract homes, where Eve and Duncan were recently involved in a sting operation to entrap a gang of home invaders that went violently wrong. It was why Duncan had a hairline scar on his cheek and Eve endured a persistent low-level ringing in her ears. She didn't mention her problem to anyone. They'd both just returned to active duty and she didn't want to give the captain an excuse to keep her at a desk one minute longer.

"Did the burglar take anything besides food?" she asked. "Computers? Money? Cell phones?"

"Just a blue cable-knit wool sweater that I kept in my office. Sometimes the AC can get too frosty," Ewell said. "Oh, and a Harry Bosch novel I was reading at lunch."

Duncan nodded. "You should change the name."

Ewell said, "I don't understand."

"Maybe if you didn't call it a break room, he wouldn't break in. It's almost like you're asking for it."

Ewell put his hands on his hips, signaling that a reprimand was coming. Eve noticed that the pleats of his slacks were sharp enough to draw blood. "There's nothing funny about this, Detective. Our employees feel violated."

Eve spoke up before Duncan could reply and escalate the situation.

"Please forgive my partner. He's retiring in two weeks. It makes him giddy." It made her worried. She was twenty-six, the youngest robbery-homicide detective in the department's history, and she'd come to rely on Duncan's experience to make up for her own lack of it. "I can assure you that we are taking this burglary very seriously."

"Then shouldn't you be taking an impression of the shoe print?" Ewell pointed to the base of the hill, where several perfect shoe prints were pressed into the moist dirt. "We have a broken sprinkler, so this area is always muddy. He left tracks all over the break room carpet. You can run the shoe prints through If Tread."

"If what?" Duncan asked.

"I-F-T-R-D, the International Footwear Tread Reference Database. I saw it on *NCIS* last night. The treads are like fingerprints. You can ID the shoes in seconds, locate the local store he bought them from, geo-track the RFID chip in the credit card he used, and find out where he is right now."

Duncan scratched the faint scar on his cheek in apparent bewilderment. "What do you mean, geo-track?"

Ewell sighed. "You can use GPS to pinpoint his exact location. Then you can use the store's surveillance video to run his face through facial-recognition software, cross-match it with the DMV photo database, and bam, you have him."

"Wow." Duncan nodded, impressed, and looked at Eve. "I could have made my job so much easier if I'd started watching *NCIS* years ago."

She glared at Duncan, who was needlessly teasing Ewell, making trouble. "Can you please get the impression kit from the car so we can lift this shoe print?"

"Sure." Duncan ambled over to their car, a plain-wrap Dodge Charger, and popped the trunk.

Ewell shook his head at Duncan's back and shifted his gaze to Eve. "It's a good thing he's retiring. He's totally out of touch."

"Don't be fooled, Mr. Ewell. People underestimate Columbo, too," she said.

"Columbo is fictional," he said.

"I'm just making a point," she said. "Why didn't the alarm go off during the burglary?"

"He broke the glass and climbed in without opening the window. The window frame is alarmed, but not the glass itself, and we don't have motion detectors. We have him on video, though. He's wearing a hoodie and gloves, so forget about fingerprints. CSI might be able to lift some hair and fibers. When is the team getting here?"

"Unfortunately, they don't respond to property crimes of this nature." Eve handed him her card. "Could you email me the video and photos of the muddy footprints?"

"I'd be glad to." He ran his finger over the embossed sheriff's badge on her card. "How long do you think it will take to get a hit from If Tread and act on that?"

"Things don't move as fast as they do on TV and the crime lab is pretty backed up. They have to prioritize cases, so it could be quite some time."

Likely decades, if ever. Hundreds of rape kits had been sitting on shelves for years, waiting to be tested. Nobody would ever take the time to analyze forensic evidence in the theft of frozen Jimmy Dean sausages from an office break room.

Ewell stiffened with anger. "Does he have to kill someone before this crime gets attention?"

"Let's hope it doesn't come to that," Eve said as Duncan returned holding what looked like a large cookie cutter in one hand and a bag of Sirchie Shake-N-Cast in the other.

"But it could," Duncan said, handing her the cookie cutter. "It's not a big leap from stealing Doritos to homicide. Nacho cheese is a well-known gateway drug, especially if it's the flaming-hot stuff."

Ewell was no fool. He knew he was being ridiculed. "I have work to do. Water is an essential resource. Unlike some people, we never rest."

He marched back into the building, Duncan looking after him with a grin.

Eve pressed the cookie cutter over the footprint, creating a square border around it. "I'm glad you're amusing yourself."

She held her hand out for the bag of Shake-N-Cast, which contained a unique plaster powder inside and an "easy-break" capsule of water premeasured to create just the right amount of slurry to capture the impression of a single shoe- or footprint.

"Are you really going to waste valuable plaster taking an impression that will never be analyzed?"

The Shake-N-Cast cost about eighteen dollars a bag but the money didn't come out of her pocket, so what did she care? She tipped her head to the security camera mounted in the building's eaves. "I'm sure he's watching and I'll still be working here after you retire. I don't need to be on another bureaucrat's shit list. I am on enough of them already."

He handed her the bag, which she crushed between her hands, breaking the capsule of water inside. Then she shook and gently kneaded the bag to mix the contents.

A paramedic unit and fire truck roared by, heading south on Las Virgenes Road, sirens wailing. After it passed, Duncan said, "Be sure to share this compelling case with the *Ronin* writing staff in our meeting tonight. It could be a two-part episode."

Any mention of the TV show being developed about Eve's exploits made her uncomfortable and reminded her how intricately her career was entwined with the media.

A little over eight months ago, while Eve was off duty and bike riding along Mulholland Highway, she saw actor Blake Largo, who played the invincible Deathfist in a string of globally successful movies, beating a woman in a restaurant parking lot. Eve stepped in, he took a swing at her, and she put him on the ground in one smooth move, an incident onlookers livestreamed with their phones. The video of a lean, blue-eyed, pixie-haired young woman in a skintight bike jersey and shorts easily subduing Deathfist went viral, making her a popular sensation at a time when the Los Angeles County Sheriff's Department was being rocked by one ugly, headline-making scandal after another. Eve used her widespread popularity to convince the sheriff, who was desperate to distract the public from the scandals, to promote her to robbery-homicide, making her the youngest woman in the department's history to wear that badge. The strategy worked, pushing the scandals out of the daily news cycle. It was a win for the department, the sheriff, and Eve.

The first homicide case she solved ended with another viral video, this time shot by a firefighter, of her running from a raging wildfire in Malibu Creek State Park with a child in her arms. That captivating image, coupled with the bizarre case behind it, led Hollywood producers to scramble to develop a TV series based on her. She hated the idea but agreed to cooperate to control how she was portrayed. But mostly she did it because she needed the money to pay the legal fees in a $10 million wrongful-death suit filed against her by the widow of a deputy who'd killed himself after Eve exposed his involvement in covering up a rape.

Eve had arranged for Duncan to become a technical adviser on the TV show when he retired so she could concentrate on doing her job, which now meant tearing open the perforated top of the Shake-N-Cast bag and pouring the liquid mix into the cookie-cutter mold to capture the burglar's shoe print.

"Don't mock the show," Eve chided Duncan. "You're going to make more as a technical adviser than you ever did as a detective. Frankly, I'm surprised you aren't feeling an immediate emotional connection to this burglary."

"Why is that?"

"I know how much you love Double Stuf Oreos." Eve balled up the empty Shake-N-Cast bag and looked for a garbage can. They had some time to kill. It would take thirty minutes for the plaster to set so they could lift it from the ground, and then another twenty-four hours for it to harden enough at her desk to send to the lab, not that she ever would.

"Actually, I'm delighted we got assigned this break-in instead of a deputy," he said. "Hunting a junk-food burglar who likes to read crime novels is a nice, low-key way to spend my last weeks on the job, especially after what you've put me through."

"What is *that* supposed to mean?" She lobbed the empty bag into a garbage can by the lobby door.

"I've sustained more injuries in the months I've been partnered with you than I have in my thirty years in the department. I don't want to become a cliché, the retiring cop who gets killed the day before he walks out the door."

"So take your banked vacation time, retire today, and avoid working the next two weeks altogether."

"If I wanted to do that, I wouldn't have come back after getting my face slashed and my arm broken on our last big case."

"So why *did* you come back?"

"I want to go out the way I came in: doing my job." His work phone vibrated in his pocket with a distinctive ring that was different from his personal cell. He took it out and answered, then listened for a few seconds. His expression darkened. "We'll be right there."

"What is it?" Eve asked as he pocketed his phone again.

"Captain Dubois. Hikers found a seriously injured woman in Malibu Creek State Park. She's been shot."

The park entrance was only two miles south on Las Virgenes Road from where they stood. The two of them dashed to the car. Eve got into the driver's seat, started the ignition, hit the lights and siren, and peeled out.

CHAPTER TWO

All of Los Angeles County was like a vast Hollywood studio back lot, with movies and TV shows being shot everywhere, but Malibu Creek State Park actually was one for decades, before Twentieth Century Fox donated the land to the state in 1975.

The craggy mountains, rolling hills, deep canyons, vast meadows, and oak forests had doubled for such places as the Scottish Highlands, the Philippines, deepest Africa, rural Maine, war-torn Korea, the Swiss Family Robinson's island, the paradise of Shangri-La, postapocalyptic Earth, and various alien planets. *How Green Was My Valley, Logan's Run, Doctor Dolittle, M*A*S*H, Lost Horizon*, and *Planet of the Apes* were all shot there.

Now a woman had been, too.

The park entrance was a few yards south of the intersection of Las Virgenes Road and the famous Mulholland Highway, the rural two-lane road that snaked from the eastern edge of Calabasas, southwest along the steep contours of the Santa Monica Mountains above Malibu Creek State Park, before dipping south and ending in the crashing surf at Leo Carrillo State Beach.

Eve made a sharp right into the park, came to a hard stop at the guard shack, and lowered her window to speak to the park ranger, a young man in a crisp uniform wearing a wide-brimmed hat. She flashed her badge at him and introduced herself.

"Where's the injured woman?"

The ranger gestured to the west. "She's in the dry creek bed, near the rock pond. Head straight down the road toward the campground, past the second parking area, and you'll see a dirt road to your right. That's the old Crags Road. Take the right and follow the road until you see the fire engine and paramedics. A ranger is waiting for you at the scene."

Duncan leaned across Eve so the ranger could see him. "Lock down the park. Nobody in or out besides law enforcement, park rangers, and emergency medical personnel."

"The park is over eight thousand unfenced acres."

"Do what you can," Duncan said and sat back.

Eve sped on, past the parking lots, and turned onto the dirt road, which followed the northern boundary of a large meadow and on through an oak canopy, the trees blackened where they'd been licked by flames. She was surprised by how resilient the trees were and how quickly nature reclaimed the scorched earth with new growth.

The road spilled out to a wide clearing, a dirt parking area with four portable bathrooms that overlooked the dry, chalk-white creek bed and a wooden bridge. To the west, the creek ran into the brush and rocks between two steep ridges.

A park ranger's pickup, a fire engine, and a paramedic unit were parked in the lot. Eve parked beside them. She and Duncan got out and walked to the embankment above the dry creek bed, where two paramedics crouched over a bloody naked woman sprawled on her back. A couple of hikers in their twenties stood off to one side, watching in grim fascination.

Eve turned to Duncan. "Where's the ranger?"

"Good question. I'll get a statement from those two." He gestured to the couple. "You handle the victim."

Eve went down to the creek to get a closer look at the woman, and recognized her immediately. The victim was Zena Faust, an activist blogger for the *Malibu Beat* who was a harsh critic of the Lost Hills sheriff's station, local politicians, developers, and celebrities. And Eve thought Faust was usually right.

It was always disturbing for Eve to see the victim of a violent assault, but this time it was someone she knew. It was shocking, even more so, it seemed to Eve, because Faust was completely naked. The injured woman couldn't have been more exposed or vulnerable than she was at that moment. Her arms were sleeved with tattoos and her ears, nose, lips, and nipples were pierced with either rings or studs. Her upper body was peppered with small circular wounds, clearly the result of a shotgun blast at relatively close range. Faust's right leg was twisted at an unnatural angle.

Eve knew the paramedics, too, from a prior case. They were Jamie Dundas and Rick Gage. Jamie injected something into the IV line in Faust's arm while Rick splinted her broken leg.

Eve used her phone to photograph Faust, her position in the creek, and the wounds on her body. She'd learned from past experience how important crime scene photographs, taken immediately upon arrival, could become in an investigation. Details she didn't see now, in the chaos of the moment, would be clear on the photos. She pocketed her phone and crouched beside Faust.

"Zena, it's Eve Ronin. Do you remember me?"

Faust looked up at Eve, her eyes wide and terrified. But Eve saw the recognition.

"You have to help . . ." Faust's voice was weak, her breathing raw. It sounded as if she were sucking air through a bag of broken glass. Eve glanced at her chest, at the blood bubbling out, and wondered whether pellets had punctured a lung.

"I will, I promise. Can you tell me what happened?"

"Not me. Kim. My girlfriend. You have to help her. She's still back there."

"Back where?"

"The pond. We were swimming last night . . . He shot us when we came out."

Eve glanced to the west, where the creek bed disappeared into the wooded ravine, and she noticed drops of blood on the white calcified rock. It was a trail that told a grim, violent story.

"Who shot you, Zena?"

"I don't know. I didn't see him. I just ran . . . until I fell and couldn't get up again. Find Kim. Please."

Faust began wheezing for air and grimaced in pain. Jamie Dundas turned to Eve.

"She's in no condition to answer questions now," Jamie said. "Talk to the ranger. He went looking for the other victim."

In other words, Eve thought, leave us alone and let us do our job.

Eve stood up and saw a ranger staggering out of the ravine along a creek-side trail. He appeared to be in his twenties and seemed shell-shocked. She hurried over to him.

"I'm Detective Eve Ronin, LASD. Did you find the other victim?"

"I found her body." He tipped his head in the direction he came from and lost his balance. Eve caught him and eased him down to a sitting position on the embankment.

"Relax. Put your head between your knees. Take deep breaths." She looked over at Duncan, who had his back to her, talking to the couple, and beyond him, she saw two LASD patrol cars and an ambulance coming down the road toward them. She turned back to the ranger. "Do you want me to get you one of the paramedics?"

He shook his head. "I just need a minute. I'm a little light-headed, that's all."

"Okay, stay here. I'll be right back."

Eve headed for the pond. She walked along the edge of the trail so she wouldn't disturb any footprints. The trail followed the creek on one side and the base of a steep ridge of boulders and crumbling sandstone on the other.

12

She followed the trail over rocks and between trees, down to a pond surrounded by boulders of various sizes and set against a dramatic stony outcropping. But it was more than that. Somehow all the elements combined perfectly to create a place that seemed truly magical, like a Hollywood set rather than a real place. It was beautiful, totally unexpected, and yet familiar to her, even though she'd never been there before.

That was because she'd seen this pond, sometimes with waterfalls, tropical plants, and other production designer tweaks, on-screen a hundred times before.

She was in Movieland, and the tweak this time was a corpse.

The dead woman was naked and lying on her back, her upper body on shore, the rest of her in the water. A shotgun blast had blown away the left side of her face and shredded her ear. Her left shoulder and chest were also perforated with pellets.

Eve knew that there could be hundreds of pellets packed into the wadding of a shotgun shell. The more pellets expelled by the shell on firing, the greater the chances were of hitting the target . . . and the farther away the shooter was from the target, the wider the dispersal of pellets would be. The shotgun-blast injuries of the two women suggested to Eve that the shooter had been close in front of them, perhaps only ten or fifteen yards away.

Eve looked up and, on the other side of the pond, saw two towels and some women's clothes casually draped on a boulder, as if tossed there in the couple's hurry to undress and get in the water.

She pulled out her phone. There was no signal. She took a few photos to document the scene, then headed back, careful to follow the exact route she took coming in.

The ranger who'd found Kim was still sitting on the ground when Eve got back. The ambulance and two LASD patrol cars had arrived in her absence. The two hikers were walking back toward the campground on Crags Road. Duncan was talking with two uniformed LASD deputies, Tom Ross and Eddie Clayton, and the paramedics were lifting Zena Faust from the creek bed onto a stretcher held by two ambulance drivers.

Eve stopped beside the ranger and put a hand on his shoulder. "Are you feeling better?"

He nodded. "I'm sorry. I've never seen anything like that before."

"You have nothing to apologize for. What's your name?"

"Mark Weston."

"Okay, Mark. How many people are camping in the park right now?"

"Maybe a dozen overnighters. More or less. It's a weekday and the park gates would have just opened for the day about now, under normal circumstances, though there could be people who came in on foot."

"This portion of the park is a crime scene, from the campground to the pond and all the trails leading in here. It's too big an area for us to tape off and secure, so we're going to need rangers posted at every entrance, road, and trailhead to keep people out. Can you arrange that?"

"It's not my call," he said. "I'll radio the superintendent."

Weston got up slowly, Eve helping him to his feet, and went to his truck to get on the radio. Eve walked over to Rick Gage and told him about the body by the rock pond.

"I need you to go back there and officially confirm that she's dead," she said. "Take the creek bed in so you don't disturb any possible footprints on the trail. And don't touch anything besides the body. I want to limit the contamination of the scene as much as possible."

"I understand," the paramedic said. He picked up his medical kit on the off chance that Eve was wrong and headed down the creek bed.

Eve went over to Duncan, who was in the middle of giving instructions to the two deputies.

"Call for some more units. We need to know who else is in the park and campground. I want IDs, license plates, everything. Nobody leaves, everyone gets interviewed. Assume every tent and vehicle is a possible crime scene. Understood?"

"You got it," said Deputy Clayton, who was known among his fellow deputies as "Shades" because he rarely took off his wraparound sunglasses. He went over to his patrol car and Deputy Ross started to go with him, but Eve stopped him with a gentle tug on his shirtsleeve.

Ross was an ex-marine and hadn't lost his military bearing. He was very self-contained, and ordinarily a man of few words. Eve felt a special fondness for him because he'd once put himself at personal and professional risk to protect her. He'd even carried her in his arms when she was too injured to stand and, in some ways, feeling as scared and powerless as Zena Faust did now.

"Tom, I'd like you to accompany the victim in the ambulance to the hospital," Eve said. "Her name is Zena Faust."

"She hates everyone at Lost Hills station," Tom said. "She won't want me anywhere near her."

"Go with her anyway. Just by being there, she'll know that she's safe and not facing all of this alone."

Tom nodded. Assignment accepted. "What was she doing here?"

Duncan replied. "Camping with another woman. The couple who found Faust in the creek saw them pitching their tent yesterday afternoon. I don't know where Zena's friend is."

Eve gestured behind her. "I do. Her body is fifty yards further up the ravine, by the pond, where they were skinny-dipping last night."

"Her body?" Duncan said.

Before Eve could explain, she saw Jamie Dundas climb into the back of the ambulance and the two attendants getting ready to leave.

"Get going, Tom. Make note of anything she says, and when you get to the hospital, make sure the trauma nurse opens a rape kit, checks her for GSR, and collects anything under her fingernails. I'll catch up with you there later."

Tom jumped into the back of the ambulance, taking a seat beside a startled Jamie Dundas, and closed the door behind him. The ambulance sped off, siren wailing, though the only traffic they might face on Crags Road was a squirrel.

Duncan watched it go. "Do you think Faust was raped? Or shot her girlfriend and then herself?"

"I'm just covering every base." Eve had learned some painful lessons over the last few months about the unexpected directions a case could go. "Her girlfriend's first name is Kim. We'll probably find her ID with Zena's, either in their clothes by the pond or back at their campsite."

"Can you tell how Kim was killed?"

Eve glanced back toward the rock pond and saw Rick Gage approaching, his nod confirming what she already knew.

"Shotgun blast to the face and upper body. Zena was hit, too, but I don't know if it was pellets from the same shot or if the shooter fired twice."

Duncan seemed troubled. Eve assumed it was because his last two weeks on the job just got a lot more complicated and unpleasant. He said, "You call in CSU and the ME and I'll talk to the captain about activating the Malibu Search & Rescue Team."

"What do we need them for?"

"To help gather possible evidence. CSU will want to search at least fifty yards in each direction from here." Duncan looked south at the high, craggy mountains. "And that includes some very rough terrain."

"I'm sure Captain DuBois will appreciate the suggestion," Eve said. "And pretend he came up with the idea himself."

Mel Dubois, the acting captain, was previously a lieutenant from the Court Services Division and before that was a gang enforcement supervisor. Eve felt that he was woefully unfamiliar with the unique cultural and geological challenges of the Lost Hills sheriff's station's jurisdiction, a patchwork of unincorporated areas, state parks, national parks, and cities without police departments of their own. It was an area bordered by Santa Monica Bay to the south, Ventura County to the northwest, and the City of Los Angeles to the northeast and east. That made the LASD the law in the Santa Monica Mountains, Malibu, Westlake Village, Agoura Hills, Hidden Hills, and Calabasas, where the station was located.

Smack in the middle of that jurisdiction were Malibu Creek State Park and the Santa Monica Mountains National Recreation Area, patrolled by their own rangers and park police.

It was a political and jurisdictional nightmare. Conflicts were common and ugly. Dubois was the fourth captain of the station in a little under a year. Eve thought that he was the least prepared of all of them to handle the job, not that she was in a position to criticize him. It was widely believed, at Lost Hills and throughout the department, that she didn't deserve her job, either.

"I'm beyond caring about politics now," Duncan said.

"You never cared," Eve said. "That's why you're retiring as a detective instead of a captain."

"This job is all I ever wanted but now I'm not sure I was ever fit for it."

The comment surprised her. It was the first time she'd ever heard him express even a hint of insecurity about his skills as a homicide detective. "What is *that* supposed to mean?"

He waved her off. "Go. Get on our radio. I'll use the one in the patrol car that Tom left behind."

On her way to their car, Eve intercepted Gage again as he was gathering his supplies and packing up his paramedic vehicle.

"Hey, Rick, can you tell how long the other woman has been dead?"

Her question seemed to startle him. "I'm surprised you'd trust my take on anything, Detective."

He was referring to a recent medical emergency they'd both worked and it pained her to think she might have been responsible for any negative professional blowback against him.

"Please call me Eve. And we *all* made mistakes on that case."

"But you wouldn't have made yours if I hadn't made mine."

"Nobody blames you," she said. "Well, I certainly don't."

"Thanks. Half of her body has been lying in cold water, so that skews the timing of some natural postmortem processes, like rigor and decomp. I'm not a medical examiner, but judging by her massive head trauma, I'd say she died instantly and that her body has been there for hours."

That pretty much confirmed what Faust told her, but Gage had probably heard what she'd said, too. "What can you tell me about Zena Faust's injuries?"

"I'd guess that she has a collapsed lung and maybe a concussion. She thinks she may have blacked out for some time . . . or just fell asleep. It's possible she has some internal bleeding, too. Only thing I know for sure is that she's got a broken leg, probably from tripping and falling on the rocks."

"So she'll live?"

"Barring any unexpected complications, yeah, she's lucky to be alive."

"Thanks."

Eve went back to her plain-wrap Dodge Charger, slipped into the driver's seat, and got on the radio to the dispatcher to summon the crime scene unit and medical examiner to the scene. While she was talking, the fire department vehicles left and she saw two more LASD patrol cars enter the park. She was just getting off the radio when Duncan sat down in the passenger seat beside her and closed the door.

"There's something you need to know, Eve."

She put the microphone handset back into place and turned to face him. "Okay."

He waited a long moment, then looked out at the creek bed where Zena Faust was found. "I'm responsible for this. I might as well have pulled the trigger myself."

CHAPTER THREE

Eve followed Duncan's gaze, using the moment of silence to try to figure out what was going on with him and coming up with nothing. His statement was absurd.

"I've got a few questions," she said. "But before I ask them, would you like me to read you your rights?"

"That isn't funny," Duncan said. "A woman is dead because I didn't do my job."

"I don't believe that."

"You're partly right, I'm not solely responsible." He gestured to the ranger, who was standing outside his truck and staring down at the creek. She presumed that Weston was waiting to hear from his bosses or was sticking around to secure the scene. "This is on him, too. He knew. So did his superintendent. So did a lot of other people."

"Knew what?"

"About all of the other shotgun shootings in and around the park. This is the sixth one but the first involving a serious injury or death. But I knew it was inevitable."

"I didn't hear about any previous shootings."

"Nobody has. They began over a year ago, long before you got here." Duncan took a deep breath. "It started with someone taking potshots at a few cars on Las Virgenes and on Mulholland, then at a motor home in the campground, a house bordering the western end of the park, and a couple making out in their parked car."

"It's amazing that no one was hurt."

"I didn't come into it until the motor home was shot at, and that's only because they drove their RV to the station to report the shooting, mostly because they wanted the paperwork to be sure their insurance company would pay for their damage. I starting asking around and was shocked to hear about the earlier cases."

"Nobody reported the shootings?"

"They reported them to the park rangers, who didn't share them with us. Or anybody else."

She could see how that was possible for the shootings that occurred within the state park, but not the ones that happened on the surrounding roads. That was LASD territory.

"What about the shootings on Las Virgenes and Mulholland? Didn't those victims call 911?"

"They did, but since the callers all reported that the shots came from somewhere in the hills, which is the park, the 911 operator referred them to the park police, and they bury everything they can."

"Why would they do that?"

"Because over three hundred thousand tourists a year visit Malibu Creek State Park and that generates a lot of business in Calabasas, Agoura, and Malibu. Nobody wants to scare away those tourists and their dollars by suggesting the park might be dangerous. But when someone shot into a family's living room a few weeks later, that scared one of the rangers enough to quietly tip me off."

"Was it Weston?"

Duncan nodded. "He was terrified and so was I."

She could understand why. "You were worried that the shootings were all connected."

"I knew they were. I just couldn't prove it and I was afraid that while I was trying to, someone would get killed. I wanted to warn the public about the danger. So I shared my concerns with Captain Moffett."

Moffett was in charge of the Lost Hills station when Eve first arrived, but after presiding over a stakeout that went disastrously and fatally wrong, he was transferred to a command position at the Men's Central Jail. It was a demotion that was characterized publicly by the department as a "lateral move," but that didn't fool anyone. His replacement, Captain Roje Shaw, transferred over from Compton, but he abruptly retired only days later, after he, too, supervised a bungled operation that led to two deaths, several injured deputies, and a brush fire. That was more the result of bad luck than incompetence or a failure in command, but Eve didn't blame him for bailing out. Dubois was quickly appointed acting captain while the sheriff searched for the right person for the job.

"Did Moffett want to bury the shootings, too?" she asked.

"No, he actually agreed with me, but it wasn't his decision to make. So we went to headquarters together to present our argument to Assistant Sheriff Nakamura, who listened to what we had to say and then immediately shut us down."

That didn't surprise her. Eve had dealt with Nakamura herself and was glad he was no longer with the department. "You mean he shut you up."

"I understood why. We didn't have any hard evidence that the shooting incidents were related. He argued that by warning the public, and implying there was a serial shooter, we'd spark a panic that would be 'counterproductive.'"

"So what did you do?"

"I followed orders. I stayed quiet and kept working the case. But I didn't have any leads, and there were no more shootings, so the investigation stalled. And then I got partnered up with you," Duncan said. "Almost immediately, there was the Kenworth family massacre, then the wildfire that swept through here, then we had more homicides to solve, and I never looked back. I thought it was over. Actually, I didn't think about it at all. I forgot about it. Now a woman is dead because of my inaction."

"You did all you could."

"I should have warned the public. But I didn't. So Zena Faust and her girlfriend didn't realize the risk they were taking by camping in this park."

Eve thought back to her own unpleasant encounter with Assistant Sheriff Nakamura, which in many ways led to his departure. "Nakamura was right."

"About what?"

"He once warned me that my stubborn belief in one theory of a crime would blind me to other possibilities."

"The corrupt, self-serving prick was trying to distract you from the truth to save his career, remember?"

Eve did. The sheriff had actually given her Nakamura's badge as a memento. She kept it at home in her junk drawer. "Yes, he was, but that aside, it was still good advice."

"You're taking pointers from crooks now?"

"You don't know that the killing last night has anything to do with the previous shootings."

"Yes, I do," Duncan said. "They all involved a shotgun."

"A lot of people use shotguns."

"It happened in the park."

"Not all of the other shootings happened in the park," she said. "You said so yourself. They were on Las Virgenes Road or on Mulholland Highway."

"They were all in or around the park."

"So is every homicide we investigate. It's an eight-thousand-acre park, the biggest park in any metropolitan area in America, and it's in the center of our jurisdiction. Everything else is squeezed into the fringes."

"You're just trying to make me feel better," Duncan said. "But what you're actually doing is pissing me off."

"Because I'm making sense."

"Because you're pretending to be the voice of reason when we both know you're the most unreasonable person in this car."

"I used to be," Eve said. "Until now."

Duncan looked past her. "Uh-oh. Here comes trouble."

She turned to her driver's side window and saw a state park vehicle, a Ford Explorer, speeding their way, kicking up a big cloud of dust in its wake. "Who is that?"

"Trisha Kalb, the park superintendent. Technically she's a peace officer, just like us, but she behaves like a politician," he said. "Did you ever see the movie *Jaws*?"

She turned back to him. "Of course I did."

"She's the mayor of Amity."

That told her a lot. The mayor, played with smarmy perfection by Murray Hamilton, was the guy who wanted to keep the beaches open despite the presence of a man-eating shark.

Kalb pulled up beside their car so that her rolled-down driver's side window was beside Eve's. She was in her forties, wearing a crisp Park Service uniform and flat-rimmed ranger hat, and had a deep tan from a life working outdoors. She wore no makeup and her hair was tied in a tight ponytail that pulled too hard on her face, making all the skin taut. It hurt Eve just to look at her.

Eve rolled down her window, too, but before she could say anything, Kalb spoke up.

"Who do you think you are telling my rangers to shut down the park?"

Well, we're off to a good start, Eve thought. She decided to take a relaxed approach to the direct assault.

"I'm reasonably certain that I'm Eve Ronin, a Los Angeles County sheriff's detective, and that I'm investigating a homicide and a shooting."

"You don't have the authority to close my park. You don't look like you even have the authority to order a drink."

Duncan leaned forward so Kalb could see him clearly. "Actually, I'm the one who gave the order, Trisha. This is a crime scene and we're containing it."

"You know better than that, Duncan. This is a state park, under state authority—"

Duncan interrupted her. "In unincorporated Los Angeles County. Our jurisdiction."

"It's not so clear-cut, it's—"

He talked over her again. "You can go after people for tossing beer cans in the creek, or carving their initials in a tree, or throwing rocks at squirrels, but this is a murder and that's our job. The park is a crime scene. If you've got a problem with that, take it up with the sheriff."

"Oh, I will," she said. "In the meantime, the body is down there, at the rock pond. That's your crime scene, not the whole damn park. There's no reason to seal everything clear back to Las Virgenes and up to Mulholland."

"We don't know how the shooter got in or out of the park or even if he's still here," he said. "So until we do, this end of the park is closed."

"If you go to that unnecessary extreme, it makes a tragic, isolated incident appear to be a major crisis and will spark a press and social media frenzy," Kalb said. "Let's be reasonable, Duncan. I'm sure you can investigate this and keep a low profile at the same time."

Before Duncan could answer, they heard a rumble and then a Sheriff's Department helicopter flew in low overhead, coming in for a landing in the empty parking area near the front gate, the sight bringing traffic on nearby Las Virgenes Road to a standstill.

"Shit," Kalb said, staring at the helicopter. "Why don't you send up balloons and bring in a marching band while you're at it? Is subtlety beyond you people?"

Eve was surprised by the arrival of the helicopter, too. The radio in the car crackled. Eve answered the call. It was Deputy Clayton, alerting them that a CSU advance team had arrived on the chopper and that a patrol car would be bringing them right out to the scene. Eve acknowledged the message, then looked at Trisha Kalb, who was glowering at them.

"You should be pleased," Eve said.

"I don't see why."

"The crime scene investigators are based in Monterey Park, a good hour or more away in rush hour traffic. The fact that headquarters immediately sent a team here by chopper demonstrates how seriously they're taking this case and how quickly they want it resolved."

"You don't understand the impact even a temporary closure will have," Kalb said. "The wildfire and the damage it caused closed us down for months. We've only been open again for a few weeks. People have just begun to come back."

Duncan said, "And so has the shooter."

"This incident has nothing to do with those random, unrelated acts of hooliganism," Kalb said.

Duncan shook his head. "You're wrong. It's another in the string of shotgun shootings and now it's escalated to murder."

For an instant, Eve thought Kalb might jump out of her car and climb through their window to strangle Duncan.

"If that reckless, baseless speculation shows up in the press, I'll know exactly where it came from," Kalb said, pointing a finger at him. "And I'll have your badge for it."

"You can have it in two weeks with my compliments," Duncan said.

CHAPTER FOUR

An LASD patrol car pulled up behind their three vehicles. Eve got out to greet the arriving team, her action cutting off the discussion with Trisha Kalb. Duncan and Kalb joined her.

Nan Baker emerged from the patrol car wearing a full Tyvek jumpsuit, gloves, and booties and carrying her shoulder kit and camera. The CSU leader was an African American woman in her forties, built like a linebacker, and willing to mow down anybody in her way. She was accompanied by forensic investigator Lou Noomis, who was reedy and tall, and Deputy Medical Examiner Emilia Lopez, a short woman who wore glasses too large for her tiny face. Noomis and Lopez were also dressed head to toe in Tyvek. Eve quickly handled the introductions all around.

Nan addressed herself to Kalb.

"More of my team are being brought in by chopper and our ground units are on the way with additional equipment and personnel. We'll be setting up an evidence collection tent here but the mobile command center unit will be in the upper parking lot." She gestured in the direction of Las Virgenes Road. "I want to restrict foot and vehicle traffic here as much as possible, though it's probably way too late to prevent contamination."

Eve gestured to Mark Weston, who was still standing outside his truck. "Nobody except that ranger, me, and a paramedic have been to the pond since the shooting was reported."

"But how many first responders have been where we are standing now and down in that dry creek," Nan said to her, "both of which are natural and obvious paths to and from the crime scene?"

Nan had a point, and Eve knew it. But it pissed her off anyway.

"I'm sorry about that, but all they knew at first was that a woman was injured in the creek and needed emergency medical care," Eve said, trying hard not to sound defensive. "They weren't aware of the murder yet."

"I understand. I'm just explaining myself so we're all clear on why I am doing what I'm doing." Nan turned again to Kalb. "My team will work the areas closest to the victims in the creek and at the pond. We will thoroughly map and photograph every piece of evidence, including the body, before anything is moved or collected. We'll utilize drones and laser scanners to assist in that effort." Nan turned now to the ME. "After the mapping is done, Emilia, you will be able to remove the body. But I'd like you to do an initial examination of the injuries to the victim, particularly the dispersal and penetration of the shotgun pellets, so we can derive from that a rough idea of the shooter's position."

Emilia Lopez nodded. "Of course, Nan. Whatever you need."

That all sounded fine to Eve, but she had work to do, too. "I'd like to look at any IDs or cell phones that might be among the two victims' clothing as soon as possible."

Nan glared at her. They were outside, and it was about eighty degrees, but Eve could swear the temperature suddenly dropped to freezing.

"Thank you for that reminder, Detective Ronin. It might not have occurred to me, after fifteen years spent processing hundreds of homicide scenes, that you might want that material."

Eve felt herself flush with embarrassment and saw a glint of pleasure in Kalb's eyes. Nan continued with her briefing.

"We will be expanding our search for evidence to the most likely and natural points of entry and exit to the pond." She turned to Kalb. "We'll go where the evidence points us, but we'll also heavily rely on your knowledge of the park, as well as the participation of your rangers in the actual search."

Duncan spoke up. "We'll be deploying Malibu Search & Rescue to help you out, too."

Kiss ass, Eve thought.

"Thank you, Duncan," Nan said.

Kalb abruptly held up her hand in a halting gesture that made Nan flinch in anger.

"Hold it right there," Kalb declared. "You're talking about a vast area and an enormous amount of man-hours. We need to discuss a more reasonable, scaled-down option to do this."

Nan shook her head in adamant refusal. "We can do this right or we can half-ass it. And since I have to own the consequences of that decision in court, I will testify to the exact limitations, if any, imposed on our efforts and by whom. Then the public can decide how that individual's decision impacted either the conviction or acquittal of the defendant. Your call."

Nan stared defiantly at Kalb.

The superintendent's face reddened. When Kalb spoke again, her voice was as tight as her face. "How long do you think your work is going to take?"

"I haven't visited the actual crime scene yet, but based on experience, I'd say two full days. Lou?" She glanced at Noomis, who had an enormous Adam's apple that looked like he had a baseball stuck in his throat. It was hard for Eve not to stare at it.

"Judging by the terrain here," Noomis said, "I'm thinking it'll be closer to three."

Kalb was now not only angry, but incredulous. "You want to shut down the most popular area of the park for *three full days*?"

Eve was glad she was wearing a thin Kevlar tank top under her blouse so she'd be safe from any shrapnel from Nan's inevitable explosive reply.

"What I want is to be home in my pajamas making cookies for my kids and then watching *Love It or List It* with my husband in my big, fluffy, king-sized bed. Instead, I will be here, on my knees in the mud, for fourteen straight hours, flop-sweating in this Tyvek suit, gathering evidence, after which I will be stuck in a hotel room, eating a cold fast-food dinner. This is not about what I want, Ms. Kalb. It's about doing the job right. Now, if there is nothing else, we need to get to it."

Nan didn't wait for a response. She turned her back on Kalb and headed carefully, and slowly, along the edges of the path toward the rock pond, followed by Noomis and Lopez.

Trisha Kalb pivoted abruptly herself, marched back to her Explorer, and drove off fast, kicking up dirt. Ranger Weston remained standing where he was, and Eve thought he seemed relieved that it hadn't occurred to anybody to include him in the contentious discussion.

Duncan looked at Eve and sighed. "There are some things you never learn."

"What is that supposed to mean?"

"We both know how CSU does their job. The only reason Nan explained her process was for Kalb's benefit. All you had to do was listen patiently and quietly. You don't always need to say something."

"Unless it's to kiss Nan's ass."

"Yes, and it's even better when doing it helps her get what she wants from someone else."

Aha, Eve thought. Now his kiss-ass comment made sense to her.

"That's why you said you've got Malibu Search & Rescue on board," she said. "To motivate Kalb to get *her* rangers involved."

"It's important to remember that if Nan is happy, ultimately you will be, too, because our case will succeed or fail based on her work."

"What about our investigative skills and deductive genius?"

"It's worthless if evidence is overlooked or tainted," he said. "Let's check out Zena's campsite and see if the deputies have learned anything."

◆ ◆ ◆

They got back into the car and Eve drove them to the campground, which was bordered by Las Virgenes Road to the east, a range of steep hills to the south, a valley of grassland and dry streams to the west, and a parking lot and the administration office to the north.

The sixty-two campsites were arranged in an oblong oval with a cinder-block restroom building located in the center. Each site had a firepit and picnic table. Deputy Eddie Clayton was stationed on the road leading into the campground. Eve rolled down the window as she approached him. He was leaning against his cruiser, his arms crossed under his chest.

"Hey, Eddie," she said. "How many campers are there?"

"Twelve people," he said. "Three couples, one family of four, and two individual males. That tally includes the two shooting victims."

"Any suspects?"

"I don't think so, but you'd have to ask Deputy Snell or Deputy Lavors. They've been doing the interviews. Snell is securing the victims' tent until CSU can process it and Lavors is still talking to people. I pulled the short stick and got guard duty."

Eve smiled. "Like hell. You'll take any opportunity to work on your tan."

Duncan leaned forward. "Which campsite belongs to the victims?"

"Fifty-nine. Turn left at the fork, it's on the west side of the road."

Eve followed the directions. The campsite was farthest from Las Virgenes Road and had a spectacular view of the meadow, oak woodlands, and mountain peaks known as Goat Buttes in the distance. A dome-style quick-pitch pop-up tent with a zippered door was located under a fire-blackened oak tree, near the picnic table. Deputy Snell sat on the picnic table, drinking a bottle of water. Two camping spots over, Eve saw the couple who'd found Faust. They were sitting in the open tailgate of their car, backed up to their large tent. Eve and Duncan got out and approached Snell. He had a scrunched face, as if a vise were pressed against his head and chin, so he seemed to be perpetually wincing.

Eve said to him, "Did you find any IDs or phones in the tent?"

Snell turned to Duncan. "I didn't uncover any IDs, wallets, phones, or car keys in the tent. The vehicle is locked and registered to Kim Spivey, who lives in Reseda. The campsite reservation was made yesterday online by Zena Faust, using her credit card. They arrived at three p.m."

Duncan didn't say anything. Eve asked, "Did anybody hear or see anything unusual last night or this morning?"

Again, the deputy ignored Eve and spoke to Duncan.

"Nobody heard any gunshots or saw anything or anyone suspicious. The only campers who noticed Spivey and Faust were those two"—he gestured to the couple who found the body—"who saw them set up camp."

Duncan nodded. "I got their statements already."

Eve glanced at the handful of other occupied campsites. "What can you tell us about the other campers?"

Snell looked at Duncan. "There's another couple in campsite ten. They're in a pickup truck with a camper bed." He pointed to it. "They're aging hippies in their seventies from Spokane, Washington, on a road trip. Their camper reeks of pot. They've been here for three days and planned to leave tomorrow for San Diego. There's a family of four, two adults and two children under the age of ten, in a thirty-foot trailer parked in site sixteen." He pointed out that one, too. It wasn't hard to spot. "They're day-trippers from Fresno and planned to leave this morning. There are also two individual males, camping alone. One is a marine on leave from Port Hueneme, hiking the Backbone Trail, who was camping here for the night. The other is a homeless guy. Smelly

Bob. We've seen him around before. My partner, Ed Lavors, is talking to him now."

The two deputies had been busy and thorough. Eve appreciated that but was irritated that Snell was ignoring her, though she wouldn't give him the satisfaction of complaining about it. "Do any of these people have a weapon or an arrest record?"

Snell replied to Duncan. "The marine has a Glock, which is registered, and a nasty-looking Rambo knife. No arrests. Smelly Bob also has a knife, not as nasty, and priors for drunk and disorderly, shoplifting, and lewd conduct. He likes to jerk off in front of Albertsons supermarket."

Duncan sighed. "Is there a reason you're ignoring my partner?"

The question didn't throw Snell at all. Without breaking eye contact with Duncan, he took a swig of water before responding.

"Once upon a time, there was a party girl who liked to get high and fuck strangers on the beach. Two off-duty deputies gave her what she wanted. Now, because of that man-hating bitch"—he pointed his empty water bottle at Eve without looking at her—"the deputies are in prison, another deputy ate his gun, and my former partner is now a security guard at a Big Lots in Temecula. Good men were ruined and families were destroyed by Ronin. She's the only person in the department I don't trust to have my back. Nobody does."

Another Great White, Eve thought.

The Great Whites were a clique of tattooed Lost Hills station deputies, several of whom she'd arrested for their crimes. She was convinced that at least two other Great Whites, driving old patrol cars, had tried to kill her on a coastal highway north of Ventura by forcing her off the road into the sea. She was lucky she'd survived, but whoever the deputies were who had come after her were still out there. They could be anyone with an LASD badge.

"Bud Collier was your partner?" Duncan asked.

"Yeah. A great cop. Saved my life twice on the street."

A great cop? Eve thought. Collier was a Great White member who had set them up for almost certain death by intentionally delaying backup when she and Duncan were in an undercover situation that went bad, leaving them alone, and unarmed, against three armed, violent felons in a Calabasas McMansion.

Duncan stepped up to Snell and pointed to the scar on his face. "I got this because Collier didn't have my back."

"You got hurt because you were at that bitch's side. Unintended collateral damage. It's a good thing you're leaving, Donuts. Nobody is safe around her."

"Eve didn't take Collier's badge. *I did.* And he's lucky I didn't shove it up his ass when I beat him up in the locker room," Duncan said. "As I recall, you were there when I did that. You didn't stop me."

"Because it wasn't my fight."

Duncan took another step forward so they were only inches apart. "Because you're gutless. You didn't have his back. But Eve did. She's the one who stopped me. Have you looked him in the eye since that day?" Now Snell shifted his gaze, finding something fascinating to study at his feet. "That's what I thought. Because he knows you're a coward and so do you."

Duncan turned and got back in the car. Eve joined him, looking at Snell, who was glowering at them both, through the windshield.

"I want him out of here," she said.

"What good will that do? If we send away every deputy who dislikes or distrusts you from the park, only Eddie Clayton will still be here."

"Gee, thanks."

"Snell doesn't have to like you. He did his job today, and did it thoroughly, that's what matters. Drop me off with Smelly Bob and Deputy Lavors. I'll stick around here and coordinate things while you go to the hospital and see if you can get anything more out of Zena."

Eve put the car in drive and pulled away. "I like that plan. We can compare notes at lunch."

"Did you have to mention lunch? Now I'm hungry."

She drove slowly around the oval. "You're always hungry."

"Bring me back a carne asada nacho burrito with extra meat and cheese from the hospital cafeteria."

"There are a hundred restaurants I can stop at, but you want me to bring you hospital food? Nobody likes hospital food."

"Oh, that reminds me," he said. "Get me one of those little cups of lime Jell-O they only give to patients. I love those."

She gave him a look. "You're kidding."

"Why did you think I visited you in the hospital?"

"Because you were worried about me?"

"Hell no," he said. "It was strictly for the cuisine."

CHAPTER FIVE

She left Duncan at Smelly Bob's ratty tent, which was held together with strips of duct tape and plastic sheeting, and then she drove out of the park, heading north on Las Virgenes toward the Ventura Freeway. Her phone rang the instant she hit the road. She answered the call on speaker.

An officious woman said, "Please hold for Gabriel Montlake."

Eve hated being put on hold, especially on calls she didn't even make. But Montlake was the defense attorney recommended by Rebecca Burnside, a shrewd Los Angeles prosecutor, to defend Eve against the lawsuit filed by the family of the suicidal deputy. So Eve put up with the aggravation.

She got on the freeway, heading east, and was passing the Parkway Calabasas exit a few moments later when Montlake's assistant spoke again.

"Mr. Montlake, I have Eve Ronin for you."

There was a click, and then Eve heard the gregarious voice of the lawyer, a man she hadn't even met in person yet. She'd only seen his jowly face and wild white hair in the *Los Angeles Times* and, occasionally, as a legal pundit on CNN.

"Eve, glad I caught you. Is it a good time to talk?"

"My morning has been murder, but that's the nature of my job. I've got a few minutes. Tell me what's on your mind." She hoped he could tell her quickly. He charged $500 an hour for his time.

"I've reviewed the lawsuit against you. It's pretty straightforward. Pruitt's widow is coming after you for $10 million for violating her husband's civil rights, specifically for intentional infliction of emotional distress, and wrongful death."

She got off the freeway at the Valley Circle exit in Woodland Hills and hit the stoplight in front of the Motion Picture and Television Country House and Hospital, a sprawling senior living community and hospital, where her father, television director Vince Nyby, lived in a bungalow. She hadn't visited him and had no plans to ever do so. The facility was located across from the entrance to Old Town Calabasas, the eastern border of her jurisdiction.

"I didn't kill Pruitt," she said.

"True, but you could be responsible for his death if you relentlessly harassed him until he couldn't take it anymore."

"I only spoke to him once, outside his home," she said. "That hardly qualifies as relentless."

"But they'll argue you confronted him there because you wanted to use his family as emotional leverage, to apply pressure on him."

"Yes, I did, to talk to me about his role in covering up a rape and murder, not to blow his own head off."

The light turned green and she made a hard left up the street, then another left onto the overpass, crossing above the freeway and heading north into West Hills, a residential suburb of Los Angeles.

"Under California law," Montlake said, "you're responsible for Pruitt's death if your harassment was intended to cause injury."

"I told him the facts, that he was going to prison, no matter what, and it would destroy his family," she said. "But if he helped me, if he did the right thing, it could reduce his penalty and be a step towards redemption."

"He saw another way out," Montlake said.

"I couldn't have known he'd do that and it wasn't my intent," she said. "Isn't that the bottom line? I wanted his testimony, not his corpse."

Montlake sighed. "There are several arguments I can make to the court to seek a dismissal at this stage. I could say that you have qualified immunity as a police officer, so the case is moot. And we could admit that yes, you harassed Pruitt but, as a matter of law, the plaintiff can't establish that your actions were the legal and factual cause of his suicide."

"What are the chances of those arguments working?"

"The sheriff's department claims you acted on your own, outside your official capacity, so they aren't responsible. You might win that fight in a separate lawsuit against the county, but probably not as grounds for dismissal of this suit."

Okay, she thought. That argument was a long shot.

"And the other approach?"

"There has to be a connection, legally and factually, between your actions and Pruitt's suicide. People take their own lives for lots of complicated reasons. So we might be able to convince a judge that even if you did harass Pruitt, his suicide was provoked by many other things and long-standing psychological issues," Montlake said. "Not only that, but his wife didn't overhear what you told Pruitt, and she admits that he didn't say you were harassing him. The only living person who actually knows what was said is you. So how can she prove that what you said caused his suicide?"

"That sounds like a strong argument to me," Eve said, driving past shopping centers and fast-food outlets. "Let's go for it."

"I will," Montlake said. "But we'll probably lose."

She slapped the steering wheel in frustration. It felt like the whole conversation was a waste of time and $250. "Why?"

"The judge usually likes a look at the evidence before making a decision about dismissal. None of that is in. So once all of the witnesses have been deposed and all the documents have been reviewed, we'll move for summary judgment in our favor."

"Okay," she said, tentatively. "What are our odds of winning at that point?"

"Pretty good."

Burnside had told Eve that Montlake was the best, the lawyer she would hire in Eve's shoes. So what choice did Eve have? "All right. What do you need from me?"

"A $20,000 retainer and your signature on some documents."

That was her entire option fee for the TV series pilot. Once Eve gave him the money, she'd have only a few hundred dollars left in her savings account.

"Will I recoup my legal fees from the other side if I win?"

"Nope," he said.

"So I lose no matter what. It's just a question of how much."

If the TV series didn't go forward, or was quickly canceled, her detective salary wouldn't cover her living expenses and legal fees. She'd be so deeply in debt that she could end up living in a tent beside Smelly Bob's.

"There's another option, one I strongly urge you to consider," Montlake said. "Settle with the Pruitts. Don't let this case go to court."

"Why would I want to do that?"

"Because this matter would conclude with no legal determination, no judge's ruling, about whether you acted in the course of your job."

"How does that benefit me? I'll be broke."

"Only temporarily. The county arbitrarily decided, without any sort of due process, that you acted on your own, and then they settled with the Pruitts. The county's judgment about your actions carries no legal weight," Montlake said. "Without a court decision that you went rogue, and that your actions were directly responsible for the suicide, the county would have to reimburse you for your fees and settlement costs. The only way the county could avoid that would be to take you to court and prove to a judge that your actions were outside your official capacity as a detective. That's a hard, expensive road to travel and the law is tipped on your side, so the county will settle with you. You might even make a few dollars on the deal."

"I am not settling with the Pruitts," she said. "I'd be admitting that I drove him to suicide."

"No, you wouldn't and both sides would expressly state that in the settlement agreement."

"A statement doesn't fool anyone," Eve said. "Everyone would consider me guilty. I can't accept that. So that option is off the table."

She turned right onto Sherman Way. There was a row of old, decaying RVs parked across the street from West Hills Hospital. At first glance, it appeared to be a homeless encampment. That was partly true. But Eve knew the RVs were primarily occupied by woefully underpaid orderlies, who weren't earning a living wage, and young doctors, who were working off crushing medical school debt and had no money left for rent. Every few days, the RV community would move to another street near the hospital.

"Okay," he said. "But win or lose with the Pruitts, you could potentially recover your costs, plus damages, by suing the county for their failure to defend you."

She liked that idea, but it would cost her even more money. "Would you take that case on contingency?"

"Nope."

"You would if you were sure you could win."

He laughed. "That's a good deduction. There's a reason you're a detective."

Eve drove into the hospital parking lot and took a spot reserved for "official vehicles" near the entrance to the emergency room. "Have your assistant email me the paperwork to sign and the details on wiring you your retainer."

"Will do."

It wasn't even noon yet and her day was already shit.

Eve had been in the West Hills Hospital emergency room so often, as a cop and as a patient, that just about everyone on staff had met her, but that's not why they let her in without having to flash her ID. Her sister, Lisa, three years younger than her, was a nurse there, so they also knew her as a member of a coworker's family. Lisa and Eve both had their mother Jen's piercing blue eyes, but that's where their resemblance ended, since they had different fathers. Lisa was a few inches shorter than Eve, rounder everywhere, and had naturally curly black hair.

Eve spotted Lisa in her blue scrubs and white running shoes, chatting at the nurse's station with Tom Ross. They both saw her coming at the same moment.

"Eve," Tom said, "you didn't tell me your sister was a nurse here."

"I haven't told you anything about my personal life."

"Soon it won't matter if you've told anybody," Lisa said. "The world will see it all on the TV series. I hope the actress who plays me can capture my lovable, inquisitive nature, sharp intellect, and raw sensuality."

Tom smiled at Lisa. "That would be impossible."

Lisa smiled back at him. "Aren't you the charmer."

Eve groaned. "Where can I find a barf bag?"

"On an airplane," Lisa said. "We use bedpans here."

"You aren't a character in the series," Eve said. "Nobody in our family is."

"Why not?" she asked.

"To respect your privacy."

"Nobody asked me if I wanted my privacy respected."

"The studio would also have to buy the rights to your life story," Eve said.

Lisa's father was a grip, a member of a film crew responsible for arranging the lights, laying camera tracks, and moving the walls of the sets around. Their mother, who worked for decades as an extra, one of the nonspeaking people in the background of scenes, had dated him for only a month or so before he disappeared from her life.

"I'll take whatever they'll give me," Lisa said. "Even if it's just spare change."

"The studio is too cheap to step up. Besides, Mom would want to play herself. It's awkward enough already that she's getting a small role."

"Chris Evans," Tom said.

Eve looked at him. "What?"

"That's who should play me."

"That will never happen," Eve said. "For one thing, he's an A-list movie star and this is episodic TV. Two, you aren't a character in the show. And three, if you were a character, it would be a minor part that wouldn't attract a star."

"Ouch," Tom said. "There aren't any deputies in the show?"

"Of course there are, but they aren't going to be based on real people," Eve said. "Speaking of which, can we come back to reality, please? What more do we have on Zena Faust?"

"She didn't say anything to me in the ambulance," Tom said. "She hates me, or I terrify her, or both."

Lisa touched his arm. "I don't see how that's possible. You're instantly likable."

Eve looked around. "Where is that bedpan?"

Tom turned to Lisa. "Thank you. But Faust hates the Lost Hills sheriff's station. She trashes us every day in her *Malibu Beat* blog. She thinks everyone there is corrupt or inept or homicidal or all three, except maybe for Eve."

Eve said, "Deputy Wayne Snell says I'm a bitch that nobody trusts, so it cuts both ways."

"Do you believe him?" Tom asked.

The deputies who'd vandalized her car, and who tried to kill her in Ventura, were still out there and she knew there were probably a lot of other deputies who hated her, not only for the deputies she'd arrested, but for leapfrogging over more deserving and experienced detectives to get into Lost Hills robbery-homicide. So yes, she absolutely believed Snell. It would be foolish and dangerous not to.

"I know that I can trust you, Duncan, and Eddie with my life," she said. "And that's about it."

"There are others who stand with you," Tom said. "More than you think."

She hoped he was right. Because in two weeks, Duncan would be gone.

"You two are scaring the crap out of me," Lisa said. "I mean, if cops can't trust each other, who are we supposed to count on?"

Eve immediately regretted being so candid in front of her younger sister. She'd always felt an almost parental responsibility to protect and reassure her two siblings and she'd just blown it with Lisa.

"The Los Angeles County Sheriff's Department is one of the top law enforcement agencies in the nation and I am proud to wear the badge," Eve said. "They will keep you safe."

"But you just said you don't trust anyone there."

"To have *my* back, but not when it comes to protecting the public," Eve said. "They believe I am a traitor and a danger to the department."

"I don't know how you can stand that," Lisa said. "I couldn't work here if I thought my colleagues distrusted me. Or if I couldn't trust them. Patients could die as a result."

"I don't think about it. I focus on doing my job. So, Lisa, how badly is Zena Faust injured?"

Lisa answered the question. "She's got a lot of shotgun pellets in her right arm and chest, a collapsed lung, a fractured tibia, and a nasty bruise on her forehead. The doctor inserted a chest tube to release air from her chest cavity and allow her lung to reinflate. Her leg is in a splint for now but we'll be putting a cast on it soon. And we've dressed dozens of wounds."

"Is she going to have surgery to remove the pellets?"

"I don't think so. Digging them out will just cause more damage and the body will naturally push out the pellets that aren't too deep." Lisa reached over the counter of the nurse's station and came up with a baggie full of tiny steel pellets, like ball bearings. "But there were some we were able to pluck out with tweezers."

Eve took the baggie and examined the pellets. "It's bird shot."

She wasn't a ballistics expert by any definition, but she could recognize what she was holding, primarily because of the size and number of pellets. They appeared to be about 5 mm, which meant they were used for birds and small game. The pellets were small so they wouldn't decimate the game and, by extension, the meat.

Tom took the bag from Eve and studied the pellets, too. "She's lucky she wasn't more seriously hurt."

"I think her girlfriend took the brunt of the blast," Eve said, then glanced at Lisa. "Can I talk to Faust now?"

"Sure, but I don't know how coherent she'll be, considering what she's been through and all the drugs we've pumped into her. She's in exam room one right now."

Eve nodded and looked at Tom. "I'll give you a ride back to the park after I'm done talking with Faust."

Lisa said, "Shouldn't he stay at the hospital, just in case whoever shot her comes back to finish the job?"

Eve wondered if Lisa was really concerned about Faust's safety or just wanted more time to flirt with Tom. "I think she's safe. The shooter could have killed her while she was lying helpless in that dry creek and he didn't."

But that left Eve with an intriguing question. Why *didn't* he finish her off? Faust was helpless and easy prey, lying in the creek bed with a broken leg. Perhaps, Eve thought, he spared Faust because she wasn't the intended target. It was Kim Spivey he wanted to kill. And he'd succeeded.

It was something to think about.

CHAPTER SIX

Eve entered the exam room. The back of the bed was raised, propping Faust up in a sitting position. Faust wore a loose-fitting, oversize patient gown. A bunch of tubes ran in and out of her body to the IV bags, a catheter collection bag, and monitoring equipment arrayed around her bed. Oxygen tubes taped under her nostrils helped with her breathing, and her splinted broken leg was slightly suspended on a pulley system. Her eyes were bloodshot, her cheeks were tear streaked, and her lips were chapped. But Faust's brown eyes were focused and fierce.

"Kim is dead." Faust spoke with a ragged, weak voice, breathing as little as possible to push out the words. "Isn't she?"

"I'm very sorry," Eve said as she approached her bedside. "I will do everything I can to find the person who shot you both, but I need your help. Can you answer a few more questions for me?"

Faust nodded.

Eve pulled over a chair and took out her phone. "I'm going to record our conversation to be sure I don't miss any details. Is that okay?"

Faust nodded again.

Eve stated the time, date, location, and who was present in the room, then asked her first question. "What were you doing at the park?"

"We just wanted to get away for two days without battling traffic or driving for hours to go somewhere," Faust said. "The park seemed like a quick escape, but it's mobbed on the weekend, so we figured we'd have it all to ourselves on a weekday."

"When did you get there?"

"She picked me up at my place in Topanga and we got there about three."

"Did you talk to anyone?"

"Just the ranger at the gate who gave us our permit."

"Then what?"

Faust took a moment to gather her strength and to wince through some pain. "We hiked a bit, saw the rock pond, and thought it would be even more beautiful at night. So we came back to the tent, had some dinner, messed around for a while, then went back to the pond at about eleven thirty."

"What did you do with your wallets and ID when you went to the pond?"

"We locked them in Kim's car and took her keys with us."

"What else did you have with you?"

"Just our phones and some towels," Faust said.

"What route did you take to the pond?"

"The trail through the meadow. We didn't take the road, though that would have been easier. But you aren't supposed to go to the pond at night, and we didn't want a ranger to see us, so we were kind of creeping there. That was half the fun."

"Were you carrying flashlights or using the lights on your phones to find your way?"

"We used our phones, but only for a second or two. We were tripping and giggling and staggering the whole way." A tear rolled down her cheek, prompted by the memory.

"Were you two drinking before?"

"We had a few beers. Smoked some weed. But yeah, we were a little wasted. Good wasted, if you know what I mean." She gave Eve an appraising look. "You probably don't."

Faust was right. Eve had never been high, or drunk, in her life. Her mom, and her younger sister and brother, believed it was a control issue, that Eve couldn't stand the thought of being even slightly uninhibited. Which was true. That didn't mean she wouldn't have wine, beer, or a cocktail, but she could stop at one and make it last through a meal or other social occasion.

Eve asked, "Did you see anyone else? Or get the sense that you were being watched or followed?"

"No. It felt like we were the only two people in the world."

"What happened when you got to the pond?"

Faust paused again and wiped away some tears. "We took off our clothes, went swimming, played around. It was wonderful."

"How long were you there?"

"Maybe half an hour or so before we started getting cold and got out, holding hands." The tears were streaming from her eyes now. The physical act of talking was painful for her, but not as much as the memory. But Eve had to know exactly what happened.

"Were you side by side?"

"No, she was a bit in front of me, and to my right, kind of pulling me along with her to get me to hurry up . . . We were eager to get back to the tent and snuggle . . . and we were almost out of the water, maybe up to our ankles, when there was this blast from the shore . . . so bright, so loud."

Faust went silent for a moment, reliving the horrible experience.

"When you say 'the shore,'" Eve asked, "where exactly was the shooter?"

"Directly in front of us, but kind of above, too, in the darkness. I felt a thousand stings . . . and her blood on my face. I knew that's what it was because it was so much warmer than the water. She fell, he fired again, and I ran to my right, into the brush, tripped over something, fell on some rocks, hit my head, and blacked out . . . I don't know for how long, but when I woke up, I felt that some time had passed. I was dizzy and nauseous and covered in sticky blood. I didn't know whether it was mine or hers . . . but I knew my leg was broken from the intense pain . . . so I began to drag myself along the creek toward the campground. I tried yelling for help . . . but I couldn't get my breath . . . and I was so cold, shivering all over. I thought the night would never end . . . that I would die out there."

The struggle of saying it all, of getting it out as quickly as she could, seemed to exhaust her. She held her hand to her chest and grimaced, squeezing the last of her tears from her eyes.

Eve waited her out. She wasn't ready to leave yet. There was more she needed to know. For several minutes, the only sounds in the room were the beep of the EKG machine and Faust's labored breathing. But when Faust's breathing seemed to slow, to become less ragged, Eve spoke again.

"You called the shooter 'he.' Did you get a look at him?"

"No. I didn't see anyone."

"Then how do you know it was a man?"

"I don't for sure," Faust said. "It's just a feeling."

"Did you see his shape or hear his voice or anything else that might have given you the impression that the shooter was a man?"

She shook her head. "All I heard and saw was the blast . . . and Kim falling. I ran for my life and left her there with him. I'm a selfish coward."

"You did the right thing, Zena. There was nothing you could have done for her. She was dead before she hit the ground. Did the shooter chase after you?"

"I don't know. I was in a panic and then I fell, knocked myself out, like I already told you. Maybe that's what saved me. It kept me still and quiet while he was looking for me."

It was possible. It was also very dark. The shooter might not have wanted to use a light, if he had one, and risk drawing attention to himself or the crime scene in case anyone had been drawn by the sound of the shotgun blast.

"Do you have any enemies, Zena?"

Faust grinned. "I'd laugh if it didn't hurt so Goddamn much. I've got more enemies than friends. Just look at my blog."

"Can you narrow it down for me?"

"For starters, everybody you work with at Lost Hills station."

Eve knew the feeling. "Anybody in particular?"

"I'm the one who revealed that Captain Mendoza was sexually harassing a female deputy. He hates me."

That was before Eve's time. Captain Moffett had just replaced Mendoza when Eve arrived at Lost Hills.

Faust continued. "I exposed the deputies who give favorable treatment to celebrities for drunk driving and wife beating. They hate me, too."

That also happened before Eve showed up, though one Lost Hills detective, Stan Garvey, was notorious for kissing up to famous athletes, music industry stars, and big-name Hollywood talent, including writers, producers, directors, and talent agents. He hated Eve for scoring a TV series deal, one of his big dreams.

"It goes on and on," Faust said, "all the way up to writing about the deputies you arrested for rape and the boys club in the department that protected them for years. I've also been looking into Captain Moffett's surprise reassignment to Men's Central Jail and Deputy Collier's resignation, but nobody's talking." Faust narrowed her eyes at Eve. "Weren't Moffett and Collier both involved in your botched undercover sting and the shooting at the Commons?"

Eve could feel Faust slipping into reporter mode and was tempted to tell her that everything they were saying was off the record, at least as far as publication was concerned, but decided that would be cold and inappropriate.

"Everything you're talking about was some time ago. Is there anything you've said or done recently that could have provoked someone to hurt you now? Perhaps someone outside of the Lost Hills station?"

"I've been hammering Derek Hayes, the movie studio exec, the last few weeks over the ways he's lied and gamed the system to restrict public access to the beach in front of his house. He said he'd ruin me. But they all say that. So did Paul Banning, the greedy asshole who shaved off the top of a hill at Las Virgenes and Mulholland for his megamansion, then cut a bunch of oaks because he still wasn't happy with his view."

Banning immediately went to the top of Eve's suspect list. He lived directly across the street from Malibu Creek State Park. He could have easily walked into the park, and out of it, without detection.

Faust took a moment to gather her breath again before continuing. "And there's half of the Calabasas City Council, who I'm sure Robinson Properties is bribing to get the New Positano project pushed through. They'd all like to shut me up before I can expose their corruption."

"How about Kim? Did she have enemies?"

"Just one," Faust said. "Curtis Honig."

Eve knew the name. Honig was the disgraced movie producer convicted in New York of sexually molesting his staff and raping dozens of actresses.

"How is Kim connected to him?"

"Kim is a yoga instructor now, but ten years ago, she was one of Honig's assistants and the first woman to accuse him of sexual assault. But she's a nobody, and a lesbian, so she was ignored until a famous straight movie star went public with the same story," Faust said. "Kim testified to the Los Angeles grand jury a few weeks ago and now Honig is being extradited from New York to stand trial here this month. He certainly has the money to hire a hit man."

Eve made a mental note to check if any of the other women who'd testified against Honig had been attacked before or after his New York trial. "A lot of women that he victimized have come forward over the last few years. What good would it do him now to have Kim killed?"

"Revenge," Faust said. "It all began with her."

Eve gave Faust a moment to rest and herself time to think about what she'd heard. Faust had so many enemies, it would be tough to narrow it down to a few likely suspects, though Banning looked like a strong possibility. But perhaps the shooter wasn't someone Zena Faust and Kim Spivey already knew. It could have been someone they'd encountered in passing yesterday and had offended, intentionally or otherwise.

Eve asked, "Did either of you have any heated encounters yesterday? Maybe cut someone off on the road? Chew out a waiter? Reject a come-on? Argue with someone at the park?"

Faust shook her head. "I was writing at home until Kim picked me up and she'd spent her day packing and getting supplies for our little getaway. If she'd had a fight with someone, she would have told me about it."

Eve could feel Faust's energy dissipating. They didn't have much more time to talk.

"Do you know the password to Kim's phone? I'd like to have it so we can see if she got any threatening emails or texts she might not have told you about."

Faust gave her the password, then said, "When do I get my phone, ID, and credit cards? The hospital billing department was on me even before the ER doctors."

"As soon as possible, probably in a couple of hours. Who knew you and Kim were going to be camping at the park?"

"Anyone who follows my Instagram or Twitter feeds. I posted some pictures and stories from the park when we got there. Those are the last pictures I'm going to have of us together. At least they were happy ones." She looked imploringly at Eve. "Do you think Kim suffered?"

Eve shook her head. "She died instantly, without fear or pain, knowing only the peace she felt being with you."

"I really want to believe that."

"I do," Eve said.

"Get the person who did this," Faust said.

"I will." Eve gave Faust a reassuring smile and left the room.

CHAPTER SEVEN

There were half a dozen TV news choppers circling over Malibu Creek State Park when Eve arrived with Tom. On the east side of Las Virgenes, an army of satellite broadcast vans filled the parking lot at King Gillette Ranch, which was as close as the Park Service was letting the media get to the crime scene.

Eve parked at a picnic area near the campground, where Duncan was waiting at a table. She and Tom got out of the car, each of them carrying take-out bags from In-N-Out Burger and a tray of soft drinks. Tom carried his over to Eddie Clayton, who was at a nearby table, and Eve joined Duncan.

"Where's my hospital burrito?" he asked.

She sat down across from him and began removing their burgers and fries from a bag. "I made an executive decision. I got you your favorites off the In-N-Out Burger secret menu instead. They make much better food than a hospital cafeteria."

"A hospital cafeteria is a higher level of cuisine than In-N-Out. They don't have a drive-through window. That should tell you something."

"It tells me it's a hospital, not a place to eat. But I brought you these." She pulled several lime Jell-O cups from one of the In-N-Out paper bags. "I stole them off a patient food cart."

Duncan broke into a big smile. "You've redeemed yourself."

Duncan dug into his three-by-three animal-style burger (three mustard-infused beef patties, three slices of cheese) and animal fries (french fries slathered in melted cheese, chopped onions, and their secret burger sauce) while Eve worked on her regular cheeseburger, fries, and a Coke.

As they ate, Eve filled Duncan in on what she'd learned, ending with Faust's comments about Paul Banning, the owner of a nearby house. She looked over at Banning's house, which was on the north side of Mulholland Highway, from King Gillette Ranch. The massive white, two-story Spanish-Mediterranean hacienda was sprawled along the top of a hill that had been cleaved flat and denuded, making it stand out and overwhelm the natural landscape. Eve could understand why people were upset by it.

"If Banning saw Zena's Instagram post, and knew she'd be right across the street last night, it might have been an irresistible opportunity for him, if he was mad enough," Eve said. "We still need to read her blog and see just how hard she's been on Banning, but he strikes me as our strongest suspect."

"Only because we don't have any others yet. Besides, there's a big stumbling block with him."

"How do you know? We haven't even begun to investigate him."

"I kinda have," Duncan said, wiping a gob of secret sauce off his chin with a napkin.

"Kinda? What does that mean?"

"He was one of those earlier targets I mentioned. Over a year ago, when his house was still being built, someone took a shot at his Porsche as he was leaving the jobsite, peppered the car with bird shot. He made his fortune in the debt-collection business and assumed the shooter was someone who owed him money."

"That doesn't rule Banning out as a suspect in this murder," she said.

"It makes him unlikely to be the serial shooter."

"We don't know that there is a serial shooter."

"I do," Duncan said.

"So you're dismissing him as a suspect because he doesn't fit into your preconceived notion of the crime."

"No, I'm just saying there's a stumbling block."

"It's you. Not him."

"In two weeks, that won't be a problem, will it? You'll just have to humor me until then." Duncan spotted some secret sauce on his tie and tried to wipe it off. Eve looked past him and saw Ranger Weston walking over, holding a brown paper evidence bag.

He held it out to Eve. "Your CSI people asked me to bring this over to you. It's a set of car keys and two cell phones from the clothing left at the pond."

She took it from him. "Thanks. Help yourself to some fries. In fact, take the whole thing."

"Gladly." Weston picked up her plate of fries and an unopened packet of ketchup, and walked back to his truck.

Eve reached into the bag, took out one of the cell phones, and punched in the code that Zena Faust gave her. It unlocked the device. Duncan gestured to it with his cup of Coke.

"Kim's phone?"

Eve nodded, scrolled briefly through the previous day's texts, but saw only exchanges between Faust and Kim, making arrangements for the camping trip. There were a few others between Kim and some of her clients, rescheduling yoga appointments. Eve set the phone aside. She'd take a deeper dive later.

"You could have offered the fries to me," Duncan said.

"You need to save room for the Jell-O."

"There's always room for Jell-O. It's liquid. It goes in an entirely separate compartment than solid food."

Eve thought for a moment. "Okay, let's say you're right, that there's a connection between this murder and the previous shootings."

"I was talking about Jell-O, and the physiology of the human body. I need a second to shift mental gears." Duncan took a sip of his drink. "All right, let's talk about the shooter."

"Maybe the shooter isn't the connection."

"What other connection is there?"

Eve pointed to Banning's house. "What better way is there for Banning to rule himself out as a suspect in *this* shooting than to copy the one that happened to him?"

"You're saying this shooting is a one-off copycat crime."

"It's possible," she said. "But he screwed up and killed the wrong woman."

Duncan pondered that while eating a french fry. "You're also saying it was a crime of opportunity, that it didn't occur to Banning to do this until he saw Zena Faust's post on Twitter or whatever."

"Yes."

Duncan ate another fry, feeding his thought process. "He'd need to already own a shotgun to pull it off."

"Lots of people own shotguns. That's not a big leap."

"Yes, it is. It's the kind of convenient coincidence that only happens on TV cop shows."

"My life is one," Eve said. "Or it soon will be."

"But this is the real-life part," he said. "We don't get to have it so easy."

"Easy would be if one of the campers was covered with gunshot residue and had the shotgun in his sleeping bag."

"No such luck. While you were gone, all the campers were swabbed for GSR and consented to searches. We got nothing, so I thanked them for their cooperation, apologized for the inconvenience, and let them all go."

"Any word from Nan yet?"

He shook his head. "The ME hasn't left with the body, and Malibu Search & Rescue is here, standing around in the group camping area, waiting for their marching orders, so Nan must still be mapping the crime scene."

"So, in the meantime, let's take a look at Zena's blog and then go knock on Banning's door."

"After I have my Jell-O. Want one?" He held out a cup to her.

"I'd rather have an enema."

"You could have if we were eating at the hospital cafeteria," Duncan said. "But it's not offered at In-N-Out."

"Maybe it's on their secret menu," she said. "It could be how In-N-Out got their name."

Eve spent the next few minutes going over Faust's website on her phone. It didn't take long to confirm that Faust had been hammering Banning and movie mogul Derek Hayes pretty hard the last few days. But she'd also written harshly about Calabasas city councilman Clark Netter and developer Gilbert Robinson, among others.

Eve set down her phone and saw that Tom Ross was still sitting at the next table with Eddie Clayton. She waved at Tom to come over. He picked up his Coke and approached their table. She handed him the evidence bag.

"Here's Zena's phone and the keys to Kim's car. Can you get Zena's ID from the car and take it, and her phone, to her?" Eve asked. "It will give you another opportunity to flirt with my sister."

"Lisa has already left. Her shift just ended and she's going home to squeeze in a shower and a nap."

"How do you know that?"

"Because she wants to be fresh and rested for our dinner tonight," he said.

"You do work fast."

Tom smiled. "You mean she does. She asked me out."

That didn't surprise Eve at all. Lisa wasn't shy, especially when it came to men. "There's one more thing you can do before you go."

Eve got up, went over to her car, and took out the evidence bag from the hospital that contained Zena's clothing, the baggie of shotgun pellets removed from her wounds, and other forensic evidence. She handed it to Tom, who'd followed her over.

"Can you please take this evidence out to the CSU team? Make sure they log it."

"Will do." He nodded and headed off to a patrol car.

Duncan joined her at her car and gestured to the huge house on the hill. "How do you want to play this?"

"You already have a relationship with Banning, so I'll follow your lead."

Duncan held out his hand. "Then it's better if I drive up and they see me on his gate camera."

She gave him the keys, they got in the car, and they drove out. They didn't have to go far. They crossed Las Virgenes, headed north for a few yards, then made a right onto the eastbound Mulholland Highway, then an almost immediate left to a shared community gate in front of a long, winding private road.

The road served three massive homes that had been built on unnaturally flat pads carved off the top of the rolling hills leading up a ridge, where Banning's house dominated a promontory overlooking Malibu Canyon, the Santa Monica Mountains, and Malibu Creek State Park.

Duncan leaned out of the driver's side window, reached for the keypad, and pressed the button reserved for Banning's property. A woman's voice answered.

"Yes?"

"This is Detective Duncan Pavone with the Los Angeles County Sheriff's Department. I'd like a word with Mr. Banning if he's around."

"Of course, Detective, come right up."

The gate yawned open and they made a left up a winding driveway of pressed concrete that was designed to resemble cobblestone. They drove up to the house, where a new Ferrari, a Rolls-Royce, a Mercedes, and a Bentley were parked like artwork in the motor court, arrayed around a burbling fountain of frolicking nude women etched in marble.

An actual woman was waiting for them at the fountain. Unlike the statues, she was all sharp angles, both in her physical features and the cut of her business suit. She was in her late twenties, perhaps early thirties, and seemed European to Eve, though she couldn't pinpoint a particular nationality.

The woman stepped up to greet them as they emerged from their car. "I'm Jayda Montaro, Mr. Banning's executive assistant. He's out back, if you will follow me."

She led them along a stone path that followed the western contours of the house.

"This place is huge," Duncan said. "It's even larger than it appears down there on earth." He waved his arm out at the park below.

"It's seven thousand square feet," Jayda said, "not counting the underground garage or the detached guesthouse, on a two-acre pad."

Eve said, "Which was a beautiful oak-lined hilltop, until it was stripped and graded to build this."

"This was the northwestern corner of the five-hundred-acre Stashower Ranch. The previous developer who owned this property was going to build seventy-five homes here. Instead, Mr. Banning and his investing partners built only twenty estate homes on a hundred acres and donated the remaining four hundred acres as permanent open space, guaranteeing that it remains a pristine habitat for wildlife."

It was a nice parry, Eve thought, and well rehearsed. But Jayda neglected to mention that Banning also got hefty income tax credits, property tax reductions, and one additional benefit from the donation that would drive up the prices of the twenty remaining properties. So Eve mentioned it.

"He also got an inherent guarantee that nothing will ever be built that obstructs the views or invades the privacy of these twenty home-owners, making the properties even more valuable." Eve had learned all that from the solid reporting on Faust's blog.

Jayda turned and smiled at Eve. "So it's a win for everybody involved. Mr. Banning crafted the perfect arrangement, which is a testament to his business acumen."

That's when they reached the backyard, where two men sat under a vast pergola, an outdoor living room with barbecue, wet bar, refrigerator, firepit, flat-screen TV, overhead fans with palm-frond-style blades, and a panoramic view of Malibu Creek basin, the Santa Monica Mountains, and the rolling hills to the north. All that was missing, Eve thought, was a throne where Paul Banning could sit to survey his kingdom.

One of the men, who Eve assumed was Banning, got up and strode over to them, his right hand outstretched. Banning was tall, fit, and smoothly tanned, the even, rich finish resembling the paint job on one of his cars. His teeth were bright white and perfect. He wore a loose-fitting untucked silk shirt and slacks and had a thick gold watch on his wrist that looked heavy enough to be used for weight lifting.

"Detective Pavone. This is a surprise."

Duncan shook his hand. "I apologize for disturbing you, Mr. Banning."

"Not at all. You've already met Jayda. This is my associate Gene Dent." Banning tipped his head toward the man sitting at the table under the pergola. He was pale, pudgy, and wore an ill-fitting suit. "Gene, remember a year ago when someone took a potshot at my car?"

"Of course I do," Dent said. "I also remember the insurance company sobbing over the $50,000 repair."

"This was the detective on the case," Banning said, then turned back to Duncan. "Frankly, I thought you gave up months ago."

"Detective Ronin and I would like to speak with you privately, if you don't mind."

"No worries." Dent grabbed the Louis Vuitton messenger bag at his feet and got up. "I have a plane to catch and I could use a head start on the traffic."

Jayda said, "I'll see you out."

"Safe travels, Gene." Banning shook his hand and watched him leave with his assistant. Eve noticed a pair of binoculars on the table, along with three glasses of wine and a platter of tiny quiches.

Banning turned back to the two detectives. "Now you have me worried. Does this have something to do with my family? Has my wife or daughter been hurt?"

"Oh, no, nothing like that," Duncan said. "I didn't mean to scare you. I should have known better."

Banning smiled. "It's okay. So what is it?"

"I'm sure you've noticed all the activity down at the park this morning."

"It's hard not to with all the TV news choppers flying around. We could barely hear ourselves talk." A helicopter streaked by above them, circling the park, as if to underscore his remark. "What happened?"

"There was a shooting last night that might be tied to yours," Duncan said.

Banning looked out at the park. "All of this attention is for a car? It must have been a lot nicer than mine."

"It wasn't a car that got shot up this time. A woman was killed and another was seriously injured."

"My God, that's horrible. I'm sorry to hear that," Banning said. "But I don't understand what I can do to help. I never saw who shot at me. I didn't even realize it was a gunshot until I got to my office and saw all the holes."

Eve said, "Were you home last night?"

He seemed to her to be startled by her voice. She hadn't spoken yet, so maybe he'd forgotten that she was there.

"Yes, but I didn't hear anything, if that's what you're asking. Sound carries from the road, of course, but there's so much traffic, and cars backfiring all the time, it just becomes white noise. We don't notice it."

"Do you own a shotgun?"

Now he seemed taken aback by her directness. "What?"

63

"One of the victims was Zena Faust."

"She's dead?" Banning asked.

"She's the one who survived," Duncan replied.

Eve cocked her head and studied him. "You look disappointed."

Actually, she thought he looked confused, which was what she was going for with her questioning, to put him off balance.

"You think I shot her?" He gave a weak, forced chuckle. It came out more like a cough. "That is absurd."

"Zena doesn't think so," Eve said.

"She pointed you to me?"

Duncan said, "She claims that you're furious over the extensive coverage her blog has given to the protests over the construction of this house, how it's an obscenity that desecrates the scenic corridor, and her accusations that you violated building codes, paid off inspectors, cut down legally protected oaks."

Banning waved that off. "I expected all of that bullshit the day I broke ground, if not from her, then from some other wacko."

Eve said, "I'll bet you didn't expect Faust to reveal that when you were a teenager vacationing in England, you were involved in a hit-and-run that cost a child his arm . . . and that you fled to the Dominican Republic, which has no extradition treaty with the UK, to avoid arrest."

Banning glared at Eve. "That tragic accident was settled thirty years ago. Do you know the real reason why Zena Faust is coming after me? It's not about my house. It's about hers."

"I don't understand," Duncan said.

"I dabble in real estate investments, but I'm primarily in the debt-collection business. She owed tens of thousands of dollars and my company forced her to sell her house to pay off the debts," Banning said. "She hates me. I wouldn't be surprised if she was the one who shot up my car."

That was interesting information, Eve thought. It revealed that Faust had her own agenda, one that might color anything she told them.

Banning turned to Eve. "Yes, I own a shotgun. You're welcome to it. Take my DNA, too, while you're at it."

Eve gave Duncan a look. Her life really was a TV show. "We will."

A helicopter swooped in low overhead, down toward the park, so loud that it would have drowned out any conversation and drew their attention. Eve saw the sheriff's department seal on the side of the chopper and watched it land in the parking area.

Now that they could be heard again, Duncan spoke to Banning. "We mean no offense, Mr. Banning. We're just being thorough and exploring all the possibilities."

"But it doesn't make any sense to suspect me," he said. "How could I have known that Faust was down there?"

"She posted about it on social media."

"You think I follow her online?"

Eve said, "Absolutely."

She picked up the binoculars from the table, held them to her eyes, and looked to see who would emerge from the chopper. The zoom was incredible.

"These binoculars are so powerful you could have seen her when she arrived," Eve said. "And if she had anything from lunch stuck between her teeth."

Sheriff Richard Lansing stepped out of the chopper. *Shit*, Eve thought. Lansing was in his late fifties, the son of a preacher, and wore his uniform and badge the way the pope wore his white cassock and cross.

She handed Banning his binoculars. "We have to go. We'll send a crime scene investigator up to collect your shotgun and swab the inside of your cheek. Stick around until then."

Duncan smiled at Banning. "Thank you for your cooperation. We appreciate it."

The two detectives headed for their car. As soon as they were out of earshot, Duncan said, "We make a good team, perfectly in step, like Fred Astaire and Ginger Rogers. I'm going to miss that."

"Me too."

"Why are we rushing off?"

"Lansing just landed."

"Of course he did. Because of all of them." He gestured to the satellite trucks parked below at King Gillette Ranch. "He can't resist a camera."

They got into the car and Duncan drove them down the road to the gate.

Eve asked, "How do you feel about Banning as a suspect now?"

"He's got means, motive, and opportunity."

"And a shotgun," Eve added.

"I stand corrected on that point," Duncan said. "But I still think we have a serial shooter at work."

"Based on what?"

Duncan paused at the gate, waiting for it to open. "My gut. And it's impressive, as you may have noticed."

"'Impressive' is not the word I would have chosen."

CHAPTER EIGHT

Duncan drove up to the park headquarters, which was in an old two-story Colonial-style home adjacent to the campground. Various official vehicles, from the Park Service and the LASD, as well as the medical examiner's van, were parked in front of the house.

"Welcome to Mr. Blandings' Dream House," Duncan said to Eve as they got out of the Dodge Charger.

"Who is that?"

"Not who, what. It's a famous 1940s comedy. Cary Grant and Myrna Loy build their dream home in rural Connecticut. Hijinks ensue. This was the house."

"Is this how it looked in the movie?"

"There weren't any police cars or morgue wagons in the original."

"Well, there certainly will be in the reboot," Eve said.

Lansing and Kalb emerged from the park office. Kalb had a smug look on her face. Lansing said something to her, then walked alone over to Duncan and Eve.

"I was just about to call you two," Lansing said. "I've been getting an earful from the mayors of Calabasas and Malibu, the state parks commissioner, the district's state senator, and the chair of the Los Angeles County Board of Supervisors. They all want this park open."

"We're investigating a murder," Duncan said.

"Yes, but look at this production," Lansing said. Eve thought that was an interesting choice of words, given where they were standing, in a park that was once a studio back lot, and outside a house built for a film. Now it was all the location for a murder in Movieland. "You'd think it was the Kennedy assassination."

"We could be dealing with a serial shooter."

Lansing wagged a finger at Duncan, as if he were chastising a child. "I don't want to hear even the slightest hint of that spoken, not unless you have solid physical evidence to back it up." The sheriff waited. Duncan was silent. "That's what I thought. So what we have at the moment is an isolated incident in an isolated spot. I don't see any reason why this park can't be reopened."

Eve could think of one. "We don't know how the shooter got in or out or if he's still here."

"Malibu Creek State Park is twelve square miles of mountains, canyons, and grassland, none of it fenced. We could bring in a hundred officers and spend a month in here and never know the answer to those questions," Lansing said, then nodded toward their car. "Let's go see Nan."

Duncan still had the car keys, so he drove the three of them down Crags Road to the clearing at the dry creek that led to the rock pond. A tent had been erected there, where forensic technicians were cataloging evidence they'd collected, and a designated pathway of plastic sheeting, held down with stakes, led from the clearing to the pond.

The three of them got out of the car, signed in with the deputy securing the scene, and followed the path to a spot overlooking the pond. Numbered yellow placards were placed in various spots where evidence was waiting to be collected and a dozen forensic investigators were on their hands and knees around the pond, taking photos or digging carefully in the dirt. Kim's body was still there, covered with a sheet, Nan standing in the water in galoshes nearby.

Nan spotted the sheriff, Eve, and Duncan and approached them with her hands up in a halting gesture. She remained standing in the water.

"Stay there, don't come down here. We're still working the rest of this area," she said, referring to the shoreline in front of them. "We don't often see you at crime scenes, Sheriff. What can I do for you?"

"You can update me on where you are with your investigation."

"We've just completed our mapping of the scene and are releasing the body to the medical examiner. We've been able to determine, based on the angle, dispersal pattern, and impact depth of the shotgun pellets into objects, as well as the recovery of the spent wad, that the shooter was standing over there . . ." She pointed to a slight slope leading down to the portion of pond where Kim's body was. "We've isolated some footprints that may or may not belong to the shooter. And further up one of the trails, which could have been used for his escape, we've collected some fresh vomit. We can extract DNA and more from that."

"Great," Lansing said. "So let's get your team out of here so the public can enjoy this beautiful park."

"We're just getting started," she said. "We still have much more work to do."

He made a show of looking bewildered. "What else is there?"

"Lots of things. For instance, we don't know the path the shooter took to enter or leave the pond."

"Is that necessary to know?"

Eve could tell Nan was trying to control her temper. When Nan spoke, it was slowly, and evenly, patronizing the sheriff.

"It might lead us to evidence of his vehicle, and that might indicate the make, and model, and if it was parked or running, which could help us identify the assailant or determine if he was acting alone. But there's still much more to do right here. There's a large amount of footprints, footwear prints, and trash, probably left behind by numerous visitors over a period of days, but any of it could also have been left by the shooter. We still have to collect and process it all. We also need to wait until nightfall to begin other testing."

Lansing smirked, which only seemed to irritate Nan further. "What can you possibly accomplish in darkness that you can't do now?"

"This is not a restricted, enclosed space like a vehicle, house, or apartment. We can't control the light," Nan said. "We need darkness to use alternate light sources to expose any bodily fluids that might have been left behind but that are invisible to the naked eye. The dried fluids will glow when exposed to ultraviolet, infrared, or different color bands of light."

Lansing sighed with obvious frustration. "So you can be out by morning."

"We still have to thoroughly inspect all possible trails in and out of here for evidence and collect it," Nan said. "That's best done in daylight."

"Fine," he said. "You have until noon tomorrow."

Nan took a deep breath, and Eve knew the tirade that was coming.

"There are two ways we can do this job, thoroughly or—"

The sheriff interrupted Nan. "Half-assed. I know. I've heard your speech fifty times before. Your notion of 'half-assed' would qualify as an exhaustive investigation compared to the way crime scene units work anywhere else. You're the best of the best."

"Flattery won't get you anywhere with me or change the time required to fully process this crime scene."

"Noon tomorrow. Not a second longer." The sheriff turned and walked back to the car, passing Emilia Lopez and two of her attendants as they came down the trail with a body bag to collect the corpse. Duncan and Eve lingered with Nan for a moment.

Nan glowered at the sheriff's back until he disappeared in the trees. "Now we're going to have to pull an all-nighter here and try to cram another day of work into just twelve hours, which is impossible. And people get sloppy when they're tired."

Eve said, "I'm sorry."

"Save your apology for the victim's family. You'll need it if your case crumbles because of the mistakes made today. Is there something else you need? I have work to do."

Eve told Nan about Paul Banning, his shotgun, and his willingness to consent to a DNA swab.

Nan agreed to send someone up to his house to collect the evidence, then added, "But don't get your hopes up, even if his shotgun is the murder weapon."

"Why not?"

A flash of irritation crossed Nan's face. "Shotguns that shoot pellets have a smooth bore, which means that any casings we find can't be matched back to a specific weapon the way bullets can be from a rifled firearm."

Eve felt stupid, a common occurrence around Nan. "Right. Thanks. I forgot about that."

Duncan and Eve started to walk away as Lopez and her team began to lift Kim's corpse into the body bag. Eve was glad she didn't have their job.

Duncan said, "You have no idea what Nan is talking about, do you?"

"I'm never ashamed to admit my ignorance, except that right now she's pressed for time and wouldn't appreciate wasting any of it on educating me."

"Wise decision. A rifled bore has grooves that add a stabilizing spin to the bullet, improving accuracy and creating scratches that can be matched like a fingerprint to a specific weapon."

"I suppose pinpoint accuracy isn't as important when you're blasting a target with a thousand pellets, especially at short range."

"The smooth bore also increases speed, which is handy if you're shooting at something that's moving fast like a duck, a turkey . . ."

"Or a Porsche," Eve said.

"That's right."

They found Lansing leaning against their Dodge Charger, his arms folded under his chest, but he didn't seem to Eve to be upset that they'd kept him waiting.

Lansing looked at Eve, as if he were reading her thoughts. "I wanted to give you a minute to commiserate with Nan over what a coldhearted political bastard I am."

"That was very considerate of you, sir," Eve said.

"Where are you two on your investigation?"

"It's early stages." Eve filled him in. When she was done, Lansing took a moment to think before he spoke.

"I'm not surprised someone took a shot at Zena Faust. She prides herself on making enemies. I think you'll find the killer's name in one of her articles."

"I don't think so," Duncan said. "Why would he use bird shot? Why not a bullet?"

"Why not an axe, a knife, or a flamethrower? You can ask the killer that when you find him."

Eve said, "Or her."

Lansing shook his head, dismissing her notion. "Women don't use shotguns. Not in Los Angeles. Too messy."

"With respect, sir, that's an unproven, broad generalization."

"No, that's hard-earned knowledge gleaned from years of experience, which you don't have yet," he said.

They all got back in the car, Eve in the back seat and the two men up front, and returned to Mr. Blandings' Dream House. But Lansing didn't get out right away. He looked across Las Virgenes Road at the King Gillette Ranch and all the press vehicles parked there.

"Nobody talks to the press but me, is that understood?"

Duncan nodded and Eve said, "I hate talking to the press."

Lansing turned in his seat to look back at her. "You love it, but you aren't the one I am concerned about." He glanced at Duncan, who held up his hands from the steering wheel in surrender.

"My wife won't let me go on TV. She says the cameras add twenty pounds to you and I'm fat enough," Duncan said. "What are you going to tell them?"

"That a camper, who we aren't identifying until we can notify next of kin, was killed in a shooting, but we believe that it's an isolated incident, the park is safe, and the public isn't in any danger."

"We don't know that's true," Duncan said.

"That's why I'm saying that 'we believe,' not that 'we know,'" Lansing said. "But what I *do* know is that we don't gain anything by terrifying people, most likely for nothing."

"And if someone else gets shot?"

"Then I'll say we made a mistake."

Duncan glanced at Eve in the rearview mirror before he spoke again. Eve shook her head, warning him against saying something he might regret. He shifted his gaze to the sheriff.

"I'm sure that will make whoever gets shot feel a lot better," Duncan said. "Unless they're in the morgue."

The sheriff patted Duncan on the shoulder. "I'm going to miss you, Donuts."

Lansing got out of the car and so did Eve. She slid into the passenger seat as the sheriff walked up to Mr. Blandings' house and was met by Trisha Kalb on the front step.

"I don't think he's really going to miss me," Duncan said.

"There's nothing more we can do here right now. Let's go back to the station, notify Spivey's next of kin, and write up our reports. Then we can head out to the studio for our meeting with the *Ronin* writing staff."

Duncan turned the car around and headed for the gate. "What about dinner?"

"You just had a late lunch and you're already worried about dinner?"

"I like to know where my next meal is coming from," Duncan said. "It's a natural survival instinct."

"They're serving us dinner at the meeting," Eve said.

"I think I'm going to like the TV business," he said.

CHAPTER NINE

The Lost Hills sheriff's station was a one-story brick-and-cinder-block building on the south side of Agoura Road, on the western border between the cities of Calabasas and Agoura Hills, facing the Ventura Freeway. The helipad and the fenced-in rear parking lot for employees' cars and official vehicles were up against the northernmost hills of Malibu Creek State Park. Those hills were untouched by the wildfire and thick with chaparral and clusters of oak trees on the slopes and the folds between them.

Eve and Duncan spent the next few hours in their cubicles, filling out the piles of obligatory paperwork that came with their job. Then they got into her Subaru Outback for the drive to the TV studio.

She rolled down all the windows as she drove out of the station's parking lot. She was convinced the Subaru's interior, despite being thoroughly cleaned a dozen times, still reeked of the dog shit it had been stuffed with by the same unidentified deputies who'd spray-painted TRAITOR BITCH on the passenger side of the car. At least the graffiti wasn't visible under the new paint job.

The studio was an old warehouse on Balboa Boulevard, close to the western runways of Van Nuys Airport. Aircraft parts were manufactured in the warehouse until the late 1980s, when the property was converted into soundstages and production offices that were rented to various TV shows and movies. The entire street was lined with similar light-industrial buildings.

Duncan looked disappointed as she parked in front of the warehouse, which didn't have any signage outside besides the address painted in large numbers on the front wall. There was nothing about the building that indicated to anyone driving by that movies and TV shows were shot there.

"When you said that we were going to the studio," Duncan said, "I was expecting a studio."

"You mean a big, grandiose front gate, rows of soundstages, a back lot of fake streets, and actors milling around everywhere dressed as Roman gladiators, cowboys, showgirls, and astronauts?"

"Something like that."

"The big studios, like Universal and Paramount, are massive and impressive, especially the ones with roller coasters and dinosaurs, but they are also very expensive places to shoot. This is the real Hollywood. The valley is filled with anonymous soundstages like this."

Eve's mother, Jen, had spent years working in them, mostly sitting around for hours, reading romance novels while she waited to be summoned by an assistant director to fill out the background of a shot while the actors performed their scenes. One day Jen might have been a nameless nurse passing by in a hospital corridor while two surgeons argued over how to save a life. The next day, she could have been one of a hundred terrified passengers belted into their seats as a stewardess argued with a hijacker. But in every situation, Jen was merely human decor, something with a pulse to dress up the set while someone else did the acting. Jen yearned to have dialogue, to be an actor in the forefront, not the background. Her yearning, with the exception of a few bit parts over the years, went largely unfulfilled.

Once Eve got her driver's license, she became not only her mom's full-time babysitter but also her personal driver. Jen said she needed the driving time to concentrate on getting into character, even though she rarely had any lines.

Eve felt like she'd visited every soundstage in the valley when she was a teenager. She'd definitely been to this one a few times but she'd never imagined she'd return again for a TV show about her. It didn't feel real.

"The TV series *Hollywood & the Vine* was shot here," she said. "The original, not the new reboot."

"How do you know that?"

"Mom worked on it," she said. "So did my father."

They got out of the car and went into the lobby, which hadn't changed since the days when aircraft parts were made in the building instead of TV shows. The floor was scratched linoleum, the white walls were decorated with yellowed pictures of various small airplanes, and the front office was separated from the door by a faux wood–paneled counter with a linoleum countertop.

Nobody was at the desks, but they were met at the door by Simone Harper, the executive producer and writer of the show. She was an African American woman in her thirties, casually dressed in a T-shirt, jeans, and sneakers, the standard uniform of TV writers of both sexes. But Eve suspected that Simone dressed that way to disarm people or, in the case of her writing staff, to put them at ease so they wouldn't be intimidated by her during the creative give-and-take of coming up with stories.

That's because Simone was one of the most powerful writer-producers in television, creator of the Emmy Award–winning hit series *Playing Doctor*, a drama about a headstrong young woman who takes over her late father's medical practice in an isolated corner of Alaska even though she isn't actually a doctor. Simone's first job as a staff writer was on *Hollywood & the Vine*, so Eve thought that being back in this building again, this time as the showrunner of her own series, had to be strange and meaningful for her, too.

"It's so great to see you." Simone hugged Eve and then offered Duncan her hand. "And I'm delighted to finally meet you, Duncan, though I feel like I already know you."

"I could tell from the script," Duncan said.

Eve wasn't sure if he was being sarcastic or not and, she guessed, neither was Simone. But the producer's polite smile didn't waver.

"Let's chat in my office for a minute before we meet the writers." She led them up a freestanding staircase to the second floor.

"I thought *you* were the writer," Duncan said.

"I wrote the pilot, and I'm the executive producer, but we have a writing staff for the rest of the episodes, though ultimately I'll revise every script to maintain a consistent voice for the show."

Simone's office was a large windowless room with a big desk on one end, and on the other, a collection of mismatched couches and coffee tables facing several large dry-erase boards covered with multicolored handwritten scrawl. Eve assumed the scrawl was outlines for future episodes but she didn't want to take a closer look to find out.

It was hardly an office befitting a woman of Simone's wealth, power, and stature in the TV industry, though Eve figured that she probably had a much nicer setup at her company headquarters on the Warner Brothers' studio in Burbank, where the interiors of *Playing Doctor* were shot.

Eve pointed to a fake window with a fake view of a tropical beach that was hanging on the wall behind Simone's desk, which was piled with scripts and papers.

"I like the view," Eve said.

"I asked the prop department for a window with a view and that's what I got," Simone said.

"It beats the real view," Eve said, guessing it would either be an alley or an airplane runway.

"Fantasy and escapism is our business and that window is a constant reminder," Simone said, then beckoned them with a wave of her arm to the two guest chairs in front of her desk. "I really appreciate you coming here, Eve. It's one thing for the staff to meet you on the page and another in person."

"I'm not that Eve Ronin."

"I'm glad you understand that, because we got some network notes on the characters. I've had to make some changes in the latest draft to address them." She handed them each a script from the pile on her desk. The pages were an assortment of different colors that reflected the dates of each revision.

"What kind of changes?" Eve asked.

"The network found Eve a bit too abrasive and unlikable, so I've had to soften some of her edges."

Duncan flipped through the script. "I wish you could do that to her in real life."

"I doubt that's necessary," Simone said. "Overall, most of the changes they asked me to make in the script are designed to give us room to reach a broader audience and to create new stories."

Eve said, "For instance?"

Simone looked at Duncan. "I've made Eve's partner twenty years younger than you are, but he's still got years of experience."

He shrugged. "I am young at heart, so it still fits."

"We've made the captain a gay Asian American man because the network felt he came across as too one-dimensional," she said. "We've also tweaked Eve's backstory. She was still raised by a single mother but, instead of Jen being a struggling actress, she is now a waitress at a Denny's in the valley, one of many menial jobs she's cycled through. Also, Eve doesn't know who her father is and, on some level, she is still searching for him, and that mystery is part of what drives her as a detective."

"I know who my father is," Eve said. "So do you."

"But our Eve doesn't," Simone said.

"So why not go one step further and change her name?" Eve said. "I wouldn't mind. In fact, I'd be much happier if you did."

"We won't do that because you, and your story, are what inspired this series and the pilot is based on your first homicide investigation. You are the big hook," Simone said. "But beyond that case, and maybe the one with the skeletons in Bone Canyon, we have to make up stories because you haven't solved enough cases yet to sustain a TV series."

Duncan held up the script. "You should have based the series on me. I have plenty of cases."

"No offense, but there have been enough cop shows about white, middle-aged, male homicide detectives. But we're going to stay honest to your reality." Simone glanced at Eve. "Especially yours."

"I have no idea what that means," Eve said.

"Yes, we've made some changes. However, we want to be true to the essence of who you are and the work you do and tell stories that reflect both your ideals and real police work," she said. "That's what we hope to get from you tonight and as the creative process goes on. Shall we begin before the dinner gets cold?"

"I vote yes," Duncan said, standing up. "What are you serving?"

"Barbecue ribs, brisket, and some salads delivered from Bludso's in Hollywood," Simone said. "I hope you don't mind."

"I never mind barbecue," Duncan said. "You could barbecue a bowl of Captain Crunch and I'd be happy."

"More like ecstatic," Eve said.

Simone led them down the hall to a windowless conference room where four women, ranging in age from their twenties to late thirties, and one man, who looked to be in his late fifties, sat around the table, though three seats at one end remained unoccupied. The writers already had food on paper plates in front of them and, from the looks of it, had been eating for a while. The barbecue ribs and sliced brisket were in large aluminum platters on a table against one wall, along with a bowl of potato salad, some paper plates, plastic cutlery, and piles of napkins, containers of sauce, and an assortment of canned soft drinks.

Simone introduced everybody, filled her plate with salad, and took the seat at the head of the table. Eve helped herself to a couple of ribs, potato salad, and a drink and took an empty seat on one side of Simone.

The lone male writer, his name was Archie, sat across from Eve and next to the empty seat meant for Duncan. Archie looked at Eve, up and down, and said, "You're even younger than you look on TV."

"Should I take that as a compliment?"

"You should be selling Girl Scout Cookies." Nobody laughed or even smiled. Archie glanced around the table and shrugged. "Sorry. I'm still getting used to being the only man in the writers' room."

Simone said, "We all know what that feels like, Archie, but in reverse. That's why we're being so patient and understanding."

"I think you mean tolerant," said Valerie, an Asian woman with a shaved head.

Jackie, a heavyset white woman who gave off a motherly vibe, said to Eve, "Is this what your experience is in the LASD? Do you feel like the only woman in a world of clueless, entitled men?"

"There are other women in the department," Eve said. "The biggest obstacle I face is resentment, not because I am a woman, but because of my youth and inexperience and the widely held belief that I don't deserve to be in homicide."

"Is there truth to that belief?" asked Yvette, a woman who sat with her feet up on her chair, hugging her knees to herself.

"Yes," Eve said. "I have to prove myself every day."

Simone looked at her. "To the other detectives or to yourself?"

Eve could see now that this was going to be a very unpleasant experience for her. She didn't like discussing her feelings.

"Mostly to myself," she said.

Duncan sat down carrying two plates piled high with meat slathered with barbecue sauce and carefully set them on the table so the food wouldn't topple. "She's done an exceptional job, and I'm not just saying that because she set me up with this consulting gig for my retirement."

"Detective Pavone?" Carol held up her hand, as if waiting to be called on in class, which fit, since she looked like she'd just graduated from college. "Why did you welcome her when your colleagues didn't?"

"I didn't. I felt the same way everyone did, only to a lesser degree, since I knew I wasn't going to be stuck working with her for very long. I'm retiring, so I didn't care." Duncan tucked a napkin into the collar of his shirt and surveyed his plates, trying to decide what to start eating first. "But I didn't like how she got her promotion and I was sure she didn't deserve it. Turned out that she's got a real knack for the job, but she's raw and inexperienced. There's a lot she has to learn. Honestly, I feel like I am abandoning her when she needs me most."

Eve was surprised by his admission and a little embarrassed by it, too. "This is beginning to sound like a group therapy session."

Simone and the other writers laughed, sharing knowing looks with each other.

"That's what writers' rooms often become, Eve," Simone said. "The best stories are the ones that force you to bare a part of your soul to write them."

Archie said, "That's certainly what made our scripts on *Vampire Cop* so compelling."

Jackie asked Eve, "Why did you become a sheriff's deputy?"

Eve leaned forward so she could look down the table at Jackie. "My little sister will tell you it's because I'm the oldest of three children of a single parent. Life at home was total chaos and uncertainty. I hated it. So I tried to impose order in our lives and keep things from regularly spinning out of control. But I failed because I had no real authority over anyone. So I found a job where I could succeed at it."

"That's what your sister thinks," Simone said. "But what do you think?"

"She's probably right. The way I see it, I have two jobs: maintaining order and restoring order. My private life is still a mess, but in my job, I feel like I have some control over the chaos."

Duncan set down the rib he was devouring, leaving sauce on his cheeks, to say, "That isn't even remotely true. You have no control at all. None of us do. It's foolhardy to think otherwise."

Simone studied Eve, as if that alone would reveal important truths about who she was. "What was the chaos at home?"

"I'd rather not get into it," Eve said. "Especially since you're probably going to be working with my parents."

Archie raised an eyebrow. "We are?"

Simone shifted her gaze to him. "Her mother is an actress and her father is an episodic TV director I worked with when I was a baby writer. It's how I got the jump on every other producer in town who was chasing Eve's story."

"Who is he?" Archie asked.

"Vincent Nyby," Eve said. "He's directing the pilot."

"He is? I thought he died years ago," Archie said, then saw the horrified expressions on the faces of his fellow writers and quickly added, "I don't mean to be rude."

Eve waved off his concern. "No worries."

Her response seemed to intrigue Yvette. "Really? I would be offended if Archie said that about my father."

"You're offended by everything I say," Archie said.

Yvette ignored him and pinned her gaze on Eve. "How do you feel about your father working on the show? And why do you two have different last names?"

She has good instincts, Eve thought. *Like a shark.* It would make Yvette a good writer for the show, but Eve really didn't want to answer her questions. She was thinking about how to dodge them when her phone vibrated in her pocket.

She took out her phone, glanced at the screen, and saw a notification that she'd received an email and video attachment from Wallace Ewell, the Las Virgenes Municipal Water District bureaucrat. It was just the pretense she needed to escape this interrogation.

"I'm sorry. We have to go," Eve declared and stood up. "An urgent lead just came in on an important case we're working and we've got to chase it down right away."

Duncan quickly swallowed a mouthful of brisket and wiped his face with a napkin.

Simone stood up, too. "Of course, I totally understand. Thank you for coming by. We hope to see a lot more of you."

Duncan also stood, but had a forlorn expression on his face. He didn't want to leave his dinner behind. Eve realized that she hadn't touched her barbecue ribs but it was too late now. She wasn't taking it to go.

"Mind if I take some leftovers?" Duncan asked Simone. He didn't have Eve's reservations.

"Go ahead," Simone said. "Take whatever you want."

He hurried over to the table along the wall, sealed one of the aluminum platters of brisket with aluminum foil, and carried it out of the room with him. He didn't dare look back to see if anybody objected. Eve followed him out and headed for the stairs as fast as she could without running.

"Slow down. What's the big news?" Duncan clutched the tray to his chest as if someone might try to pry it from his grasp. "Did Nan find something?"

"No, nothing like that. I just received the security camera video from the water district guy."

"So why are we leaving? The discussion was just getting interesting."

"I'd rather have a root canal without anesthesia than answer any more of their questions."

She dashed down the stairs and out of the building. If Duncan didn't hurry up, he'd have to call an Uber.

Thanks to the negotiating skill of Linwood Taggert, her big-time talent agent, Eve had final say over how she was portrayed in the TV series. Having that control had eased some of her worries. But now, on the drive back to the Lost Hills station, she told Duncan that she was thinking she'd rather have nothing to do with the show at all and just leave all the creative decisions to him.

"You can't ignore the show," Duncan said, sneaking a piece of brisket from the tray and popping it into his mouth. "It's going to be out there. People are going to meet you and expect you to be *that* Eve Ronin. So she'd better be someone you like."

"How am I going to do my job and compete with fictional me every day?"

"It's been done before."

"How do you know?"

"I did some research before I let you drag me into this," he said. "Back in the 1970s, NBC aired a TV series about LAPD homicide detective John St. John while he was still on the force. It was called *Jigsaw John*. It didn't affect his work at all. The show was canceled after a few episodes but he stayed on the job for another twenty years, going on to catch the Night Stalker and the Freeway Killer."

"That's encouraging," Eve said.

"Did you know the Gene Hackman movie *The French Connection* was based on Eddie Egan, a real NYPD cop who was still on the job when the film came out?"

"No, I didn't. What happened to Egan?"

"He immediately retired and became an actor," Duncan said. "And spent the rest of his life playing cops on TV."

"Okay," Eve said. "Now you're terrifying me."

"I'm just saying you'll find a way to deal with it."

"Becoming an actor is not one of them," she said. "I can promise you that."

Eve hated herself for agreeing to be involved in the show, but she kept reminding herself it was the only way she could pay her legal fees. It really was, because she knew that she'd never sue the LASD to get the money, even if it was certain that she'd win. It was bad enough that so many deputies believed she was out to get the department without her actually *doing* it.

All she wanted was to be an actual sheriff's department detective, not an actor playing one on TV. Or, worse, a woman trying to play one in real life and giving an unconvincing performance.

CHAPTER TEN

She dropped Duncan off at the Lost Hills station and then headed toward home, a two-story street-facing condo on the north end of Las Virgenes Road, on the other side of the Ventura Freeway, only a mile or two away, so close by that she often biked to work.

Eve stopped at the T intersection of Agoura Road and Las Virgenes, where she faced what was once a sheep ranch nestled against the hills but now was one of the last big undeveloped parcels in Calabasas.

The weed-choked land was dotted with seemingly hundreds of tall story poles, tied together with colored streamers to represent the contours of proposed buildings, arrayed around a billboard for "New Positano—A Robinson Development." The billboard depicted 180 condos and six thousand square feet of retail space, all designed to resemble a quaint, centuries-old coastal Italian village of tightly packed whitewashed stucco buildings, crowding the slopes around a cobblestone open square and an enormous burbling fountain of Poseidon and his trident.

A Disneyfied re-creation of Positano, a picturesque village clinging to the cliffs on Italy's Amalfi Coast, seemed to Eve like a ridiculous thing to build in the dry, fire-scarred hills of Calabasas, originally a Spanish settlement. But, in a strange way, it was architecturally consistent. All the streets in the gated residential communities on the ridge above were named after Italian towns and cities. And there was the Commons shopping center, the city's default "downtown" on the other side of the hills, that was modeled on a rural village in Tuscany and had a clock tower that supported the world's largest Rolex.

The way things were going, she thought, soon movies set in Italy would be shot in Calabasas instead to save money. The city would become a de facto Hollywood back lot, enjoying a lucrative new revenue stream from issuing location permits. Maybe that was their secret plan all along. It was surprising to Eve that Zena Faust hadn't already pursued that possible conspiracy theory on her blog.

If Eve turned left and took the overpass over the 101, she'd be home in two minutes for dinner and a good night's rest.

But she thought rest was overrated and, more often than not, felt more like laziness to her. She chose instead to turn right and go to Malibu Creek State Park, putting off dinner and dragging out her work day even longer into the night.

Less than ten minutes later, she was parked beside the CSU tent in the clearing above the dry creek. A deputy had her sign in and told her the CSU team was still conducting their alternate light source tests.

She used the light on her phone to follow the trail to the pond, which was bathed in the eerie blue glow cast by the flashlight-like devices held by the camera-toting CSU investigators along the shore. The investigators were wearing plastic goggles with orange-colored lenses that allowed them to see the biological stains illuminated by the light from their devices. But Eve couldn't see anything besides the blue glow.

Nan wore a pair of goggles and, by way of a greeting, offered Eve a matching pair. "Good timing. Pissmaster Noomis has sniffed out a discovery."

Eve had met Noomis at her first homicide crime scene and that's when he'd first demonstrated to her his skill at identifying a urine sample as human, or from another animal, by the smell.

"I don't want to think about how he developed his mastery." Eve put on her goggles and followed Nan to the far eastern edge of the pond, where Noomis was crouched, examining a tree trunk.

"I have two kids, a dog, a cat, and a hamster," Nan said. "I'm not too bad at it, either."

Now that Eve had goggles on, she could see sparkles everywhere. It looked to her like Christmas tree lights had been strung among the trees, rocks, and bushes, mostly at ground level. The tree that Lou Noomis was studying was covered with luminous orange spots, but one was wider and higher than the others, an arched slash of radiant color.

A digital camera with an orange lens filter hung around Noomis' neck, and he held one of those unusual flashlights, which had a design that reminded Eve of a stealth plane, matte gray with even, smooth surfaces and only a few blunted edges.

Nan said, "Hey, Lou, look who showed up to see what you've found."

Noomis turned from the tree and smiled when he saw Eve. "You're interested in urine?"

"Not in general," she said.

He held out his stealth flashlight to her. "Do you mind holding the SPEX HandScope for me?"

Eve took it and kept the beam aimed at the tree while Noomis shot some pictures of what was illuminated on the trunk.

"It's fascinating," Noomis said. "This tree tells a story in urine."

"I'd prefer to read the book or see the movie," Eve said.

"The tree has been regularly marked by people and animals, mostly coyotes, dogs, and bobcats. It's coated with piss, as are a lot of boulders, bushes, and trees here. But this wider, higher sample is clearly the most recent. It's human and it's male."

"You can tell that from the height of the sample?"

"Yes, but also the quantity of urine, the spray pattern, the amount of residual pH, which creates the intensity of the glow, and, of course, there's the distinct smell," Noomis said. "He had a full bladder, but he wasn't in a hurry to empty it, so he was relaxed, not freaked out. He had a strong, consistent flow, released in a calm, steady manner. No flourishes, so we're probably dealing with a healthy adult."

"Flourishes?" she asked.

"Target shooting, distance shooting, and painting with the pee stream. Those are typically juvenile behaviors. Adults just want to do the job."

Eve glanced at Nan. "Men have a lot more fun peeing than we do."

Was that a smile or grimace that Eve saw on Nan's face? It was too dark for her to be sure.

Noomis went on. "I'm guessing from the smell and pH that he drank mostly water and fruit juices yesterday, no alcohol or soft drinks. I'll swab the bark and collect a piece of it, as well as some of the dirt at the base."

Nan said, "There is no presumptive field test for urine, like there is for semen, so we have to send a sample of whatever we find to the lab for testing and analysis to confirm that's what it is. But Lou is right 95 percent of the time."

"I just have a nose for it," he said. "We all do, but most people teach their brains to ignore it, after initial detection, because it's unpleasant. Unfortunately, I can't do that. I walk down a street or into a men's room and I smell it all. Cities are drenched in piss, especially Paris."

"Why Paris?" Eve asked.

"Outdoor, open-air pissoirs used to be everywhere and are an ingrained part of the French culture, even when there aren't many to use anymore. So people feel free to piss everywhere. And they do."

"I'll scratch Paris off my vacation list."

Noomis lowered his camera and stood up. "Venice is nice. Lots of canals to urinate in. No residual odor."

He must be a wonderful date, Eve thought and handed the SPEX HandScope back to him. "Thanks for your help."

"It's my job," he said. "And my passion."

Eve walked away with Nan to leave him to his passion. "Can we get DNA from the urine Noomis has found and the vomit you collected earlier?"

"Yes, and a lot more," Nan said. "But it will take fourteen to twenty-one days."

"Can't it be done faster?"

"Of course it can. But it depends."

"Depends on what?"

"Who is shot and the circumstances. If the president of the United States, Beyoncé, or Mark Zuckerberg are killed, or if a terrorist with an AK-47 walks into a kindergarten and mows down a dozen children, you can get DNA results in a day," Nan said. "But in most cases, you have to convince the lab to make your urine and vomit a higher priority than all of the other biological evidence they are testing from all of the rapes, murders, and other crimes in California. They'll need to believe it's urgent and that the public is in imminent, violent danger if the unknown offender isn't found ASAP."

"Assuming we can make that argument," Eve said, "how quickly can we get results on this and the vomit?"

"Forty-eight hours. But look around."

Eve did. The area was alight in the festive glow of semen, blood, piss, dung, snot, and saliva.

Nan continued. "There are samples everywhere. Some are human, some are animal. We won't know for sure until the lab tells us. My point is, there's no way of knowing which samples are the important ones. The lab will have to test them all."

"Let's prioritize the vomit, and the recent piss, and anything close to where the killer was standing."

"Why? From what we can determine, the gunman was standing at the north end of the pond when he shot the victims," Nan said.

"But the urine is on the west side of the pond and the vomit is on the southeast side."

"So you're saying they came from three different people?"

"Or maybe the same person at different times last night. I don't know. What I'm saying is that your arbitrary method of choosing which samples to prioritize is useless and pointless."

Ouch. Eve was getting really tired of being chastised and lectured by Nan.

"Fine," Eve said, taking off her goggles. "So how would you do it?"

"I wouldn't," Nan said. "Let the evidence tell the story."

Oh joy, one more lesson, Eve thought.

Nan took off her goggles, too. "But you're right about one thing."

"What's that?"

Nan smiled. Eve was sure of it this time.

"Peeing is never any fun for women," Nan said. "In fact, that may be the title of my memoir."

"I want a signed copy." Eve smiled and handed Nan her goggles. "See you tomorrow."

She walked back up the trail, away from the strange sparkle of every living thing that had ever visited the rock pond.

IKEA could have used Eve's apartment as a spread in their catalog. Every piece of furniture had come from a single shopping trip to their Burbank store and a long, profane day assembling it all with a collection of ridiculously small Allen wrenches.

The first floor was taken up by her "open concept" living room, dining room, and newly remodeled kitchen. The laundry room was a stacked washer-and-dryer unit in a closet under the stairs. The only artwork was her bike, which was parked behind the couch near the front door. The bathroom, guest room, and master bedroom were upstairs.

She ate some Grape-Nuts out of the box, washed it down with a Diet Coke, then went upstairs for a shower.

It had been an incredibly long day, but she wasn't ready to sleep. Instead, she got into bed, activated Kim's phone, and scrolled through her texts. Almost immediately, she found an exchange between Kim and Raylene Bradley, a local wildlife and nature activist, known for demonstrations throughout the valley and for leaving the corpses of dead animals, poisoned by rodenticide, on the steps outside city hall or on the hoods of council members' cars. The text exchange read:

RAYLENE: How much is Zena being paid by Gilbert Robinson to trash me?

KIM: You're paranoid and demonizing everybody. Zena believes in the same causes you do. That hasn't changed. But you have. You don't understand the damage you are doing.

RAYLENE: Coyotes, hawks, owls, and bobcats are being killed by poisoned rats and their habitats are being paved over by greedy developers. I'm fighting for them while she's being paid off to attack me. The blood is on her hands now.

KIM: See? That's what I mean. You've gone nuts. Nobody wants anything to do with you anymore, or your causes.

RAYLENE: Shut her up or I will . . . and it won't be pretty.

Raylene ended the exchange by sending Kim a picture of a dead emaciated bobcat.

That, Eve thought, *is what we call a clue.*

Eve got up at six and had a granola bar, a banana, and a cup of hot tea for breakfast. While she ate, she checked the latest local news on the *Los Angeles Times* website. The Malibu Creek State Park shooting was on the virtual front page, but the victims weren't named. Although the shooter was still at large, Superintendent Trisha Kalb said the shooting was an isolated incident, that the general public wasn't in any danger, and that the park would be open by noon that day.

Eve rode her bike to the station, walked in the door at 7:15 a.m., and was surprised to see Duncan already at work in his cubicle, a large cup of McDonald's coffee within reach, the air around him redolent with the lingering scent of Egg McWhatevers, maple syrup, and hash browns. Otherwise, they had the squad room all to themselves.

She walked over to him and leaned on the divider between his messy, paper-strewn cubicle and her neat, orderly one. "I didn't expect to see you in so early."

"I got a full eight hours sleep. I'll bet you got maybe four."

"Two," Eve said.

"Let me guess," Duncan said. "You went straight to the crime scene again after you dropped me off and then spent all night going through Kim's phone and Faust's blog."

"When I start investigating a homicide, I go all-in."

"You become obsessed."

"I become focused," she said.

He shook his head. "You can't sustain that, physically or emotionally. I keep telling you that. The way you're going, I'll outlive you."

"And yet, here you are, in early, too, working the case."

"Only because I'm cheap and there's a three-hour difference between here and New York. I wanted to talk to one of Curtis Honig's prosecutors before they went into court but I didn't want to pay for the long-distance call."

"Did you reach them?"

"Yeah, an ADA named Joel Goldman. I got his take on the possibility that Honig hired a gunsel to take out Kim Spivey."

"A *gunsel?*"

"It's the same as a *gunman*, but more fun to say. Goldman told me that Honig's lawyer is mobbed up, and probably knows plenty of gunsels-for-hire, but if Honig wanted to silence his accusers, he'd do it by bribing them with money or acting jobs . . . or the threat that they'd never work again . . . not with violence."

"Which is also the method he used to coerce them into sex."

"That's right and Goldman doesn't think Honig would change his methods now. Not only that, but they are watching Honig's money and he doesn't have any left to hire a gunsel. He's spent it all on lawyers," Duncan said. "Does Kim have any other enemies?"

"I went through her emails and texts going back a few weeks and the only threat I found was aimed at Zena Faust. It came from Raylene Bradley." Eve read the exchange out loud to him.

"Wow," Duncan said. "I didn't see that twist coming."

"You know Raylene?"

"Oh yeah. Raylene Bradley and Zena Faust are both angry women, raging at the world, seeing conspiracies everywhere."

"That's sexist."

"It's the truth. Anytime there's a protest around here, Raylene and her Malibu Nature Strike Force is leading it and Zena is there, too, hyping it up. It's worked out well for both of them."

"In what way?" Eve pulled up her chair and sat down.

"Thanks to all the publicity Zena helped whip up over the protests, Raylene succeeded in pressuring the City of Calabasas to stop culling coyotes whenever somebody's puppy gets eaten," Duncan said. "She also convinced the politicians in Sacramento to outlaw some of the rodenticides that poison the animals that eat the dying rats, decimating the food chain."

"So they are all about the wildlife."

"And stopping anybody from building anything in Calabasas," Duncan said. "I think they've protested everything that's gone up. But they have managed to block every attempt over the years to develop the open space at Agoura Road and Las Virgenes."

"You mean New Positano."

"That's just what the latest project is called. There have been a dozen others since I've been here." Duncan finished up his coffee, tossed his cup at the trash can across the room, and missed. It would have been a lot easier to drop it in the can under his desk, but that would have been too simple. It also explained the coffee and food stains on the wall all around the other can.

"But this time," he went on, "Raylene may not be able to stop it. Supposedly the council is split two to two over approving New Positano with one guy, Clark Netter, supposedly still undecided. It shows Raylene doesn't have the juice anymore to get things done."

"Because of Zena Faust's editorial?"

"Raylene did it to herself. Kim Spivey's text was right. Raylene has gone insane. It started with an incident a year or so ago, when a coyote out in La Cañada mauled a three-year-old girl playing in her backyard. Her mother had to snatch the kid from the coyote's jaws. The La Cañada city council reacted by wiping out the pack of coyotes that lived in the hills behind the family's house."

"I can understand why they did that," Eve said. "But it must have outraged Raylene and her group."

"It sure did. Raylene showed up at their next city council meeting covered in fake blood, called the council members murderers," Duncan said. "She also accused the mother of beating her daughter and blaming the injuries on an innocent animal."

"My God," Eve said.

"Raylene had to be dragged, howling like a coyote, out of the council chambers by police. She's only gotten worse since then, harassing anybody who opposes her, committing acts of vandalism. Our deputies are regular visitors to her place . . ."

And then something occurred to him. Eve saw the realization on his face.

"What is it?" she asked.

"She lives in a mobile home right across the street from Malibu Creek State Park."

Without another word, they both got up and headed for the door.

CHAPTER ELEVEN

In Eve's mind, Las Virgenes Road was the Las Vegas Strip of Calabasas, not because it was lined with casinos, but because of the wildly divergent theme-park architecture that would soon be along the route.

A bright-white re-creation of an eighteenth-century Hindu temple, complete with a massive pyramidical tower, elaborately decorated with parapets, niches, and sculptures, already stood on the southeast corner of Las Virgenes and a narrow side road in sharp contrast to the rolling hills and blackened oaks. A replica of a coastal Italian village, except with a Holiday Inn and Winchell's Donuts, almost seemed low key to Eve by comparison. Erupting volcanos, an Eiffel Tower, and the Statue of Liberty might not be far behind.

She shared this observation with Duncan, who reminded her that before Calabasas city hall was built a few years ago, the lot it was on was used to store a fifty-five-foot tall, 1/24th-scale model of the Eiffel Tower, as well as the Statue of Liberty and other international landmarks, created by a Hollywood prop house for a defunct theme park in Southeast Asia. So the precedent had been set for the Las Virgenes Strip.

Eve turned left onto the narrow road. Directly behind the Hindu temple, surrounded by oak trees, chapparal, and steep hills to the south, was a tiny mobile home park, consisting of only a dozen units, with a sign out front with lettering made from seashells. The sign read **HANG**

Ten Village. She made a right into the village and headed for the mobile home at the end of the cul-de-sac, abutting the hills.

Hang Ten Village was built in the 1960s as a community for surfers, hippies, beatniks, and nudists. She thought it hadn't changed much in the ensuing years. Surfboards were still visible in most of the yards. But instead of just Volkswagen Beetles, vans, and camper-shelled pickups parked in the carports, there were a few Teslas and Priuses. And as Eve and Duncan stepped out of their LASD plain-wrap Ford Explorer, Eve could hear plenty of wind chimes tinkling in the breeze that, even at this early hour, carried a hint of marijuana. It was so anachronistic, Eve thought, it was almost another themed development off Las Virgenes: Hippieland.

Raylene's mobile home had a wooden front deck covered with flowerpots, wind chimes, bird feeders, dream catchers, and whirligigs. Eve and Duncan went to the front door and he rang the bell.

The door was opened by a completely naked woman Eve recognized as Raylene Bradley from photos on Faust's blog. Raylene was in her forties, evenly tanned from head to toe, but the most striking thing about her was the starburst tattoo around her left nipple.

"Can I help you?" Raylene asked, not the least bit self-conscious about her nudity.

Duncan said, "You can start by putting on a bathrobe."

"Fuck you."

Raylene started to close the door but stopped when Duncan said, "We're homicide detectives from the Lost Hills sheriff's station."

She opened the door again. He flashed his badge. "I'm Duncan Pavone and this is my partner, Eve Ronin."

Raylene looked at Eve. "Deathfist. I've read about you." She tipped her head at Duncan. "Is he one of the good guys or the bad guys?"

Eve said, "He's the best detective in the department."

"That isn't saying much." Raylene stepped to one side. "Come on in."

They entered the living room, which was separated from the kitchen by a low counter with two wicker barstools. The living room couch, easy chairs, and end tables were also wicker. The kitchen table was hand-hewn wood, but the four chairs were wicker with thin cushions. The walls were covered with sheeted wood paneling, and there were woven baskets everywhere, holding magazines, books, candy, seashells, and potpourri. Sand candles of all shapes and sizes were on every table and countertop.

A shirtless man stood in the kitchen, behind the counter, chopping fruits and vegetables and dumping them into a blender. His long pony-tailed hair was sun-bleached blond, his nose was crooked, and there was a nasty scar under his left shoulder.

"Who are they?" he asked.

Raylene said, "Five-O."

"What do they want?"

"Me to put on a bathrobe," she said.

The man grinned at Eve and Duncan. He was missing a few of his front teeth. "Our house, our rules. I'm Chase Orkett, Raylene's boy toy. We're about to have breakfast if you'd like to join us. There's plenty for everyone."

Duncan approached the counter and looked at all the fruits, vegetables, and nuts on the cutting board. There was also a sheet of wheatgrass, which looked like a square of sod in a cake pan. "You have salads for breakfast?"

"Smoothies. This morning we're having wheatgrass, apples, bananas, dates, bell peppers, broccoli, parsley, celery, beets, and hemp seeds," Orkett said, beginning to trim the wheatgrass with sharp-tipped rose clippers. "The mixture reduces inflammation without tearing up your stomach, increases energy, and generates more fulsome erections."

"An Egg McGriddle will do the same thing," Duncan said, "and I already had mine."

Eve stepped up beside Duncan and saw that Chase Orkett was naked, too.

"We're investigating the shooting that occurred on Monday night in Malibu Creek State Park," she said. "Two women were shot, one of them was killed."

"We saw it on the news," Raylene said, standing by the kitchen table. "What's that got to do with us?"

Eve turned to her. "You knew both victims. Zena Faust was injured and Kim Spivey was killed."

Raylene abruptly sat down at the table. Eve's first thought was that she was taking a big risk sitting naked on a wicker chair, even with a thin seat cushion.

"Oh my God," Raylene said, holding a hand to her chest. "That's awful. Poor, sweet Kim. How badly was Zena injured?"

"How badly would make you happy?"

Orkett dropped his rose clippers. "What the hell is that supposed to mean?"

Eve ignored him and kept her gaze on Raylene. "You threatened Zena only hours before she was shot."

"No I didn't," Raylene said.

"You texted Kim and told her to shut up her girlfriend or you would and that it wouldn't be pretty. And to illustrate your point, you sent her a picture of a dead bobcat."

"Turns out you were right, it wasn't pretty," Duncan said. "Kim's face was blown off. Nothing but mush."

Raylene took in a sharp breath.

Orkett stepped out from behind the counter holding a chopping knife at his side. "Who the fuck do you think you are coming into our home and accusing her of murder?"

Eve and Duncan put their hands on their holstered guns and faced him.

Duncan said, "We're homicide detectives, sport. Drop the knife, unless you'd like a .38-caliber vasectomy."

Orkett hesitated.

Raylene stood, holding up her hands. "Hey, hey, everybody just lower the fucking temperature. Chase, put down your knife and finish making those smoothies. We could all use them."

Orkett dutifully tossed the knife on the counter and stepped back behind it. Eve and Duncan relaxed, taking their hands off their guns.

Raylene took a deep breath, exhaled it slowly, then sat down again. "That text wasn't a threat. I didn't mention any violence. Haven't you ever told someone that you're angry with that you're going to kill them?"

"Sure," Eve said. "But I've never punctuated it with the picture of a dead animal."

"You have to understand the context."

Eve pulled out a chair and sat down at the table. "Okay, help us with that."

Orkett ran the blender, so no one could speak for a minute. Eve wondered if it was intentional, to give Raylene a moment to think about what she was going to say.

"For centuries, Malibu Creek State Park was the ancestral home of the Chumash tribe, before they were driven off the land and it was turned into a private country club for the rich and then a movie studio back lot," Raylene said. Duncan, sensing he was in for a long story, sat down, too, with a big sigh. "The Chumash believe there is a spiritual bond between the people, the wind, the water, the earth, and all the animals that live here. I am 1/30th Chumash, so defending the mountains and the wildlife is not just my passion, it is in my blood." She pointed to the tattoo on her left breast, the sun with her nipple in the center. "Do you see this?"

"It's hard to miss," Duncan said.

"It's the Chumash tribal sun," Raylene said. "It's an expression of my commitment to that fight."

Orkett brought over two smoothies in tall milkshake glasses, setting them down in front of Eve and Raylene, then he pointed to his right shoulder, where he also had a tattoo of the sun. "This is mine. I'm not a member of the tribe, but I got inked in solidarity a few years ago when we went up to the Chumash Casino in Santa Ynez to see Rick Springfield's show." He pointed to his other, scarred shoulder, where he had the words "I Wish I Had Jessie's Girl" tattooed. "The greatest song ever. It has so many levels. Think about it."

Raylene took a sip of her smoothie and went on.

"The battle, which I've taken beyond these mountains to all of Southern California, is not about me. It's about the cause, it's about the beauty of the land and the innocent animals that are at stake. Our petty personal differences don't matter. That dead bobcat should be what we're fighting against, not each other. That's what I was saying with that picture."

"That's not how I read it," Eve said and took a sip of her drink. It was delicious, full of complex flavors, dense and yet deeply refreshing.

"It doesn't matter how you read it," Raylene said. "I know that's how Kim did."

Duncan said, "Maybe so, but I'm sure her opinion changed once she saw a shotgun aimed at her face."

Orkett came to the table carrying two more smoothies. "Are you listening to a fucking word she's saying? Raylene wasn't threatening anybody and she sure as shit didn't shoot Kim or anybody else."

Orkett set a smoothie glass down hard in front of Duncan, spilling some on the table, then took a seat at the table himself with his drink. Eve knew there was no way Duncan would even taste his smoothie, not unless it was made with ice cream and Oreos.

Eve took another drink of hers, then asked Raylene, "Why did you text Kim and not Zena?"

"Because Zena is irrational and unreasonable, that's obvious from what she wrote. She's not going to listen to me. But she'd listen to Kim."

Duncan asked, "How did you know Kim?"

"She was my girlfriend, long before she met Zena."

Duncan raised an eyebrow and glanced at Orkett, then back at her. Raylene noticed the reaction and seemed irritated by it.

"I love people, Detective, not genders," she said. "Genitalia means nothing to me."

"That's not entirely true." Orkett winked at Duncan, man to man, and took a sip of his smoothie. Duncan just stared at him.

Eve faced Raylene, because Orkett was making her sick. "How did your relationship with Kim end?"

Orkett raised his hand and waved it. "She met me."

Raylene said, "Don't misunderstand. It wasn't an affair. Kim and I had an open relationship. We could separate sex from love. But then, one day I saw him at the beach . . ." She smiled at the memory and reached for Orkett's hand, giving it a squeeze.

"I was still a professional surfer then," he explained to Eve and Duncan. "I drew a big crowd that day."

"Watching him on the waves was revelatory," Raylene said, still holding his hand. "I saw a person who was one with nature, and one with the water, in perfect harmony."

Orkett sighed. "Until a wave smashed me against some rocks a couple years ago. Tore up my shoulder. Knocked out my teeth. Now, I sell insurance with my brother-in-law in Van Nuys and only surf for fun."

"With him, I couldn't separate what I felt physically from what I felt emotionally anymore," Raylene said to Eve, woman to woman, as if it were something Duncan wouldn't understand. "He's my body-and-soul mate."

"Kim didn't have hard feelings?"

"None. In fact, Zena and Kim were right there with us—me and Chase and the Malibu Nature Strike Force—when we marched outside the gates of Vista Grande to protest their use of rodenticide traps. And they laid down with us in front of the bulldozers when developers wanted to raze a dozen heritage oaks in Calabasas to build a car dealership. Zena's blog was our megaphone and the other media in town picked it up."

Duncan grunted. "But not anymore. Now Faust thinks you're a nutjob. She wrote that stunts like leaving a dead coyote on a city councilman's front porch hurts the causes you're fighting for."

Raylene dismissed his comment with a toss of her head. "She's sold her soul. Trident Publications just bought her blog and guess who their biggest advertiser is? Gilbert Robinson, the developer of New Positano."

"Sounds like you had a lot of reasons to want Zena dead," Duncan said. "Only oops, the wrong woman got killed."

Orkett pointed a finger at Duncan. "You're an asshole."

"I'm just getting started, sport." Duncan grinned and looked at Raylene. "Did you know Zena and Kim would be camping in the park?"

"Of course I did," Raylene said. "Zena doesn't take a crap without memorializing it with a selfie on Instagram. You want to know who killed Kim? I'll tell you. Zena did."

Eve said, "Zena was shot, too. There's no way she did this."

"I didn't say Zena pulled the trigger, but Kim's murder is still on her. She thrives on generating hate. You could spend the rest of your life talking to her enemies."

"That's true," Eve said, "but the same could be said of you."

"The difference is that I am fighting for a cause," Raylene said, cupping her tattooed breast and offering it up for emphasis, as if it weren't already in their faces, then letting it go. "Zena is fighting for likes, hits, and retweets. You kill me, nothing changes—the cause is bigger than I am. It endures. You kill Zena and the hate stops."

"Everything you're telling us just makes you look more likely to be the shooter."

Orkett said, "Maybe that should tell you something, lady."

"A straight-out confession would clear up any confusion." Eve looked at Raylene. "Where were you last night?"

"Right here," Raylene said.

"Can anybody confirm that?"

"Just Chase," she said.

"Not only can I confirm she was here," Orkett said, looking Eve in the eye, "but I was inside her, more than once, and in more than one place."

Eve met his gaze. "Do you own a shotgun?"

"Just the one between my legs." He smiled back at her. "Gee, I hope I didn't offend you."

"Not at all. It's just hard to believe."

"What do you mean?"

"Well, until you mentioned you sold insurance, I was sure you made your living as a castrato."

"A *what?*" Orkett started to get up from his seat, but Raylene gave his hand a firm squeeze.

"Cool it, Chase. They are just doing their jobs."

But Orkett was still glaring at Eve. "Fuck that. We invited them into our home, offered them our hospitality, and stood before them naked in every way and they still called you a killer, even after you told them you loved Kim once."

"I still do . . . just not the way I once did."

The emotion felt honest to Eve, and so did the pain. Eve had heard enough and was tired of Chase Orkett. She stood up and Duncan did, too.

"I'm sorry for your loss," she said to Raylene. "Thank you for the smoothies and your cooperation."

"Is that all?" Raylene asked.

"Instead of asking," Orkett said to Raylene, "you should be telling." He looked at them. "We're done."

"For now," Duncan said and they walked out.

Once they were back in the Explorer, Eve started the car to get the air-conditioning going and grinned at Duncan.

"A .38-caliber vasectomy?"

He grinned back at her. "It was a great line, wasn't it? I also liked that castrato reference you made, though it went right above his head."

"I was aiming between his legs."

Duncan laughed. "That's another good one. We should be writing this stuff down for the show."

"Hell no." Eve stared at Raylene's mobile home. The shutters were closed, so she couldn't see what they were doing in the house. "They were trying awfully hard to make us uncomfortable by walking around naked."

"My guess is that they stripped when they saw us arrive in our car. Even unmarked, it screams cop."

"We're homicide detectives. We see a lot of corpses in this job. Did they really think seeing two live naked people would throw us off our game?"

Duncan shrugged. "Raylene is all about trying to shock people. I would have been disappointed if she didn't try something. Do you believe what you said to her, that she's looking real good as our shooter?"

"Yes, I do. She lives in the center of where all the previous shootings occurred. We know she hates Zena Faust. And we know she hates Paul Banning for building his obnoxious house and ruining the scenic corridor. Now we just have to connect her to the other shooting victims."

"We also need evidence," he said, "and there isn't any."

"Yet," she said. "But if it's not her, she's right about Zena's large number of enemies. We need a way to narrow down the list."

"Unless Zena was a random victim of a serial shooter, in which case all the time we spend tracking down her enemies, or investigating Raylene, is chasing our tails."

"So we're back to the same problem," Eve said.

"We need evidence," Duncan said, "and there isn't any."

"Yet," she said again.

"Maybe Nan has something for us," Duncan said. "She must be nearly ready to pack up and go."

"Good idea," Eve said. She turned the car around in the cul-de-sac and drove out of Hang Ten Village, past the Hindu temple, and onto Las Virgenes Road for the short ride north to the entrance to Malibu Creek State Park.

CHAPTER TWELVE

Eve stopped their car at the Malibu Creek State Park gate to identify themselves and she was surprised to see Trisha Kalb in the guard shack with the ranger. Kalb nudged the ranger aside and came to the window to speak to the detectives herself.

"We're opening this park to the public at 12:01," Kalb told Eve. "Tell your people I don't want anything left behind at the rock pond."

"They are crime scene investigators," Eve said, "not crime scene cleaners."

"You mean there might still be brains and blood out there?"

Duncan leaned forward in the passenger seat to join the conversation. "Along with all the usual urine, semen, shit, drool, and vomit left by park visitors, human and otherwise."

Eve added, "You should see that pond at night under ultraviolet light. It's disgusting."

Kalb said, "It's called nature."

"So are brains and blood," Duncan said. "So you have nothing to worry about."

Eve smiled and drove on before Trisha Kalb could say anything more.

◆ ◆ ◆

Nan and three members of her team were at the clearing, packing their things into two CSU trucks. She was inside the tent, cataloging each bagged item of evidence as it was boxed up for lab analysis or evidence storage.

Eve and Duncan approached her and waited for her to acknowledge their arrival. She looked like she hadn't slept at all.

"Come to make sure I skedaddle on time?" she said.

Duncan said, "We're checking in to see if you made any last-minute discoveries."

"Aren't you optimistic."

"It's what's kept me sane all of these years," he said.

"We've collected lots of shotgun pellets and the two wads, as well as some cigarette stubs, soft drink cans, candy wrappers, and dozens of various biological samples. Some of that stuff may have come from the shooter or none of it. The pond is a very popular area. We still don't know how the shooter entered or left the park or if he was alone or with an accomplice," Nan said. "But we did lift a few different, but distinct, footwear impressions from the general area where the shooter was standing and from the two paths the shooter might have taken to or from the rock pond."

"That's something," Eve said.

"It's more than that," Duncan said. "We can run the impressions through If Tread, fire up our orbital satellites, locate him within seconds, and then send out a patrol car to arrest him without us ever leaving our desks."

"You've been watching too much television," Nan said and then looked at Eve. "If I see any of those bullshit high-tech forensic scenes on your show, I will set fire to your house. Angela Bassett is playing me, right?"

"Rihanna," Eve said.

"Perfect," Nan said.

Eve and Duncan thanked Nan and got back into their Explorer. But as Eve was backing up to leave, Emilia Lopez called Duncan from the medical examiner's office. He put the call on speaker and Eve kept on driving, taking them through the park and on toward the station.

"I've completed my autopsy of Kim Spivey and there were no surprises. She was killed by a single gunshot to the face and neck, causing catastrophic trauma to her brain and puncturing her carotid artery, resulting in devastating blood loss," Lopez said. "There were dozens of bird-shot pellets in her head and upper torso. The penetration and spread of the pellets suggests she was about ten to twenty yards from the shooter. She had low levels of tetrahydrocannabinol and had less than 0.01 percent alcohol in her system. She was buzzed, but not significantly impaired, at the time of her death."

"Thank you for the executive summary," Duncan said.

"What do you know about her next of kin?" Lopez asked.

"Her parents live in Phoenix. Yesterday, I arranged for a team of detectives there to notify them."

"Have you heard from anyone in her family?"

"Not yet," Duncan said.

"If they contact me, is there anything about her death that I shouldn't reveal to them?"

"Please don't go into any detail about the ballistics, specifically that the ammo was bird shot," Duncan said. Eve knew he was requesting this because he wanted to avoid inspiring any copycat crimes and to hold back information only the real killer would know as a way to weed out the crazy "false confessors" who sometimes came forward in highly publicized cases.

"Understood, though there is still quite a bit of it in the body. The mortician will see it," Lopez said. "And if they cremate her, he will sort out the pellets from the ashes."

"Hopefully by then we'll have caught the killer and it won't be an issue anymore."

"Okay, then I don't see any reason to hold the body, do you?"

"No, I don't."

They said their goodbyes. He ended the call, then sighed.

"Death notifications are at the top of the list of things I won't miss about this job. I'm glad I got a pass on this one."

Eve turned left onto Agoura Road, heading east, past the Good Nite Inn, which was still open for business even though half of their building, the part facing the Ventura Freeway, had burned down in the wildfire and still hadn't been demolished or rebuilt. But nobody stayed there for the ambience anyway. Most of their clients only wanted a bed for an hour or two, a night at best.

"What are you going to miss most about the job?" she asked Duncan.

"The arrests. Nothing feels better than justice." He paused for a moment. "Oh, that was good. Why aren't you writing that down?"

"I'm driving. Why don't you write it down?"

"That seems a little self-indulgent," he said.

She turned left into the Lost Hills station parking lot and immediately spotted a familiar red 1990 Mazda Miata convertible parked there. The personal plate read REDHOTY.

"Oh shit."

"What's wrong?" Duncan asked.

Instead of driving through the gate to the official lot, she parked beside the Miata out front. "That's my mother's car."

Duncan grinned.

"Stop it." Eve got out, marched up the steps, and entered the station lobby to find her mother, Jen, standing at the front counter, talking to Deputy Weaver, the young desk officer who'd just transferred over after a stint working at the county jail, something every deputy went through before landing an assignment.

"Mom," Eve said. "What are you doing here?"

"Research," she said, her voice scratchy from years of smoking Marlboros. Supposedly she'd quit, but everything she owned still reeked of cigarettes. Men inexplicably found her voice very seductive.

"She's been here all morning," Deputy Weaver said, sounding very tired. Eve knew how he felt. She'd been there for only five seconds and her shoulder muscles were tightening up from the stress, or perhaps in anticipation of it.

Jen was wearing a loud, busy blouse from Chico's that accentuated her surgically enhanced curves and tight capri pants that went out of style in the 1960s, back when she was born, but she was on a one-woman crusade to revive them by example. She had a huge canvas tote bag over one shoulder and was holding a notepad and pen in her hands.

"What are you researching?" Eve asked.

"My character on the show, of course."

"You have one line, Mom. It's 'I'll see if the detective is available.'"

"But there are shadings that have to come through in my expression, voice, and body language to convey the full richness and complexities of Maggie's character."

"Who is Maggie?"

"Maggie Malloy, the character I play," Jen said.

"The role doesn't have a name. Or a sex. All it says in the script is 'Desk Deputy.'"

"Before Maggie was working the front desk, she was a homicide cop. But then a serial killer murdered her family and she couldn't do the job anymore . . . but she also couldn't let go of her badge. It's all she has left."

Duncan said, "That sounds rough."

Eve looked over her shoulder at him. "She made it up. It's not in the script. It's only in her mind."

Jen ignored Eve and smiled at Duncan. "You must be Duncan Pavone."

He held out his hand to her. "It's a pleasure to meet you, Mrs. Ronin."

She shook his hand. "Call me Jen. We're like family. Can I call you Donuts?"

Before he could answer, Eve said, "Mom, this is where I work. You can't hang out in the lobby, harassing the deputies and eavesdropping on conversations."

"It's a public space and I'm sure Jeff doesn't mind."

"Jeff?"

Deputy Weaver raised his hand to identify himself. "She's had me say 'I'll see if a detective is available' a dozen times."

"So I can get the nuances right," Jen said.

The tightness in Eve's shoulders was spreading to her neck. If this conversation didn't end soon, she would have a headache that a handful of Advil wouldn't cure. "You're done here, Mom. There are no nuances."

"Of course there are. All of Jeff's experiences on the street are in every word," Jen said. "I need that authenticity."

Eve knew that Weaver had no street experience, but she didn't want to embarrass him by pointing that out. "You don't have to bother the desk officer for that. Your daughter is a homicide detective, remember? If you have questions, ask me."

"I want to do a ride-along. What's your schedule like today?"

That's when Wallace Ewell, the bureaucrat from the Las Virgenes Municipal Water District, came through the lobby door carrying a large cardboard box and smiled when he saw Eve and Duncan standing in front of him.

"Just the people I was coming to see. You ran off and left this behind yesterday." He lifted up a flap on the box to show them the plaster shoe-print cast inside. "This is important evidence. How could you just leave it sitting in the dirt?"

Eve took the box from him. "Sorry about that, Mr. Ewell. We got called to a shooting in Malibu Creek State Park and have been busy investigating that ever since."

"So our burglary doesn't matter anymore?"

Duncan stepped forward. "A woman was killed, sir. That takes priority over the theft of Oreos and a double-knit sweater."

But Ewell wasn't intimidated. He met Duncan's eye. "Everybody counts or nobody counts, that's what Harry Bosch says."

"Oh, I like that." Jen made a note on her pad. Eve wanted to slap the pad out of her hands, but she'd have to drop the box to do it.

Duncan said, "So you want me to tell the dead woman's parents that I'd really like to catch her killer, but first I've got to find a guy who stole some Cheez Doodles?"

"Are you telling me nothing else gets investigated—rapes, burglaries, car thefts, whatever—until you catch this killer?" Ewell said. "What kind of police force is this?"

Eve spoke up, eager to end this argument. "Of course he's not saying that, sir. He's just very passionate about solving this homicide."

"I wish there was someone passionate about solving burglaries, too." Ewell walked out and would have slammed the door behind him, if that had been possible.

Eve noticed her mom taking more notes. "What are you writing?"

"Duncan's Cheez Doodles comment was great. It really drove home the emotional truth."

"I'm full of great lines like that," Duncan said. "But today I've really been on a roll."

Eve's neck muscles were becoming crowbars. "That was a private conversation, Mom. Not one word of it gets shared. Understood?"

"What about the ride-along?"

"Go home. I will call you later."

"No, you won't." Jen sighed, dropped her notepad into her giant tote bag, and glanced at Duncan. "Do your daughters call you?"

"Every week."

Jen turned to Eve. "There's a lot you can still learn from him."

She kissed her daughter on the cheek and walked out.

Duncan smiled, watching her go to her Miata. "I like her."

Eve turned to the desk deputy. "I'm sorry about that."

"I have nuances," Deputy Weaver said.

"I'm sure you do," Eve said. "I meant no offense."

But clearly the damage had already been done. She'd made another enemy in the department.

Thanks, Mom.

Eve went to the door leading into the station and Deputy Weaver hit the button to unlock it. Duncan held open the door and Eve walked through, carrying the box. They walked down the hall toward their squad room. But as they passed the open door to the captain's office, DuBois called out to them.

"Can I have a word, Detectives?"

They turned back and went into his office, Eve with dread. Nothing good ever came out of a meeting with the captain, and the timing of this one didn't bode well.

Dubois stood behind his neat and tidy desk. He had a thick gray bow-tie mustache that was a stark contrast to his buzz-cut hair. His face reminded Eve of the cartoon character on the canisters of Pringles potato chips.

"We can't have your mom camped out in our lobby, Detective Ronin," Dubois said. "There has to be a wall, topped with broken glass and barbed wire, between your work here and your personal life."

"I understand, sir. It won't happen again," she said.

"Did you see the *Malibu Beat* this morning?"

Duncan stepped forward. "We were out interviewing a suspect. Why?"

Dubois swiveled his computer monitor around so they could see the screen. "Zena Faust tells the whole story of what happened in the park. She even took selfies of her injuries and talks about the bird shot that's still in her body."

It was infuriating, but Eve wasn't surprised. Faust was a journalist. "She wanted to break her story before someone else did."

"She went too far," the captain said. "She shared details that could compromise the investigation. She's even got a sidebar with her 'list of prime suspects.' You need to tell her to shut up."

Eve saw an opportunity here and took it. "Now it's even more crucial that we get the DNA results from the urine and vomit collected at the scene as soon as possible. Can you put in a word with the lab, sir?"

"Sure, but it won't do much good. You know how many shootings there were in Los Angeles County the last two days? It's first come, first serve."

Duncan said, "Unless it's an actor, rapper, or politician who gets shot."

"And the sun rises in the morning and sets at night. That's the way it is." Dubois gestured to Eve's box. "What's in there?"

"A shoe-print impression from the water district office break-in the other day."

"Stick with the shooting. Give that and whatever you have on the case to Crockett and Tubbs. They just got back in. They're working a burglary last night at a real estate office. Maybe they're connected."

"Yes, sir." Eve took that as a dismissal. She and Duncan walked out and into the squad room, where detectives Wally Biddle and Stan Garvey, better known in the station as Crockett and Tubbs, were in their side-by-side cubicles.

Garvey was African American and reputedly coined, and actively spread, the team's nickname out of his love for *Miami Vice* and the stylish Hollywood sheen the TV cops had. He was a sharp dresser and spent all his free time working security on film sets, movie premieres, and private celebrity weddings and parties. There were more screenplays on his desk than police reports. The walls of his cubicle were covered with photos of him with actors, athletes, and rap stars. Eve knew he was jealous of her TV show, and furious that she was achieving his dream and yet wasn't taking full advantage of her opportunity.

Biddle was a clean-cut, coat-and-tie version of Chase Orkett, a California native in his forties who gave up his dream of being a competitive surfer to become a cop. But with his blond hair, parted down the middle, and perpetually sunburned nose, he still looked like he'd be a lot more comfortable in board shorts and flip-flops than in his Men's Wearhouse off-the-rack suit.

Eve dropped the box with the shoe-print cast on Garvey's desk.

He looked at the box like it was a pile of fresh horse dung. "What's this?"

"A shoe-print impression from a break room break-in at the water district office two nights ago," Eve said. "I'll send you the surveillance video, too."

Duncan added, "We're a bit behind in our paperwork. We'll write up our report and get it to you two in a few minutes."

Biddle said, "Why should we care?"

"The captain says it's your case now," Duncan said.

"This is so exciting," Garvey said with a sigh.

"We love getting your table scraps," Biddle said.

Eve sat down at her desk, glad Ewell would now be someone else's problem. "Don't blame us. Blame Dubois."

Garvey put the box on the floor. "When have you two ever been given a case because we were too busy working something else? Or been assigned to do our scut work while we take the lead in a homicide investigation?"

Biddle peeked in the box. "Maybe it'd be different if we had tits and a TV show."

"Or were retiring," Garvey said.

Duncan took off his coat, draped it over the back of his chair, and sat down. "Yes, it would."

That stopped them cold. Garvey and Biddle shared a look, then Garvey turned to Duncan.

"Wait, what? You're agreeing with us?"

"You're getting screwed because I've got seniority and she's got youth and fame. But soon I'll be gone, and fame and youth are fleeting, so your day will come."

Biddle nodded. "You have a point, Donuts. We just have to wait you out."

"The way things are going," Duncan said, "it won't be long."

Eve turned in her chair. "How do you figure that? My youth and fame aren't nearly played out. I'm still in my twenties and my TV show hasn't been produced yet."

"The way you work, you're going to burn out or get fired in a few months," Duncan said.

"He's right," Biddle said.

"And most shows get canceled after a couple episodes and are instantly forgotten," Duncan continued.

"That's true," Garvey said. "I'm feeling better already."

"Me too," Biddle said.

Crockett and Tubbs went back to their work. Eve got up and leaned over the partition between her cubicle and Duncan's.

"Gee, thanks."

"I'll make it up to you. I'll catch up on our paperwork while you go talk to Zena Faust. Straighten her out. Then go home early, get some sleep. You look like a zombie."

"How about I do the paperwork and you talk to her?"

"I would, if only for the opportunity to eat some hospital food, but she likes you," Duncan said. "She thinks I'm one of the bad guys."

"I'm beginning to believe she's right," Eve said.

"Ah, you love me. I'm full of emotional truth."

CHAPTER THIRTEEN

Eve rode her bike home, got into her Subaru, and drove out to West Hills Hospital, where she found her sister in the ER, doing some paperwork at the nurse's station.

"What are you doing here?" Lisa asked.

"I need to talk to Zena Faust. Can I buy you lunch afterwards?"

"It's got to be the cafeteria, the Subway across the street, or whatever food truck is parked outside. I can't wander far, we're shorthanded."

"Fine with me. Can you tell me where Zena is?"

Lisa gave her the room number on the third floor. Eve took the elevator up and found Faust's room. The door was wide open, so she strode in without knocking or announcing herself.

Faust was sitting up in bed, still plugged into machines and IVs, but typing furiously on her phone with her thumbs, a skill Eve hadn't mastered. Her bruises were black and had spread, like oil slicks, across her body. Faust had to be in a lot of discomfort, but she seemed to Eve to be a lot more energized than the last time they'd talked.

"Have you caught Kim's murderer yet?" Faust asked without looking up from her tiny screen or pausing her furious typing.

That was something else Eve couldn't do—type and talk at the same time.

"Nope, and your blog post today doesn't help."

"I'm grieving. Expressing my feelings helps me deal with it."

"I understand your pain, but you're disclosing too much and making it harder to do our jobs."

Faust stopped typing and set her phone down on her lap. "All I did was say I got shot, and that my lover was killed, and that my heart is broken."

"You shared details of the crime that only you and the killer knew and now anybody with Google can know them, too," Eve said. "As a result, we can't trip up a suspect for having knowledge he isn't supposed to have or verify that what he's saying is the truth."

"Like what?"

"Like exactly how the shooting went down, the weapon that was used, and even the ammunition. We were withholding that from the media."

"Sorry," Faust said, unconvincingly.

"Don't apologize to me. You and Kim's family are the only ones hurt by it."

"It's not going to make a difference. The killer already knows we're onto him."

"He does?"

"I gave you a list that his name is on," Faust said.

"You published the list, which also was not helpful," Eve said. "Now all those possible suspects have a heads-up that we're coming for them."

"They should already know. You are talking to them, aren't you?"

"You didn't tell us that Paul Banning took your house."

"Because it's irrelevant," Faust said.

"He says that's why you're attacking him on your blog," Eve said, "not because he graded a hill and cut down some oaks to build a huge house."

"Like I said, it's irrelevant."

"Not if you are using us to harass your enemies," Eve said.

"That's *exactly* what you should be doing," Faust said, "because one of them killed Kim and filled me with bird shot."

She had a point, Eve thought.

It seemed to Eve that Faust's anger had clear health benefits, helping her push past the physical and emotional pain she had to be feeling. Even her breathing sounded less labored. Eve couldn't really blame Faust for feeling the way she did, or acting on it through the only channel she had, her writing. But despite the trouble Faust was causing, Eve reminded herself that Faust was the victim, and had suffered a tremendous loss.

"Is there anybody else on your list that you have a personal issue with?" Eve asked.

"Everything I write is personal."

"Does that go for your editorial about Raylene Bradley, too?"

"What does she have to do with anything?"

"I'm just wondering why she isn't on your suspects list," Eve said. "You called her irrational and paranoid on your blog."

"She's not on the list because we fight for the same causes and she loves Kim. She wouldn't hurt her."

"So the fact that you're sleeping with Raylene's ex, and accusing her of being too crazy to lead the fight for the causes she cares about, must feel like a double betrayal to her."

Faust shook her head. "It wasn't Raylene. It was a man."

"It was dark outside. You couldn't see who it was. Maybe she couldn't see who she was shooting at."

Faust kept shaking her head as Eve talked, silently disputing every word as it came out.

"I've given you a fucking road map to the asshole who shot me and killed Kim and you want to talk about Raylene? Do your job."

"I can't if I have to worry about you blowing our investigation by talking too much or by withholding information."

"You're not making any sense," Faust said, picking up her phone and starting to type with her thumbs again. "One minute you say I'm saying too much, the next not enough."

"Don't play games with me, Zena, because the only one who loses is you. We both know the only reason you wrote that story was because you were afraid of getting scooped by the *LA Times* on your own story," Eve said. "Okay, now you've beat them. Find something else to write about. And if there is anybody else we should be looking at, or anything you haven't told us about your relationships with the people on your list, now is the time to tell me."

Faust didn't lift her eyes from the screen and just kept typing, as if nobody else were in the room.

"Fine. Get well soon."

Eve walked out.

◆ ◆ ◆

Lisa was waiting for Eve in the ER.

"I'm starving," Lisa said.

"Me too."

"Let's go." Lisa headed for the exit to the parking lot, the doors sliding open for them automatically. So it was Subway or a food truck for lunch.

"Where are we eating?"

Lisa pointed to a yellow food truck parked near one of the entrances to the parking lot. "The Grilled Cheese Truck. Four cheeses on homemade sourdough."

"They should park that in front of my condo 24/7," Eve said. "I'd never cook again."

"How did it go with Zena?"

"It's hard enough solving a case without the victim working against you."

"Now you know how I feel."

Eve walked alongside her sister across the parking lot. "What do you mean?"

"Patients almost never do what we tell them is best for their health and then complain when they just get sicker or their injuries don't heal. It's incredibly frustrating."

"So you're saying what we do is futile."

"All it takes is one win, one life saved, and all the other bullshit doesn't matter."

They reached the truck and ordered off the very simple, limited menu. Eve paid and they waited for their order to come up.

Lisa took a big sip from her Coke. "The other day, you said you trust Tom with your life. Did you mean it?"

"I did and I do."

"Even though he has a Great White tattoo on his shin?"

The Great Whites were the secret clique of Lost Hills sheriff's deputies that Eve had exposed in her investigation of a rape case, which led to a deputy killing himself and the lawsuit against her. Secret LASD cliques, each associated with a particular jurisdiction or special unit, had been around for decades and the tattoos were an expression of a deputy's sense of brotherhood, pride, and devotion to the neighborhood or unit. However, in recent years, it seemed that every deputy or detective charged with a horrible crime was also a member of a clique, prompting one federal judge to call them "gang members with badges."

"How do you know Tom has the tattoo?" Eve asked. Lisa grinned. "Geez, you slept with him on the first date?"

"I don't get many opportunities for sex. I work long hours and when I'm not, all I have time for is laundry, grocery shopping, and sleep."

The cook called their order, which gave Eve a moment to think about how she felt about Lisa sleeping with one of her coworkers. It was awkward. But it wasn't uncommon for first responders to date one another. That was almost the only circle they moved in and few outside it understood the life they led. There was comfort in that familiarity.

Eve and Lisa got their grilled cheese sandwiches and sat down at the curb to eat them.

Lisa side-eyed her sister. "Don't worry, it's not serious."

"If your relationship goes bad, I could lose Tom and be left with only one deputy I can trust in the whole department."

"I've only known him a short time, but I am certain that Tom wouldn't turn his back on you, even if I tear out his heart and run over it with my car," Lisa said. "He's not that kind of man."

Lisa was right. And that, Eve knew, was why they both trusted him, though in different ways.

"Now you know why I am not worried about his tattoo," Eve said. "It doesn't mean the same thing to him as it does to the other men who have it."

They ate in comfortable silence for a few minutes, before Eve spoke again. "Mom came by work today."

"Did she want you to fix a parking ticket?"

"Worse. She's prepared a whole ridiculous backstory for a nameless character in the pilot who has one line of dialogue. I am going to regret insisting that she get a speaking part. No, I already regret it."

"It's a great gift you're giving her. You're making Mom's dream come true after years of struggle and disappointment," Lisa said. "You should be happy that you were able to do that for her."

"She's going to make that impossible."

"She wouldn't be Mom if she didn't," Lisa said.

After lunch, Eve went home, intending to change and take a bike ride along Mulholland to clear her head. But once she walked through the door, she was suddenly very tired. So she changed her plans. She kicked off her shoes and trudged up the stairs to take a nap. She was halfway up when her doorbell rang.

Shit.

She knew better than to open the door or put her eye to the peep-hole. It was a good way to get shot. Instead, she took out her phone and checked the doorbell video app to see who was there.

It was a man in his seventies, with a full head of white hair, a bushy mustache, and a deeply lined face. He wore a paisley red ascot and a maritime-style blue blazer over his white polo shirt, a fashion choice that reminded her of the perpetually jolly Thurston Howell III, the millionaire castaway on *Gilligan's Island*.

But he wasn't Thurston Howell. He was her father, Vince Nyby.

They lived only a few miles away from each other, but she'd never told him where she lived—specifically to avoid this moment.

Eve thought about pretending she wasn't home, but that would be cowardly and he wouldn't be standing out there if he didn't already know she was inside. So she'd just look childish and stupid.

Eve went to the door and yanked it open. "How did you know I'd be home?"

"Hello to you, too," he said, giving her a big smile. When she didn't reciprocate, he sighed and gave in. "I called your office and your partner told me you were out for the rest of the day. So I figured you'd either be here or bike riding on Mulholland."

"How did you know where I like to ride?"

"It was in the *Los Angeles Times* article about your fight with Blake Largo that made you a star."

"I didn't read it," Eve said. "And I'm not a star."

"You will be, thanks to me, which brings me to why I'm here," Vince said. "Can I come in, or do you want to have this discussion on the front step?"

"I'd rather not have it at all," Eve said, but she stepped aside to let him in anyway. He walked past her into the living room. She closed the door, though she was tempted to run out into the street instead.

"Nice place. Beautiful kitchen," he said. "You live so close by. We should really see each other more often."

That clueless remark made her want to shoot him. "Take the hint, Vince."

"I'm your father. It wouldn't hurt to call me Dad."

It would hurt, more deeply than he knew. "How can you, the definition of an absentee father, walk in here and tell me that I should call you Dad and see you more often? Are you senile or insane?"

He held up his hands in surrender. "I'm not telling you anything, hardnose. I'm just making polite suggestions. No need to get all riled up over nothing."

"Nothing." She rolled her shoulders, trying to loosen up the muscles tightening into rebar. It had never been this fast or this bad before. And it had never happened with anyone but her mom. One more reason to hate this bastard. "How many children do you have, Vince?"

"I don't see how that matters."

"Nine. You have *nine*. With seven different women. How many of those women did you marry? Zero. How many of those children have your name? Zero. How many of those kids did you visit?"

"I visited with them all, at least once a year. Sometimes more."

"I'll bet you only showed up for their birthdays or on holidays with a gift-wrapped Barbie doll for the girls or a Hot Wheels car for the boys. But even that ritual only lasted until their senior year of high school, because you were terrified that if you attended graduation, or showed up afterwards, you might be asked for money to help with college," Eve said. "Though I'm sure there were a few of your offspring, like me, who decided in their teens that they didn't want to see your face again."

"None of that is not true. You have no idea how difficult some of the women made it for me to see my children," he said. "I fought very hard. But, sadly, I couldn't win every battle."

"Mom never prevented you from seeing me," Eve said.

"But she made it very difficult with her hostility and by always demanding money or acting jobs from me whenever I came by."

"Of course she did, because you wouldn't pay child support and she was a single mother struggling to raise three children."

"Only one of them was mine," he said.

"And those deadbeat fathers weren't supporting their kids, either." Her mom had terrible taste in men, and poor judgment, and was the maker of most of her own troubles, but Eve wasn't going to concede a thing to this man. For the sake of this discussion, her mom was a saint.

"What Jen did was implied extortion and it put you in the middle," Vince said. "So I stayed away. I made that personal sacrifice to spare you the pain of being used as a weapon against me. But I've never stopped loving you."

"How many of your children are in your life now?"

"You are," he said with a smile. "That's what matters."

"This is a business arrangement, Vince. Nothing more." And she'd been forced into it against her will, or at least that was how it felt, especially now.

"It's also our chance to make up for lost time," he said, "to really get to know one another."

"Oh, I know you too well already," Eve said. "You're only here because you want something from me, something that's worth facing my bitter wrath. So what is it? It must be pretty important to you."

He paced for a minute, torn. He wanted to ask for it, whatever it was, but he also didn't want to prove her right. She liked seeing his pain. He had no choice.

"I made this series deal happen. I brought you and Simone Harper together, on the understanding that I'd direct the pilot."

"You and I didn't have any understanding. That was between you and her."

"And she's broken that promise, one you know she made," Vince said. "She's brought in a young woman to direct."

"That's not my problem," Eve said.

"It's your show. You can make her honor her commitment."

Eve laughed. "Oh, come on, Vince. How many court orders to pay Mom your overdue child support did you ignore? What about the honor of *that* commitment? Now you know how it feels."

"If you won't do it for me," he said, "then do it for yourself."

"What are you talking about?"

"Simone made me a promise and she's breaking it, on a show about you and what you stand for, that wouldn't exist if not for me."

"This show was going to get made with or without you or Simone Harper," Eve said. "You're giving yourself far too much credit."

"Even so, if you really believe in honor and integrity, then you can't abide this and live with yourself. Because it was done in your name. I know you, hardnose. Better than you think I do."

He smiled at her and walked out the front door, leaving her standing there, seething.

Seething took a lot of energy and she didn't have any left. She went upstairs and took a nap, paying her sleep debt to herself. It was after 7:00 p.m. and dark in her bedroom when she woke up.

Eve took her laptop, went downstairs, and microwaved some frozen fried shrimp for dinner and ate it while checking her email.

There was a note from Daniel Brooks, a forensic anthropologist she'd had a brief romance with in January while they worked on a case. But shortly afterward, he went off to Tarawa, an atoll in the North Pacific, to exhume and identify the remains of hundreds of American soldiers killed in a 1943 battle with the Japanese. His expedition had already gone on several weeks longer than planned but he'd kept in touch.

She found herself looking forward to each of his emails and the photos he sent with them. This time, he included a picture a coworker had taken of him asleep in a hammock strung between two palm trees and over the gentle surf rolling up a perfect beach. His Australian bush hat covered his face, and one of his legs dangled over the side of the hammock, his big toe touching the water.

"There's room in this hammock for two," he wrote. "We're finishing up in a few days. Everybody will be leaving. Why don't you come out and join me? We'll have this corner of the atoll to ourselves. We can pretend we're castaways."

It was a romantic idea, but she couldn't imagine herself doing it, certainly not while she was in the middle of investigating a major homicide case.

She put off replying to Daniel and instead started googling the details on the other people on Faust's suspect list, like Gilbert Robinson, the developer, and Derek Hayes, the movie studio exec. They were rich, powerful men. She had a hard time believing they felt so threatened by a blogger that they'd shoot her.

Eve checked out Faust's blog, and a huge headline filled her screen.

SHERIFF'S DEPT & PARK SERVICE COVER-UP LEADS TO MURDER: SERIAL SHOOTER ON A BLOODY RAMPAGE

Her first horrified thought was, *Oh shit, what has Duncan done?*

But as she read the article, she was relieved to discover that Duncan had nothing to do with Faust's story. Her previous article about the shooting had prompted four people to reveal to her that somebody had shot at them, too, nearly a year ago.

According to the article, the other victims were:

Jay and Joy Dube, who were camping in their motor home, when they were awakened at 3:00 a.m. by someone shooting out their windshield and destroying all the little potted plants on their sweeping dashboard shelf.

Chloe Stark, a self-proclaimed "internet porn star," who was filming a masturbation video in the park for her website subscribers when someone shot her camera, which was on a tripod. The camera was destroyed and, with it, one of her hottest performances.

And Marco Fitch, a construction worker who was driving north on Las Virgenes Road when someone took a shot at his pickup truck. He didn't realize he'd been shot at until he reached his jobsite, a hotel being constructed beside the Las Virgenes on-ramp to the eastbound Ventura Freeway, and got a look at the damage.

They all claimed that they'd reported the shootings to park rangers or sheriff's deputies, who either suggested they were mistaken or dismissed the incidents as "petty vandalism." A park ranger allegedly told the Dubes their windshield exploded from "severe temperatures" and a "prior ding in the glass," something that "happens all the time." Marco Fitch called 911 and was chastised for reporting a "nonemergency," and he was too dispirited after that to go to the sheriff's station to file a report. And Chloe Stark claimed that rangers threatened to slap her with an expensive citation for shooting a film in the park without a permit if she pursued her "unbelievable" complaint.

All of the victims told Faust that they were unaware that anybody had been shot at before, or since, their own incidents. The last line of her article was a question:

> How many other shooting victims are the Sheriff's department and State Park authorities hiding from us? How many more people have to die before the truth comes out?

It was a little after 9:00 p.m., but she called Duncan anyway. He answered after a few rings with a sleepy voice.

"It's past my bedtime," he said.

"You'll want to get up for this. Zena Faust has been contacted by other people who were shot at in and around Malibu Creek State Park last year."

"Who?"

She read him the names and told him their stories.

"I only know about one of these incidents," Duncan said. "The couple in the motor home. Chloe Stark and Marco Fitch are news to me."

"That doesn't mean these others were actually shot at or, if they were, that it was with a shotgun, or the same kind used in the previous shootings. These could be totally unrelated incidents or totally false."

"But we have to find out," Duncan said.

"Yes, we do. I just wanted you to be prepared for what we're going to walk into at the station in the morning."

"A category five shitstorm," Duncan said. "Get some sleep."

But she'd had a nap just two hours ago, she was wide awake, and she was furious at Zena Faust. She could sit there fuming, or she could do something about it.

She chose action, as she always did.

It was shortly after nine thirty when she marched out of the elevator on the third floor of the West Hills Hospital. She was immediately intercepted by a nurse.

"Visiting hours are over," the irritated nurse said.

"Not for me." Eve flashed her badge and continued past her into Zena Faust's dark room, where the blogger was asleep, still in a sitting position.

Eve turned on the lights, awakening Faust, who only half opened her eyes.

"Why do you keep taking my blood?" she said. "Can't it wait until morning?"

"I don't want your blood," Eve said. "I want answers."

Faust opened her eyes, and took a moment to focus them on Eve. "Go away. I'm tired."

"Why didn't you tell me about the other shooting victims when I was here earlier?"

"I didn't know about them yet," she said.

"Why didn't you call me the instant you heard from them instead of publishing their stories first?"

The question seemed to wake Zena, making her fully alert. She sat up straighter in bed and looked Eve in the eyes. "Because I won't participate in a cover-up."

"What are you talking about?"

"Don't bullshit me, Eve. The reason why you didn't want me publishing the details of what happened to me was because you knew there were other victims out there, that there's a mad sniper on the loose, and that it would all come out."

"That's not true," Eve said, feeling on the defensive now, and realizing that coming here, in a fit of anger, was a very bad idea.

"Are you saying you didn't know there were other shootings?"

Eve wasn't just talking to the victim of a violent crime now, but a reporter. She had to be very careful how she responded.

"We hold back key details of unsolved crimes, facts that only the perpetrator or victim know, for good reason. But you've shared those facts with the world, so now anybody can use them to embellish or make up stories or fill in the blanks in their memories. You've made it substantially more difficult for us to find who shot you and killed Kim."

"You already told me that line of bullshit and you didn't answer my question," Faust said. "Come to think of it, maybe you just did."

"You know I've only been at the Lost Hills station for few months," Eve said. "I wasn't here when these other shootings supposedly happened."

"But your partner, Duncan Pavone, was," she said. "The couple whose motor home got shot up told me that he called them months later to ask them more questions."

But Faust hadn't reported that in her story and Eve wondered why. Was she holding it back for a bigger, more damaging exposé?

"I don't know anything about that," Eve said, and it was true.

"Does Pavone think there's a serial killer on the loose?"

"First it's a mad sniper on the loose, and now it's a serial killer. You're sensationalizing what happened. One person, Kim Spivey, has been killed. No others."

"That we know of," Faust said. "We didn't know about any of the shootings, either, so we went camping in the park and now Kim is dead. How many others will die because you kept your mouths shut?"

"How many will die because you opened yours?"

Faust glared at her. "Can I quote you on that?"

Eve ignored the urge to flip her off. Instead, she just walked out with the uneasy, guilty feeling in her gut that it wasn't Zena Faust who was in the wrong. It was her.

CHAPTER FOURTEEN

Zena Faust's story broke too late to make it into the print edition of the *Los Angeles Times*, but it was the lead story on their website, as well as sites for the local TV stations, when Eve got up at 6:00 a.m. and checked.

She decided to drive to the station because riding up on her bike would make her easy prey for any reporters camped out in the parking lot. It turned out to be a wise decision.

When she arrived at 7:00 a.m., camera crews from various Los Angeles–area TV news shows were already gathered outside the Lost Hills station. The nicely coiffed men and women were milling around with their camera operators, ready to report live on Zena Faust's revelations when the national morning news shows briefly cut away to give their affiliate stations a few minutes to share their local headlines and weather.

The employee gate opened and she drove to the back of the station, parking beside Duncan's decade-old, but immaculate, Buick Regal sedan. She got out, went to the station's back door, slid her card-key through the security lock, punched in her code, and went inside, walking down the short corridor, past the holding cells and locker rooms, to the detectives' squad room. Duncan was at his cubicle, drinking from a 7-Eleven Big Gulp cup.

"When did you get in?" Eve asked.

"About twenty minutes after you called me."

"You've been here all night?"

He patted a foot-tall stack of files on his desk. "I've compiled files on all the cases I know about and what little I could find on the new ones Zena Faust mentioned in her article. I couldn't find crime reports in our system for them."

Eve pulled over her chair and sat down beside him. "I spoke to Zena last night after her article was posted."

"What did she tell you?"

"That she's exposing the cover-up."

"Good for her," Duncan said.

"Except there wasn't a cover-up," Eve said.

"Yes, there was."

The squad room door flew open and Captain Dubois burst in, angry. "I take it you've seen the *Malibu Beat* blog post and the mob of press out front."

"Yes, sir," Eve said.

Dubois looked accusingly at Duncan. "Did you know anything about this article or contribute to it in any way?"

"If I did, I would have told her about all of the cases," Duncan said. "But she only mentioned one that I was previously aware of, and two new ones, which is terrifying enough. It suggests there could be many more."

"Those two could be nothing," Dubois said. "I don't want either one of you talking to Faust again. We're cutting her off."

"That could be counterproductive," Eve said. "What if she gets more tips or remembers more details of the attack?"

"If she does, we can read about it on her blog. The sheriff will be issuing a statement within the hour reiterating that there isn't a serial shooter."

"We don't know that," Duncan said.

"There is no evidence that there is."

Duncan pointed to his computer screen. "It's right on her blog. The incidents match the MO of the cases I've already investigated and the rock pond shooting on Monday night."

"That's because yesterday Faust shared with the world the key details of the case and inspired these loons to come out," Dubois said.

Perhaps Chloe Stark, the self-anointed porn star, might have been looking for notoriety by attaching herself to Faust's shooting, but Eve didn't think the other victims who came forward, a couple of campers and a construction worker, fit the loon profile. She felt they were probably just concerned citizens, trying to help by publicly sharing their own similar experience.

"But if only one of the incidents is legit, that helps us see a pattern," Duncan said. "We need to look into these new reports, and reopen the investigation into the prior shootings, to know for sure if they are connected or not."

Dubois shook his head. "If you start talking to those people, you add credence to Faust's theory, which is bullshit. So don't do it or word will get out fast. That's an order from on high. Focus your attention on Faust's enemies. God knows she has plenty of them."

Dubois walked out.

Duncan sighed and stood up from his desk. "We have our orders. But let's have breakfast at Chez McDonald's first. My treat. You can even order the Big Breakfast, with all the extras."

"You're taking this well," Eve said.

"Because it's only temporary. Dubois and Lansing can pretend the previous shootings didn't happen, but either the victims will step forward themselves or the cases will come to light in some other way," Duncan said. "So the cases will be reopened and we will reinvestigate them. I just hope nobody else gets killed in the meantime."

The McDonald's was nearly empty, doing most of their business at their drive-through window.

But Duncan ordered the Big Breakfast, which he didn't like to eat on his lap, for fear of spilling maple syrup all over himself, so they ate inside. Eve ordered a Bacon, Egg, and Cheese Biscuit and a Coke. They were sitting down on the hard plastic benches of a window booth when Eve's phone rang. It was Nan, so she put it on speaker.

Nan said, "We've identified the murder weapon as a 12-gauge smooth-bore shotgun firing number 5 bird shot."

"The most common shotgun in America," Duncan said.

"We've also identified some shoes from the dozens of footwear impressions we collected. There are three sets that I think are the best contenders to be the shooter's, based on how fresh they were, the proximity to the victims, and where additional impressions from the same shoes were found on the probable entrance and exit points from the scene."

Eve asked, "So are we looking for a man or a woman?"

"Could be either or both. One set is Trailmaster, a man's hiking boot, size twelve. It's one of the most common. But this particular tread pattern was discontinued over a year ago. One set is a pair of women's Hoka Gaviota walking shoes, size seven and a half. And the other is a man's running shoe, Adidas, size eleven. They all have distinctive striations and wear that will allow us to positively match them to a pair of shoes, if you ever find them."

"Were any of these shoe prints found near the biological samples you collected?" Eve said. Duncan might have asked the same question if his mouth wasn't full of pancakes.

"Both the Hokas and the Adidas were close to the urine and the vomit. The Trailmaster was only near the urine. All three were at the spot where the shooter stood."

Duncan swallowed his mouthful of pancakes. "What was in the vomit?"

"Fruits, vegetables, beef, casava root, some undigested hemp seeds and corn kernels, blood, and some drugs."

"Casava root?"

"Most likely boba, the little balls in pearl milk tea."

Eve said, "There were hemp seeds in Raylene and Chase's smoothies."

"So was the entire garden section of a nursery," Duncan said. "But no beef or corn."

"Just because they drink smoothies and protect coyotes doesn't mean they're vegetarians," Eve said.

"Hemp seeds are common ingredients," Nan said. "Lots of smoothies have them. I had some in mine this morning and I've been known to have a hamburger at lunch, too. That doesn't make me the shooter."

"Point taken," Duncan said, sopping up some maple syrup with his deep-fried hash brown patty. "What drugs did you find?"

"Nothing illegal. Esomeprazole, an acid reducer, and acetaminophen, a nonsteroid anti-inflammatory, which make sense to find together."

"Not to me," Duncan said, swallowing his bite of mapled hash browns.

"Blood in the vomit is a symptom of a peptic ulcer, which is caused by stomach acid, bacteria, or anti-inflammatory drugs, like acetaminophen, and that would also explain the esomeprazole," Nan said. "On the other hand, the blood could also be a symptom of tears in the esophagus, which is common among alcoholics."

Duncan said, "So we're looking for a drunk who likes salad bars and hamburgers."

Eve added, "Or a CEO under a lot of stress who pops Advils for her headaches and Nexiums for her heartburn."

"You know the brand names for those drugs?" Duncan said.

"Of course I do. Intimately. I'm a homicide cop whose partner drags her to a lot of greasy fast-food places."

"So now we have another suspect profile. A cop."

Nan said, "And there are countless other possible profiles, too. These results won't help you find a suspect, but they will help you prove the person you find is the right one."

"What about the urine on the tree that Noomis sniffed out?" Eve asked.

"It's human and it's male. We didn't detect any drugs or unusual medical conditions in the sample. Beyond that, there isn't much I can tell you. Urine can be fragile evidence."

"What does that mean?"

"Urine deteriorates quickly and there's a high risk of contamination from being out in the open," Nan said. "On top of that, it was left on a tree, which, being a living thing, can alter the properties of the sample."

Duncan pushed his empty paper plate away and stifled a burp before speaking. "So, basically, the forensics on the puke and piss don't point us to any suspects."

"They might if we can pull DNA results from them," Nan said, "but even then, you might still be required to do some actual detective work."

"Not me," he said. "By the time the DNA results show up, I'll be on a golf course in Palm Springs, enjoying the six-month anniversary of my retirement."

Eve said, "Not if we can get the sheriff to tell the lab this an urgent, high-priority case."

"If he thought it was," Nan said, "I'd still be at the crime scene, packing up."

Duncan smiled and met Eve's gaze. "Yes, but don't you love these young, naive detectives, so full of optimism and false hope?"

"It's exhausting." Nan clicked off.

Eve looked down at her untouched egg biscuit. She'd lost her appetite.

Duncan nodded at her tray. "Are you going to finish that?"

"No, and neither are you." She picked up her tray, slid out of the booth, and walked toward the trash can by the door.

"Why not?" Duncan said, following after her with his tray.

"I'm watching your cholesterol." She was about to throw the egg biscuit out when she saw a homeless guy sorting through the trash can outside the door. He was unshaven, dirty, thin, and wearing three shirts and torn jeans. She left the tray on the garbage can but kept the biscuit, still in its wrap, and carried it outside with her.

The man looked up as she emerged. "Going through the trash isn't a crime."

"I didn't say it was," Eve said, wondering how he knew she was a cop. She reached out her hand, offering him her egg biscuit. "It's untouched."

"Why didn't you eat it?"

"I wasn't as hungry as I thought I was."

He took the biscuit from her. "That's a problem I've never had."

She didn't know what to say to that, so she didn't say anything, and just kept walking into the parking lot to their car.

CHAPTER FIFTEEN

They drove out to Malibu, where the beaches were technically open to the public, but a line of gated, often guarded, billionaire-owned mansions created an elegant Berlin Wall between the people and the precious strip of sand.

Movie mogul Derek Hayes, who was at the top of Faust's suspect list, lived in one of those homes on Pacific Coast Highway, a few miles south of the intersection with Malibu Canyon Road, the southern terminus of what was known farther north as Las Virgenes.

With the exception of a closed four-car garage, and the wide driveway that served it, most of Hayes' home was hidden behind a high wall and a solid, heavy wooden gate. But today the gate was open and a moving truck occupied one of the two southbound lanes. An LASD patrol car and a plain-wrap Dodge Charger were parked behind it.

Security guards in tailored suits, wearing earpieces and dark sunglasses, watched the movers lug boxes and furniture out of the house and into the truck. While out in the street, Deputy Wayne Snell directed traffic on PCH around the truck and Detective Stan Garvey supervised the movers.

"Would you look at that," Duncan said as Eve pulled behind Garvey's car.

"Now that's service," Eve said. She and Duncan got out and approached Garvey, who didn't look pleased to see them.

"What's going on, Tubbs?" Duncan asked.

"Derek Hayes is moving," he said.

"I can see that. Why are you and a deputy here?"

"Hayes runs Pinnacle Studios and has a lot of valuable items," Garvey said. "It's a security risk."

Eve pointed to the guys trying hard to look like Secret Service agents. "Isn't that what they're here for?"

"Look, the guy lives right on PCH, his moving truck is a traffic hazard, and if there was an accident or, God forbid, someone tried to rob him, it could cause a major, deadly incident. We're being proactive," Garvey said. "For the safety of the entire community."

Duncan nodded. "Proactive, preventative policing."

"Exactly. Stopping serious accidents and major crimes before they happen. It's an important part of what we do."

Eve said, "How often do you provide this important service for people who aren't zillionaires, celebrities, or Hollywood power players?"

"We'd do the same thing for anybody on PCH."

"Of course you would, because zillionaires, celebrities, and Hollywood power players are the only people who can afford to live here," Eve said. "What about a family living on Old Topanga? Would you stop to direct traffic and provide security for them?"

"So you'd prefer we wait until a distracted commuter, tuning their radio to NPR, slams into the moving truck and dies? Or an armed gang with automatic weapons tries to steal one of Derek's Hockneys and gets into a shoot-out with rent-a-cops that covers the asphalt in corpses?"

"That's vivid. Sounds like a movie," Eve said. "Are you pitching that to 'Derek' now or after the move?"

"Screw you," Garvey said.

Duncan said, "Did the captain send you and Deputy Snell here?"

At the mention of his name, Snell glared at them both.

Garvey shifted his attention to Duncan. "We happened to be in the neighborhood and saw the potential for big trouble."

"And an opportunity to build bridges with the community."

"That's right. It's how you establish trust between the department and the people we serve."

Eve said, "You mean the rich people who green-light movies."

"Yeah," Snell said, waving a Ferrari past the truck but looking at Eve as he did it, "the same people you're giving blow jobs to every day to get your TV show. The only difference between you and Detective Garvey is that he earned his badge and doesn't have to betray other cops to get ahead."

Eve glanced at Garvey, who shot a grin at Snell. She said, "You agree with him?"

Garvey looked back at her, his grin turning into a smirk. "I think two cops sucking hard at Hollywood's tit are in no position to be giving me any shit for offering a courtesy to a studio exec."

He was right, she thought. From now on, people would assume she was more interested in Hollywood than in doing her job. She'd have to work even harder to prove herself, that she was doing more than providing credibility for a TV character, that she was a real cop.

Duncan stepped up to Garvey. "You can justify a deputy stepping in to direct traffic around a potential hazard but there's no reason for a robbery-homicide cop to be here."

"I don't have to justify anything to you, Donuts. I don't work for you."

"No, you don't. You work for the captain, who sent us here to interview a suspect in a homicide," Duncan said. "Should I tell him we ran into you? You think he'd buy your proactive-policing argument?"

"I was just leaving anyway," Garvey said, shouldering past Duncan and getting into his car. He drove off, nearly rear-ending their Explorer on his way out of his spot.

Duncan and Eve walked to the front of the house, flashed their badges at the security guards, and went through the open gate, a cobblestone courtyard combining two separate homes into a single larger compound behind the wall. The homes were contemporary, with lots of windows, and were cantilevered over the beach.

They walked through the open double doors of the main house into a vast two-story great room that opened out to the beach and a glass-walled deck that made it appear that the man standing on it, talking on his cell phone, was floating over the surf.

He turned to face them as they approached and Eve held up her badge as both a greeting and introduction.

Derek Hayes had a full head of black-and-gray hair that matched the continuously maintained three-day's growth of black-and-gray stubble on his tan face. His silk shirt was opened wide to flaunt his muscled, gray-haired pecs. Eve supposed it was a show of his virility going into his early sixties. He wore suede loafers, with no socks, and the pant legs of his beige Versace gabardine slacks were rolled up as if he were ready for a stroll along the berm. But she doubted he ever wore that expensively casual outfit anywhere closer to the sand than the deck he was standing on.

He finished his call and smiled at them.

"What can I do for you, Officers?"

"Detectives," Eve said as she and Duncan joined Hayes on the deck. "Eve Ronin, and this is my partner, Duncan Pavone."

"I know who you are," he said to Eve. "How could I ever forget? You cost me a billion dollars, maybe more."

"How did I do that?"

"By making an invincible action hero kiss the ground with one slick move. Now nobody wants to see Blake Largo as Deathfist again."

"Or maybe they just don't like actors who abuse women."

"Either way, we can't sell the three *Deathfist* movies we already made anymore and we can't recast the part with another actor because the character is toxic."

"That's heartbreaking," Duncan said, "but we have more important things to discuss with you."

Hayes smiled. "What could be more important to me than the *Deathfist* series?"

"A murder," Eve said.

"That was a murder," Hayes said. "Of a billion-dollar, global, multimedia movie franchise and maybe even my studio, too."

Movers carefully carried a painting of a French farmhouse, and another of a vase of roses in the California sunshine, through the living room and out to the truck, and she realized that Garvey wasn't kidding about the Hockneys. She'd seen the artist's work at the Getty.

"Do you know Zena Faust?" Eve asked.

"You mean the lunatic who included me in a list she published of suspected murderers? The woman I'm going to sue into poverty? Yeah, I'm vaguely aware of her."

"Zena says you threatened her after she revealed you built a fake four-car garage and driveway," Eve said, "and painted the rest of the curb red, just to keep people from parking in front of your house."

He shrugged. "I was protecting my home and my family. How would you like it if anybody could park outside your front door?"

"Anybody can," Eve said.

"Can they also walk past your bedroom window and into your backyard?"

Duncan looked out at the water. "Your backyard is a public beach. You knew that when you bought the property and the one next door. And you knew that there was an existing easement between the two properties that required you to provide access so people on PCH could get to the sand."

"That's a matter of contention," Hayes said.

"And while you were being contentious," Eve said, "Zena revealed your fakery and that you blocked the path with boulders on the beach and a locked gate on PCH."

"I was protecting the house from erosion and the public from injury," Hayes said. "It's easy to paint me as the rich asshole who wants to keep the beach for himself. But she didn't report the other side."

"There's another side?" Duncan said.

"The state, by creating strict and insane limitations on coastal real estate development, made it so only the richest people could afford to live here and, at the same time, essentially made us responsible by default for maintaining and protecting the beach," Hayes said. "We pay huge state and local taxes. But we also pay, out of our own pockets, to prevent erosion, remove safety hazards, and keep the beach clean from trash, sewer runoff, and a thousand other things. We're the stewards of the California coastline, keeping it pristine, and protecting the marine life, and the entire damn ecosystem, from being destroyed."

"By the public," Eve said.

"We're protecting them, too." Hayes stepped up to the waist-high glass wall that lined the deck and gazed down the coastline of billionaire homes with pride.

Duncan stepped up beside him. "From what? Sunburn and beach rash?"

Hayes turned his back to the water and faced his empty living room and, beyond it, the moving truck and the traffic on the busy highway.

"All of those people parking and walking on PCH, one of the busiest highways in the nation, pose a dangerous safety issue. You want to see chain-reaction pileups and families getting mowed down? By reasonably limiting access, we're also saving lives."

"So you're actually doing a great public service by keeping the beach to yourself," Duncan said.

"People could still get to the beach," Hayes said. "They just couldn't do it by parking in front of my house and going through my yard."

The nearest access was a mile away, but Eve knew that argument was moot now. "But now they can," she said. "You lost your battle with the state. The Supreme Court ruled against you, forced you to open the walkway, and fined you a million dollars."

"They did, which is why I am moving," Hayes said. "With a $15 million profit in my pocket from the sale."

"You didn't sell for the return on investment," she said. "You did it because you don't want to share the sand."

Hayes grinned at her. "But it sure helps take the sting out. We loved it here, but we no longer have any privacy or security. Our lives are in real danger in this house, thanks to Zena Faust."

Duncan said, "She didn't file the lawsuits that forced you to open the pathway."

"No, but during the height of that legal battle, when emotions on the other side were irrationally heated and protestors were outside my door, she ran that article about my garages and the no-parking zone."

Eve said, "You mean your fake garages and fake no-parking zone."

"The next day someone took a shot at my car, which could have killed my stepdaughter. If I was going to shoot Faust, which I didn't do, it would have been then, not months later."

Eve shared a look with Duncan. *Another shooting?*

He shifted his gaze to Hayes. "Is your stepdaughter around?"

"You just missed her. Ashley went with her mom to our new place to get it ready for the movers."

"Okay," Duncan said. "What can you tell us about the shooting?"

"It was about six months ago. Ashley took my Rolls to go to the movies in Calabasas with her friends, early on a Saturday morning. They wanted to catch the first show. She heard a loud bang around Mulholland, but she assumed it was some mow-and-blow Mexicano's pickup truck backfiring. You know how crappy those trucks are. But when she got to the Commons, she saw the damage. I'll show you."

Eve said, "You haven't repaired it?"

"It would cost a hundred grand to fix and jack up my insurance rate into the next solar system. Besides, my stepdaughter thinks the bullet holes add character, so I gave the car to her."

"How old is she?" Duncan asked.

"Seventeen."

"And you gave her a Rolls-Royce?"

"Used. With bullet holes," Hayes said. "She doesn't mind. Says it gives her street cred. She sings rap, you know. You should see her TikToks."

He led them through the living room and across the courtyard to the next house, where the real garage was. Parked inside the garage were a blue Lamborghini Aventador, a Rolls-Royce Cullinan, and a gray matte-painted, de-chromed, de-glammed two-door Rolls-Royce Dawn with a spray of shotgun pellet holes in the front passenger side of the car.

"It's a good thing this car is built like a Sherman tank," Hayes said, "or it could have been deadly."

Duncan examined the holes, running his hand over the sheet metal. Eve knew what Duncan was thinking. One more shooting to add to the list, more evidence of his theory that a serial shooter was at work.

"Did she call the police?" Duncan asked.

"After the movie, she saw a deputy at the Commons eating a slice of pizza outside of Fresh Brothers and reported it to him. That's the last I heard about it."

Or that anybody did, Eve thought. The shooting was buried.

"Why didn't she call the police before the movie?"

"She was already late for the show. Besides, what would you have done, send a search party into the Santa Monica Mountains? Come on. He was long gone."

Duncan pointed to the front of the car with its impressive grille. "Can you please pop the hood for me?"

Hayes did. Duncan leaned inside the engine compartment and poked around. Eve had no idea what he was doing but picked up the questioning in the meantime.

"What makes you think you were specifically targeted, rather than being picked at random?"

"The timing," Hayes said. "Faust's nasty one-sided article ran the day before and that morning somebody took a shit on my front porch. I also have a very distinctive car, but the windows are too tinted to see who is actually driving."

So it was circumstantial, she thought. It could just be someone who hated rich people.

Duncan straightened and held his open right hand, palm up, to Eve. It contained three pellets of bird shot. Hayes took a look, too, and frowned.

"I've had that car detailed at least three times since the shooting . . . and they still missed those? They did a shitty job."

Duncan took an evidence baggie out of his inside coat pocket and poured the pellets into it. "Be glad they did. It's evidence."

"So why didn't the deputy at the Commons collect it?"

"I don't know," Duncan said.

"You could ask him." Hayes pointed to the closed garage door. "Ashley told me that he's the deputy out in the street, directing traffic."

Snell.

Eve and Duncan approached Deputy Snell on PCH, where he was still directing traffic. They stood safely between the parked patrol car and the rear of the truck so they wouldn't get hit by any of the speeding cars.

Just to be irritating, Eve asked Snell the first question. "Do you remember seeing a Rolls-Royce that was all shot up at the Commons a few months back?"

Snell pretended not to hear her. Or see her.

Duncan said, "Detective Ronin asked you a question, Deputy. You can answer her, or we can drag your ass back to the station and you can answer the captain."

Snell frowned, but gave in. "Yes, I do, but it didn't happen there. The shooting was on Las Virgenes."

"Tell us what happened," Eve said.

"I was having lunch at the Commons and some rich, spoiled girl in a Rolls, who thought I was her personal assistant, demanded that I write up a report immediately on an incident that'd happened a few hours earlier. It didn't seem so urgent to her when it happened, so I told the stuck-up brat that she could drive to the station and ask to see a deputy or she could wait until I was done with my lunch. So she waited."

"Did you take the report?"

"Yes," Snell said.

"Did you tell anybody about it?"

"Like who?"

"Your watch commander. A detective. The captain," Eve said. "Somebody got shot."

"No, a car got vandalized. Not a drop of blood was spilled," Snell said. "If somebody got shot, I would have said something. But this kind of thing happens all the time."

That got Duncan's attention. "Cars getting shot up?"

"Expensive, show-off-your-money cars getting keyed, spray-painted, tires slashed or windows smashed, and yeah, sometimes shot up."

"While people are driving them?" Duncan said. "That's attempted murder."

"She didn't think so. If she did, she would've called 911 right away instead of waiting to see Spider-Man save the world again."

"Do you know who the stuck-up brat was?"

"I don't know and I don't care."

Duncan thumbed over his shoulder toward the house. "Derek Hayes' stepdaughter. You don't remember her, but she remembers you: the deputy who made her wait around while he leisurely ate a slice. Now her dad knows who you are, too."

Snell looked like he'd just taken a sip of sour milk. He'd been directing traffic on PCH to curry favor for nothing. Derek Hayes would never forget what Snell did to his daughter.

"Karma," Duncan said, "will always piss on your new shoes."

CHAPTER SIXTEEN

Eve and Duncan were driving south on PCH, toward the Interstate 10 on-ramp in Santa Monica, on their way to see Gilbert Robinson, the developer of New Positano and a suspect on Zena Faust's list.

It felt very strange to Eve to be running an investigation like this. Ordinarily, they'd develop their own suspects, based on the evidence, not from a list that somebody handed to them. But the evidence wasn't pointing them to anyone yet and the captain had given them their orders, so there they were, beginning what would probably be an hour-long drive out to Robinson's office in Pasadena.

"Now we've got one more shooting to add to the list," Duncan said. "I wonder how many others there are that we don't know about."

"It doesn't make any sense," Eve said.

"It's all about not scaring people away from the park and business away from Calabasas, Malibu, and Agoura. That's why Snell's report on the shooting wasn't flagged by the watch commander or the captain for further investigation."

"Not that. I meant this case. Paul Banning and Derek Hayes, two of the people on Zena's suspect list of possible shooters, are both obscenely rich, have obnoxious houses, and have good reasons to hate her. But that's not all they have in common. They are also shooting victims themselves," Eve said. "Those are facts. I'm just not sure what they tell us."

"I am," Duncan said. "It says there's a common thread that ties them all together. We just don't see it yet. To do that, we need to investigate all of the shootings, not just Zena's. That means going back and talking to each victim."

"We've been ordered not to talk to them."

Duncan looked at her. "Since when do you follow orders?"

"I always do," Eve said.

"Except that time you drove into the middle of a wildfire."

"That was different."

"This is my wildfire," he said.

Eve's phone buzzed, and the caller ID showed it was Deputy Tom Ross. She put the call on speaker.

"Hey, Tom, you've got me and Duncan. What's up?"

"I'm up on Piuma Road, above Monte Nido," Tom said, referring to a narrow, winding road that ran along the steep hills of the Santa Monica Mountains National Recreation Area above a rustic, old Calabasas neighborhood nestled in a deeply wooded canyon. "A car went over a cliff on a sharp turn and started a small brush fire. Are you far away?"

"We're on PCH, about to hit Santa Monica," she said. "Why?"

"The driver is dead and the paramedics say he was blasted by a shotgun."

Eve turned on the police flashers hidden behind the front grille of their plain-wrap Explorer and looked for the first opening in northbound traffic that would allow her to safely make a highly illegal U-turn.

"Have you told the dispatcher?"

"Not yet. I wanted to be sure that you and Duncan caught the case."

Eve saw a brief opening in the traffic.

"Hold on a second." Eve turned on the siren, wrenched the wheel hard to the left, and made a tire-screeching U-turn into the northbound lanes, prompting several drivers to slam on their brakes, more in surprise than to avoid collisions. She weaved through traffic at high speed back toward Malibu Canyon Road and raised her voice so Tom could hear her over the siren. "Close Piuma Road for a hundred yards in both directions and contain the scene. Don't let it get more contaminated by the first responders than it already has been. We're on our way and we'll call it in." She touched the disconnect button on her phone and stole a quick glance at Duncan, who'd gone pale. "It's not your fault, Duncan."

He reached for the mike without looking at her. "I'll call it in."

It didn't take long for the firefighters to put out the flames, not that there was much to burn besides the demolished Mercedes and the deeply rooted heritage oak that had abruptly stopped its disintegrating rollover tumble.

That's because in January, mere weeks after the firestorm that rampaged west from Topanga Canyon and barely missed this spot, a weed-abatement crew swooped in and cleared the dry, overgrown brush on the steep hillside to protect the hamlet of homes below from future fires. The crew's work exposed the parched earth and the decomposing corpse of a murdered woman. Her body was found in roughly the same spot as the flattened, barely recognizable Mercedes that Eve and Duncan saw from where they stood on Piuma Road with Deputy Tom Ross.

Deputies had cordoned off the road in both directions, though there was rarely much traffic on it anyway since most of the surrounding hills for miles from that point and continuing southwest were parkland. The fire department vehicles and paramedic unit were still on scene.

Eve noticed there was wreckage from the car, and what appeared to be clothing, strewn down the hillside.

"What do you know about what happened?" she asked Tom.

"Forty minutes ago, a driver saw the smoke in the ravine and the broken guardrail, pulled over, and spotted the car down there. He called 911. We responded at the same time as the fire department."

"Were there any witnesses?"

"Not as far as we know," Tom said. "Nobody called in the gunshots, either."

Duncan pointed to the homes down below. "We'll need deputies to canvass the homes down there, and the few up above, and get any security camera video the residents might have of cars that were on the road at the time. Do we have an ID on the deceased?"

"The paramedics didn't pull his ID, but I got the license plate from a firefighter and ran it." Tom checked his notebook. "The car is registered to Clark Netter, who lives at a Piuma Road address that's about half a mile up, around that bend."

Eve had heard the name before. "Why do I know that name?"

Duncan sighed, an exhalation that conveyed a deep weariness, not of labors performed or pain endured, but of those yet to come.

"He's a Calabasas city councilman." Duncan grimaced. "I should have retired a month ago."

Eve headed over to the paramedics, who were being pulled up by the same ropes they'd used to rappel down to the Mercedes from a winch attached to a fire department rescue vehicle. The paramedics were Jamie Dundas and Rick Gage, the same team who'd responded to the rock pond shooting. Once the paramedics were back on the road, Eve went up to them.

"How bad is it?" she asked.

"As bad as anything I've ever seen," Rick said. "But I don't have Jamie's experience."

"It doesn't get much worse," Jamie said. "The victim took a shotgun blast to the left side of his head. He was probably dead before the car went over the edge. If he wasn't, the crash certainly would have done the job. There was nothing we could do besides pronounce him dead. He's all mangled up, he suffered extreme traumatic injuries, but you can see the pellet wounds and there are holes all over the upholstery."

Eve gestured to their rappelling equipment. "Rig me up and give me some rope. I need to see for myself."

Jamie regarded her with open skepticism. "You know how to rappel?"

"I was a Girl Scout," Eve said.

"I thought all they did was sell cookies," Rick said.

Duncan came up behind Eve. "Can you picture her selling cookies?"

Jamie said, "Let me get out of this harness and set you up."

Duncan pulled Eve aside, out of earshot of the paramedics. "Can you rappel?"

"I did the rock wall in the food court at the Topanga mall once," she said.

"I'm serious," he said.

"I also earned a Girl Scout high-adventure patch in outdoor survival skills."

She'd taken a daylong rappelling course on some rock formations in the Santa Susana Pass, near the Simi Valley Freeway. She'd also learned how to tie some knots, and make soap out of plants.

"How old were you?"

"Fifteen." She didn't remember anything about the course but hoped it would come back to her. The general principles weren't so hard to understand.

Duncan frowned. "We could wait for the car to be pulled up."

"That will take hours," she said. "One of us has to go down there and it's not going to be you."

"I'll tell the paramedics to stick around."

"What for?"

"You," he said.

◆ ◆ ◆

Eve suited up in the harness, with some help from a gruff, square-jawed firefighter named Grisby, who had some nasty burn scars on his neck.

"Just what we need, a freakin' Girl Scout," he said. Obviously, word of her impressive qualifications had spread among the first responders. "Remember, keep your legs about a shoulder-length apart, your knees slightly bent, and don't look up. It doesn't matter where you've been, look at where you're going. There's jagged debris from the car all over the hillside. I don't want you getting impaled because you were taking a selfie."

"I got it," Eve said, leaning slightly back from the edge of the cliff to test the length of rope that was looped through the harness in front of her, then around her waist, and that she held in her right hand to use as a brake. She wore a helmet and leather gloves that the firemen had supplied for her.

Grisby took one more look at her equipment, tugged at carabiners and checked knots, then nodded his approval. "Okay, take it slow and easy."

That was her plan. She moved to the edge of the cliff and hopped slowly down the hill, looking down at the obstacles in her path and testing the brake to find her natural rhythm. She sidestepped around rocks and debris and almost immediately noticed something unusual.

Charred one-hundred-dollar bills were scattered like dry leaves all over the place. She braked and bent over to pick one up. It seemed real to her, and there had to be at least a few thousand dollars' worth of bills nearby. She also saw two suitcases, one broken wide open, the other still intact. That explained the clothes and toiletries amid the debris. She stuffed the bill in her pocket and continued down to the vehicle, which was pancaked upside down against the tree trunk.

Eve maneuvered herself to the driver's side of the Mercedes and peered inside. Netter's body was enmeshed in the dashboard, the roof, and parts of the engine. It was hard to get a full sense of his body, but she could clearly see the bird-shot damage to his head. It was very similar to the injuries that Kim Spivey had sustained.

She saw a wedding ring on his left hand and a Rolex watch, which could be helpful in identifying him. Eve braked her rope, took out her phone, and snapped some pictures, documenting the scene. Then she pocketed her phone, released the brake to give herself some more slack, and swung herself close to the car, grabbing hold of part of the frame with her gloved hand. Steadying herself, she carefully pulled his wallet from his bloody pocket. The leather wallet was covered with blood. She eased it open to his driver's license, which was clean inside a clear plastic pocket. It was Clark Netter.

She slid the wallet back into his pocket, then shouted up to Grisby that she was ready to come back up.

Eve found Duncan in their Explorer, typing on the dash-mounted laptop computer. The driver's side window was rolled down and she leaned on the sill to talk with him.

"It's definitely Netter," she said. "And a shotgun was involved."

"I did a quick check on him online. He's married with two children, both in college. In his day job, outside of politics, he works as a financial manager in Beverly Hills," Duncan said. Eve knew that the elected Calabasas City Council positions were not full-time work and paid only about $6,000. "He must have been on his way home."

"From an out-of-town trip," Eve said. "There are suitcases scattered on the hillside and there's money blowing around that we need to collect."

Duncan looked up at her. "Cash?"

She held out an evidence baggie containing the hundred-dollar bill that she'd picked up. "From what I could see, all hundred-dollar bills. We need to make sure none of the first responders pocketed any. Is there a way to broach it that won't offend all of them?"

"Nope, so I'll handle it," he said.

"Why you?"

Duncan got out of the car with a groan, clutching his right knee. "Because I'm lovable and retiring and you're abrasive and sticking around. I'll do that and coordinate things here. You go visit Netter's house and tell them about his death before his family learns about this from somebody else. His wife's name is Hallie."

"Someone lovable should really be the one to tell her. How about we swap?"

"I've done my last death notification," Duncan said and walked away before she could present an argument.

Eve got in the Explorer and drove up to the house. She didn't have to go far. It was the first home past the curve, about a half mile away. The nearest neighbor was perhaps a quarter mile farther east.

There was an elaborate wrought-iron front gate, with lots of curls and swirls in the design, set between two high brick pillars. A speaker was mounted outside, with a ringer button and an embedded camera. Eve pressed the button and a woman answered.

"Yes?" The woman was out of breath and sounded a bit harried, as if she'd been interrupted in the middle of doing a dozen other things. Eve thought it was amazing how much could be conveyed in a single word.

Eve held up her badge to the camera. "I'm Eve Ronin, a detective with the Los Angeles County Sheriff's Department. Are you Mrs. Netter?"

"Yes, I am. What is this about?"

Definitely harried, Eve thought. Even irritable.

"I need to talk with you, face-to-face."

The gate opened. Eve drove up the very short driveway to the large two-story home, a prime example of an architectural style that she'd heard described as "modern farmhouse hacienda." The house looked to her like the ugly offspring from a drunken one-night stand between a farmhouse and a Quonset hut.

Eve got out and went to the door, which looked like it was sheathed in aluminum and was as welcoming as a meat locker or morgue drawer. It underscored for her the grim reason for her visit.

Hallie Netter opened the door in a sweat-soaked tank top and shorts, beads of sweat rolling down her brow. Her colored blonde hair was pulled back in a ponytail for exercise. She was in remarkable shape for a woman that Eve guessed was in her fifties but hardly looked it.

"Sorry I'm drenched in sweat," Hallie said. "I was riding the Swiss Alps on my Peloton."

"I like to bike, too, sometimes right past your door," Eve said. "Piuma is a beautiful ride."

"I need the exotic locations or I'll get bored, and I like the air-conditioning, though it didn't do me much good today."

Eve hated small talk. "Can we sit down?"

"Of course, I'm sorry, come in." Hallie beckoned her in, then led her to the living room. It was very contemporary and cold, all white everywhere, except for the black, hard, unwelcoming leather-and-chrome furniture. Eve sat on the couch. It was like sitting on concrete.

Hallie remained standing. "I don't want to get sweat on the upholstery."

"Are you expecting your husband back this afternoon?"

"He should be here anytime now, if you'd like to wait for him. He's on his way back from Las Vegas."

"On business?"

Hallie nodded. "For Calabasas. Another boring conference for local government officials. This one was on septic tank and sewer issues . . . or was it cell phone ordinances? I don't remember. He seems to have a different one every month. It's a schlep to Las Vegas, but it gives him an excuse to lose money at blackjack."

"Does he drive," Eve asked, "or take a plane?"

"He drives. It's only four hours or so . . . and it ends up being faster than flying when you factor in getting to the airport two hours in advance, then waiting for a taxi or Uber when you arrive. He actually likes the drive, says it gives him a chance to think . . ." Hallie's voice trailed off and she crossed her arms under her chest. The boobs were fake, Eve noticed, but better done than her mom's. "I don't mean to be rude, but what exactly is this about?"

Eve nodded toward the easy chair that was between them. "Could you please sit down?"

Hallie did, but sat on the edge of the seat, just to placate Eve. "Oh God. Has something happened to Susie or Shane? Is that why you want to talk to us both?"

"Your children are fine." At least she hoped they were. She didn't know one way or the other. Eve took a deep breath. "Your husband has been in a car crash. He went off the road into a ravine."

Hallie caught her breath and put a hand to her chest. Eve wondered why people did that when they were shocked. "Is he hurt?"

"I'm sorry. There's no easy way to say this. He didn't survive."

Hallie became very still but her lower lip began to tremble. "Where did this happen?"

"Right here, up the road," Eve said. "Just beyond the turn."

Hallie bolted to her feet. "I need to go see him."

Eve jumped up and blocked her path to the door. "I'm sorry, but you can't yet."

"Why not?"

"The area is closed off," Eve said. "It's a crime scene."

"What do you mean, a crime scene? Was he hit by a drunk driver? Someone speeding?"

"He was shot," Eve said.

Hallie covered her mouth and ran off. Eve followed to a small bathroom down the hall, where Hallie fell to her knees in front of the toilet, lifted the lid, and vomited into the bowl.

Eve crouched beside her, put a hand on her back, and gently patted her. It felt like the right thing to do, but also incredibly stupid and useless.

Hallie vomited again, then leaned back from the toilet. Eve reached for a towel and handed it to her. Hallie wiped her mouth and sat cross-legged on the floor, hugging herself, like a terrified child.

"I'm sorry," Hallie said. "The exercise. The shock."

"It's okay." Eve stood up, found a second hand towel, drenched it with cold water in the sink, wrung it out, then sat down beside Hallie and dabbed her face and neck. When Eve was a kid, her mom would do that for her whenever she threw up. It always made her feel better.

"Thank you," Hallie said.

Eve pressed the wet towel against the back of Hallie's neck. "Let's just sit here for a minute. Take it easy. I'm in no hurry."

The house rumbled as a helicopter flew low overhead. She guessed it was probably the LASD chopper, bringing in the CSU, and landing at the scenic overlook another mile or two up the road.

"Yes, you are," Hallie said. "You have to get those bastards."

Those bastards, Eve thought. Interesting choice of words.

"You know who did this?"

"Of course I do. The Malibu Nature Strike Force, the Save Calabasas Coalition, the Mountains Protection Society, all of those eco-psychos. They've been terrorizing us for weeks. Protesting outside our house. Sending us hate mail."

"Why?"

"Because they see Clark as the swing vote on the council regarding the New Positano project, though it's no secret he's going to vote for it at Wednesday's meeting," Hallie said. "Or how he would have if they hadn't killed him."

"Did he have any other enemies?"

"Aren't those enough?"

Eve removed the towel and tossed it in the sink. "When did your husband go to Las Vegas and where was he staying?"

"He left on Tuesday and was staying at the Wynn."

"Did he mention anything about winning at blackjack?"

"Yeah, when he called early this morning to say he was heading home," Hallie said, tears welling up in her eyes. "He said it was his lucky night."

She began to cry. Eve reached for some toilet paper and handed her a square. Hallie took it and wiped her tears away.

"Is there somebody you can call to be here with you?"

"My daughter lives in Santa Monica," Hallie said.

"The road up here is closed and will be for a while. We'll have her brought up. Is there a neighbor who can stay with you in the meantime?"

"The Suttons. They are the next home up the street. We house-sit their dog when they go out of town."

"Okay, let's give them a call."

Eve helped Hallie to her feet and went with her to a phone in the kitchen. In the meantime, Eve called to arrange for Hallie's daughter to be picked up and stayed with Hallie until the neighbor arrived.

CHAPTER SEVENTEEN

Eve returned to the crime scene on Piuma Road. Nan was already there with some of her team and Emilia Lopez, suiting up to rappel down to the car to begin their work. Duncan walked up to the Explorer and Eve rolled down her window.

She motioned to Nan. "They got here fast and you can bet this time Lansing will let Nan work this scene as long as she wants, no resources spared."

"He'd argue that the circumstances are entirely different," Duncan said. "An elected official has been assassinated."

"It's not right. Every murder investigation should be treated equally."

"Do you think if you'd stopped an ordinary guy, instead of an action-movie star, from beating up his girlfriend that the video of the takedown would've gone viral or that you'd be a robbery-homicide detective now?"

"I'd still be a deputy investigating burglaries in Lancaster and I probably never would have made it to robbery-homicide," Eve said while Nan rappelled down the hill with ease, followed shortly after by one of her team. "But if I did, it certainly wouldn't be at Lost Hills. Maybe Acton."

"Now you know why all the other deputies hate you."

"That was never a mystery to me."

"So you already know equality doesn't exist," Duncan said. "At least not in law enforcement."

"Where it should," she said. "If it does anywhere."

"It's all about politics. I never learned how to play the game. I never wanted to. But you've already proven that you're a master."

"If that were true," she said, "I wouldn't be so hated."

"I meant politics on a grand scale. It's the interpersonal aspect you need to work on. Speaking of which, how did it go with Hallie Netter?"

"She thinks someone in Raylene Bradley's group killed her husband. The councilman was the swing vote on the New Positano project."

"Swinging to yes," he said.

"She thought so."

"So do most people. Netter liked the tax dollars and other fees Calabasas rakes in from hotels, so the developer added one to the project as a sweetener to secure his vote."

"Or his killing has nothing to do with New Positano and he was shot at random."

"What makes you say that when you've been handed a perfectly good motive?"

Eve held up her phone. "Raylene has an alibi."

"You talked to her already?"

"I didn't have to. While I was waiting for a neighbor to come stay with Mrs. Netter, I checked Raylene's social media feed. She's in Orange County, at the Aliso Viejo city hall, covered in fake blood, protesting their trapping of coyotes. All the local TV stations have sound bites with her."

"The shooter could have been one of her followers."

Eve watched Emilia Lopez rappel down the hill. "You said yourself that her followers aren't following her anymore."

"All it takes is one," Duncan said. "With a shotgun."

"But you don't think so."

"No, I don't, and it terrifies me."

"Why?"

"Because if the shooter is picking people at random," Duncan said, "it's going to be impossible for us to guess who he's going to shoot next."

Eve and Duncan went back to Lost Hills station, opened the files on all the previous shootings, and spent the next few hours putting the information up on whiteboards and bulletin boards so they could see the whole case in front of them.

On the dry-erase board, they listed the names, ages, and addresses of all the victims, brief details on each shooting, and where and when they occurred.

On the bulletin board, they spread out a map of the Lost Hills jurisdiction, specifically the portion bordered by the 101 freeway to the north, the Pacific Coast Highway to the south, Kanan Dume Road to the west, and Topanga Canyon to the east. The patchwork shape of Malibu Creek State Park was in green and right in the middle of the map. They put colored pins at the location of every shooting incident.

Captain Dubois came in, and for an instant, Eve felt like a child caught stealing candy from the pantry. He crossed his arms under his chest and took a long, silent look at their boards.

Eve braced herself to be reprimanded for breaking his order to ignore the previous cases and concentrate on Faust's list of suspects.

"Heard anything new from the scene on Piuma Road?" Dubois asked.

His question was a relief and, by not commenting on what he was seeing, a tacit acknowledgment that a serial killer investigation was inevitable now that two people had been shot dead.

"CSU is still down at the car, but there's debris and cash all over the hillside," she said. "They've collected about $5,000 so far."

"Terrific. A politician dies with a car full of cash. That's going to spark lots of ugly speculation. Keep it to yourself. The same goes double for the type of murder weapon . . . Nobody needs to know it was a shotgun."

Duncan said, "You can't cover this up forever."

Eve could have slapped him for missing the subtle underlying message that Dubois was giving them and provoking him instead.

Dubois scowled at Duncan. "Do you ordinarily go around sharing key details of a homicide with the public before the investigation is over?"

"Only if it might save another person from being killed."

"If and when it could, I'll be the first person to go to a microphone and warn everybody. But we aren't there yet. Not even close," Dubois said. "The sheriff doesn't want CSU rushing this . . . They need to go over every inch of this crime scene. We don't want to miss the smallest detail."

Eve saw an opportunity and took it. "Then we'll need the DNA results from the Malibu Creek State Park shooting ASAP to compare against any biological samples that we collect here."

"I'm way ahead of you, Eve. The sheriff spoke personally to the lab. They are putting a rush on them. We should have something within forty-eight hours."

"He did that?" Duncan said. "Even though he doesn't think the shootings are related?"

"The evidence will decide that."

"Finally, something we can all agree on," Duncan said.

"I don't need your agreement, Duncan. I need you to follow orders and just do your job until the end of next week. Do you think you can do that?"

Dubois walked out without waiting for an answer.

Eve turned to Duncan. "He's right about keeping the details quiet for now. It's what's best for the investigation."

"Yeah, I know that. But it's still a cover-up. There's a serial killer out there shooting people."

Biddle and Garvey came in. They both looked irritated.

"The captain called us in from the field," Biddle said. "Told us to drop everything and to assist you two in your investigation."

"Again," Garvey said.

"Would you rather be chasing down the break-room bandit," Duncan said, "or helping us nail a serial sniper?"

Biddle asked, "Have you got any proof it's a serial killer and not random, unconnected incidents?"

Eve pointed to the boards. "We're hoping it's here but that we just aren't seeing it. Maybe you will."

Garvey snorted. "You're willing to take that chance?"

"I don't care who solves this case," she said, "as long as it gets solved."

"I'd like it to happen before I retire," Duncan added. "I don't want these people on my conscience for the rest of my life."

Biddle picked up a yellow pad from his desk, pulled a pen from his pocket, and pointed to the boards. "So take us through it."

They did. The list of people involved in shootings over the last eighteen months were:

Paul Banning (age 40s)—Debt collector, real estate speculator. Porsche shot at outside of his home, Las Virgenes & Mulholland. [Morning]

Ashley Hayes (20s)—Stepdaughter of movie studio exec. Rolls-Royce shot at on Las Virgenes. [Morning]

Neil Sturgis & Vanessa Pate (teens)—Young couple. Audi parked in campground shot at while couple making out inside. [Late Night]

Harriet Winstead (60s)—Interior decorator. Rear, park-facing windows of her home shot out. Malibou Lake. [Late Night]

Gloria Trucco (50s)—Agoura Hills alpaca rancher. BMW SUV shot at on Mulholland. [Morning]

Jay & Joy Dube (60s)—Married, retired couple, traveling. Motor home windshield shot out. Malibu Creek State Park Campground. [Late Night]

Chloe Stark (20s)—Amateur porn actress. Camera shot to bits while filming video, Malibu Creek State Park. [Morning]

Marco Fitch (30s)—Construction worker. Pickup truck shot at on Las Virgenes Road on way to hotel jobsite. [Morning]

Kim Spivey & Zena Faust (30s)—Yoga instructor and blogger/journalist. Shot at Rock Pond, Malibu Creek State Park. [Late Night]

Clark Netter (50s)—Calabasas city councilman / financial manager. Mercedes shot at on Piuma Road. [Morning]

There was a five-month gap between the teenage couple getting shot at in November of the previous year and the rock pond shooting of Zena Faust and Kim Spivey that week. Within that time frame, a cataclysmic wildfire burned through a hundred thousand acres, much of it in the Santa Monica Mountains, which Eve and Duncan thought could account for the lull.

When Eve and Duncan were done explaining everything, Biddle's pad was full of hastily scrawled notes, numbers, and dates. He ticked through his notes and said:

"By my count, six people got shot at in their cars, three people got shot at while on foot in the park, and one was in her home. No pattern there. The shootings all occurred either in the morning or at night, so the killer is occupied in the afternoons. That could be something."

Garvey said, "The victims range in age from teenagers to senior citizens, so no pattern there, either. The cars that got hit were a Porsche, an Audi, a Rolls, a BMW, and a Mercedes. All European cars. That's a pattern. But the pickups and the RVs could be American-made, so maybe it's not."

Biddle said, "Raylene Bradley sent Kim Spivey a threatening text, and her group was singled out by Hallie Netter and Derek Hayes. That's not a pattern, but it's a connection."

"But Faust ruled Bradley out as a suspect," Garvey said. "And Banning thinks Faust could've been the one who shot his car."

"Now you see why we're confused," Eve said.

"And these are just the victims we know about," Duncan said. "There could be a dozen more shootings that haven't come to light yet."

Garvey said, "The only thing these shootings have in common is that they were all done with a shotgun firing bird shot. But since we only have evidence recovered from a couple of the incidents, that's just a guess."

Eve looked at the map. "There is one more thing these shootings have in common. They were committed by someone firing from park land."

Biddle shook his head. "You only know that's true for the couple making out in their car, the wannabe porn star, the retirees in the motor home, and Faust and Spivey."

"I know it for all of them," Eve said, touching each pin on the map as she spoke. "The back windows of Harriet Winstead's home at Malibou Lake were shot out. The windows face the park, so that's where the shooter had to be. Whoever shot Clark Netter was above Piuma Road. That's park land. Whoever shot at Paul Banning's car as he left his house had to be across the street, so either in King Gillette Ranch or Malibu Creek Park. Same goes for whoever shot at Hayes' Rolls-Royce as his stepdaughter was driving up Las Virgenes. And Gloria Trucco's truck was shot while she was on a stretch of Mulholland that bisects the park."

Duncan studied the map and nodded. "She's right. So the shooter knows the park well and knew exactly where to place himself to take his shots."

"But was he lying in wait for someone to just come along," Biddle said, "or was he targeting these specific people?"

"If he was targeting them," Garvey said, "how did he know when they would come strolling along or driving by? I don't buy it. I think it's one guy and he's just taking potshots at people that piss him off for some crazy-ass reason. Maybe he doesn't like pricey European cars, nature freaks, and lesbos."

"Do you want to confess now, Stan," Biddle said, "or later?"

Duncan's phone rang. He answered it, listened for a moment, and said, "We'll be right there." He hung up and turned to Eve. "Nan has a preliminary report for us."

Biddle said, "While you're gone, we'll start going through incident reports filed over the last two years, see if there are any possible cases that were overlooked as pranks or vandalism. I don't want to be surprised or embarrassed by anything we should already know."

That made a lot of sense to Eve.

Biddle's comment was still on her mind, and irritating her, a few minutes later as she drove with Duncan on Las Virgenes Road toward Piuma Road. She was about to pass the Malibu Creek State Park gate when she made a sudden, last-minute right turn onto the entrance road. The tires squealed and it felt like the Explorer was about to tip over.

Duncan clutched the dashboard. "What are you doing? Trying to give me a heart attack?"

"You're retiring soon, so it's time for me to establish my own professional working relationship with Trisha Kalb."

"Right now?"

"Especially now."

Eve rolled up to the guard gate and flashed her badge at the ranger, a man she hadn't met before, and introduced herself. "We're here to see Trisha Kalb."

"Is she expecting you?"

"Nope." Eve drove on, not waiting for the guard to call in, and headed for Mr. Blandings' Dream House.

"Uh-oh," Duncan said.

"What's the 'uh-oh' for?"

"Remember what I said about your interpersonal political skills?"

"Yes."

"It's about that," Duncan said.

Kalb was already standing outside the administration offices when Eve pulled up and put the car in park. Eve unbuckled her seat belt but kept the motor running.

"Stay here," she said and got out, meeting Kalb on the front step.

Kalb's hands were on her hips. "What's so important that you couldn't call?"

"Have you heard about what happened to Councilman Netter?"

"He was killed in a car accident on Piuma Road. The road is county owned. It's park land above the road, but it's private open space below, where his car landed, so it's none of our business."

"It will be when word gets out that he was killed by a shotgun blast," Eve said, "fired by someone in the park."

"You don't know that."

"We do," Eve said. "What we *don't* know is exactly how many other people have been shot at in the park in the last two years."

"That's because the state park police has jurisdiction here and they don't have to share every little thing that happens with the sheriff's department."

"They can share it now or they can wait for the court order tomorrow."

"What court order?" Kalb asked.

"The one I am going to get the district attorney to obtain if I don't have those shooting reports on my desk tonight because, Trish, I don't want to look clueless when the victims come forward."

"You're getting nothing from me and I can assure you that the sheriff is going to hear about this."

"Everybody will. Wake up, Trish." She snapped her fingers in Kalb's face. "A city councilman has been assassinated by a sniper hiding in your park. So get your head out of your ass, grab a shovel, and dig up the incident reports you've buried or not only will I get a court order,

I'll make sure every TV reporter in LA is there when I pick it up and when I serve it."

"You can't," Kalb said. "You don't have the authority or the pull. Who the hell do you think you are?"

"Haven't you heard?" Eve got right in Trisha's face. "I'm the Deathfist."

Eve turned around, got back in the car, and looked at Duncan. "How were my interpersonal political skills this time?"

"Exceptional," he said.

Eve backed up the car, made a sharp U-turn, and continued on to the crime scene.

CHAPTER EIGHTEEN

Eve and Duncan arrived to find TV news choppers circling overhead and one side of Piuma Road lined with media trucks. Two dozen reporters stood crowded behind the yellow-taped police line.

Farther up Piuma, at the crime scene, forensic investigators scoured the hill above the road, while others dangled on ropes along the cliff, working slowly in a grid pattern, documenting and collecting evidence. A few other experts walked the roadway, looking for skid marks and anything else that might tell the story of what happened or point to whoever was responsible.

The fire department vehicles were gone, replaced by LASD patrol cars, a CSU mobile command trailer, a tent where evidence was logged, a tow truck to pull up the crushed car, and a flatbed truck to take it away. Klieg lights were being set up for the night and deputies maintained a perimeter, making sure the crime scene wasn't breached by reporters or civilians.

Duncan walked up to Tom Ross, who was keeping an eye on the evidence tent and the command center. "How did the door-to-door go?"

"Nobody saw anything and they didn't hear anything, either. A homeowner down on Woodruff Road is tearing up his backyard hardscape and has had jackhammers going on all morning."

"Any security camera footage?"

Tom shook his head. "There are two main ways to this spot. One is to take Piuma Road east from Malibu Canyon, the other is to take Cold Canyon Road south from Mulholland. There aren't a lot of homes on those routes. Most of them are set way back and don't have their cameras pointed at the road."

"Thanks for the legwork anyway," Duncan said.

"It's our job," Tom said.

Eve moved to Nan in the tent, where clothing, suitcases, and evidence baggies of shotgun pellets and hundred-dollar bills were laid out on a table to be tagged, logged, and photographed before being taken to the command trailer for storage and transport.

"Looks like you are setting up for the long haul," Eve said.

"At least another day here," Nan said. "This is a very difficult and dangerous crime scene. The car tumbled down steep terrain, spreading debris the whole way. It all has to be documented and collected by investigators on ropes. That's slow going. Once that's done, then we can drag the vehicle up, bring it back to base, take it apart, and process it."

"What about Netter's body?"

"The fire department helped us extract the corpse, which wasn't entirely intact, from the wreckage and the medical examiner has brought it to the morgue for autopsy. We retrieved these items from his pockets."

She motioned to some clear plastic evidence bags on the table that contained a bloody set of house keys and two phones with broken, blood-smeared screens—an iPhone and a cheap disposable, sold for as little as ten dollars in gas stations.

"Duncan, take a look at these," Eve said. He came over and she pointed to the phones. "How many people do you know who travel with an iPhone and a burner?"

"Only the ones I've put in jail," he said.

That was her thought, too. "This was a man with secrets."

"And a lot of money." Duncan picked up an evidence bag full of hundred-dollar bills, some of them burned, some bloodstained, some crisp and new.

Nan said, "We've collected $10,300 in nonsequential hundred-dollar bills so far. Most of it was in a suitcase that was ejected from the vehicle and split open. We're still collecting bills from the hillside. The money appears to be genuine, but we'll contact a currency expert to be sure."

Duncan put the bag down and picked up the one containing Netter's watch. It had come through the crash unscathed. "The only Rolex I've seen that's bigger than this is the one in the Calabasas clock tower."

Netter's watch had clearly been built to last, Eve thought. Rolex could use it as a selling point. *You might not survive a car crash, but your watch will.* "Do you have a rough idea of how the shooting went down?"

Nan shrugged. "I can take a guess, based on the victim's injuries, the spread and depth of the gunshot pellets in the vehicle, taillight fragments near the broken guardrail, the absence of skid marks on the asphalt, and where we discovered the shotgun wad. But don't hold me to it."

"Duly noted," Duncan said.

"He was heading westbound, approaching the curve, when he was shot twice from up there"—she pointed to the hillside, park land covered in dense chaparral, sage scrub, and mustard grass—"killing him instantly. The car rolled backward, smashed through the guardrail, tipped end over end, popping the trunk and expelling the contents, then it rolled over twice before coming to rest against a tree, the vehicle nearly flattened and sparking a small fire."

Eve was still studying the hillside, imagining the sniper crawling through it, finding the right spot. "That's thick, weedy brush the shooter was hiding in."

"Full of ticks, ants, spiders, and mosquitoes," Duncan said.

"I don't think he just lucked into the spot," Eve said. "He scouted it in advance."

Nan nodded. "I think you're right. We found his sniper's nest and it was too perfect. His position was only ten or twenty yards from the driver's side window and yet allowed him to remain well hidden. He was nestled in deep, lying on the ground, waiting for the target to arrive. Judging by how flattened the plants are, he was there for some time, at least an hour."

Duncan said, "I don't suppose the shooter left behind any cigarette stubs, a water bottle, candy wrappers, or some bodily fluids?"

"Not that we've found. We also haven't spotted any usable footwear impressions yet," Nan said. "But he made a clear path through the brush to an existing trail. He could have hiked in on the Backbone Trail or had a car parked somewhere along the road. We're investigating turnouts up and down the road, but a lot of hikers have parked in those spots. I am not hopeful about finding usable evidence there."

Eve picked up a baggie full of shotgun pellets. "Was the murder weapon the same one used at the rock pond?"

"I don't know but it was definitely the same ammunition."

There was a noisy commotion down at the crime scene line. Eve looked back and saw Zena Faust being pushed in a wheelchair by another woman toward the crime scene tape strung across the road. She looked terrible, all swollen, bandaged, and bruised. Her right leg was in a cast, jutting out in front of her on an extension on the chair.

Eve marched over to the barricade and faced Zena, whose broken leg extended underneath the crime scene tape. "What are you doing here, Zena?"

"My job," she said.

"There are plenty of reporters here. Shouldn't you still be in the hospital?"

"Shut away, drugged up, and silenced," Faust said. "I'm sure that's exactly what you'd prefer, because you don't want me, or anyone else, revealing the truth."

"What truth, Zena?"

Faust raised her voice so the reporters could hear her. "That we're standing in the kill zone of the Malibu Sniper and that Councilman Netter is the latest victim."

How does she know already that it was a shooting? Eve wondered.

The act of raising her voice, though, seemed to have taxed Faust. She winced in pain and clutched at her chest. Eve crouched down so they were eye to eye.

"You really should go back to bed, Zena. You aren't ready for this. You've been shot."

"Yes, I have." Faust noted the media coming closer and summoned the breath to raise her voice again. "How many more people have to be seriously injured or killed by the Malibu Sniper before you start being honest with the public about the danger?"

Kate Darrow stepped up to the line, her cameraman right behind her. She had the face, body, hairstyling, makeup, and wardrobe of a movie star playing a TV reporter, but Eve knew she was the real deal in every way. Smart. Tough. Well informed.

"I'm hearing from my sources that Councilman Netter was shot," Darrow said. "Was it also with a shotgun?"

"The investigation into the circumstances of Councilman Netter's death is ongoing. We're not ready to make any comments at this time."

Eve started to walk away, and Darrow fired a question at her back.

"Is it open season on anyone near Malibu Creek State Park . . . or is the sniper only targeting specific people?"

That pissed Eve off. She turned to face Darrow, making sure the camera saw that she was taking her on directly.

"Trying to bait me with sensationalized questions crafted to scare your viewers and create a promo for your evening newscast is not only offensive, it's irresponsible. I thought you were a better reporter than that, Kate. I guess I was wrong."

Eve walked back to the evidence tent, where Duncan stood, watching the show.

"I wish I knew the answer to Darrow's question," he said.

"So do I." She headed for their Explorer and he fell into step beside her.

"But you've proved, once again, that you're a natural politician."

"Why do you say that?"

"Because you made Darrow feel ashamed about a question you're asking yourself."

Eve stopped and faced him. "Are you suggesting I am insincere?"

Duncan smiled. "I'm suggesting you'll probably be elected sheriff someday."

The files that Eve demanded from Trisha Kalb were on her desk when they got back to the station. There were six single-page incident reports. Four were shootings they already knew about—the amateur porn star, the homeowner, the teens making out, and the couple in the motor home. But two were new.

Stony Jarrett, a wildlife biologist for the state, was shot at in the park, and a homeless person, with an encampment in one of the ravines, reported that someone shot up his shelter while he was sleeping inside, barely missing him. The homeless man hadn't been seen in months, but Jarrett was still working in the park.

Biddle and Garvey hadn't found anything yet, but they were still looking, and simultaneously compiling stats on "shots fired" calls that turned out to be other things, like firecrackers. It was dull, unglamorous, time-consuming work and Eve appreciated that they'd volunteered to do it.

She started working on the reams of paperwork and reports they were required to prepare and file on every step of their investigation. While she began on that, Duncan contacted the phone company to get the process started on obtaining the list of calls Clark Netter made over the last few days on both phones. Duncan also reached out to various banks to track Netter's recent credit card activity.

Duncan insisted they go home at 8:00 p.m. and he wouldn't let her take any work with her. He argued that she needed her rest, that she should learn to conserve her energy to be at her best for herself and the victims she was pursuing justice for.

Eve couldn't argue with that and went home without even a pen from the station in her possession.

She took a long shower, had a bowl of Grape-Nuts for dinner, and turned on the TV to catch the local news. Her comment to Darrow didn't make the cut in her taped report from the crime scene, but that didn't surprise Eve.

Various Calabasas city leaders were interviewed about Clark Netter, expressing their shock over his death and praising his community service. So did longtime Los Angeles City Council member Ricardo Villegas, who offered a tearful tribute to Netter, his former chief of staff before he quit to go into the private sector and pursue a political career of his own on the side. Then they showed a clip of Lansing's press conference from LASD headquarters.

"Our hearts and prayers go out to Councilman Netter's family, his friends, his coworkers, and the citizens of Calabasas," he said. "I can assure you that we are dedicating the full resources of the department to rigorously and thoroughly investigate the circumstances of his tragic death."

Darrow called out a question: "You mean his murder. There were homicide investigators at the scene."

To illustrate her point, the report cut away to footage of Eve and Duncan at the site before returning to Lansing for his reply.

He said, "We treat every death situation like this as a homicide until the evidence proves otherwise."

Zena Faust was at the press conference, too, and shouted out a question. "Clark Netter was shot in the face. What does that prove to you? Or do you think he shot himself while he was driving?"

Her question didn't shake him. "The investigation is ongoing and it would be inappropriate for me to comment or speculate until we have all the facts."

Eve turned off the TV. They were in for some hell tomorrow. Lansing was bound to take out his frustrations on her and Duncan. She went up to bed so she'd be rested for it but couldn't get to sleep. She kept thinking about the conversation she had with Garvey and Snell outside Hayes' house, and all the comments Duncan made the rest of the day about her being political.

It wasn't fair, she thought. Politics had nothing to do with her actions. She was just doing what she believed in, which was honoring the badge and what it represented. She'd leveraged her popularity to get a promotion from Lansing only so she could do more important work, not out of ambition, and certainly not for the attention. She didn't court Hollywood, they came to her. She didn't do anyone any favors to get the TV series deal. That would go against all of her principles and compromise her integrity.

All she ever wanted to do was her job.

But thinking about Hollywood, and her integrity, and favors, reminded her of the unpleasant conversation with Vince. She hated to admit it to herself, but he was right.

He'd played her perfectly, the manipulative prick.

She picked up the phone and called Simone Harper, the executive producer of the show, at home before she could reconsider.

Simone answered, and Eve said, "I hope I'm not calling too late."

"Not at all. I do my best writing between eight p.m. and two a.m. I saw you on the news. This case you're working has the makings of a great episode."

The idea that her life was now fodder for weekly episodes made her nauseous, but she wasn't going to think about that now. She was feeling enough stress already.

"I heard that Vince isn't directing the pilot."

"The network is under a lot of pressure to be diverse and hiring an old white guy for the job, who is also your father, just wouldn't play well," Simone said. "Besides, they felt a young woman would be a better fit creatively on this project. She's also Asian and gay, which gives her a particularly unique perspective. I'm very excited about working with her."

"You promised him the job."

"I promised him I would try, but ultimately, it's not my decision. The network wouldn't approve him."

"I could make the case that he's being denied the job because he's old," Eve said. "That's ageism, every bit as bad as other forms of exclusion."

"So is nepotism," Simone said, with some edge in her voice.

Eve had to admire her for that jab. Simone wasn't intimidated and she was also right. Nepotism wasn't a good look, either.

"You knew he was old, white, and my father when you, not me, promised him the job. You have to honor that promise."

"He can do episode two," Simone said. "The network is fine with that, just not the pilot."

"He's directing the pilot or there won't be one," Eve said. "I'll walk away, taking my name and my story with me. I'll kill the series before it even starts."

"I thought you hated him," she said.

"I do," Eve said. "This is how I show it."

"By fighting for him against your own best interests?"

"He never fought for anyone but himself. So every time I fight for someone, every time I stand for something besides myself, I'm proving I'm not him."

Eve startled herself with that admission. She had no idea where it came from, or that she felt that way until now, but she knew it was true.

Simone said, "You know he's playing you, right?"

"Of course I do."

"That doesn't make you angry?"

"I've been angry at him since the day I was born," Eve said. "I'm used to it."

"The network doesn't like to be strong-armed," Simone said. "They could cancel the pilot over this."

"I can live with that, too."

Eve said good night to Simone and ended the call.

A part of her hoped the network would kill the show, though it would almost certainly mean she wouldn't be able to afford to defend herself against the lawsuit.

She could lose everything, all for her father, who'd given her nothing, who'd never had any interest in her until he could get something from her.

Did she really think her sacrifice would teach him anything? That he'd have some life-changing revelation and realize his shortcomings as a man and as a father?

Hell no.

The best she could hope for was that he'd help her get a job as a security guard at the motion picture home.

Not that she'd ever ask him for anything.

I'm so stupid.

CHAPTER NINETEEN

The first thing Eve saw when she drove into the Lost Hills station employee parking area the next morning was Sheriff Lansing's black Expedition. His driver Rondo sat in the front seat, his tinted window rolled down, his expression as implacable as a marble statue, his eyes hidden behind sunglasses as dark as a black hole. He was a huge man, and everything about him seemed square and hard to Eve, like a brick that some mischievous witch, with a flick of her wand, made into a man.

Eve parked beside the car and walked up to the Expedition. "Morning, Rondo. I have a quick question for you." His expression didn't change. He could have been dead. "Is Rondo your given name or a nickname?"

"Ronin," he said. "Is that really your name?"

"It's really mine, but it wasn't really my mother's. Her given name was Ronan, with an *a* instead of an *i*. But then she saw some Japanese samurai movie and thought Ronin would be cooler, that it would get her more work as an actress, so she had it legally changed."

"Did it work?"

"Nope," Eve said.

"But the name fits you well."

"So? Rondo?" Eve let her voice trail off, hoping to encourage a reply.

He turned, and she assumed he was looking at her now, though it was hard to tell. "It's my given name. My parents were musicians. Rondo has a lot of meanings in music, but generally it's a piece that's fast, colorful, and rich in character."

"It's also a great name for a tough guy," she said.

"I also play the harpsicord," he said.

She smiled. "Don't let that get around."

"I don't," he said. "So if it does, I'll know who it came from."

That's when Duncan arrived in his Buick Regal and parked beside Eve's car.

She walked over to greet him as he got out. "You can take that old Buick to car shows. It's mint."

"That's my retirement plan," he said. "Go from one car show to another, soaking up the envy."

"I'm relieved to hear that you have a backup plan, because the TV series could be over before it starts."

She told him why.

"Are you sure that you did it for the principle," Duncan said, "or because you're afraid of how the show will change your life?"

"My life will probably be worse either way," she said.

"Then it's a win-win for you," he said and they headed into the station.

They didn't get past the open door to the captain's office. Dubois called them in, where Lansing stood waiting in front of the captain's desk. Lansing didn't bother with a greeting. He got right to the point.

"The murder of Councilman Netter has sparked a media firestorm and outrageous speculation that, frankly, has local governments severely rattled. What have you learned so far?" They told him what they knew about the case, and when they were done five minutes later, he said, "So you have nothing."

Duncan said, "We think it's the same shooter who killed Kim Spivey and was involved in at least ten other incidents."

"It could be," Lansing said. "Or it could be a copycat provoked by Faust's article. Or it could be a bunch of kids taking potshots for fun. Or it could be a street gang moving into the area. The fact is, you don't know. I've been on the phone all night with the mayors and city council members of every municipality this station serves and they all agree: the cases aren't connected."

Eve asked, "What do they know that we don't?"

"They know what they want to believe, and what we and the state park police tell them," Lansing said. "We don't want people afraid to be near Malibu Creek State Park."

"Why not?" Duncan said. "It would certainly cut down the number of targets and deaths."

"So would shutting down the roads, closing the park, and ordering homeowners to shelter in place or evacuate. Is that what you want?"

"I want people to know the danger," Duncan said, "to be alert and cautious."

"Good. Because we're having a community meeting at nine a.m. tomorrow morning at the Calabasas Library to educate the public and that's what I want you to tell them. All the local mayors will be on the stage, as well as State Senator Holbrook, State Park Superintendent Trisha Kalb, Captain Dubois, myself, and you two," Lansing said. "Make it clear they should be alert and cautious, whether they are near the park or anywhere else. Because the danger is the same. That is the message you are going to deliver, while underscoring that it's irresponsible and inaccurate to suggest, based on the scant evidence we have, that there's a serial sniper at work."

"What if we are asked about specific cases?" Eve asked.

"Share only the generalities and deflect. I know you can do that, I saw you on the news last night. You handled Faust and Darrow brilliantly. I couldn't have done it better myself."

Duncan said, "That's what I told her."

"You have the full resources of this department, whatever you need, and the power of my office behind you," Lansing said. "Call me if any whips need to be cracked or walls need to be smashed."

"Thank you, sir," Eve said.

"Study up on the cases today so you don't look stupid tomorrow. Know the names and dates. Dazzle the public with your knowledge of the facts, though don't share anything meaningful."

"We wouldn't dare," Duncan said.

"The public will be reassured seeing an experienced veteran homicide detective and a famous, highly skilled young investigator on the case," Lansing said. "I know that I am."

That sounded like a dismissal to Eve, so she headed for the door and Duncan followed.

Out in the hall, Duncan said, "So, you're young and hot."

"So, you're old and grandfatherly," Eve said.

"They are going to eat us alive tomorrow."

"Yep."

They went into the detective squad room and stood in front of the whiteboard, which needed to be updated to include the two new shooting incidents that Kalb had shared.

Duncan sighed. "We have a lot of reading to do."

"You do. You were the primary detective on the cases before I got here, so you do the reading and take the lead tomorrow. No sense both of us being stuck at a desk today."

"What are you going to do?"

"Netter's hobby was being a city councilman, but he earned his living as a financial manager. I'll visit his office. Maybe he made a few enemies. Also, the files from state park police are thin, just one-page incident reports. I'd like to learn what they left out . . . or didn't bother to discover. I'll start with Stony Jarrett, the state wildlife biologist."

"Okay, while I'm studying the files, I'll also follow up with the cellular service providers on Netter's iPhone and burner phone data dumps, and I'll have Crockett and Tubbs see if anyone on Zena's list of suspects might have a reason to kill Clark Netter."

"Good idea," Eve said and looked at all the names on the board.

There were so many victims. And, in Faust's case, too many suspects. Eve was certain there had to be something that tied them all together. Even if the shooter thought he was picking people at random, he wasn't. There was an order to everything, and she wouldn't stop until she found out what his was.

Eve found California Department of Fish and Wildlife biologist Stony Jarrett's truck at the end of Simes Lane, a narrow, cracked asphalt road deep in La Sierra Canyon, off Mulholland Highway, bordering what was once the Seminole Hot Springs and Mineral Baths. In its heyday, between the 1920s and late 1940s, the resort typically drew a thousand people each weekend to their mineral baths, swimming pool, and whirlpools, the 116-degree water pumped from a spring 2,600 feet underground. By the 1950s, though, mineral baths lost their allure and the resort was demolished to make way in 1967 for a mobile home park, which was now in ashes, incinerated only a few months earlier by the wildfire.

Stony Jarrett's truck bed was replaced with built-in animal cages and utility cabinets. An antennae array was on the cab's rooftop and big off-road lights and grilles were mounted on the front.

Stony was in his forties and leaned against the truck, a cowboy hat on his head. He wore a Kevlar vest over his khaki uniform shirt, carried a holstered sidearm at his waist, and held a strange device that looked like a garage-door opener with a TV antenna attached to it.

He was studying the readout on the device as Eve got out of her car and walked up to him. "Detective Ronin?"

"Thanks for meeting me," she said.

Stony looked up from his device. His skin was like a worn leather chair. She'd never seen so many lines in a man's face. "You caught me just in time. I was about to hike up into the hills and cell reception in this canyon is lousy."

She pointed to the strange device in his hand. "Is that why you have that?"

He held it up to her to see, as if that would make its purpose obvious. It didn't.

"This is a signal locator for the tracking devices we've attached to the various mountain lions in the park. I'm tracking P72, making sure she's left her den so I can check on her cubs."

"Are you carrying the gun in case she comes back?"

"It's not for her," he said. "I'm worried about the predators that carry guns, which I'm assuming is why you want to talk with me."

"Do you often get shot at?"

"It only takes one shooting to make you take precautions."

"Tell me what happened," she said.

"Oh, this was about a year ago. I was tracking P74, a rogue mountain lion that got too much of a taste for blood. He massacred a rancher's herd of alpaca and his dogs just for the fun of it. Didn't eat any of 'em."

"You were hunting it?"

"Not exactly. A week earlier, I'd passed along the state depredation permit to the rancher, Lane Trucco, which gave him the right to shoot it next time it came on his property. I was opposed to it. But the order came from on high."

She felt a chill, but it wasn't from the temperature. She knew the Trucco name. Someone shot at Gloria Trucco's truck while she was driving on Mulholland. That meant that two people involved in the depredation permit, Stony and Trucco, were shot at. Was it a coincidence or a clue?

"Do you know Gloria Trucco?"

"Sure, she's Lane's wife," Stony said. "She was furious about the killings. She wanted that lion's head above their mantelpiece."

"Why were you opposed to Trucco shooting the mountain lion? Would you have preferred to do it yourself?"

"I didn't want the lion shot at all. We're supposed to protect the mountain lions. The cat doesn't know we've imposed a law on him that he can only kill to eat, but I understand Trucco's point of view, too," Stony said. "Trucco lured him into a trap baited with a dead deer, and shot him. Or at least he thought he did. The mountain lion ran off. I wanted to see if P74 was injured and put him down if he was."

"Who knew where you were out there?"

"Nobody, except my supervisor. I don't park my truck anywhere near where cubs or mountain lions are so no one can follow me to a den," Stony said. "Anyway, I was deep in a ravine when someone shot over my head, obliterating a bush. Scared the shit out of me."

"Was it a warning shot . . . or did he miss you?"

"I'm not sure. I dove for cover and he took another shot where I'd been standing. I actually had a cell signal, so I called 911. The operator transferred me to the park police. I gave them my exact GPS coordinates. I figured if they got there quick enough, we could track him down and corner him. Tracking is my business."

"How close did you get to catching him?"

Stony chuckled, but he didn't seem very amused to Eve. "It took them ninety minutes to get there, and when I say 'there,' I mean down where I parked. They called to say they'd meet me at my truck. I was afraid if I stepped out I'd get shot. But the shooter was long gone."

They either didn't take him seriously or didn't want to confront the situation. Both reasons perplexed her. "Did they come back to the scene to collect evidence?"

"Not with me. They told me I must have been mistaken, that this kind of thing doesn't happen here. I said, 'It just did.' I'm surprised they even filed a report. I guess they had to do it to justify their mileage."

"Who do you think was shooting at you?"

"Best guess? The Mexican Mafia. I probably got too close to one of their pot farms."

His answer surprised her. "I thought the pot farms were all out in the Antelope Valley and Mojave Desert now."

"Sure, but there's also plenty of them still hidden here, and for good reason. The park has the advantage of being in the middle of an urban area, close to major freeways, easy access to buyers and sellers, and the plants are almost impossible to spot, unless you are up close. During the wildfire, it smelled like a huge frat party up here."

"I didn't notice," Eve said. She'd been preoccupied at the time, running from the flames with a child in her arms. It could have smelled like hot chocolate and she wouldn't have noticed.

"The gangs also like to use these mountains to get rid of bodies," he said. "It's a good place to toss or bury a corpse."

She nodded in agreement. "We found the skeletons of a lot of gang members up here after the wildfire burned away all the brush."

"I'm sure it's only a small fraction of the bodies that are actually up here. If it wasn't the Mexican Mafia shooting at me, or some gang members getting rid of a body, then maybe I got too close to a homeless person's encampment. You'd be surprised how many people are living off the grid in the park and they are fiercely protective of their territory."

"How do they survive?"

"They have vegetable gardens, set traps for small game, and they hunt."

"With shotguns?" Eve asked.

"Sure. They also scrounge scraps from restaurant trash cans, steal food from campsites, shoplift from grocery stores, and break into homes and businesses around the park."

That could explain the break-in at the water district headquarters, Eve thought, and why the guy only took food, some clothing, and a book to read.

Stony went on. "But you'd be surprised how many of them actually have jobs. I know a woman who works at the Jack in the Box on Kanan and lives in a tent up here. Keeps it real clean and orderly. She can't afford rent in LA on what she earns, certainly not in a safe neighborhood."

"Does she have a shotgun?"

"A switchblade," Stony said.

"What about the Malibu Nature Strike Force and groups like them?" Eve asked. "Could they have targeted you?"

"They were furious with me, and I don't blame them, for giving Trucco the depredation permit. But they wouldn't hurt me. I'm a wildlife biologist. They know I'm on their side."

"Or they pegged you as a traitor," she said.

"Their whole thing is protecting animals from being harmed," he said. "I'm an animal, too. Besides, I was just the messenger."

"Why do you think the state park police didn't want to follow up on your report?"

"It's all about keeping up the image that there's nothing to fear when you're surrounded by the beauty and tranquility of nature," Stony said. "But the fact is, nature is brutal, and while you're distracted by all that beauty and tranquility, it will kill you."

Eve motioned to his Kevlar and his gun. "You seem prepared."

"Survival of the fittest, that's nature, too," Stony said. "Next time someone shoots at me, I'm shooting back."

Eve believed he would, too.

CHAPTER TWENTY

The financial management firm where Clark Netter worked was in a Century City high-rise that looked to Eve like a steel-and-glass penis.

The top-floor offices were as stark and cold as Netter's house and every employee she saw was wearing black. Eve assumed the staff was in mourning over the death of one of the partners.

Akiko Sakurai, one of the surviving partners, wore a sleek black dress that made her look to Eve like an assassin in a Netflix movie rather than an accountant. The woman was in her thirties, with long jet-black hair and perfect makeup, and sat at her glass-and-chrome desk, a stunning unobstructed view to the Pacific Ocean behind her. Eve sat facing her and that amazing view, which was meant to convey Akiko's power and high stature.

"Clark came here after working as chief of staff for Los Angeles City councilman Villegas, who is one of our clients, by the way," Akiko said. "Clark's political experience, and later his work on the Calabasas City Council, gave him invaluable, keen insights into many industries and a deep understanding of complex budgets."

"He must have been deeply loved here," Eve said.

Akiko cocked a brutally tweezed black eyebrow. "Why do you say that?"

"Everyone in the building is wearing black."

"Oh, that's not for him. I mean, his death is shocking, tragic, and very sad, but we all love black. It's very fashionable now and it's become our company style, instantly setting us apart from everyone else in our space. It also conveys how serious, dependable, and solemn we are in the way we handle our clients' finances."

"It also conveys death," Eve said.

"In some ways, managing money is like managing death. It's a fact of life that evokes fear, dread, fascination, and misunderstanding," Akiko said. "It's also something that's deeply influenced by religion, race, and culture, and that many people prefer be handled in the shadows."

"I wouldn't like being in the dark about how my money is handled." She'd be lucky, she thought, if she still had any money after the Pruitt lawsuit was over, especially if she'd just gotten her show canceled before it had even started.

"Everyone is different, Detective. Some people have more faith in us than they do in themselves when it comes to investing, living within their means, and making sure all the bills get paid on time."

"But nobody likes losing money, especially when it's because of someone else's mistakes or bad advice."

"We aren't perfect," Akiko said.

Eve's phone buzzed. She checked the screen. It was Linwood Taggert. Her agent at Creative Artists Agency. He could wait. Forever. She put her phone away.

"Who are the clients who thought Netter wasn't perfect? Are there any who might be angry enough to want him dead?"

"Are you familiar with Tommy Jory?"

"Vaguely." All she knew was that he was a movie star who played a comic book superhero who threw cars and buses at bad guys.

"He's suing us for $30 million. He claims that Clark spent his money without consent, made horrible investments, failed to pay taxes, took kickbacks from every third party he hired, didn't pay his bills, and borrowed money against his assets without his knowledge, ultimately forcing him to sell off his properties, cars, boats, and art to stay afloat."

"Does he have a case?"

"Jory has a pathological compulsion to spend money, faster than he can earn it, buying exotic cars, designer clothes, a castle in Eastern Europe, a yacht, erotic art, rare comic books, a small jet, and a Caribbean island, among other things, while also indulging his sexual desires with high-priced male, female, and trans prostitutes and staging massive, decadent parties that would make Caligula blush," Akiko said. "Of course Jory went broke. We advised him that filing a lawsuit would force us to reveal all of his profligate, obnoxious, and sordid spending in explicit detail."

"That must have pissed him off."

"He threatened to fly a plane into our building," Akiko said.

"Did you report the threat to the FBI?"

Akiko shook her head. "Clark had his plane repossessed instead."

Eve was finishing her second of two slices of thin-crust cheese pizza at Lamonica's NY Pizza in Westwood Village when her phone buzzed. She checked the screen. It was Duncan. She swallowed her mouthful of pizza and answered the call.

"Hey," she said.

"Where are you?"

She didn't want to tell him the truth or he'd ask her to bring him back an entire pie and it would stink up the Explorer.

"Clark Netter's office in Beverly Hills. I'm coming back with another suspect to add to the list, as if we don't have plenty already." She was referring to actor Tommy Jory. He might not have a plane anymore, but he could have a shotgun.

"I got the data dump from Netter's iPhone," Duncan said. "Nothing unusual popped up in his texts, emails, or call logs. He disabled GPS tracking but he was obviously unaware that the phone company tracks him anyway and that the records are available to law enforcement."

"Why would he care about that possibility? Did he rob a bank while he was out of town?"

"He drove to Las Vegas on Tuesday morning, then went between the Wynn and the Côte d'Azur several times on Wednesday, and then drove straight back on Thursday, except for a stop for gas and Skittles in Yermo, which I've also confirmed with his credit card transactions."

"You didn't call just to tell me he bought Skittles."

"I glanced at his GPS history going back weeks. It shows lots of trips back and forth between his home, his office, and Calabasas city hall," Duncan said, "but it also shows several visits to a house in Woodland Hills."

"Who owns it?"

"It's a rental property. The current tenant is an offshore company, Eagle Ventures LLC, that paid a year's rent in advance. The transaction was all handled online."

"It could be a totally innocent corporate rental, a place for their executives to stay while conducting business in Los Angeles."

"I don't think so," Duncan said. "I also got the calls, texts, and photos from his burner phone. They are all to and from one person. Jayda Montaro."

"Paul Banning's assistant?"

"Small world, isn't it?" Duncan said.

"What kind of texts and photos were they?"

"X-rated," he said. "I can now testify under oath that Clark Netter was circumcised and that Jayda likes Brazilians, and I'm not talking about the people."

"Was it all sexting?"

"They also made arrangements to get together in Las Vegas in her room at the Côte d'Azur," Duncan said. "He bought the phone three days ago and should have thrown it out the window on his way home through the desert. But I'll bet she's tossed hers by now."

"I'll ask her," Eve said.

Forty minutes later, Eve pulled up to Banning's gate and flashed her badge to the camera. It seemed like everybody in LA lived behind a gate except her. Jayda's voice came over the speaker.

"Good afternoon, Detective Ronin. Unfortunately, Mr. Banning isn't here at the moment. He's away at a meeting. He'll be back around four p.m. if you'd like to come back."

"It's you I'm here to see." There was a long silence. "You might as well get this over with now, Jayda. Or I could park a patrol car out here until you leave and bring you into the station to talk."

It was a lie, she didn't have the right to bring her in without charging her with something, but Eve was banking on Jayda not knowing that.

The gate opened and Eve drove up to the house. The assortment of cars on display around the fountain of nude women had changed. Now it was a Ferrari, a Corvette, and a Tesla. Eve wondered if Banning ever drove the cars or just used them as his very expensive version of garden gnomes.

Jayda was waiting for her at the fountain, arms at her sides, balling her hands in and out of fists. She wasn't happy, bracing herself for a fight, figuratively if not literally.

Eve got out of the car and walked up to Jayda, who spoke first.

"What is this about?"

"Clark Netter didn't throw away his burner phone before he got home. We have every email, text, and photo that was on it," Eve said. "So use your imagination."

"I've worked for Paul Banning and observed him making lots of complex deals. One of his rules is: don't negotiate with yourself."

"What does that have to do with this conversation?"

"I'm not answering a question you haven't asked. I am not going to use my imagination. You will have to use yours."

Eve glanced at the fountain and wondered how Banning's wife and daughter felt about the statues of the nude women splashing around.

They didn't look like Italian Renaissance Venuses to her, more like surgically enhanced *Baywatch* lifeguards.

"Were you having an affair?"

Jayda flexed her hands some more. "'Affair' is a broad term. You'll have to be more specific."

"Were you having sex?"

"Yes," she said.

"Were you in love?"

"No," she said.

"Was that feeling, or lack of it, mutual?"

"There was plenty of feeling, but it was almost entirely sexual for us both. Clark was deeply in love with his wife and devoted to his kids."

"He had a funny way of showing it," Eve said.

"We had sex. Great sex. That's all," Jayda said. "It actually strengthened his marriage."

"Really? How do you figure that?"

"Because of me, he stayed with Hallie even though she couldn't meet all of his physical needs," she said, as if the answer were obvious. "Sex with me kept his family together."

"Jayda, you know what that sounds like to me? A desperate rationalization to soothe a guilty conscience."

"Your opinion is meaningless, Detective. Adultery isn't a crime and telling his wife about our purely carnal relationship now would only add to her pain."

"What makes you think she doesn't already know about it?"

"Because Clark only used burner phones to contact me and we'd meet once or twice a month when he was in Las Vegas for a conference or on business," Jayda said. "He'd stay in one hotel, I'd stay in another, and we'd get together in my room. We were never seen in public."

"What about the house in Woodland Hills?"

"We never slept together here," Jayda said, "but if we had, it certainly wouldn't have been in a house in Woodland Hills."

"Why? Is the neighborhood beneath you?"

"No room service," Jayda said.

So, Eve wondered, if Jayda was telling the truth, what was Netter doing at that house in Woodland Hills?

"Did he have another lover?"

"I think between me and his wife, his needs were met." Jayda smiled. "And often exceeded."

Or Jayda was wrong, Eve thought, and two women weren't enough for him.

"You had to spend a lot of time and money on travel, and go through a lot of aggravation, just for sex with this guy," Eve said. "I'm sure there are easier, and cheaper, ways for a woman like you to get laid."

"I lead an extremely busy life and I have high standards, and very specific physical needs, that few men are able to satisfy. Clark was one of them," Jayda said. "So yes, it was worth it and a good fit for my lifestyle."

"Do you still have the burner phone you two used to communicate?"

"I don't use a burner," she said. "I don't have a husband to worry about."

"Don't delete any texts or emails you two sent or received. We may need them and you wouldn't want to be charged with destroying evidence."

"You'll need a warrant for that," Jayda said.

"I do?" Eve said. "That's good to know. Thanks. How did you and Clark meet?"

Jayda shook her head and balled her fists some more. "I'm done indulging your prurient interest in my sex life. What does any of this have to do with his murder?"

"I don't know yet," Eve said, but thought it was very interesting that Jayda drew the line at talking about how they met.

"So you're just fishing," Jayda said.

"I'm investigating," Eve said, and decided to take a different approach. "Tell me about the last three days. When and where did you see him?"

"I arrived on Tuesday night. I saw him then, and again on Wednesday night, both times in my suite at the Côte d'Azur."

"Nothing unusual happened before or after?"

"No, it was like every other time. I was satisfied."

It was odd to Eve that she didn't mention Netter's big blackjack winnings. "Can you think of any reason why someone would want to kill him?"

"No, and it's a pointless question," Jayda said. "He was shot at random by the Malibu Sniper."

"Don't believe everything you read or see on TV."

"Are you saying there's no sniper?"

"I'm saying we don't know who killed Clark Netter or why," Eve said. "You don't seem very shaken about his death."

"Because I'm not sobbing in front of you? What happened to him is horrible and tragic. I'm sad about it—he was a good man and I'll miss the fun we had. But my heart isn't broken, and yes, Detective, I have one. Surely you aren't in love with every man you sleep with."

"I'd like to be," Eve said.

"Men will sense that. It makes you appear weak and needy."

"I think it makes me appear human."

She turned, got back in her car, and drove down the long driveway. Jayda didn't want to talk about how she and Netter met. But now that was something Eve was determined to find out, because it obviously was significant and troublesome. Why else would Jayda want to hide it?

The driveway ended at Mulholland, where Eve had a choice. She could turn right, and go to Lost Hills Station. Or she could turn left, and go to the crime scene.

She turned left.

CHAPTER
TWENTY-ONE

Netter's crushed car was on the flatbed truck and Nan stood on the street, watching it being secured, as Eve walked up to her.

"Come to check up on us?" Nan asked.

"I was in the neighborhood. Found anything new?"

"We've recovered $24,600. If there was more out there, it's either ashes or in someone's pocket. We've lifted partial footwear impressions at the turnouts up and down the road where a car might have been parked, but I can tell you now none of them match those recovered from the rock pond."

"So you haven't found anything that might help us."

"Well, I don't know if this will help you or not, but I think it's kind of interesting," Nan said. "We found a tracking device in the car."

Eve couldn't believe Nan didn't understand the importance of the discovery. "Of course that's helpful. Why didn't you tell me that to start with?"

Nan smiled at her with a certain deviousness. "Now you know how it feels."

It was payback, for Eve playing Columbo on a prior investigation instead of simply telling Nan what she'd found. Eve knew she deserved it.

"You've made your point," she said. "I won't indulge myself again."

"It was more like showing off." Nan reached into her pocket, pulled out a baggie, and handed it to Eve. The baggie contained what looked like a large thumb drive. "Whoever installed this tracking device didn't try very hard to hide it. The tracker was plugged into the OBD-IT port under the dash."

"What is an OBD-IT port?"

"Mechanics plug their computers into it to access the car's electronic data. The benefit of plugging a tracker into it is that it's constantly powered and can use the car's own GPS and Wi-Fi system to gather and send data," Nan said. "The downside is it's easy to find if anyone is looking for it or if you take your car in for service."

Eve's phone vibrated. She checked it. Linwood Taggert again. She ignored it, pocketed her phone, and handed the tracker back to Nan. "Can you tell from the device who put it there or who is watching?"

"There are two kinds of trackers—passive and active. A passive tracker logs data that is downloaded later. An active device delivers real-time data. This appears to be a hybrid," Nan said. "If it's in passive mode, anybody with access to the car, and the password to the device, can download the travel history. If it's active, it's accessing Wi-Fi, and whoever wants to follow the target in real time needs to use a proprietary app, unique to the device manufacturer, to get the live data."

"So to keep a constant watch, the spy has to register their device," Eve said, "which means providing the serial number and a credit card to pay the company for the service."

"That's right. Unless it's a law enforcement agency that's doing the spying."

She hadn't thought about that. "Is it?"

"I don't know yet. I need to open the tracker up. That's where I'll find the serial number and details that will help me identify the brand or if it's government-issue."

"Please let me know as soon as you do," Eve said, "so we can serve a warrant on the app company to tell us who was watching."

"You're assuming this tracker was active. If it was passive, it probably won't be registered."

"And we won't get a name. We'll have to hunt down where it was bought."

"That might be difficult," Nan said. "There's no brand name on this. There are hundreds of different brands, many of them slapping their names or logos on identical devices made by the same Chinese manufacturers, and they're sold everywhere."

"We'll just have to hope it's active," she said. "Or that it belongs to someone with a badge."

Eve walked back toward her Explorer and, to her surprise, Nan walked with her. It was odd because, up until now, it always felt to Eve like Nan was eager for her to go away.

"You can hope," Nan said. "I'm long past that."

"You have no hope? That's depressing."

"On the contrary. I stick to the facts in front of me and act accordingly. I've found that leads to less disappointment and more happiness."

Now Eve understood what this walk-and-talk was about. She stopped at the Explorer and faced Nan. "How old do I have to be before people stop offering me life lessons?"

"It's not age, it's experience."

"There's another one," Eve said, but with a smile, to show there was no bitterness or anger behind the remark.

"It won't be long, Eve. You've crammed more experience into the last few months than most detectives I know have in decades."

"I have the scars to prove it," she said.

"That's why I don't understand people who complain about their scars. I wear mine with pride. You should, too."

"You couldn't resist throwing another lesson in there, could you?"

Nan smiled. "Nope."

Since Eve was in the neighborhood, she decided to drop in on Hallie Netter and ask her some questions based on what she'd learned about her husband over the last twenty-four hours.

Once again, Eve found herself facing another gate. She rolled down her window, pressed the buzzer on the keypad, and held up her badge to the camera. The gate opened without Eve having to say anything this time.

She drove up to the door, got out, and was met by a woman who looked like a younger version of Hallie Netter. Her eyes were bloodshot and ringed with dark circles. She'd probably been crying a lot, Eve thought, and sleeping very little.

"I'm Detective Eve Ronin. I'm investigating your father's death. You must be Susie. How is your mom?"

"How do you think? She's devastated. We all are. My brother is flying in from Boston today. Helicopters and drones are circling the house at all hours," Susie said, glancing up angrily at the sky. "We can't even grieve in private. It's been hell."

"I'm very sorry. Please let us know if there is anything we can do to help."

"You can hurry up and arrest the bitch who shot my father."

That was specific, Eve thought. "Which bitch is that?"

"Raylene Bradley," Susie said. "She loathes my father. She whipped up half of Calabasas into believing he's evil."

"It wasn't her. She was in Aliso Viejo, protesting at a city council meeting, when your father was killed."

"So talk to her lunatic followers, those self-important hypocrites who think any developments besides the gated communities they all live in, which the hills were razed to build, are bad," Susie said. "They don't realize that it takes tax dollars to keep a city afloat and you can't get taxes from weeds and trees. But you can from hotels and other businesses.

All my father wanted was a reasonable balance between nature and development and was killed for it."

Hallie walked up behind her daughter in the foyer. She had the same bloodshot, dark-ringed eyes. They really were the past and future of the same woman, Eve thought, both tormented by grief.

"You have to forgive Susie," Hallie said. "She's an urban planning major at USC. She believed in the compromise Clark was trying to strike."

"No apologies necessary. I need to ask you a few more questions."

Hallie motioned her inside, and she and her daughter stepped aside to let Eve pass.

"What could I possibly know that could help you?" Hallie asked, scratching her chest.

"Can we talk in private?" Eve asked as Susie closed the front door.

Hallie glanced at her daughter, then at Eve. "I don't see any reason to. There's nothing you can ask me that I can't answer in front of my daughter."

"Did you know your husband disabled the location services on all of his iPhone apps?"

Hallie led Eve into the stark living room and offered a seat on the hard couch. "Why would I know that or care?"

Eve decided to stand. She didn't want to be the only one sitting, the two women staring down at her. "Because it suggests that he didn't want anyone tracking his movements."

Susie said, "Or maybe he just didn't want to drain his battery, or get bombarded with ads based on where he happened to be, and only turned it on when he needed it, like for directions."

"That's possible," Eve said. "Except we found a tracking device in his car. Someone wanted to know where he was at all times. Maybe that's who Clark was trying to hide from by shutting off his location apps."

Hallie scratched her chest again. Eve wondered if it was a nervous habit.

"That's ridiculous," Hallie said. "He's not an international spy. He mostly travels between work in Beverly Hills, Calabasas city hall, and home and that's about it. What could he possibly have to hide?"

"An affair? Meetings with a rival management firm? I don't know. I thought you might."

Hallie looked as if Eve had just smacked her in the face, her cheeks reddening in response to the blow. "My husband was not cheating on me or his employers. He was the most honest, decent man I've ever known."

Eve toyed with telling her that it wasn't true, but it had been less than a day since his death, Hallie's eyes were welling with tears again, and her daughter was standing right there. The truth could wait.

Susie stepped defensively in front of her mother and scowled at Eve. "My God, what is wrong with you? Isn't it obvious who put the tracker on the car? It was his killer, so he'd know when and where to shoot him. Instead, you come here and accuse my father, the victim, of betraying his friends and family."

Hallie patted her daughter's arm. "That's not what she's doing, honey."

"It's exactly what she's doing," Susie snapped, her eyes still on Eve. "Get out of our house."

"I'm sorry if my questions caused you pain," Eve said, "but they have to be asked."

"The hell they do." Susie marched to the door and opened it. "Out. Now."

Eve walked out and got into her Explorer.

That went well.

Perhaps Hallie knew about the affair, Eve thought, but didn't want her daughter to know that her dad was cheating.

It was a mistake bringing it up. It was impulsive. She knew her inexperience was showing, again, and damaging the case.

Duncan wouldn't have let her do it if he were here, which just proved how much she needed him.

As she drove back down Piuma Road, she worried about who would protect her from herself once he was gone.

CHAPTER
TWENTY-TWO

Eve spent an hour at the station briefing Duncan, Biddle, and Garvey on what she'd learned that day from talking with Stony Jarrett, Akiko Sakurai, Jayda Montero, Nan Baker, and Hallie Netter. Now it was their turn to brief her. Duncan led off.

"The ME called with her autopsy report on Netter," he said. "I learned that getting a shotgun blast in the face and driving off a cliff can kill you."

No news there, Eve thought.

Biddle said, "The only connection we could find between Zena Faust's list of suspects and Councilman Netter is that Derek Hayes is a client of his management company."

"Paul Banning is on Zena's list," Eve said, "and Netter was sleeping with Jayda Montero, Banning's assistant."

Garvey said, "But Zena didn't know that."

"Don't be so sure," Eve said. "Maybe that was going to be her next exposé, explaining how Netter got Banning's huge house approved in a protected scenic corridor. Banning had his assistant seduce a city councilman."

"We could ask her," Garvey said.

Duncan shook his head. "We do that, then it'll be tomorrow's headline story on *Malibu Beat* and reported by every news-hungry TV station in town, just as we're going into the community meeting tomorrow."

"Even if Faust did know," Biddle said, "that'd only give Banning a motive to shoot *her*. It doesn't explain the other killings."

"That's true," Eve said.

Duncan patted the stack of files on his desk. "I've been reading through all these damn files today to prepare for tomorrow. Most of the victims opposed one of Raylene Bradley's causes or did something to piss her off."

"For example," Garvey said, "blogging that Raylene's a lunatic while you're scissoring with her ex-girlfriend?"

"Yeah, but Raylene has a solid alibi," Duncan said. "She was in Aliso Viejo when Netter was shot."

Garvey shrugged. "So it's somebody else we haven't looked at yet doing the killings and we're just doing a circle jerk."

"Stan's right," Biddle said. "We've got tunnel vision. We should forget about all of the suspects we have and look at this from an entirely fresh perspective."

Eve thought that was a good idea, because everything was muddled in her mind now anyway.

"Knock yourself out, guys." Duncan stood up from his desk. "Eve and I have to go to the circus tomorrow anyway. I'm leaving." He pointed at Eve. "So are you."

Eve looked at the wall clock. It was a few minutes past five.

"It's awfully early to be calling it a day," she said.

"You got in here at eight," Duncan said. "That's a nine-hour day. Tomorrow we're going to be onstage with every politician in Southern California and facing an angry public and a vicious media horde. We need to be fresh and sharp. That means a decent meal and a good night's sleep."

"When have you ever skipped either one?"

"I'm talking about you," Duncan said.

There was no sense arguing with him, she thought. Especially when he was right. She went home.

◆　◆　◆

Eve drove up to her condo to find a clean-cut man in his twenties, wearing a nice business suit, sitting on her porch. She parked at the curb, got out, and marched up her front walk. He took out his phone and tapped in a number as he stood.

She said, "Are you a process server, a missionary, or have I won the Publishers Clearing House sweepstakes?"

"I'm an aspiring agent."

"CIA?"

"CAA." Creative Artists Agency. He handed her the phone. "You have a call."

She took the phone and held it to her ear, knowing who would be on the other end of the line.

Linwood Taggert said, "Why don't you ever answer my calls?"

Eve groaned. "Why don't you ever take a hint?"

"You should be thrilled to hear from me. When I call, it usually means money."

"In return for a piece of my soul," she said, "and a percentage of my dignity."

"Congratulations," he said. "You may not have to worry about that anymore."

"You're dropping me as a client?"

"I heard about your call to Simone last night. What the hell were you thinking?"

Eve turned her back on the aspiring agent on the porch and took a few steps away for some privacy. "She made a commitment and she needs to honor it."

"I'm not talking about that. You have an agent. You should have called me first. I fight your battles for you."

"I fight for myself," Eve said.

"If you had a brain tumor, would you cut it out of your own skull? No, you'd see a brain surgeon. When you have a TV problem, you go to your agent."

"This was a personal problem."

"You're wrong. It was business, but Vince, the asshole, made you think it was personal," Linwood said. "He used you."

Eve knew he was right, but at the same time, the show was called *Ronin*, so everything about it was personal to her. "What could you have done that was any different?"

"Everything. This needed to be handled with finesse, but you have all the finesse of the Hulk on meth. I would have had lunch with the studio president, talked him into seeing things our way, and then we would have had drinks with the network president who, three martinis later, would have left thinking that having Vince direct the pilot was his idea."

"Wasn't he the one who rejected Vince for the job?"

"Of course not," Linwood said. "That's like asking if the president of the Ford Motor Company personally hires the guys who paint the cars."

"Isn't that done by machines now?"

"Are you missing my point or are you just trying to irritate me?"

"Guess," Eve said.

"The decision was probably made by some junior development executive who never saw any of your father's shows and is afraid that if the pilot sucks, he'll be blamed for it because he approved an old hack instead of hiring a young, cutting-edge director. It could cost him his job."

"So is the network going to back out of the pilot over this just to prove they have bigger balls than me?"

"No, because I have bigger balls than all of you," Linwood said. "I am going to terrify the network."

"How are you going to do that?"

"By taking the project today to another network and getting a much better offer."

"But this network hasn't hacked out yet," Eve said.

"We're walking unless they put Vince in the director's chair and apologize to you."

"Or they'll sue us for breach of contract."

"What do you care?" Linwood said. "You have a great lawyer."

"Who I'm paying with the money from the show."

"Then he'll have a fantastic motivation to fight for you."

"Or he'll quit," she said.

"Let me handle this. Don't answer any calls from Simone, the studio, or the network until I tell you it's okay. Promise me, Eve."

"I promise."

"Good," Linwood said. "Because you're my only client I can trust to honor that."

Eve ended the call and walked back over to the aspiring agent, who was practically standing at attention at her front door. She handed him the phone. "How long were you sitting on my front porch?"

"A couple of hours." He checked his watch. "Oh good, I still have time to pick up Mr. Taggert's dry cleaning before the place closes."

"Is any of this in your job description?"

"I work in the agency mail room. Technically, my job is sorting and delivering mail. This is how you move up."

"How does this prepare you to be an agent?"

He seemed to really consider the question before he answered. "You learn how to coerce people to do your bidding . . . willingly."

"Definitely something to aspire to."

She went into her house, made herself dinner, ate an entire mini carton of Ben & Jerry's ice cream, and did her laundry while binge-watching a subtitled French espionage series on Netflix and intentionally avoiding her laptop and her phone.

It felt like a vacation, so naturally, she felt guilty for not working. But she did get to bed early and had a deep, guiltless sleep.

The auditorium at the Calabasas Library was filled with a hundred members of the community. Dozens of reporters stood along the walls except for Zena Faust, who was technically a shooting victim and sat in the front row, a set of crutches beside her.

Eve sat with Duncan behind a long table on the stage, along with Lansing, Captain DuBois, Trisha Kalb, State Senator Peter Holbrook, the mayors of Calabasas, Malibu, and Agoura Hills, and representatives from the California Highway Patrol, National Park Service, and the Mountains Recreation & Conservation Authority.

Out in the audience, Eve spotted Raylene Bradley and Chase Orkett, as well as Hallie Netter, flanked by her daughter, Susie Netter, and a man she assumed was her son, Shane, based on the strong family resemblance. Along the back wall she saw several deputies, including Tom Ross, Eddie Clayton, and Wayne Snell, ready to respond to any trouble. Finally, her eyes settled on park ranger Mark Weston, who looked as if he hadn't slept in days. His complexion was sallow and his hair was askew. If she hadn't known better, she'd have thought he'd been on chemotherapy for weeks since she'd last seen him, but it had been only three days.

The attendees were asked to submit their questions in writing to keep things orderly, but mostly so the sheriff and others could ignore the questions they didn't want to answer.

Maps that illustrated the boundaries of the different state, national, and public lands in the Santa Monica Mountains and Simi Hills, and

how the various law enforcement agencies overlapped and divided jurisdiction, were projected on the wall behind the stage.

Senator Holbrook, who was serving as master of ceremonies, took
to the podium and opened the proceedings by acknowledging the shock
and horror he felt about the murders of Kim Spivey and, only days later,
Councilman Netter.

"These horrific, senseless acts of violence in the Santa Monica
Mountains have sparked fear, panic, and troubling rumors," he said,
"and also valid concerns that key information is not being shared with
the public. There is a widespread belief that the investigation is bogged
down in bureaucracy between agencies. I feel the same way you do. That
is why we called this unprecedented community meeting to address all
of these issues honestly and directly."

The senator then introduced Trisha Kalb, who stood and spoke to
the audience from behind the table.

"I know you have concerns. I do, too. I can assure you that we're
working closely, and smoothly, with all of our partners to keep you safe.
That is our shared priority."

She was only the second speaker, and already the lying had begun.
Eve tried to maintain her poker face.

"We have National Park rangers and state park police on patrol at
all times throughout the eight-thousand-acre park—on foot, on horse-
back, on mountain bikes, and on ATVs. They are tremendously skilled
and experienced," Kalb said. "But when it comes to serious crimes, we
seek the unparalleled expertise of the sheriff's department and let them
take the lead, as they have on the rock pond shootings."

One more lie, Eve thought. This meeting was not off to a good
start.

Kalb continued. "That isolated incident is still under investigation,
but there is one thing all of us up here know with absolute certainty:
the public is in no danger. That's why our campgrounds and the entire

park remain open for your enjoyment. You are as safe there as you are in your own living room . . . maybe safer."

Eve's phone vibrated on the table. She glanced at it. It was a text from Mark Weston:

We need to talk.

She looked up and met his gaze across the auditorium. Even from here, his eyes looked sunken into the back of his skull.

Trisha Kalb sat down and the sheriff stood up to speak.

"Thank you, Superintendent. Our goal today is to share with you as much as we can without jeopardizing our ongoing investigation into the two killings."

There started to be some rumblings of discontent in the audience, but Lansing held up his hand to halt it. Eve texted Weston back a thumbs-up emoji.

"I understand there have been reports in the media of other shootings in the Santa Monica Mountains over the last year or so that did not result in serious injuries or deaths. We are actively looking into those, too," Lansing said, "but at this time, we do not see any forensic or other connection whatsoever between them."

Weston texted back:

Meet me after this show is over. Art's Deli, Studio City. I'll wait.

Weston wanted to make sure they met far away from Calabasas and anyone who might recognize them. Eve thought that was interesting. What secrets did he have to share?

Lansing droned on. "We've assigned two of our best homicide detectives—Duncan Pavone and Eve Ronin—to lead the investigation into the murders of Kim Spivey and Councilman Netter and they have the full resources of the department, and of every agency up here, behind them. The multiagency cooperation has been truly astounding."

That wasn't true, either, Eve thought. The lying came so easy to them.

"I'll let the detectives tell you more about the cases and then we'll get to your written questions," Lansing said. "We'll begin with an overview from Detective Pavone."

Duncan stood up, but Eve felt all the eyes in the auditorium on her as well.

"Thank you, sir. Over the last eighteen months, there have been twelve confirmed incidents, reported to the state park police or the sheriff's department, of persons, vehicles, or properties being shot at," Duncan said. "During that same period, there have been twenty-three unconfirmed reports of shots fired. That doesn't mean actual shootings, but people calling us to say they heard a gunshot."

Eve's phone buzzed again. This time it was a text from Nan.

Tracker is non-govt and was in passive mode.

It was followed by the brand name and serial number. That wasn't good news.

Duncan went on, using the research that Biddle and Garvey had compiled for him.

"Statistically, those numbers are in line with the average of monthly 'shots fired' calls we've had over the last decade and does not suggest a pattern or anything unusual. In these twenty-three specific cases, the causes were determined to likely be a blown transformer, backfiring cars, or people setting off firecrackers. No evidence was found of any actual shooting."

Faust stood up on her crutches, drawing everyone's attention even before she spoke, her anger as raw as her voice.

"What do you call the hundreds of shotgun pellets in my body? What do you call Kim's faceless corpse? What more evidence do you need?"

A hush fell over the audience. Duncan shifted his weight, clearly uncomfortable. "I apologize for any misunderstanding. I wasn't referring yet to what happened to you, Ms. Spivey, or Councilman Netter."

"You mean what *wouldn't* have happened to us if only we'd known there was a homicidal sniper on the loose."

The crowd immediately started shouting their outrage, their voices becoming one angry rumble of noise. Duncan held up his hands in surrender and the commotion, to Eve's surprise, actually settled down.

"Please don't all shout at once. I know you're angry and that you have serious questions. I'm here to answer them. But first you need to have the same facts we do. I was just about to discuss the confirmed cases, in general terms, and share with you—"

"A litany of total bullshit," Faust interrupted. "We've had all of that we can take already."

A middle-aged man in a jacket and tie stood up beside Faust. He was a stranger to Eve, but she could see the sadness on his face and the crushing weight of the grief he carried on his body.

"Detective Pavone, I'm Harold Spivey, Kim's father. I believe the park is a killing field and I know my daughter wouldn't have camped there if she'd known about the shootings. Nobody would."

Trisha Kalb bolted up from her seat too fast, her desire to do quick damage control undermined before she even spoke.

"You have suffered an indescribable loss, Mr. Spivey, and you truly have our deepest sympathies. But there wasn't any evidence then, and there isn't now, to suggest any ties exist between these assorted, disparate incidents."

Harold ignored her and pinned Duncan with his mournful gaze. "Do you have children, Detective?"

"Two daughters, sir," Duncan said softly.

"As one father to another, would you let your daughters go in that park or drive on the roads around it?"

The silence seemed to stretch for hours, but Eve knew it was only a few tortured seconds for Duncan. Every person in the room was watching him.

"No, sir," Duncan said. "I wouldn't."

Lansing stood. "What Detective Duncan means to say is—"

Duncan talked right over him, raising his voice.

"I believe there is a sniper in the Santa Monica Mountains, picking off people in the park and the surrounding area. Maybe it started as a prank, or a warning, but now he's killing people and we don't know why." He spoke forcefully now, his words crackling with urgency. "Anybody in the area is a potential target. So if you live or work here, be alert, be cautious, and stay indoors as much as possible. If you don't absolutely need to be here, or to drive on Mulholland Highway or Las Virgenes, stay away from Calabasas until he's caught or you could end up dead."

The whole room erupted with questions. Duncan gathered up his papers and walked off the stage. Eve got up and went with him. He went out the back door, avoiding the media he knew were parked out front, and got into the driver's seat of their Explorer. Eve got in, too.

"Feel better?" she asked.

He nodded. "At least now I might be able to live with myself."

CHAPTER
TWENTY-THREE

When Duncan and Eve came into the station, it seemed like every deputy and civilian who worked there was staring at them. Even people being processed for arrest stole a look. Word of Duncan's explosive speech had obviously spread fast. Biddle and Garvey were standing at their cubicles, shocked expressions on their faces, when Duncan and Eve walked in the squad room.

"What were you thinking, Donuts?" Garvey said. "You were only a week away from retirement. All you had to do was sit at your desk and count the days."

"Or count the killings I was responsible for by staying quiet," Duncan said, pulling out his trash can and emptying the contents into Eve's trash can instead. It struck her as a very strange thing to do.

"Making noise isn't part of your job," Biddle said. "It's quietly catching the bad guys. That's what you do."

"Did." Duncan set his empty garbage can on his chair, opened a desk drawer, and dumped everything into the can.

Garvey pointed at Eve. "She's responsible for this."

"I didn't say a word today," Eve said, watching Duncan begin removing pictures from his cubicle walls and tossing them in the garbage can.

"You've been a bad influence on him from the start," Garvey said. "Before you came along, Duncan was slow, steady, and dependable."

"Yeah," Biddle said, "a team player who kept his head down and doggedly worked his cases. But then he got partnered with an inexperienced attention whore. The Duncan Pavone we knew, good old Donuts, would never have done what he did today. It wasn't who he was."

"You're right," Duncan said, checking the bare walls of his cubicle.

"You're blaming me?" Eve said.

"Yes, I am. If I hadn't seen you repeatedly and impulsively defy authority and do whatever you thought was right, everybody else and good sense be damned, I don't think I'd have had the courage to speak up. Actually, courage had nothing to do with it. It was shame."

Biddle said, "You have nothing to be ashamed of."

"Time will tell," Duncan said.

"*We're* telling you," Garvey said. "You're the best detective in the department. Nobody comes close." He looked at Eve, his message clear.

Duncan picked up two old, yellowing files from his desk, stuffed them deep into the garbage can, then put his gun and badge on the desk.

Eve felt like crying, but willed herself not to. "You don't have to do this, Duncan."

"I'm just beating the sheriff to it. I'd finish the job if he'd let me, but we know he won't."

As if on cue, Sheriff Lansing came into the room. He wasn't in a rage. Instead, he looked sad.

"Jesus, Duncan. Do you realize the damage you've done?"

"I do, sir. My gun and my badge are on my desk." Duncan picked up the trash can. "I'll just empty the trash and be on my way."

"Hell of a way to end your career," Lansing said.

"Sure is." Duncan headed for the door. Eve went with him.

Lansing reached for her arm. "Wait, Ronin."

"I'll be right back," Eve said firmly, inviting no argument, and hurried out to the parking lot with Duncan, catching him at his Buick.

"What are you going to do now?" she asked.

"What I always planned to do, just a week earlier." Duncan used his key fob to remotely open his trunk.

"I'm not sure if the show is still going forward."

"No problem. I've got a great recliner and four hundred episodes of *Gunsmoke* I'm eager to catch up on."

"The press will be all over you now."

"They can sit on my front lawn as long as they want. I've got nothing more to say . . . and my sprinklers are on a timer that I'm not turning off." He put the garbage can in the trunk and closed it. She assumed the files hidden in the can were two cases he never solved and couldn't let go of, but now wasn't the time to ask. Instead, she gave him a hug, holding him tight.

"What am I going to do without you?" she said.

He patted her on the back. "You can start by catching the son of a bitch that's shooting people."

Over Duncan's shoulder, Eve could see a squadron of TV news choppers closing in like air force bombers, ready to drop their load of explosives.

"Here come the cameras," Duncan said. "I don't think we want this hug on the six o'clock news."

She let go of him and wiped away some tears.

"I'm not dying, Eve," Duncan said. "You'll see me again."

"It won't be the same."

"I certainly hope so," he said. "I don't need any more broken bones."

He smiled at her, got in his car, and drove off.

Eve took a deep breath and noticed Rondo watching her from the sheriff's idling Expedition, his window rolled down. It was impossible for her to tell what he thought of her display of emotion. Not that she cared. She went inside the station.

Lansing was waiting for her in the hallway and motioned her into the captain's empty office. She went inside and he closed the door.

"Duncan created the perfect shitstorm. The public is now in full-fledged panic, the politicians are furious, everybody thinks we're liars, and the press is having a feeding frenzy. Did you put him up to this?"

"You're the third person to accuse me of that," Eve said. "No, I didn't. Why would you think so?"

"Because what he did is just the kind of thing that you'd do," he said. "But since it would be career suicide, maybe you talked him into taking the bullet for you since he's only days away from retirement anyway. Or maybe the old fool volunteered to do it for you."

"If you believe that, reassign or suspend me. But think first about how it will look to the public and the media if you do."

It would look, Eve knew, like the sheriff was silencing the partner of the one man who spoke truth to power, that he was using it as an excuse to take retribution against the woman hero who'd exposed deep-rooted corruption within the department.

"I already have," Lansing said. "That is why you are going to lead the Malibu Sniper Task Force."

It wasn't the reaction she was expecting and was a surprise in more ways than one.

"Is that the official name?"

"Thanks to Duncan's outburst, now we've got to treat the cases as if they are connected, at least publicly. Privately, let the evidence alone dictate the investigation. You have Crockett and Tubbs and any deputies you want, but if you need more manpower, just say so. You'll also have the full cooperation of the state park police."

"I already do and it's truly astounding."

Lansing grimaced and she could see, in every muscle on his face, that he was trying to control his anger.

"I know how close you are to Duncan, so I'll assume this is a painful moment for you, and that's why you're mouthing off to me. But you really don't want to make a habit of it. You need me on your side. That's how you got here. Push me, and you'll be the law on Catalina Island."

Lansing walked past her, threw open the door, and marched out.

Eve took a moment to collect herself so she'd present a calm, controlled demeanor, and then went to the squad room, where Biddle and Garvey were anxiously waiting to see how the tumultuous events of the day would impact them.

She faced the two men. "The sheriff has informed me that I'm leading the Malibu Sniper Task Force and that you two are assigned to me."

Biddle looked at Garvey. "The indignities never end."

"That's true." Garvey looked at Eve. "But we're going to suck it up for Donuts, do our very best, and catch this bastard."

"That's all I want. Yesterday, you talked about coming at this by ignoring all of our suspects and starting fresh. Keep at it."

Biddle said, "What are you going to do?"

That was a good question. But for now, she had a meeting with Mark Weston at Art's Deli in Studio City. "Whatever occurs to me."

"That's not the most reliable investigative technique."

"It's all I've got," Eve said.

"The fact is," Garvey said, "you've been riding on Duncan's work since you got here. Without him to carry you, you're done."

Eve forced a smile. "See, there's the bright side in this situation. Soon I'll be exposed as a total fraud and you won't have to deal with me anymore."

"That's true," Garvey said, glancing at Biddle.

"Thanks for the encouragement," Biddle added.

"My pleasure," Eve said and hurried out for her meeting. She didn't know how long Mark Weston would wait for her to show.

Weston looked even worse up close than he had from a distance. Now, sitting in a vinyl-upholstered booth across from him at Art's Deli, she could see just how pallid his complexion was. He had an untouched corn beef sandwich and a cup of coffee growing cold in front of him.

Eve and Weston were the youngest customers in the restaurant by decades, and among the few without hearing aids, and that included most of the staff.

"Thank you for coming," he said, idly stirring his coffee with a spoon, watching the liquid swirl.

"You look terrible."

"I haven't slept in days," he said. "I can't get that dead woman out of my mind."

"It's not easy. It takes time but eventually it will recede. I wish I could say it completely goes away but it doesn't." She was still haunted, at the most unexpected times, by flashes of memory from her first homicide case, of that house in Topanga, the walls covered with blood. When those memories came, she didn't try to force away the images. She faced them head-on, as if daring them to unsettle her, and they crawled back into the recesses of her mind on their own, bruised but not defeated.

"You don't understand," Weston said. "It's not about what I saw but what I did. The guilt is eating me from the inside, gnawing at my bones." He looked up at her with imploring eyes. "It won't let me rest."

What is he about to confess? she wondered. *Is he the shooter?*

She met his eyes and spoke softly. "What did you do, Mark?"

"Nothing. That's what I did. Nothing. But I knew. We all did. For months."

"Knew what?"

"That someone was hunting people in the park," he said, looking back down into the abyss of his coffee cup. "We were all terrified. None of us went out there alone, certainly not at night or early morning. It was too dangerous."

"Was this after someone shot at a wildlife biologist while he was out tagging mountain lions?"

He raised his head. "I don't know anything about that."

"Then why were you all scared? Up until then, the sniper was only taking potshots at cars, RVs, and houses . . ." She stopped, seeing the guilt all over his face. "Oh my God. There were other people who got shot, weren't there? Before Faust and Spivey."

Weston nodded, unable to look her in the eye, seeking the safety of his coffee cup. "Nobody was killed, but people were hurt."

"When?"

"It was before the wildfire closed the park."

"How many?"

"Three that I know of. A hiker from Germany got a back full of bird shot while carving his name into a tree. A couple from Texas were shot at while cooking up a rabbit they caught. It took off the guy's ear. A woman from Oregon picking flowers in a ravine got shot in the ass. We used our own medics to treat the victims and nobody filed any reports."

So no evidence was collected, Eve thought. None of what Weston was saying could be proved, unless the news spread outside of LA and those victims came forward on their own.

"Who ordered the cover-up?" Eve asked, but she already knew the answer.

"Trisha, of course. But she was probably following directions from higher up," Weston said. "Maybe as far up as Sacramento."

"How do you know?"

Weston lifted his head and faced her. "The 911 operators are instructed to refer any shots-fired calls in or around the park directly to us, not the LASD or CHP, and that order didn't come from Trisha. It couldn't have. She doesn't have that kind of power."

There might be some records of the incidents at the 911 call center, Eve thought, if she could nail down the dates and times that they happened. But proving the incidents were anything beyond backfiring cars or false alarms, without the testimony of the victims or the rangers who responded to the calls, would be nearly impossible. She was screwed.

"You hid the violence, pretending it didn't exist, all so people would keep coming to the park," Eve said. "Which made them potential targets."

"It's bigger than that."

"I know, I know, it's also about keeping business flowing in Calabasas, Agoura, and Malibu."

"It's much more. It's about maintaining the seven-figure property values of the homes in the mountains, especially after the fire burned up four hundred structures and devastated the local economy," Weston said. "Everybody on that stage today, except for you and Duncan, are complicit. They all knew, or actively didn't want to know, that a killer is out there. They should all have to see what was left of that poor woman's face . . ."

He shuddered at the memory, not that it had ever left the forefront of his mind.

"It wouldn't make a difference," Eve said. She wondered if there really were orders from on high, or if the mindset was so baked into the culture of the park police and sheriff's department that it was standard operating practice . . . and had been for decades. They were operating on institutional memory, the bureaucratic version of instinct.

"Did you hear?" Weston said. "An hour after the community meeting, Trisha closed the park indefinitely and then resigned, effective immediately."

Eve didn't know that. One more thing the Park Service didn't share with her, the head of the Malibu Sniper Task Force. But their cooperative relationship was truly astounding.

"I suppose that's progress," she said.

"But I know it won't stop the guilt from chewing on my guts," he said.

"Talk to the other rangers and the medics. Get them to come forward and back up your story about the other victims."

"They won't. They'll want to save themselves."

"Prove to them they'll lose anyway," Eve said.

"How do I do that?"

Eve slid out of the booth and stood up.

"Meet them face-to-face," she said. "Let them get a look at you. That should do it."

CHAPTER TWENTY-FOUR

Eve brought home some takeout from Shanghai Bistro in Woodland Hills for dinner, opened a Diet Coke, and ate her Chinese food as she went through her email, ignoring dozens of inquiries from reporters, two notices from the IRS warning her of imminent arrest unless she paid her overdue taxes by gift card, and one email from an attorney informing her that she'd inherited a vast fortune from a Nigerian prince.

There was also another note from Daniel. If he was upset with her for not responding to his previous email, he didn't show it. Instead, he told her about the dig winding down and repeated his invitation to join him. If he didn't hear back in a week, he'd leave Tarawa with the rest of the anthropology team and hope to see her on his return, pending a shower, shave, and a haircut, of course.

It had been only a few months since they'd been together, but it felt like she'd changed so much since then. There were fresh scars on her body, and on her psyche, that she didn't have then. She'd killed a man. She didn't feel guilt or regret over the death, only anger that he'd forced her into doing it in self-defense. But she was a different woman now as a result.

Would Daniel sense that? Would it change their relationship? Did they even have a relationship? If so, what was it? They'd never talked about it.

Eve sent Daniel a short note saying that his invitation was very tempting, but she was working a difficult homicide case and she couldn't predict when it would be solved.

However, she was eager to see him again, whether it was in Tarawa or when he got back home.

She signed the email **Love, Eve**, then went back and deleted **Love**. Then she added it again.

Then she deleted it, replacing it with **Best Wishes**, but that sounded like a Christmas card.

She deleted **Best Wishes** and wrote **Sincerely** instead, but decided that was too stiff. She deleted it and wrote **I miss you**, because it was true, and hit "Send" so she wouldn't continue this argument with herself all night.

Her gaze drifted to her bike across the room. Sunday was ordinarily her day off, a chance to take a long ride and unwind.

God, she yearned for that right now.

She couldn't take a day off, not after what happened today, but maybe just a morning, to clear her head.

Eve asked the head of the Malibu Sniper Task Force if she could come in at 9:00 a.m. instead of 7:00, and her surly, driven, heartless boss said yes.

The next morning at 7:00 a.m. on the dot, Eve put on her ultraslim Kevlar tank top and her Lycra biking outfit, which included a special concealed-carry holster for her lower back that went under the waistband of her pants. The holster was also an ultraslim design, a neoprene base with a molded polymer shell designed specifically for her Glock.

It was unnoticeable on her, hidden by the bulge of the outer pocket on the lower back of her top, which was where she kept her iPhone, house keys, and ID during her rides. Ever since her encounter with actor Blake Largo, and later an attempt on her life, she never rode her bike without her weapon and vest. It was uncomfortable, but it was better than being dead.

The ride on Mulholland Highway would be short, west to Kanan Dume and back again, about fifteen miles round trip, just long enough to clear her head and get a fresh perspective before going into work. Her mind was muddled and a ride would give her a reboot.

She rode south on Las Virgenes, over the freeway, and through the commercial section of the roadway, past gas stations and fast-food places, past the LVMWD headquarters, to the intersection with Mulholland Highway, right below Paul Banning's estate. Here she headed west on the high road through Malibu Creek State Park, hugging the contours of the steep hills to her right and, on her left, a cliff's edge with no guardrail between drivers, motorcyclists, and bike riders and a fatal plunge to the dry, rocky watershed below.

She had the road entirely to herself. In the wake of Duncan's warning, there were none of the usual weekend drivers who loved speeding on the snaking road and seeing the spectacular mountain views in their convertibles or sports cars, or on their motorcycles. The only car she saw was a new Dodge Challenger parked at a hillside turnout near the Malibu Creek overlook, otherwise it was deserted. Not even the squirrels were coming out of hiding.

With the blackened hills and desolate road, she could pretend she was the last woman on a postapocalyptic Earth, an actress riding through another forgotten Movieland set that had become part of real life in Calabasas.

The emptiness made the ride even more of an escape. She was able to take the tight curves without having to worry about slamming head-on into a car as she came around the other side. But her head was still full of the case, the victims, the suspects, and the interviews. Purging it wasn't a matter of concentration but of letting go, giving in to her motion. It hadn't happened yet. But she had faith that it would.

Eve rode through Malibu Creek State Park, past Malibou Lake, and all the way to the charcoal ruins of the old Troutdale Fish Farm at Kanan Dume Road, where she stopped for a moment to rest before turning back.

She'd caught her one and only fish at Troutdale when she was eight, using a bamboo pole and some corn. It was a thrill, even though it was impossible not to catch a fish there. The two twelve-foot-deep ponds were roiling with hungry trout. But little Eve didn't know that. It was a happy memory, a fun day of fish scales, melting Eskimo Pies, and sunburns shared with her mom, her sister, and her infant brother.

But now the bait shop, shady trees, and wooden benches were gone, devoured by flames. The dry cement ponds were filled with charred wood, dirt, and mosquito larvae. The past had burned down. The days of easy catches were over.

She wondered what young Eve would think if she'd been able to look up from her bamboo pole and see adult Eve, straddling a bike and wearing a Glock and a Kevlar vest under her shirt. Would it have made her happy or sad?

Eve rode back home the way she came, only this time, she traveled along the southern edge of Mulholland Highway, straddling the line between asphalt and a sheer drop into the craggy ravines below.

She pushed herself hard, going for speed, and within a few minutes, she was finally lost in the perfect balance and the pure, exhilarating motion, freed from herself and her thoughts, the wilderness wide open in front of her. This sense of being truly centered, and yet racing forward, was a state of mind, body, and soul that she wished she could always achieve. It was better than sex.

She heard a loud gun blast, felt a thousand stings, and lost her balance, but not her forward momentum, tumbling head over heels into the air and over the cliff.

Eve hit the ground hard and rolled downhill, over jutting rocks and through prickly brush, until she slammed into something immovable, cracking her ribs, knocking the air out of her, and shocking her mind into total awareness.

Her eyes flashed open. She was curled against the base of a charred oak tree a quarter of the way down the slope and facing the bottom of the deep ravine, watching her bike crash down the hillside and shatter on a pile of boulders at the bottom.

The tree had saved her. Just like the tree that had stopped Clark Netter's car from landing in someone's backyard. But it hadn't saved him.

Eve turned her head and looked up. Mulholland Highway was only ten or fifteen yards above her and she knew instantly what happened.

I was shot.

This was the second time that someone tried to kill her by forcing her off the road. They got away before.

Not again.

Without stopping to think, or to assess her injuries, she let her fury drive her. She scrambled up the hillside, grabbing at rocks and shrubs for handholds, gritting her teeth against the intense pain in her left leg and the stabs of agony in her sides with each breath.

Eve peered over the cliff edge onto the asphalt. The road was empty. Whoever had shot at her was up in the hills. He'd be fleeing now.

But where?

She rose quickly, favoring her right leg, but her left leg buckled under her weight, and she nearly toppled backward into the ravine before regaining her balance. Aware that she was an open target, Eve staggered across the road, dragging her injured left leg, and hugged the opposite hillside for cover.

Eve wiped the sweat from her brow, then looked at her hand. The moisture on her face wasn't sweat. It was blood. She thought about removing her battered helmet but was afraid it might be the only thing holding her head together.

She took a quick glance at her body to appraise the damage. The left side of her Lycra top was riddled by the shotgun pellets that were absorbed by her Kevlar vest. No open wounds there, but definitely some cracked ribs. Her bare left leg was covered in dirt-caked blood, the flesh shredded by shotgun pellets and sliced by the sharp rocks and thorny shrubs that she'd hit in her fall. It felt like a molten spike had been hammered into her knee, but she could tolerate that. All she required of the limb now was for it not to buckle again.

Eve drew her Glock. She was counting on the sniper escaping downhill because it would be easier and faster for him. She hoped he was going to the Challenger she'd seen earlier parked in the turnout around the next bend. But she was going to the turnout regardless. It was her only way into the hills if she intended to chase him, and she certainly did. Her injuries be damned. She wouldn't stop, not until she had him.

Eve reached the turnout and peered around the edge of the hillside. The Challenger was still parked there, facing a wooded fold between two steep hills and the foot trail leading into it. She staggered into the open, her gun at her side, keeping the car in front of her for cover.

Beyond the trailhead, there was some movement in the brush, a sparse cloud of dust filtering up.

Someone was coming, and coming fast.

She wiped the blood from her eyes, raised her gun, and took aim at the opening.

A man wearing a hoodie, wraparound sunglasses, and dirty jeans emerged, a 12-gauge shotgun down at his right side, against his leg. Eve could have shot him right then, and been justified doing it, but she wanted him to see her first.

"I'm hard to kill," she said, startling him.

He raised the shotgun. She fired at the same instant he did.

His errant blast took out the Challenger's grille. Her careful shot hit him in the right shoulder.

He jerked, dropping the shotgun, and stumbled back into the narrow canyon, out of sight amid the trees. She limped after him, holding her gun out in front of her in case he had a knife or another firearm.

"I'm also a great shot," she said, moving implacably forward. "You're right-handed. If you have a gun, and try to shoot me with your left hand, I'll put you down before you get the chance. Guaranteed."

She kicked the shotgun aside, putting her weight on her bad leg, and nearly fell. That was dumb. If he'd tackled her then, she would have been finished.

But he didn't.

She continued into the canyon, her eyes following a trail of blood in the dirt that led to a tree up ahead.

"Be smart. Crawl out." She knew he wouldn't crawl, that her friendly suggestion would just piss him off.

That's what she wanted.

He whirled out from behind the tree, a gun in his wobbly left hand, and she shot him in the left knee, dropping him before he could fire. He writhed on the ground, shrieking in agony. His gun was in the dirt beside him. She wiped the blood from her eyes and limped up to him, but didn't kick the gun out of his reach.

Eve recognized him now, despite his sunglasses and hoodie.

It was Deputy Wayne Snell.

It was a shock to her that he was the Malibu Sniper, but at the same time, it was no surprise that he'd want to shoot her.

"You should have crawled," she said.

"And watch you get off on that? I'd rather die."

"That's still an option. I could shoot you in the head right now and say it was self-defense, that you were going for that gun, which is still within reach if you'd like to try. Nobody would doubt me. The ballistics tell the story," Eve said. "Or I could just sit back and watch you bleed to death from the injuries you already have if you don't give me what I want."

He could barely choke out the words between his sobs of pain. "What makes you think you won't bleed out first? You look half-dead already."

"The bird shot won't kill me," Eve said. "But don't worry, to play it safe, I'll put a bullet in your stomach if I start to feel light-headed. Come to think of it, I'm starting to feel a little woozy."

Snell grimaced. He was hurting bad. "What do you want?"

"A confession," she said.

"Nothing I say now is admissible," he said. "We're alone. Your word against mine."

"You just shot me, you moron," she said. "Going to prison is the best outcome you can hope for. This is about convincing me not to kill you right now."

"Okay, I shot everybody. Now call the paramedics."

"That's not the confession I want." She aimed her gun at his head. "I want the names of the deputies who tried to kill me in Ventura."

"Fuck you," he hissed.

Eve fired a shot into the dirt beside his head. He screamed.

"Wrong answer," she said. "Last chance."

"If I tell you now, I've got no leverage with the DA to bargain my charges down. So either call for help or shoot me. I really don't care."

"You're not as dumb as I thought you were." She carefully used her good foot to slide his gun away from him, then she reached into the pocket in the back of her shirt, a movement that nearly made her cry out in pain, and took out her phone. He saw that and grinned through his agony.

"I could still shoot you again," she said. His grin disappeared.

The screen on her iPhone was shattered, but it was still working. There was one signal bar. She dialed Tom Ross and kept her eye on Snell.

"Detective Ronin," Tom said. "What can I do for you?"

"You really have to start calling me Eve," she said. "Especially if you're going to date my sister."

"Is that was this is about? Am I in trouble?"

"Actually, I am." Now that the adrenaline rush from her anger and pursuit was waning, her pain was jacking up fast. "Are you on duty today, Tom?"

"Yes."

"There's a trailhead at the first turnout east of the Malibu Creek State Park overview on Mulholland. Do you know the spot?"

"I do."

"There's a new Dodge Challenger parked there. I am ten or twenty yards up the trail," she said. "I've been shot."

She heard him catch his breath.

"Why are you calling me and not 911?"

"Because Deputy Wayne Snell was the shooter. I returned fire, hitting the dimwit in the right shoulder and left leg," she said. "I want to be sure the first deputy on the scene doesn't finish what Snell started."

Snell used his good hand, which he'd been using to stanch the blood flow from his leg, to give her the finger. Blood dripped down his arm.

"I will be there in ten minutes," Tom said. "If any deputy besides me or Eddie shows up before we do, put a gun to Snell's head and hold him hostage."

"Let's hope it doesn't come to that," Eve said. She clicked off and put some distance between herself and Snell.

Eve hoped she'd remain conscious until they arrived. Because if she passed out, she was sure that Snell would drag himself over and strangle her.

CHAPTER TWENTY-FIVE

Tom Ross was the first to arrive at the scene and didn't want to leave Eve's side, but she insisted that he glue himself to Snell. She wanted a deputy she could trust on Snell at all times. So it was Deputy Eddie Clayton who rode in the ambulance to West Hills Hospital with her and promised that he wouldn't leave her until another deputy that both he and Tom trusted could take over.

Lisa met Eve's gurney as the orderlies wheeled her into the ER. "You're such a hypochondriac. You treat every little scratch like an emergency."

"I ran out of bandages and didn't feel like driving to Walgreens," Eve said. "You don't seem surprised to see me."

"Tom called ahead." Lisa led them quickly to an exam room. "But you're conscious, lucid, and have a phone. You could have done the same thing."

The orderlies gently transferred Eve to the bed and left the two women alone.

"I was hoping you wouldn't be here this morning," Eve said.

"Why would you hope that?" Lisa said, hanging Eve's IV bag on a stand and hooking her up to various machines.

"To avoid seeing that worried look on your face."

"You should be glad you have someone who loves you at your side right now."

"Am I that badly injured?"

"I've seen worse," Lisa said.

"That's reassuring," Eve said.

"See? That's why it's good to have me here."

The ER doctor came in and smiled. He was young and short, with wavy blond hair. His last name was Travis. He'd treated her after her experience in the wildfire that had raged through the Santa Monica Mountains and, a few weeks ago, the injuries she'd sustained in an explosion. "You again. You must love my bedside manner."

"Any excuse to get back in here for more of that endless compassion."

"What happened?"

"I was bike riding. Took a shotgun blast to my left side. Fell off a cliff. Smacked into a tree. Typical Sunday."

While she was talking, he checked her head, carefully parting her hair and examining her cuts. The paramedics had removed her helmet at the scene. "Were you unconscious at any point?"

"I don't think so."

"We've got to sew up that cut on your brow."

Dr. Travis lifted the blanket that was covering her. She was topless underneath, except for her sports bra. The paramedics had already cut off her bike suit with scissors and removed her vest to check her torso for injuries. Both items of clothing were collected by the deputies as evidence.

"I'm going to press some spots. Let me know if you feel any tenderness or pain," Dr. Travis said, but Eve was already in so much pain, she wasn't sure she'd be able to detect anything new. He started gently pressing spots on her stomach. "That Kevlar vest was a good investment. Do you always wear it?"

"I like to make a bold fashion statement."

"Aren't you quippy today."

"It's the drugs," Eve said.

"You aren't on any yet," Dr. Travis said. "That's just a saline drip."

Lisa said, "It's what she does when she's scared."

He touched her ribs and Eve grimaced.

So yes, she thought, *I can feel new pain.*

The doctor noticed and stopped his probing. "I don't think there are any internal injuries. We'll start with some X-rays, see what kind of damage those pellets did, and if you have any broken bones besides a few ribs. We'll also do a CT scan to rule out a concussion or subdural hematoma. I'll bring in an orthopedic surgeon, too."

That didn't sound good to Eve. "Why are you talking about surgery when you haven't seen the X-rays yet?"

"Because I don't need an X-ray to see that your left knee is a mess. I'm sure some pellets have penetrated the meniscus. They'll have to be removed right away," Dr. Travis said. "That's assuming you'd like to walk without a permanent limp or ride a bike again."

"That would be nice," Eve said.

"I'll call in a plastic surgeon, too."

Oh God, she thought. "What for?"

Lisa said, "That was my request. Plastic surgeons don't just do face-lifts and boob jobs. They can also minimize any scarring from stitching the cut on your head and removing pellets from your leg. Unless you'd prefer a Frankenstein scar on your brow to scare the bad guys away."

"Okay, but don't let Mom talk to the plastic surgeon when she gets here, or I'll come out of knee surgery with new boobs and collagen lips."

"What makes you think I called Mom?"

"You've been my sister all your life and I'm a detective." Eve shifted her gaze to Dr. Travis. "Can I please have those drugs now?"

After the X-rays and CT scan, in the hour or so before her knee surgery, Eve was interviewed by two LASD detectives from the Officer-Involved Shooting Team, and when they walked out, Captain Dubois walked in, approaching her warily, as if she were an unexploded bomb.

Eve was hydrated and on painkillers, so she wasn't feeling too bad physically or emotionally. She'd already been told that she had two broken ribs, no signs of a concussion, and that the orthopedic surgeon was reviewing her leg X-rays.

"Hell of a morning," Captain Dubois said.

"For me, too."

He forced a smile. It made him look nauseous. "You did good work today, Detective Ronin."

"It wasn't work, Captain. It was survival."

"Survival would have been calling for help and not going after him alone."

"The help might have killed me," she said.

"I am saddened you have such a low opinion of this department and your fellow deputies."

"That's what happens when deputies keep trying to murder you," Eve said, "and the department doesn't have your back."

"Really? Deputy Eddie Clayton is sitting outside your door and says he won't leave, even if I order him to."

"Eddie is one of the few people in the department that I trust."

Dubois looked her in the eye. "What about me?"

"It's too soon to tell."

Dubois nodded. "Fair enough. The forensic team is still at the scene, but for what it's worth, the preliminary ballistics seem to back up your story."

It wasn't a story. It was a factual account. But she didn't argue the fine point. It seemed petty, even if it wasn't.

"How is Snell?"

"He's here, in surgery, but before he went under, he invoked his right to remain silent and asked for an attorney. Biddle and Clayton are digging into Snell's movements over the last few months, seeing if his path has crossed with Zena Faust and Councilman Netter before, or if all of his shootings were random. Besides yours, of course."

"Do you think he's the serial sniper?"

"Don't you?" Dubois asked.

She'd had time now to think about Snell as the sniper and nothing seemed to fit. "He told me he did it, but I am not sure I believe him."

"He blasted you with a shotgun loaded with bird shot as you rode your bike through the park," Dubois said. "What more convincing do you need?"

"He hates me," Eve said. "These sniper killings may have just given him the perfect opportunity to act on it."

"Or you were getting too close."

"He wasn't even remotely a suspect," she said.

"But he didn't know that and maybe he was becoming more terrified with each passing hour. He knows how relentless you can be. We all do."

She knew it would be nice and easy to blame Snell for the killings and close the case. But she wasn't convinced. She didn't see a motive and didn't believe that he was simply doing it for a thrill. "I wouldn't disband the Malibu Sniper Task Force yet if I were you."

"That's the sheriff's decision, not mine. Regardless, a corrupt deputy tried to murder a detective. This is a dark day for the department. Your heroism aside, of course. Get well soon." He started for the door, but before he got there, he turned back to her. "I'm profoundly sorry this happened but I'm damn proud of how you handled yourself. You have my full support, Detective, whether you believe it or not."

"Thank you, sir."

Dubois walked out. A few minutes later, the orthopedic surgeon came in with Lisa. His name was Auerbach.

"The X-rays show a few pellets within the medial meniscus," Dr. Auerbach said.

"What does that mean in English?"

"It's like a rubber shock absorber in the knee. Some pellets have gone through it and penetrated the joint."

"How serious is this?"

"We can remove the pellets arthroscopically, which means I only have to make two tiny, shirt-button-sized incisions, barely visible once you've healed, to insert a fiber-optic camera to see what I'm doing and tools to remove the pellets. I'll give you a video of the entire surgery on a thumb drive that you can show the family at Thanksgiving."

Lisa said, "Don't give her any ideas."

"Will I have any permanent damage?" Eve asked.

"I don't think so," Dr. Auerbach said. "It will take some time for you to heal, and some physical therapy, but you won't be restricted in any way from being an active-duty police officer, if that's what you're worried about, or even competing in the Tour de France someday."

Lisa added, "While you're under, the plastic surgeon, Dr. Showalter, will stitch up your forehead and remove as many pellets as she can without doing more damage."

Dr. Auerbach said, "Dr. Showalter is good, but she won't be able to get them all, though some pellets will rise up and out of your skin naturally, like splinters, over time. Even so, you're going to be setting off the metal detectors at airports for the rest of your life."

She was more concerned about the attention she'd draw going through the metal detectors in the courthouse. "How bad is my leg going to look when it's healed?"

"There might be some tiny scratches or pockmarks, nothing too obvious," Dr. Auerbach said. "You can continue wearing a bikini at the beach."

"I don't own a bikini."

"You can borrow one from Mom," Lisa said.

"I don't have her boobs."

"Dr. Showalter can take care of that, too," Lisa said.

Dr. Auerbach raised his hand in protest. "TMI. The anesthesiologist will be by in a few minutes. See you on the other side."

He left the room. As soon as he was gone, Eve said, "I hope he's not talking about the afterlife."

"The recovery room," Lisa said. "He's the best. You're in very good hands."

"Do you have experience with them?" There was something about the way Lisa spoke about them that made Eve wonder.

Lisa smiled. "Not in the operating room."

That's what Eve thought. "What do you know about Deputy Snell's condition?"

"He'll live," Lisa said. "But his tennis game and golf swing are ruined."

"That won't be an issue where he's going."

"You should have shot him in the balls," Lisa said.

"That would have looked more vindictive than defensive."

"Are you a cop or a politician?"

"I'm beginning to wonder if there's much difference."

Eve was wheeled into surgery a few minutes later. It seemed like only an instant after that when she opened her eyes on a gurney in a curtained-off section of the recovery room for her privacy.

She was relaxed and her pain was at a low ebb, the physical equivalent of an irritating hum. Her knee was wrapped up in elastic bandages and a strange nozzle stuck out from under the wrapping. The gunshot wounds all over her left side were covered with large bandages. There was substantial bruising, the skin already turning black. Her future as a belly dancer was over, at least for the week.

Lisa drew open the curtain and asked, "How are you feeling?"

"Fine," Eve said. "Which is really surprising, given the damage I see."

"That's because you have more drugs in you now than a pharmacy."

"I asked Auerbach if I could just bite on a leather strap instead but he refused my request."

"Funny, he let me."

"That's more than I need to know," Eve said, holding up her hands.

"You have no sense of humor."

As if on cue, Dr. Auerbach showed up.

"The surgery went very smoothly. We got all the pellets out of your knee without too much punishment to the meniscus. You can see for yourself." He held up a thumb drive and handed it to Eve. "It's the POV from the fiber-optic camera inside your knee with my dramatic narration and a John Williams score. If you like it, maybe you can hire me to direct an episode of your show."

"You know about that?"

Dr. Auerbach smiled. "The whole hospital does. Your sister is very proud of you."

Eve pointed to the nozzle sticking out from under the bandages on her knee. "What's that for?"

"It plugs into a device that looks like a typical cooler, the kind you take on picnics, and runs ice water through a special pad on your knee to reduce pain, swelling, and your need for painkillers," he said. "You'll be taking that device home with you and using it every day."

He gave her some more instructions on postoperative care and, barring any complications, told her they'd release her in the morning with the ice machine, meds, and a prescription for several weeks of physical therapy. She'd be on crutches for at least a week.

"The ice therapy starts when you get to your room," Lisa said. "Where the sheriff and a prosecutor are waiting to see you, though I can have them thrown out if you want."

"No, I need to talk with them," Eve said. "It's Mom I'd like to avoid."

Lisa wheeled her out of recovery and Eddie Clayton got up from his chair outside the door to offer an armed escort to her room. He was still wearing his shades, perhaps against the glare of the hospital lights.

"I really appreciate you being here," Eve said to him.

"No problem," he said. "We've got to watch out for our own."

"Who has Snell's back?"

"Nobody. He's in the jail ward, cuffed to his bed, under constant surveillance in case he tries to off himself."

"He won't. If he wanted to do that, he had the chance in the hills. Instead, he took another shot at me."

The sheriff and Deputy District Attorney Rebecca Burnside were waiting in the hall outside her room. The sheriff looked pained, like he was trying to pass a kidney stone, but Burnside was her usual cool, put-together self, dressed casually in a sleeveless top and jeans. Burnside always exuded total self-confidence, which Eve knew was reassuring if you were on her side and terrifying if you were against her in court.

Lisa said, "Give us a minute to get Eve comfortable, then you can come in."

"Of course," Lansing said.

Lisa wheeled Eve into the room, leaving Eddie behind, and closed the door. "Are you sure you don't want to get some rest before you talk to them? You've just been through hell and surgery."

"I won't be able to rest until I do."

Lisa helped her onto the bed and noticed Eve wincing with pain. "Yeah, you will. You don't realize what you've been through, but your body knows."

Eve propped herself up, using a remote control to raise the head of the bed to an upright position, while Lisa hung her IV bag on a stand, along with her catheter bag on a hook below the bed, and then adjusted the sheets to hide the tubing. Finally, Lisa snapped a tube onto the nozzle sticking out of her knee wrapping. The tube went to an icebox on a table by the bed. Almost immediately Eve felt a nice cooling sensation on her knee. The low ebb of pain that she'd felt before disappeared. She needed a machine like this at home to use on her shoulders whenever she had a conversation with her mother.

"I won't let them stay long," Lisa said. "Ten, fifteen minutes, tops."

"You worry too much."

Lisa kissed her sister on the cheek, walked out, and beckoned Lansing and Burnside in, closing the door after them.

Lansing slowly approached Eve's bedside. "I've been thinking of what to say to you, but, somehow, none of it seems appropriate. I'm sorry for what has happened to you and I promise you that I will dedicate myself to ridding this department of the corruption that led to this."

But Eve knew exactly what she wanted to say, and did it forcefully.

"You will do more than that, unless you want me to publicly disclose what really went wrong in that home invasion sting operation that nearly got me and Duncan killed—that a sheriff's deputy set us up to die and that it was his partner who shot me today," Eve said. "Oh, and that they were both members of a secret tattooed gang that continues to thrive at Lost Hills even though several of their members were revealed to be rapists. And it's just one of many such covert societies of tattooed deputies that exist in every sheriff's station in the county. That would look great for the department."

Lansing grimaced. It seemed to Eve to be his go-to expression around her. But she saw the glimmer of a smile on Burnside's face.

"What do you want?" Lansing said.

"You will defend me against the Pruitts' lawsuit and officially state, for the record, that my conduct was appropriate, professional, and within policy."

"That's the general counsel's decision to make, not mine."

"Then you'd better convince him, or I will file a lawsuit against the sheriff's department for repeatedly trying to kill me."

"It wasn't the department, you know that," he said. "It was some rogue deputies."

"That's not how it will look to the public. You'll be thrown out of office in disgrace, the Feds will march in, and I'll get rich."

Lansing's grimace was becoming a snarl. "I don't like being extorted and my chances of being reelected are already pitiful after this weekend, so your leverage is shit."

"Then I guess it comes down to whether you want your legacy to be a department in ruins."

Burnside spoke up. "Sheriff, the general counsel will agree to her terms in a nanosecond. She is likely to win far more money in court, or in a settlement, than it will cost the county to pay off the Pruitts on her behalf."

Lansing acknowledged Burnside's comment with a nod but kept his eyes on Eve. "Is that all you want?"

"Not quite," she said. "I'm holding you to your promise to publicly acknowledge the corruption I found and to clean house."

"We have a deal," he said. "Now tell me what happened out there today."

She did, but didn't mention that she'd threatened to kill Snell.

Lansing paced back and forth, considering what she said, then started thinking out loud.

"Snell wanted to kill Eve because he hated her for putting his fellow corrupt members of the Great Whites in prison. The public already knows about them and those incidents. So that means we could contain a lot of the potential damage to the department from what happened today if we simply characterize his actions as personal revenge rather than evidence of systemic corruption."

Lansing's already writing the press release, Eve thought.

He turned to her. "What I don't understand is why Snell shot all of those other people."

"He didn't," Eve said.

Burnside said, "He'll have to convince me of that. Until then, I'm charging him for the murders and the shootings and if he wants even a particle of leniency, he'll give up every single deputy who came after you."

Lansing nodded his agreement. "And I'll take their badges and pensions."

But Eve knew that he wouldn't prosecute them, because it would reveal too much dirty laundry and essentially nullify the deal she'd just struck for her silence and the settlement of her lawsuit. Thinking about all of those ramifications, and the likelihood that the corrupt deputies would escape real punishment, suddenly made her feel very tired.

"That works for me," she said, but that was only slightly true. What she really meant was that she'd have to live with it.

"One more thing," Lansing said. "You're on paid leave for two weeks, minimum."

She hadn't tallied the days, but it seemed to her that she'd spent more time on medical leave since she'd become a homicide detective than she had actually doing her job. She didn't want to spend another day on leave.

"That's not necessary, sir," Eve said. "I have a few cuts and bruises, and a sore knee. I can still continue the sniper investigation."

"Biddle and Garvey will run with it," he said. "You're one of the victims now."

"Not if Snell is innocent," she said.

"You're still tainted. You can't be impartial."

Burnside nodded. "The sheriff is right."

Eve was too tired to argue. She'd do that later. "Please let me know how it goes with Snell."

"I will," Burnside said and glanced at Lansing, who subtly tipped his head toward the door. She left, but he remained behind.

Lansing looked back at Eve. "Do I have to worry about you talking to the media?"

"Not unless you decide there's something you want me to say."

"I appreciate that. We certainly have our differences, Eve. But the only thing that pisses me off more than you do is, ironically, seeing you get hurt, especially when it's by one of our own. You've proven again today that I did the right thing promoting you to homicide. You're a tenacious detective."

"I haven't caught the Malibu Sniper yet."

He shook his head. "That's not what I'm talking about. You embody everything the badge represents and you don't quit. That's a blessing and a curse for us both. Get some rest." He pointed at her. "That's an order."

She saluted him and he walked out. She fell asleep before the door was closed.

CHAPTER
TWENTY-SIX

Eve was awakened by the smell of grilled meat. She opened her eyes. It was dark outside and, except for the table lamp by her bed, dark in her room. Duncan was unpacking a bag from In-N-Out, placing a cheeseburger, fries, and a milkshake on her bed tray.

"I thought you only visit the hospital for the fine cuisine," Eve said, suddenly ravenous.

"That's true. This is for you. I know you have a delicate palate."

"Is that a chocolate shake?" She reached for it, but Duncan gently pushed her hand away from it.

"You can't have that until you've eaten all your greasy, fatty foods first."

"Gee, you're tough. Your kids must have hated you."

She grabbed the cheeseburger and tore into it. It was the most delicious thing she'd ever eaten. While she ate the burger and fries, she talked with Duncan.

"How did you know I was here?"

He pulled over a chair and sat down. "Tom called me. I'm taking the night shift protecting you."

"You don't have to do that. Nobody is coming after me. It's Snell who needs protection. There are a lot of deputies who must be afraid that he'll talk."

"He already has. Burnside told me that he's outed the two deputies who came after you on the freeway in Ventura," Duncan said. "Snell and those two are also the same ones who vandalized your car."

"What did Snell get in return for giving up his buddies?"

"Burnside will drop a few of the charges against him related to shooting you, but those were frosting anyway. She insisted that he has to plead guilty to attempted murder and allocute in front of a judge."

Eve knew that Burnside was essentially forcing Snell to make a confession in return for a measure of leniency. It would spare Snell, and the department, the cost, ordeal, and embarrassment of a trial. The department didn't want a trial any more than Snell did.

"Is she going after him for the sniper shootings?"

"It's not him," Duncan said. "She knew that going in. Crockett and Tubbs confirmed Snell was on duty, far from the scenes, when Spivey, Faust, and Netter were shot. There are also other witnesses who can corroborate that. Besides, he had no motive to shoot them. But he had plenty of reasons to hate you."

"So that's that," Eve said, finishing her fries.

"Except for one thing." Duncan cocked his head, studying her. "What did you get out of it?"

"Do you really think I would use this horrible experience for my own gain?"

"Absolutely. It's how we became partners, before I retired to enjoy the good life."

Eve reached for the chocolate milkshake. "The department will make the lawsuit the Pruitts filed against me go away."

"The department should have done that from the start. I hope you got more out of this than that."

She took a big slurp of the shake. It was the best medicine yet. "He also promised to acknowledge the existence of corrupt, tattooed cliques within the department and to root them out."

"You settled cheap."

"What more could I have asked for?"

Duncan shrugged. "Another promotion. You could be Lieutenant Ronin now."

"I need Lansing on my side. This was a deal he could agree to and not resent me forever," she said. Duncan stood and gathered her garbage from the tray table. "Where are you going?"

"To intercept your hospital dinner before it's delivered," he said. "Watching you eat has made me hungry. And there's someone outside who has been waiting to see you."

"You really don't have to stick around here."

He stuffed everything in the In-N-Out bag, then used a napkin to tenderly wipe some mustard from Eve's chin. "Say that again and I will shoot you myself."

"You don't have a gun."

"Of course I do. Ankle holster. I'd feel naked without it."

He walked out and her mother strolled in.

"The next time I visit you in the hospital," Jen said, "it better be to meet my new grandchild."

"That's a long way off." Eve hoped the drugs in her IV were effective against the pain of Mom-stress.

"So you do want children. That's good news." Jen came up beside the bed and looked at her daughter from head to toe.

"I didn't say that, Mom. What I meant is that there are many things I have to do before having kids even becomes a remote possibility."

Jen examined Eve's stitched forehead, the only wound that would potentially affect her appearance. "Then you should be more careful so you'll live long enough to do all those things and still have kids."

"Getting shot wasn't something I planned on."

"When you do have a daughter, the news you never want to get is that she's been shot. Again."

"I've never been shot before."

"You've been shot at," Jen said. "It's the same thing."

"If it were the same thing, I would have been wounded. I wasn't. That's not what sent me to the ER last time," Eve said. "The explosion did."

"That's one of the other things you don't want to hear about your daughter," Jen said, "that she's been blown up. Or that she drove her car off a cliff."

"I drove my car over an embankment," Eve said. "I rode my bike off a cliff."

"You did? When?"

"Also today."

Jen shook her head. "My God, you're Inspector Clouseau."

"I really am."

Eve started to laugh and so did Jen. Laughing hurt because of her broken ribs, but Eve couldn't stop herself, clutching her sides in pain. Jen leaned over and gently hugged her, which helped.

"I love you anyway," Jen said.

"Hold me tighter," Eve said between laughs.

Jen did. Eve wasn't sure when her laughter turned to tears, but her mom didn't let go.

◆ ◆ ◆

Eve watched the 11:00 p.m. local news with her mom and Duncan, who were both eating cups of hospital Jell-O. Duncan had stolen a bag full of them.

The lead story was about the attempt on Eve's life by a fellow deputy who tried to make it look like one of the sniper shootings. The report included a clip of the sheriff making a statement outside the Lost Hills station.

"Organized corruption in the form of covert, tattooed gangs of deputies took hold and thrived for decades within this department under my predecessors," Lansing said. "Rooting them out has been my mission from day one on the job. And over the last few months, Detective Eve Ronin has fiercely and courageously led the charge for me."

He took a dramatic pause, which Duncan filled with an observation. "I had no idea you were on a secret mission for the sheriff."

Eve said, "It was so secret that I didn't, either."

"Shhh," her mom said. "You're killing the moment."

Lansing went on. "Today, her bravery nearly cost Detective Ronin her life."

Jen snapped her fingers. "There's the moment. Beautifully done. He could have been an actor."

"He is," Eve said.

Lansing wasn't finished. "Even after Detective Ronin was shot, she wouldn't back down, subduing and arresting her attacker, a corrupt deputy aligned with the others in his secret gang that she'd already put in prison. I won't dignify his cowardice by uttering his name."

Duncan said, "Because he probably forgot it."

Lansing said, "I will be awarding Detective Ronin the Medal of Valor, our highest honor, because she embodies the excellence we strive for and the integrity, courage, and dedication to the law that the badge represents and that the deputy who shot her today desecrated. I do not condone and will not tolerate gangs of deputies, with their own immoral, racist code of conduct and repugnant rituals, to exist within my department."

Jen applauded and Lansing looked directly into the camera.

"I can assure you this assassination attempt won't stop Detective Ronin or me from removing every last vestige of corruption from this department. More arrests are imminent."

Eve turned off the TV with her remote.

"Why did you turn it off?" Jen protested. "He's praising you."

"He's making me sick," Eve said.

"Do you have something against receiving honors and compliments?"

There was no point, Eve thought, in trying to convince her mom that Lansing was using her to make himself look good and shift the media's attention from Saturday's debacle. "I'm very modest."

Jen glanced at Duncan. "She gets that from me."

Eve asked, "Is Lisa still on duty?"

"She took an extra shift just so she could be here for you."

"Good," Eve said. "Ask her to come up and get these tubes out of me. I'm leaving."

Duncan stood up from his chair. "Where do you think you're going?"

"Home. A bed is a bed."

Her mom stood up, too. "Except you can't get to yours. You live alone in a two-story condo. Your bedroom and bathroom are upstairs. How are you going to manage to get up there with your knee?"

"Just get me there and I'll figure something out."

"Your kitchen is downstairs. How are you going to feed yourself and keep that machine filled with ice water?" Jen said. "Face it, hardnose, you need someone to take care of you for a few days."

Duncan looked at Eve. "It's after eleven at night. What's your hurry to leave?"

"I am not spending a night in the hospital after a minor arthroscopic knee procedure and certainly not while a crowd of reporters grows outside, waiting to mob me when I leave in the morning. I'm slipping out quietly tonight."

"Fine," Jen said, "but you're staying with me."

"Hell no," Eve said.

"I don't mind. It will be like the good old days. I've got years of experience taking care of you."

"No, you don't. I took care of everyone, including you."

Jen waved off her objection. "Then it's time you let someone else do it. You've been a martyr long enough."

"She's right," Duncan said. "If you don't accept your mother's gracious and sensible offer, I will handcuff you to the bed."

"You don't have handcuffs anymore."

Duncan took a pair out of his pocket. "I turned in my badge. Nobody asked me for these."

Eve looked him in the eye. "You wouldn't dare."

"Try me," he said.

Lisa objected to Eve leaving, and so did the doctors, but they ultimately gave in and unhooked her from everything around her bed. They didn't really have a choice.

Eve left in her hospital gown, since she had no other clothes to wear, and carrying a paper bag containing some Vicodin to hold her until her prescription could be filled, her ID, house keys, and cracked iPhone. She took a quick glance at the phone, which was vibrating in a death rattle with calls, and saw dozens of missed calls and texts from reporters.

Two orderlies wheeled Eve to Duncan's Buick, since she wasn't ready yet to try squeezing herself into her mother's low, tiny Miata. Her ice machine and crutches were loaded into his back seat.

Duncan followed Jen's Miata to the beachfront city of Ventura, a straight shot up the freeway thirty miles northwest of Calabasas. Jen's ground-floor, two-bedroom apartment was close enough to the beach to smell the ocean but not to see or walk to it.

Duncan and Jen helped Eve into the apartment and set her down on the couch. Every inch of wall space was covered with photos or artwork, most of it depicting Jen at various ages, in various places, with various people over the years. The whole place smelled like an ashtray.

Eve was beginning to regret leaving the hospital, but before she could give it much thought, she fell asleep where she sat.

Eve awoke on the couch around 8:00 a.m. on Monday, hurting everywhere. Her knee was plugged into the ice machine and her phone, getting juice from her mom's charger, was vibrating on the coffee table with new calls and texts. She picked up the phone and glanced at the screen. Fifty more calls and texts had come in, none from anyone she wanted to talk to.

Jen was in the galley kitchen, making breakfast in a skillet on the stove. She told Eve that Duncan had stayed at the apartment until 3:00 a.m., when an off-duty deputy that Tom trusted came to relieve him. The deputy was parked outside the apartment in his personal car. She'd also prepared the guest room for Eve whenever she was ready to use it.

She brought a plate over to Eve and set it on the coffee table.

"Voilà, my famous Dangerous Eggs. Your favorite."

They were scrambled eggs mixed with whatever leftovers were in the refrigerator. They were dangerous because Eve and her siblings never knew what the ingredients might be. Sometimes it was Hamburger Helper. The dish was never her favorite.

Eve examined the plate with forensic intensity. "What's in it this time?"

"If I tell you that, it would ruin the fun."

"Food is not supposed to be fun," Eve said, picking up a fork and tentatively picking at the eggs.

"Of course it is." Jen brought over a plate of Dangerous Eggs for herself and sat down beside Eve.

"Not for adults."

"You never outgrow fun."

"That is your problem, Mom, right there, in a nutshell."

"I'd say it's yours."

Eve got lucky. The ingredients were cheese, bell peppers, and meatballs. It wasn't a scrambled-egg mix she'd ever make on her own but it was tasty and surprisingly satisfying. She had a Vicodin and a glass of milk to go along with it.

After breakfast, Jen helped Eve get to the bathroom and then gave her some clothes to wear. Jen stuffed the hospital gown into the trash. Eve wished she could shower, because Vicodin always made her sweat and, for some reason, reek of garlic, but she wasn't allowed to get her bandages wet. So she settled for a hand-wash with a wet towel. She avoided looking at herself in the mirror.

When she limped back into the living room, her brother, Kenny, called to check on her and then put Cassie, her five-year-old niece, on the phone. Cassie texted a picture of herself to Jen wearing the "Officer Friendly" badge Eve gave her years ago.

After the call, Eve and her mom settled down together in the living room and watched Barbra Streisand in *Funny Girl* and *Funny Lady*, Jen's two favorite movies, back-to-back, while sharing an enormous bowl of popcorn. Eve had seen the movies a thousand times with her mom, but there was something comforting about seeing them again.

By midafternoon, a strange thing happened. Two Ventura County sheriff's cruisers joined the off-duty deputy's Ford Taurus in front of the apartment. Eve wondered why she was getting the extra protection. She didn't get the answer until Tom arrived an hour later in an LASD patrol car and came in to see her. He looked grim and carried a paper bag.

"I see my protective detail has tripled," Eve said. "What's changed?"

"A lot. Do you want the good news or the bad news first?"

Jen answered for her. "The bad news. The good news will soothe the sting."

Tom glanced at Eve, and she nodded her agreement.

He pulled a chair from the kitchen table over to the couch where Eve was and sat down, facing her. "You made the right decision staying here."

"It wasn't my choice. I was forced into it."

"Then you got lucky. A deputy lobbed a Molotov cocktail into your condo last night," he said. "The fire department managed to contain the flames to the first floor but it's gutted down there. Your neighbors on either side of your place lost parts of their living rooms, too."

Eve was stunned.

Jen patted Eve's good knee. "That's such a shame. I never got a chance to see your new kitchen."

"I was having second thoughts about the backsplash anyway," Eve said.

"I guess we're going to be roommates for a while," Jen said. "You're welcome to stay as long as you want."

Eve decided she'd move into a hotel as soon as she was mobile, maybe sooner, if she could get room service to bring her meals and ice for the machine.

"So that's the reason for the extra security," Eve said to Tom. "The Ventura sheriff's department doesn't want any apartments torched up here."

"Sheriff Lansing called in a favor, at least that's what Captain Dubois told me when he sent me up here to brief you." He handed her the paper bag. "Here's your wallet, passport, and the charger for your phone. I got them from the bedroom of your apartment. I also have your gun safe in my trunk. I'll bring it up for you."

"Thank you, that was very thoughtful." She'd left her computer on the kitchen table, so it was gone. She couldn't think of any other valuables that needed to be recovered. It wasn't like she owned diamonds or had stacks of cash in her nightstand. "Is that it for the bad news?"

Tom shook his head and grimaced. "He firebombed your car, too."

Eve sighed. It was a massive inconvenience, and it would be hell getting anyone to give her car insurance again, but she wouldn't miss the Subaru. "Well, that should finally get rid of the dog-shit smell."

"You really have to learn how to make friends," Jen said.

Eve turned to Tom. "What's the good news?"

"We caught the deputy who did it. He's one of the two that Snell gave up to the DA. He barricaded himself in his house last night but SWAT flushed him out with tear gas this morning."

"And the other deputy Snell fingered?" Eve asked.

"He didn't put up a fight, though his wife was ready to with bug spray and an axe until he talked her down. She's a hard lady."

"You arrested him yourself?"

Tom nodded. "I put the cuffs on both of them. I have the same tattoo on my ankle that they do but we aren't the same kind of deputies or men at all."

Eve completely understood. "That's why you had to be the one to arrest them."

"It's important that the sheriff knows that not everyone who got inked did it for the same reasons that guys like Snell did or the department will lose a lot of good people."

"I'll make sure he understands," Eve said.

"Wow," Jen said. "This is great stuff about police culture. All these raw emotions are going into Maggie Malloy's backstory. She's inked, too."

Tom asked, "Who is Maggie Malloy?"

Eve said, "She's imaginary."

"I have tattoos," Jen said.

"Not like this one," Eve said.

"I can get one," Jen said and turned to Tom. "Can I see yours?"

"No, you can't," Eve said, and also turned to Tom. "Was that all the good news?"

"There's more. I saved the best for last. Biddle and Garvey have a suspect in the sniper case."

The firebombing of her apartment stunned her, but this was an even bigger shock.

"Who?"

"They don't know," Tom said.

"I'm confused," Eve said, "and I don't think it's because I'm on drugs."

"There was a break-in at the Agoura Hills / Calabasas Community Center yesterday. The guy raided a vending machine and took off," Tom said.

She knew the building. It was on Malibu Hills Road, directly around the corner from the Lost Hills station. That took some guts. "What does that have to do with the shootings?"

"He left shoe prints in the mud that Garvey discovered match the ones that you lifted from a break-in Monday at the Las Virgenes Municipal Water District office," Tom said. "And they both perfectly match ones lifted at the rock pond where the two women were shot."

Eve just gave the cast of the shoe print she'd lifted at the LVMWD office to Garvey and forgot about it. She didn't think of comparing it to the shoe prints found at the rock pond. The key evidence that could have solved the crime was in her hands from day one and she missed it.

"His tracks lead into the hills right behind the station," Tom said. "Biddle and Garvey are leading a manhunt for him right now with park rangers and a tactical unit."

"That's very good news." But Eve was pissed off that Captain DuBois hadn't informed her about any of it. She was technically still the head of the Malibu Sniper Task Force.

Movieland

Tom stood up. "The Ventura sheriff's department has officially taken over your protection but I am glad to come back when my shift is finished if it will make you feel more comfortable about your safety."

"That's not necessary, but thank you, Tom."

"I'll bring up your gun safe."

Jen saw him out the door, then turned to Eve, who was in a daze. So much had happened in such a short time. Sometimes cases were like that.

"I wonder if he's single," Jen said.

That snapped Eve out of her daze. "It wouldn't be appropriate for me to date a junior officer, Mom. In fact, it would get me fired."

"I know that. I wouldn't ever suggest such a thing. I was a juror on a murder case involving a female NYPD captain who slept with a detective under her command and allegedly killed his girlfriend to keep him to herself."

"That was an episode of *Bull*."

"But I took my responsibility to consider the evidence very seriously. A woman's life was in our hands."

"No, it wasn't," Eve said. "You were an extra, not an actual juror. You didn't have any deliberations."

"You didn't answer my question. Is he single?"

Why is she so interested? Eve wondered, and then a horrifying thought occurred to her.

"You aren't dating a deputy in my station," she said emphatically.

"Of course not," Jen said. "I was thinking Lisa could."

Eve didn't know what to say to that.

Jen studied her and then broke into a big smile. "She already is!"

"I didn't say that."

"You didn't have to, it's all over your face."

"Those are bruises," Eve said.

There was a knock at the door. Jen opened it and Tom came in carrying the gun safe. "Where do you want this?"

"In the guest room," Jen said. "First door on your left."

Tom carried it by. Jen glanced at his butt and winked at Eve, who scowled at her. Tom came back a moment later.

"Take it easy, Eve," he said.

"I don't have much choice."

Tom left. Jen turned to Eve as soon as the door was closed.

"Is he good in bed? I bet he's terrific. He doesn't look like a man who needs Siri to give him directions."

"I have no idea," Eve said.

"Lisa didn't tell you?"

"I didn't say they were dating and I certainly didn't say they are sleeping together."

Her mom grinned. "I doubt they are doing much sleeping. Strong forearms are an indicator of sexual stamina, you know."

"I don't want to have this conversation," Eve said.

"You can't because you don't know anything. But Lisa does. I'm calling her." Jen picked up her phone.

Eve groaned and covered her head with a pillow. Leaving the hospital was definitely a mistake.

CHAPTER
TWENTY-SEVEN

On Tuesday morning, Eve contacted her insurance agent and let him know the bad news and to find out what kind of coverage, if any, she still had left. She was hoping for some money for temporary relocation. But she didn't ask yet about a rental or replacement car. It would be a while before she could drive again. Her Uber app and her credit card were going to get a workout. The insurance agent told her he'd get back to her but she was afraid that she'd hear from the company's lawyer instead, telling her she'd exceeded the limits or terms of her policy and was on her own.

She moved into her mom's guest room for some privacy and spent her day watching reruns of *In the Heat of the Night* and other old cop shows on MeTV, a network that had no news division so she was spared from seeing any stories about herself or the case. It was mindless and relaxing, until her father's name showed up in the credits of a *Matlock* episode. She immediately turned off the TV and took a long nap.

Later that afternoon, her lawyer, Gabriel Montlake, called. Or, rather, his secretary did, and kept Eve on hold for two minutes. When he finally got on the line, he said: "How are you feeling?"

"It depends on why you're calling."

"The Pruitts have dropped their lawsuit against you. Their lawyer says it was an error, that you were covered under their prior settlement with the county."

That was fast, Eve thought.

"I feel great," she said.

"Except they are wrong. You explicitly weren't covered. Something has changed and I suspect it's related to what I saw on the news last night."

"I can't say, but I appreciate what you've done for me. What do I owe you?"

"Nothing," he said.

"But you spent time writing up and filing those motions."

"Not me. I had a newbie fresh out of law school do it. He needed the practice, so you did me a favor," he said. "I'm having your retainer returned in full. Consider it my way of thanking you for your heroism yesterday."

"You might want to keep the retainer for a while longer," Eve said. "I could need your help with my insurance company. My home and car were firebombed last night and the company recently paid to fix them up after some other incidents."

"That wasn't on the news."

"I didn't want to dominate the entire newscast."

"If the insurance company gives you any trouble, I will gladly crush them, pro bono. In fact, I'd enjoy it."

Eve thanked him and ended the call. Jen came into the room with her father. The *Matlock* credit had been an omen.

"When did you get here?" Eve asked him.

"While you were sleeping," Vince said. "I didn't want to disturb you."

"If that were true," she said, "you wouldn't be here at all."

Jen turned to him. "Don't mind her. Being shot makes her grouchy."

Eve said, "I am in no mood to discuss your problems, Vince."

"I don't have any. Simone called this morning and said I'm directing the pilot after all."

Jen smiled at Eve. "Isn't that wonderful?"

It was obvious to Eve that the network execs saw the news, and all that free publicity, and decided it was more important to have her on their side, and have this show, than fight over a director. What Eve didn't understand was her mom's glee.

"Why are you so excited about it?"

"The three of us will be working together," Jen said. "We'll be like a family again."

"We were never a family. He was never around." And now Vince was just standing there in his ridiculous ascot, with a dumb smile on his face. She wanted to strangle him with his ascot.

Jen said, "Why do you insist on dwelling on the past?"

"The statute of limitations never runs out on some crimes." Eve would have walked out if she could. Instead, she unplugged herself from the ice machine, grabbed her crutches and phone, and hobbled past them to the bathroom.

Jen looked after her. "Do you always have to be so overdramatic?"

Vince said, "Her mother is an actress, what did you expect?"

In the bathroom, Eve looked at herself in the mirror and was horrified by what she saw. Her face was swollen, scratched, and sticky with sweat. An ugly stitched wound on her brow oozed under her oily hair.

At least nobody would see her aching body. Her left leg, from her hip to just below her knee, was mostly in bandages. She couldn't see the wounds, but she could feel them, though the pain was mostly dulled by the ice and Vicodin. Her left buttock hurt, too, and she was glad she couldn't get a look at it. And she smelled like an Italian restaurant in a men's locker room.

She wet a towel, soaped it up, and began tenderly giving herself a sponge bath and thought about her miserable situation.

Sure, she was homeless, and looked like she'd been shot and thrown off a cliff, but at least she wasn't being sued for $10 million anymore. Her TV show was still going forward and the deputies who'd tried to kill her were out of the department.

What more could she want?

To catch the Malibu Sniper.

But Biddle and Garvey were on that, and if it turned out the shoe print was the big clue, she deserved any humiliation she received from them. There might even be an upside. If they made an arrest, and she was taken down a peg, they might be able to start their relationship anew when she got back to work.

Because her mom was right. She needed to make more friends.

She hid out in the bathroom until she was sure that Vince was gone, then came out feeling cleaner and smelling like flowers.

"You look much better," Jen said. "But you could use some makeup."

"I'm not going anywhere." Eve sat down at the kitchen table. She was tired of being on the couch and in bed.

"You're allowed to look good for yourself. Besides, you have been having visitors."

Her mom disappeared for a moment and came back with some makeup, which she lined up on the table.

"I don't see how you can be so chummy with Vince after what he did to you," Eve said.

Jen began carefully applying the makeup to Eve's face. "You get older, honey, and things change. I don't need his money to support you anymore. That struggle is over. So I've let go of the anger and bitterness. Life is easier that way."

"It's still there, you just pretend that it's not."

"Actually, I use it when I pretend. I draw on it for my acting, where it's helpful to me, just like you use yours to go after bad guys."

"That's not why I do what I do," Eve said.

"It's obviously your motivation."

"Stop talking like I'm a character and not a person."

"You're both now. You should share what you feel with the actress playing you. It will make her performance more authentic." Jen held up a mirror so Eve could see her face.

"Voilà. You're beautiful again."

She did look a lot better and, somehow, it made her feel better, too. "I really need to get some underwear, clothes, and shoes. Let's go shopping."

Eve expected her mom to object, to remind her that she wasn't supposed to walk on her leg, but instead her mom hopped out of her seat.

"That's a great idea. Retail therapy is the best therapy."

Jen drove them in her Miata, with the top down, seventeen miles south to the Camarillo Premium Outlets, a massive outdoor mall built on what was once a strawberry field between the old town and a general-aviation airport.

They went from store to store, trailed by two deputies, which Eve thought probably made shopkeepers think they were potential shoplifters.

But it was fun. Eve hadn't shopped with her mom in years and forgot what a great sense of humor she had or that they did have good times together.

They had some arguments, but only over fashion. Jen liked loud, colorful clothes that accentuated a woman's curves. Eve liked more conservative clothing that didn't call attention to herself or her body. They compromised. Eve purchased a few tops that were more colorful, and body hugging, to appease her mom and, she hoped, that Daniel might find attractive if they got together again.

They returned to Jen's apartment and ordered two pizzas delivered from PizzaMan Dan's, which a deputy brought to the door for safety. Eve told him that one of the pizzas was for them and gave him a five-dollar tip to give to the delivery guy.

When she returned to the kitchen table, her phone buzzed. It was Sheriff Lansing. Eve answered it.

"I have big news, and I wanted you to hear it from me first before it breaks publicly," Lansing said. "The Malibu Sniper is in custody. His name is Jasper Snow, and all this time the son of a bitch was living on the hill right behind the Lost Hills station."

The surprises just kept coming. She was glad the man was caught, but disappointed she hadn't contributed to the arrest.

"Are you sure it's him?"

"One hundred percent. He was wearing boots that match the prints left at the rock pond and he had a shotgun in his crude little encampment. But here is the clincher. The DNA results on the urine came in this morning and they matched a profile already in the system: his."

"What about the DNA from the vomit?"

Jen looked up from her pizza. "Do you need to have this conversation now?"

Eve waved at her to be quiet so she could hear Lansing's reply.

"It's not his and didn't score a hit in the system, so it's irrelevant. We've got his boot prints, his DNA, and the shotgun. He also has a history of assaulting people. Deputies have brought him in a few times."

"Has he talked?"

"Only to ask for an attorney," Lansing said. "But Clarence Darrow could rise from the dead to represent him and it wouldn't change a thing. It's all wrapped up. Snow's our shooter and Snell was a copycat. This nightmare is over thanks to top-notch police work."

And not all of it acknowledged. "That top-notch work began with Duncan Pavone. He knew it was a serial shooter months ago but nobody in the department or the Park Service would listen. You were ready to fire him for it, but he handed you his badge before you could."

"I didn't accept his badge as a resignation. Officially, he's been suspended for defying a direct order and starting an unnecessary panic but you're right. He's my next call. I just wanted you to know there's nothing left undone. You can rest easy now and focus on simply recuperating from your injuries."

"I'll do that. Thank you, sir." She disconnected the call.

Everything had happened so fast. On Saturday, they had nothing. And now, three days later, it was all over.

But she also knew that cases had their own momentum and it wasn't unusual for things to move at a sudden, rapid pace. It had happened to her. In the end, it was forensics, good instincts, and solid, basic police work that ended a crime spree that lasted for months. Garvey and Biddle deserved to be commended for following up on clues that Eve and Duncan had overlooked or didn't think to connect to the case.

She could rest easy now. If only she knew how to rest.

CHAPTER
TWENTY-EIGHT

That night, on the evening news, the arrest of Jasper Snow was the big headline. The sheriff declared "the sniper's reign of terror" over and congratulated Garvey and Biddle on their "extraordinary detective work." The two detectives basked in the glow of the media lights, particularly Garvey, who Eve thought hogged the microphone. He did, however, thank all the other detectives working the case, particularly Duncan Pavone for realizing, before anyone else, that they were dealing with a serial shooter. The reporters didn't dwell on the cover-up, or the corruption that Eve's shooting revealed. She was sure the sheriff was very happy about that.

Eve used her mom's computer to read Zena Faust's take on events. Zena was pleased and grateful that her girlfriend's killer was caught, but she questioned the suspiciously good timing of it happening only hours after Eve Ronin was shot by a corrupt deputy and forty-eight hours after Duncan Pavone revealed the massive multiagency cover-up of the earlier shootings. It was a powerful distraction. But it wasn't going to distract her. The other reporters might be willing to overlook those scandals, but she wasn't.

Good for you, Eve thought. *Don't back down.*

Eve had a hard time sleeping that night. She should have been relieved that Snow was caught, but she had questions she needed answered before she could accept it and close the case in her own mind.

What difference did it make? It was over and she had healing to do.

◆ ◆ ◆

Perhaps it was boredom, perhaps it was being stuck in the house with her mom, but as hard as she tried, Eve couldn't do what Lansing suggested and rest easy. Not until her questions were answered.

So first thing Wednesday morning, she closed the door to the bedroom for privacy, took a deep breath, and decided to call Garvey. Of the two detectives, he was the more likely to take her call, if only because he liked having friends in Hollywood. To her surprise, he answered on the first ring without even a hello.

"I've been meaning to call you, to tell you how gut-sick Wally and I were about what happened to you, but things were moving so fast on Sunday . . ." His voice trailed off.

"No apologies necessary, I totally understand."

"Snell and his bunch are a shit stain on the badge," Garvey said.

"They certainly are. I just wanted to congratulate you guys. That was some amazing police work."

"It's not like we are deductive geniuses or anything," Garvey said with false modesty. "We just followed the clues that were right in front of us and then we got a lucky break on the DNA results. Good timing, that's all it was."

"Don't downplay what you've done, Stan. It might have happened sooner, and faster, if I'd submitted those shoe-print impressions to CSU but I didn't," she said. "I was sloppy, and I've got to own that failure."

"It might have put us on the hunt for the guy earlier, but the case still wouldn't have broken wide open if Snow didn't have a hankering for Cheez Doodles over the weekend."

Garvey was feeling charitable in his success. But he raised a point that had nagged her since she'd first learned of the arrest.

"That's the crazy thing," she said. "He's just killed two people, he knows everybody with a badge is out looking for him now, and he breaks into a building two doors down from the sheriff's station to steal Ding Dongs."

"A man's got to eat. Just ask Donuts."

"Is that what Snow said? That he was hungry and didn't care about the huge risk he was taking?"

"He's not saying anything. His lawyer, a hotshot criminal attorney hired by his dad, is doing all the talking. He says his client didn't know anything about the shootings, that Snow lives off the grid, doesn't read the newspaper or watch TV. He says Snow takes a bath and an evening piss at the rock pond every night, that's why his DNA and footprints were there."

"What about the shotgun?"

"Snow says he found it. Can you believe that?" Garvey said. "How many times have you caught a guy with the dope or the stolen goods or the bloody murder weapon who says 'it isn't mine,' or 'I found it on the street,' or 'you planted it'?"

"Almost every time I make an arrest," Eve conceded.

"Exactly. Have those lame denials ever worked? It's hardly worth the oxygen to say the words. How dumb does he think we are?"

"It's simple desperation in the face of overwhelming, irrefutable evidence," Eve said.

"It's pathetic," Garvey said. "It's almost a confession in itself."

"How many shotgun shells did he have left?"

"None. Must've used them all up or hidden them. We've got CSU up there searching the entire hillside," Garvey said. "He was right behind our house the whole time, watching us come and go. It creeps me out."

She noticed that he'd quickly changed the subject from the ammunition, but she let it go.

"Me too. Why do you think he shot all those people?"

"Because he hates them. Not the people he shot in particular, but everybody. That he admits to—hating people," Garvey said. "His lawyer says it's why he was living in the hills. So he wouldn't have to be around anybody."

"Do you have a picture of Snow? I'd like to see the face of the man we've been chasing."

"The PIO is releasing his mug shot to the media tonight, but I'll text it to you," Garvey said. "I'm sure you've seen him around, we all have, which just makes it more frustrating that we weren't on him sooner."

"We had no reason to be," she said. "Again, you did great work. Please pass along my congratulations to Wally."

"I will. I appreciate the call, I mean that," Garvey said. "Tell Donuts we better get an invite to his retirement party."

"Tell him yourself. I know he'd like the call, especially after the way the sheriff treated him."

"That was a shit move," Garvey agreed.

"But you set the record straight, and that means a lot to me and I know it does to him, too."

"You got it. I'll call him now."

Garvey hung up. A moment later, Jasper Snow's mug shot showed up on her phone. She recognized the face. It was the homeless man she gave her leftover Egg McWhatever to outside of McDonald's a few days ago.

He was a serial killer hiding in plain sight and she'd met him.

She let that thought sit in her head for a moment and it didn't become any more believable to her.

Eve's phone buzzed a few minutes later. It was Duncan. She answered it. "Did you just get off the phone with Tubbs?"

"I did. It was real nice of him to call and to give that shout-out to me last night. He didn't have to do that and I told him so."

"He stepped up, I'll give him that."

"That was some real solid police work Crockett and Tubbs did," Duncan said.

"It certainly was," she said. "Textbook stuff."

"That's the way it is sometimes."

There was a long silence, then Duncan spoke again. "You don't believe Snow is the shooter, either."

"No, I don't," she said.

"You believe his lame, unbelievable story, don't you?"

"I do," she said.

"The shooter would have had the ammo."

"And wouldn't have broken into a vending machine next door to the sheriff's station after two killings," Eve said. "It's insane."

There was another long silence before Duncan spoke again. "I turned in my badge, I'm officially suspended, and I'm four days from retirement."

"I've been shot and I'm on medical leave."

"The case is not our problem," he said.

"No, it's not," she said. "Do you have anything planned for today?"

"*Gunsmoke* is on at two p.m."

"I'm thinking it would be nice to get out of the apartment and enjoy a change of scenery."

"Do you have someplace in mind?" he asked.

"Las Vegas. It seems like a long way for Clark Netter to go just to cheat on his wife. I can't help wondering if maybe he got into some trouble there that followed him back here."

"I could use some desert scenery myself. If we leave now," Duncan said, "we can get there in time for the all-you-can-eat lunch buffet."

"The buffets in Las Vegas are open 24/7."

"I'll pick you up in forty-five minutes," he said.

Eve had just enough time for her mom to put some makeup on her face before Duncan arrived in his Buick. They were on the road an hour after their call.

She wore her new blazer, blouse, and slacks and had her gun and her badge clipped to her belt. Her crutches were in the back seat, her ice machine was in the trunk, and she had some Vicodin in her pocket.

Duncan drove a hundred miles per hour the whole way, knowing if they got pulled over, Eve's badge would get them out of a ticket, though he'd have to wake her up to show it. She slept through the entire drive. They arrived at the Côte d'Azur Hotel and Casino on the Las Vegas strip at 1:00 p.m.

Duncan parked his Buick in the first floor of the garage, in a red zone by the casino entrance, and placed an official LASD placard on his dash. Then he got out and removed Eve's crutches, holding them steady for her as she emerged from the passenger seat.

"Thanks," she said, got the crutches under her armpits, then gestured to the LASD placard. "You think that'll keep you from getting towed?"

"Nobody is going to tow us without checking with casino security first and they're certainly watching us now." Duncan looked up at the security camera on a nearby pillar. "Say hello."

Eve took out her badge and held it up to the camera and smiled.

Duncan said, "That should do it."

Eve hobbled to the casino entrance on her crutches and the automatic doors hissed open for them.

She'd visited most of the casinos on the Strip, but not this one, for good reason. She was afraid they'd throw her out.

When Côte d'Azur opened fifteen years earlier, it was pitched as a return to a bygone era, when casinos were elegant and the people who patronized them were wealthy, refined, and impeccably dressed in tuxedos and evening gowns. It was a James Bond fantasy come to life, right down to the brassy 007 movie themes and scores playing on a constant loop in all the public spaces, interspersed with Frank Sinatra, Tom Jones, and Sammy Davis standards. The stores in the shopping promenade were Hermès, Gucci, Louis Vuitton, Cartier, Dior, and other high-end brands. Any patron who didn't meet the black-tie dress code, or was looking for buffet dining, was politely directed by hotel security to Circus Circus.

But the clientele for such an adult, exclusive resort was too narrow for the heavily indebted property to survive on in those tumultuous economic times, so while the luxurious decor, top-of-the-line amenities, and James Bond music still remained, there was now the Feast of Kings Buffet, an Old Navy in the shopping promenade, and people roaming the casino floor in flip-flops.

Eve was in no danger of getting thrown out now, assuming she could actually make it into the casino. Using the crutches wouldn't have been so difficult if not for her cracked ribs and her generally shot-up body. Every movement made her ache and seemed to tear at something inside her.

Duncan glanced at Eve struggling with her crutches as they made their way across the casino floor. "You want to wait here while I get you a wheelchair?"

"I can manage," she said.

"Using those crutches must be agony on your ribs and underarms. It hurts just looking at you."

"I am not getting in a wheelchair," she said.

"You're being ridiculous. Ironside used a wheelchair and it didn't diminish his authority as a police officer."

"Who is Ironside?"

"How can you be a cop and not know who Ironside is? One of the greatest TV cops of all time, played by Raymond Burr."

"I thought he was Perry Mason."

"He was also Ironside," Duncan said. "A cop in a wheelchair."

"You're comparing me to Raymond Burr?"

"Ironside was also surly and shot by a sniper," he said.

"Raymond Burr weighed ten thousand pounds. Of course he was in a wheelchair," Eve said. "I'm surprised he wasn't playing a cop carried around on a forklift."

"You *are* looking a little bloated today," Duncan said.

"What did you say?"

He smiled and she realized he'd managed to distract her from her pain all the way to a security station in the center of the casino. A uniformed guard looked up at them from behind the counter.

"Can I help you?" He said it so robotically, Eve wondered if he was actually an animatronic figure.

Duncan glanced at Eve. She pulled out her badge and said, "We're Detectives Eve Ronin and Duncan Pavone with the Los Angeles County Sheriff's Department. We'd like to speak with your head of security."

"Are you both armed?"

Duncan said, "To the teeth."

"Do you have IDs?" he asked. They handed him their California driver's licenses. "One moment, please." The guard picked up his phone and made a call.

Eve turned to Duncan. "Do I really look bloated?"

"Anger is the best painkiller."

The security guard hung up the phone and handed their licenses back to them.

"Nate Grumbo will be right out to see you."

Eve and Duncan took seats at two nearby *CSI* slot machines, branded with logos and cast photos from the long-running Las Vegas–set TV series. The symbols on the spinner wheels, instead of various fruits, were crime scene tape, chalk outlines of corpses, skulls, magnifying glasses, guns, knives, and photos of the cast.

After a few minutes, a man approached them. He was in his fifties, wearing a tailored suit that flattered his muscled physique and probably hid a weapon or two. He was private security and yet he radiated official law enforcement.

"I'm Nate Grumbo, head of security for the Côte d'Azur," he said, offering his hand to Eve and Duncan. He wore a gold pinkie ring.

Welcome to Vegas, baby. Eve shook his hand. "Ex-cop?"

"Ex-ATF. How may I assist you?"

Duncan said, "You can start by not towing my car."

"Your Buick is safe, Detective Pavone," Grumbo said.

Duncan glanced at Eve. "Told you they were watching."

Eve said, "We hope you were also watching Clark Netter, a visitor to your casino last Wednesday night. He told his wife that he'd won some big money playing blackjack."

"What's your interest in Mr. Netter?"

"He was killed by a sniper a block away from his home in Calabasas," Eve said. "He still had all of his cash on him."

"I suppose you'll want to see the same casino footage that the FBI screened on Thursday," Grumbo said.

"That's right," Duncan said, as if he knew exactly what Grumbo was talking about.

Grumbo led them across the casino to an unmarked door secured by a keypad lock, then down a stark gray maintenance corridor, with exposed ductwork on the ceiling and concrete floors, to another unmarked door, this one secured with palm-print and retinal scanners. He pressed his palm on the scanner and a red beam scanned his eyes.

"This is just like my front door," Duncan said.

The door opened and Grumbo ushered them into a vast, dark room filled with countless screens, on the walls and on individual manned consoles, showing hundreds of views of the casino floor, gaming tables, elevator interiors, parking areas, and hallways.

"Welcome to security command center," Grumbo said and led them to a console where a woman, wearing a headset with a mike, sat in front of a monitor and keyboard intently watching the screen. "Regina, could you please bring up the Netter file?"

She typed a few keys and a new image appeared on-screen. It was frozen on a ten-dollar blackjack table as seen from above.

"The surveillance footage covers Tuesday and Wednesday nights, but we've edited it into one montage for the FBI's convenience," Grumbo said and asked Regina to hit play. "We'll begin with Tuesday evening."

The video showed Clark Netter coming to the blackjack table, handing a hundred-dollar bill to the dealer, getting some chips, then sitting down to play a few hands.

"He played for twenty minutes and lost seventy dollars," Grumbo said, "then pocketed his chips and went to the men's room."

The video, in a series of edits from different camera angles, showed Netter leaving the table and walking into the men's room.

"We don't have any cameras in the men's room, of course," Grumbo said, talking over a time cut in the video. "He emerged five minutes later."

Netter walked out and Duncan pointed at him on the screen. "His pockets are bulging."

"You have a good eye, Detective," Grumbo said. "His pockets are full of chips. Ten thousand dollars' worth, to be exact. We know that because he went from here to the cashier to cash them in. He did the same thing on Wednesday, when he cashed out with another ten thousand in chips."

"What did we just see?" Duncan asked.

"A common and simple form of money laundering," Grumbo said.

"Don't you have to report winnings over a certain amount to the IRS?"

"Yes, but it's not so easy to track if you don't score an immediate, huge jackpot at a slot machine," Grumbo said. "You might earn winnings over hours of play, on and off, over several machines, over the course of a day or a week, then cash out by feeding your slips into a cashier machine all at once or over several days."

Eve asked, "What about table games?"

"It's even harder to track. You exchange cash for chips. People can hold on to chips for days, weeks, months, or years," Grumbo said. "We have no way of knowing when someone cashes in chips if they represent a win or simply what's left after significant losses."

While they were talking, the video continued to play as several men came and went from the bathroom. And then a pudgy, pale man in an ill-fitting suit walked out. Eve recognized him.

"Duncan, look," she said and pointed at the screen. Regina froze the image. "Didn't we meet that man at Paul Banning's house last Tuesday?"

"We did," Duncan said. "He left to go to the airport. Now we know where he was going. But I don't remember his name."

"It's Gene Dent," Grumbo said. "He paid for a drink at the casino bar earlier that evening using a credit card, that's how we got his name. The FBI was interested in him as well. You'll see him in Wednesday's video also emerging from the restroom after Netter's payoff."

Eve asked, "Did you have a guest named Jayda Montaro staying here?"

Regina typed something on the keyboard and a registration document appeared on-screen in a new window. "Yes, we did. She was here on both days."

At least Jayda had told the truth about that, Eve thought. But she wondered if the story of how Jayda met Netter had something to do with Banning, Dent, and the money laundering. "Did any of the FBI agents give you their card?"

"One of them did." Grumbo took it out of his pocket and handed it to her.

She pulled out her phone, which looked like it had been rescued from a tree shredder, and took a picture of the card. It belonged to Special Agent Dennis Oakland. She handed the card back to Grumbo.

"Nice phone," he said.

"I fell off a cliff with it in my pocket," she said.

"After she was shot," Duncan added.

Grumbo looked at Eve as if seeing her for the first time. Even Regina turned around in her seat to take another gander.

"You're the detective who was on the news," Grumbo said. "Well, that certainly explains your injuries."

"Are they that noticeable?" Eve said.

"Barely, but it's my job to notice subtle details," Grumbo said. "Are you staying in Las Vegas overnight?"

Eve and Duncan shared a look. They hadn't really thought about it. Duncan said, "Most likely."

"Then you'll be staying here," Grumbo said. "I'll arrange for a two-bedroom suite."

"That's very nice, Mr. Grumbo," Eve said. "But we aren't allowed to accept gratuities."

Technically, neither one of them was on the job, but it's what Eve would have said if they were.

"We'll charge you our regular advertised room rate, which is discounted on weekdays and comes with a free visit to the buffet," Grumbo said. "You can check our website if you don't believe me."

"Deal," Duncan said before Eve could argue.

Eve said, "We're going to need a copy of the security footage of Netter and Dent. Please hold on to it until we can get a warrant."

"That won't be necessary. I'll have it copied to a thumb drive and sent to your room. In the meantime, I'll get you a ride to the front desk in a courtesy cart and then to the buffet. You must be hungry."

"Thank you so much for your cooperation, Mr. Grumbo," Eve said.

"Call me Nate, and it's absolutely my pleasure. But everything I told you about money laundering is off the record. Purely theoretical on my part."

Duncan nodded. "Of course."

They walked out of the room and were met in the hallway by a golf cart, which carried them through a series of corridors, then out a door into the vast lobby, where marbled Grecian columns supported a soaring ceiling topped with a stained-glass dome. Masterpieces by Picasso, Matisse, and Gauguin adorned the walls behind the mahogany check-in counter.

Eve used her credit card to check in, they were given two keys, and then they were whisked over to the buffet by their courtesy cart driver.

CHAPTER
TWENTY-NINE

Eve ate almost as much as Duncan, who seemed to be going for the Guinness World Record in the hotly contested "buffet food consumed in one sitting" category.

"Zena Faust may have been right about Netter being on the take," Eve said, eating some shrimp. "Banning was obviously plying the councilman with money and sex for something."

"How come nobody ever tries to ply me with money and sex?" Duncan said while cutting into a slice of prime rib.

"It's easier to offer you a free lunch. That's how I got you to be the police consultant on my TV show."

"That's true," Duncan said. "I sell my soul way too cheap."

Eve dipped some lobster in butter. "I can understand why Banning might have shot Faust, to shut her up, but why would he shoot Netter?"

"To cover up that Netter sold his vote on Banning's project and is still in his pocket," Duncan said.

"But why kill him hours after paying him another $20,000 for a vote he hadn't made yet?"

"Maybe Banning knew the FBI was sniffing around," Duncan said, shifting his attention to his pile of fried chicken, "and the sniper shootings offered him an amazing opportunity to clean house and pin the killings on somebody else."

"It's possible," Eve said. "Banning knew about the shootings because he was a victim himself."

"So we're back to your crime-of-opportunity theory. It was Faust's camping tweet that set him off on his killing spree."

"It might explain the two most recent shootings," Eve said. "But not the prior ones."

"We're detectives," he said. "We'll just have to do more detecting. Right after I detect dessert."

Duncan drove them to the federal building, the words "Fidelity," "Liberty," and "Integrity" etched along the facade of what otherwise would be an utterly ordinary, and essentially anonymous, three-story office building. Eve wondered if the Las Virgenes Municipal Water District had hired the same uninspired architect or if dull was the only approved government style.

They locked their weapons in the gun safe in Duncan's trunk before going inside the building to avoid getting shot on the spot. They approached the front desk, identified themselves, and asked to speak to Special Agent Dennis Oakland. The desk officer asked what it was regarding.

Eve said, "Clark Netter and Gene Dent."

The man who strode purposefully out of the elevator moments later was heavyset, in his sixties, and had the bulging eyeballs of someone with a chronic thyroid condition and the yellowed teeth of someone with a serious nicotine addiction. He offered them his chubby, clammy hand.

"I'm Special Agent Oakland," he said as they shook hands. "You could have called instead of just showing up at our front door."

"We're only here for the day," Duncan said.

Eve said, "We're investigating Councilman Netter's homicide. We think it's time that we share information."

"I thought his killer was caught," Oakland said.

"We aren't entirely convinced that's true."

Duncan added, "Besides, the bribery investigation doesn't end just because Netter is dead."

Oakland smiled. "That's a federal matter."

Duncan smiled. "So there *is* a bribery investigation. Good to know."

Oakland's face reddened. "Let's go upstairs."

They rode the elevator up to a conference room, where they were introduced to another agent, Emily Riker, who was already seated at the table. The woman was in her thirties, and surprisingly pale for someone who lived in the desert, which made Eve wonder if she was a recent transfer from a cooler, grayer climate.

"How do you want to work this?" Eve said, taking a seat. Her knee throbbed with pain.

"You first," Oakland said. "What can you tell us about Netter?"

Eve told them what they knew, which was almost nothing.

"What we'd like to know," Eve said, "is if Banning was bribing Netter with money and sex or if it just looks that way."

Riker glanced at Oakland, and he nodded. She said, "Netter and Banning are players in a much larger corruption scheme that goes back to Netter's work as chief of staff for LA city councilman Ricardo Villegas."

Riker explained that Villegas was paid off by developers to push through projects in Los Angeles. Netter facilitated the bribes. Both Villegas and Netter saw an opportunity to expand their reach into other areas of Los Angeles County. So Netter quit and ran for the Calabasas City Council in a campaign financed by the same developers who backed Villegas.

"Whenever Netter gets bribed," Riker said, "he kicks back a portion of it to Villegas as a commission."

Duncan asked, "Where does Paul Banning fit into all of this?"

"He's an investor in New Positano," Oakland said. "Gene Dent is a fixer for Gilbert Robinson, the developer. They were buying Netter's vote to approve the project."

"So the FBI was preparing to arrest Netter?"

"We already had Netter," Oakland said. "We cut a deal with him weeks ago to testify against Villegas, Robinson, and Banning in return for a reduced sentence."

Riker added, "We photocopied all the cash Netter was bringing back to Los Angeles this time and were going to track it back to Villegas. But then Netter got shot, which also torpedoed our case. At first, we thought it was a hit."

Oakland said, "But there's no proof and we have no idea how they could have known that we'd turned Netter."

Eve glanced at Duncan, then back to the agents. "We found a tracker on his car. Was it yours?"

Oakland glanced at Riker, then back to the detectives. "No, it wasn't. Was it live or passive?"

"Passive," Eve said. "But whoever it belonged to could have tracked him right here."

Oakland shook his head. "We aren't stupid. We didn't invite him to the federal building."

But Eve thought about the other places she knew Netter had visited that would have shown up on his tracker data and immediately realized how the FBI connection was exposed. "You met him at a safe house in Woodland Hills."

Riker was obviously surprised. Her eyebrows nearly shot up off her face. "How do you know about the house?"

Duncan said, "The GPS data from Netter's iPhone. But the tracker would have it, too."

"Knowing that he visited some house wouldn't reveal that he was working with us," Riker said. "You checked the complicated ownership and you didn't make the connection."

"What if somebody ran the plates of the cars parked out front?" Duncan asked. "Who are they registered to?"

Oakland glanced at Riker. "Shit."

Eve gave Oakland the serial number of the tracker and he agreed to find out if a particular vendor, like Walmart or Amazon, was selling the lot that included that individual device and would let them know what he found out.

"With Netter dead," Eve asked, "what does that mean for your case against Villegas?"

"Unless we can turn someone else," Oakland said, "it's as dead as Netter is."

◆ ◆ ◆

The opulent two-bedroom suite that Grumbo reserved for Eve and Duncan at Côte d'Azur had a spectacular view of the resort's sandy beach and saltwater wave pool, its freshwater lake, and the glittering Las Vegas Strip beyond its lush tropical grounds. The thumb drive containing the footage of Netter was waiting for them on the counter of the fully stocked bar, along with a big basket of fruit, cheese, and chocolates.

Duncan plucked a caramel from the basket. "This is the life."

"Your wife is okay with you spending the night in a Las Vegas hotel room with a hot younger woman?"

"No offense, but have you looked at yourself in the mirror lately? People hold up crucifixes when you hobble past them."

Eve laughed. "You didn't answer the question."

"Gracie trusts me and she knows you."

"She's never met me," Eve said.

"She knows you by your actions. But most of all, she knows me and my values."

Eve propped her crutches against a barstool and helped herself to a grape. "Hallie Netter believed her husband was a man of unquestionable integrity. I wonder how angry she'd be if she discovered she was wrong."

"You think she put the tracker in his car?"

Eve shrugged and even that hurt. "It explains why it's passive and not active. She'd have easy access to it to download his data."

"But it doesn't put him and Jayda together."

"The sexting on his burner did. Maybe the day he was killed wasn't the first time he waited too long to trash it," Eve said. "Either way, she has as much motive as Villegas and Banning do for killing him."

"Once the Feds know who was selling the device, we can get a warrant to see if Hallie Netter bought a GPS tracker from any of them."

"Who do you think has the best shot of sweet-talking a judge into a warrant, Burnside or the FBI?"

"Me," Duncan said.

"You've been suspended."

"The judge won't know that. Besides, the sheriff lifted it on our call. I'm officially on vacation days until I retire. But if you're worried about it, I can write up the warrant and you can submit it."

"You've convinced me." Eve suddenly felt exhausted and miserable. "We can't do anything until we hear from Oakland. So I'm taking a Vicodin and a nap."

"That's so hot and young of you," he said.

"What are you going to do?"

"Get you some ice for your machine, then write up that warrant so it's ready to go. I brought my laptop with me."

"That can wait. You're in Las Vegas. Have some fun."

"Don't worry," Duncan said. "As soon as I'm done, I'll plant myself in front of that *CSI* slot machine and see if I can get rich."

Eve went to bed. She was already asleep when Duncan came in, filled her ice machine, and plugged it into her kneepad.

◆ ◆ ◆

It was shortly after 8:00 p.m. when she woke up, all of her joints stiff, her knee throbbing with pain. She'd definitely overdone it today and her body was protesting. Her skin was sticky and she smelled like she'd bathed in garlic sauce.

She went to the bathroom, and as much as she wanted to avoid her reflection, it was impossible. There were mirrors everywhere and she was horrifying to see.

What made casino owners think guests wanted to see so much of themselves?

She took a Vicodin and trudged into the living room on crutches. Duncan had left her a note on the bar telling her that he was in the casino.

Eve left the suite, took the elevator down, and found him at the *CSI* slot machines. She hobbled up and took the seat at the machine next to his.

"Any luck?"

"Yes. The Feds texted us. The lot that GPS tracker was part of was sold exclusively on Amazon," Duncan said, watching the spinning wheels settle. A chalk outline, crime scene tape, and a dagger. No jackpot this time. "I submitted a very narrow warrant request to a judge I know to compel Amazon to disclose if Hallie Netter bought a tracker. I stressed in my argument that we aren't interested in seeing any of her other purchases. So now we wait."

"That's nice, but I was talking about your luck at the slots."

"I'm down forty dollars on a hundred-dollar investment in a quarter slot machine over several hours of play," he said. "I've still got plenty of time to win big or lose it all."

"How do you feel about a dinner break?"

"The buffet isn't going to make any money on me. I'll eat their profit margin."

They headed to the buffet and he was right.

They were up early the next morning. They hit the buffet one more time for a massive breakfast, then headed home.

They were passing Baker, and the world's tallest thermometer, when Duncan's phone vibrated. It was the judge's clerk, calling to say she'd granted their warrant and would email it to him. Over the next few hours, while Duncan drove, Eve called Amazon's law enforcement coordinator and sent him the warrant. He emailed her the result as they crossed into Los Angeles County at about noon.

Thirty minutes later, they were in front of Netter's gate and were being greeted by a man's voice on the speaker outside.

"Who is it?" he asked.

Eve leaned across Duncan to identify themselves, then added, "We need to talk with Mrs. Netter."

"Mom is still asleep."

"Wake her up," Eve said. "This is important."

The gates opened and they drove up to the front door.

Duncan was helping Eve out of the car when Shane Netter opened the front door. Both Duncan and Eve had seen him beside his mother and sister at the community meeting.

"I'm Shane Netter," he said. "I'm giving my sister a break today. We don't want to leave Mom alone."

"That's a good idea," Duncan said.

"I saw you both on Saturday." Shane looked at Eve. "I read about what happened to you. I thought you'd still be in the hospital."

Duncan said, "She should be, but solving your father's murder was more important to her."

Shane seemed bewildered. "But the killer has been caught."

Eve hobbled up to him on her crutches. "There have been some new developments."

"I just want this nightmare to be over. Mom sleeps most of the day. I don't think she's ready to face the reality that Dad is gone."

They went into the house, where they were met by Hallie, who was in a bathrobe and looked horrible. The left side of her face drooped and she seemed to be in a drugged stupor. Eve was very concerned.

"Are you feeling all right, Mrs. Netter?"

"I'm fine. I should be asking you that question," Hallie said, slurring her words. "I'm surprised you are already on your feet."

"Just one foot."

Both women sat down this time, facing each other on opposite hard couches in the living room, while Duncan and Shane remained standing.

"What got you out of bed?" Hallie asked Eve.

Shane answered before Eve could. "She says there's been a new development in Dad's murder."

Hallie said, "The killer hasn't been released, has he?"

"No," Eve said. "Jasper Snow is still in jail for the shootings but we don't think he killed your husband."

"I don't understand," Hallie said. "If he didn't do it, who did?"

It looked to Eve like half of Hallie Netter's face was melting, not that she was in a position to criticize anyone's physical appearance today. "The last time I was here, you scoffed at the idea your husband could be having an affair. You said he was the most honest, decent man you've ever known and had nothing to hide."

"That's right," she said.

"If that's true," Eve said, "why did you put a GPS tracker in his car?"

"I don't know what you're talking about." The droopy side of Hallie's face began to twitch.

"You're lying. We served a search warrant on Amazon. We know you bought the tracker."

Shane stared in shock at his mother. "Dad was having an affair?"

"Of course not, they've made a horrible mistake." She was slurring her words even worse than before.

"His lover's name is Jayda Montero," Eve said to Shane. "They hooked up whenever he was in Las Vegas. But that's not all your mother discovered."

"Stop!" Hallie stood up, her entire face twitching wildly, and started to pitch forward.

Duncan caught her and yelled to Shane, "Call 911. Now!"

"I'm fine," Hallie said, still in Duncan's arms. But her words came out garbled. Shane hadn't moved.

"Do it!" Duncan yelled at him again.

Shane ran to the kitchen phone and Duncan gently lowered Hallie to the couch. "Take it easy, Mrs. Netter. Help is on the way."

Duncan looked at Eve. This was not the reaction either one of them expected.

CHAPTER THIRTY

Eve and Duncan sat in the hospital cafeteria, where Duncan treated himself to lunch, while they waited for news about Hallie Netter.

Duncan took a bite of his Salisbury steak, which looked to Eve like it was created in a petri dish, and said, "I wonder if the hospital has thought about franchising the cafeteria. You know, into shopping mall food courts, places like that."

"I don't think there's a big, popular demand out there for hospital food."

"It's untapped potential." He took another bite. "I've even got a slogan: 'You Don't Have to Be Sick to Treat Yourself to This.' Or 'Don't Wait Until You're Dying to Experience a Taste of Heaven.'"

"How do you feel about airplane food?"

"It's comforting," he said.

"Comforting?"

"It reminds me of those delicious frozen Swanson TV Dinners I used to eat when I was a kid," he said. "The fried chicken was my favorite, with the whipped potatoes, mixed vegetables, and apple cobbler."

"They weren't delicious."

"Have you ever tried one?"

"How good can something called a 'TV Dinner' be?" she said, and then Lisa came into the cafeteria and joined them.

"How is Mrs. Netter?" Duncan asked. "Was it a stroke?"

"Lyme disease, from a tick bite," Lisa said. "Neurological conditions like cranial nerve palsy can happen several weeks after a bite, but in rare occasions like this, it can hit within a few days."

Eve said, "How do you know she got the bite a few days ago?"

"The doctor found the two bites, one on her chest, another on her thigh. They get a distinct bull's-eye appearance at first and that's how hers look. Rash and fatigue are usually the early symptoms," Lisa said. Eve remembered Hallie scratching her chest the last time she saw her and her son mentioning she'd been sleeping a lot. "But her son says half her face was slack yesterday. She told him it was from sleeping so much on one side. That's not normal. I don't understand why she didn't see a doctor herself."

"I do," Eve said. "Her husband was shot seven days ago by a sniper lying in the brush above the road. That's when she got bitten. She probably googled the symptoms, guessed what the cause could be, and knew how damning it would be if we found out about it."

Duncan reached into his pocket and handed Eve a set of handcuffs. "You go arrest Mrs. Netter. I'll get the warrant to search her house for the shotgun."

Eve started to get up and felt a bolt of pain, as if someone had shot her in the knee again.

Lisa helped her the rest of the way up and grabbed her crutches. "You were supposed to stay off your knee."

"I've been mostly sitting for the last few days," Eve said.

"Let me get you a wheelchair," Lisa said.

"No, thanks. I'm not Ironside."

"Who is Ironside?" Lisa asked.

"Never mind," Eve said and shambled to the ER on her crutches, Lisa standing close by in case she toppled over.

Eve asked Lisa to leave when she reached the exam room and went in to find Shane standing beside his mother's bed. Hallie Netter was on an IV and whatever was in it had helped. She looked better now. Half her face was still droopy, but the twitching had stopped.

Shane stepped between Eve and the bed. "She's in no shape to answer questions right now."

"That's because she has Lyme disease from being bitten by a tick seven days ago," Eve said. "The same day your father was killed."

"What's your point? That it was the worst day of her life? She already knows that," Shane said. "This is just God putting salt in her open wound."

Eve ignored him and looked at Hallie. "The medical evidence is irrefutable, Mrs. Netter, along with the purchase of the GPS tracker and everything else."

Shane said, "What else? What are you talking about?"

Eve held up her cracked iPhone for Hallie and Shane to see. "Before we go any further, I need to inform you that I am recording this conversation and I should state, for the record, that Shane Netter is also present."

"Present for what?" he said.

"Her arrest," Eve said.

"This is crazy," Shane said. "What are you arresting her for?"

"Murder," Eve said, then recited Hallie's rights and asked if she understood them.

"Yes," Hallie said.

Shane pointed at Eve. "Your senseless harassment of my mom is cruel and barbaric. My sister is right. You people are monsters. Don't say a word, Mom."

"She doesn't have to, Shane. We know what happened." Eve looked at Hallie. "You were enraged about your husband's affair and the sniper shootings gave you a chance to do something about it. He called you from Las Vegas and told you when he'd be home. You figured you had about four hours to get into position. To be on the safe side, you got there a couple hours ahead of time to find the perfect spot. You waited in the thick brush for your husband to drive up the road, then you shot him in the head. His car went off the cliff and you ran back to your house. That's why you were sweaty and out of breath when I came to your door, not from biking the Alps on your Peloton."

Shane looked at his mom, who was staring at Eve. "Tell her it's not true. That it's crazy."

Eve met Hallie's gaze. "After that, you were basically trapped in your house for two days while our forensic team worked the crime scene and your kids have been with you ever since. You haven't had a chance to ditch the shotgun. We're searching your house now and we're going to find it."

That was a lie, but Hallie didn't know that. She slumped her head in resignation. It was all over.

Shane took her hand. "Mom? Say something."

When Hallie raised her head, there was anger in her eyes as she looked at Eve. "It wasn't the affair that bothered me. I could have lived with that. It was the bribes. If he admitted to those, he'd go to prison and we'd lose everything." She turned to her son. "We'd have been destitute. We wouldn't have been able to pay for Harvard for you or USC for your sister anymore."

Shane let go of his mother's hand. "You . . . *murdered Dad?*"

"I did it for you," she said.

Shane backed away from his mom in horror.

"He didn't give me any choice. Don't you see? Your futures, your lives, would have been ruined. But if he was dead, the FBI had no case. You had a chance of coming out of this unscathed."

"Unscathed? *You killed our dad.* That's a wound that will never heal." Shane left the room and Eve could hear him vomiting in the hall. Apparently, vomiting under stress was a family trait. She hoped Hallie wasn't going to vomit now, too.

"Where is the shotgun?" Eve asked.

"Under my bed."

"Where did you get it?"

"We've had it for years," Hallie said. "We use it to shoot rabbits, otherwise we'd have no grass left."

That might also explain some of the "shots fired" reports deputies had received from people over the last year, Eve thought. "How did you find out about the bribes?"

"I've been aware of those since he worked for Villegas, not that Clark ever came out and said it. But it was the visits to the house in Woodland Hills that worried me. I gave the address and the license plate numbers of the cars outside to a private detective I hired online."

Eve could see how it played out. "The PI told you about the off-shore ownership of the house and that some of the cars belonged to the federal government."

"I realized that Clark was flipping Villegas. What a stupid, gutless decision," Hallie said. "I thought Clark was a smart, strong man. It just shows you never really know anyone. So I did what any mother would do in my situation."

"Most mothers don't murder the father of their children."

"A mother will do anything to protect them."

Eve slipped one handcuff on Hallie's wrist and the other to the rail of her bed. "And I'm protecting everybody from you."

"I want to make a deal," Hallie said.

"What do you have to offer?"

"Clark wasn't just Councilman Villegas' chief of staff. He was his most trusted confidant. His fixer," Hallie said. "Villegas has done far worse than accept bribes from developers. I also know Clark. He kept insurance in case Villegas ever turned against him. I know where it's hidden."

Eve went out into the hallway, where an orderly was mopping up Shane's vomit, and called Special Agent Oakland.

When he answered, she said, "I have a gift for you."

◆ ◆ ◆

The mood was tense in Captain Dubois' office. Lansing was there, pacing in front of the captain's desk and so were Biddle and Garvey, sitting in the two office chairs. Nobody seemed particularly happy with Eve and Duncan, who sat side by side on the couch, facing the others.

Lansing pointed at Duncan. "You were on vacation days until retirement." He pointed at Eve. "You were on medical leave. But you both decided to conduct a rogue investigation on a closed murder case anyway."

Eve was tired, hurting all over, and not in the mood to be lectured for doing the right thing. "If we hadn't, sir, Jasper Snow would have been prosecuted for a crime he didn't commit and Councilman Netter's actual killer would have gone free."

Dubois said, "You should have notified me of your concerns, or Detectives Biddle and Garvey. Instead, you called Duncan, who was on forced vacation leave in lieu of suspension, and went off on your own merry way, falsely representing yourselves as detectives on official duty."

"You were all certain that Snow committed the two killings," Eve said. "Would you have taken our concerns about the case seriously without any evidence to back them up?"

"Of course we would," Dubois said.

"I don't think so," Eve said.

"It doesn't matter what you think," the captain said. "We have a chain of command. We have procedures. We have rules. But you treat them as suggestions. You do not get to choose which rules and procedures you want to follow. You obey them. And if you don't, there are serious consequences for misconduct."

Garvey spoke up. "Not for her. Not before and sure as hell not this time. Let's be honest about that. Look at her. You really think you can get away with punishing a detective who was shot by a deputy and two days later, despite her wounds and her place getting firebombed, caught the killer of a city councilman? She has your balls in a vise and knows it."

That was true. But she'd heard all of these complaints about her behavior before. The way she saw it, she was being criticized for conduct male cops would be respected for, especially if it resulted in closing big cases, as it had for her. So none of their whining meant anything to her.

Biddle said, "She's also jeopardized our case against Snow. Now his lawyer is going to argue that the other shootings Snow is charged with were committed by someone else."

"Maybe they were," Eve said.

Garvey slapped his knee. "There it is."

"There *what* is?" she asked.

"The real reason you're limping around on this crusade, which is obvious to everybody in this room."

"Justice," she said.

"Ego," Garvey said. "You can't accept that somebody else besides you solved the Malibu Sniper case . . . so you're going to do everything you possibly can to undermine it. You can't stand the spotlight being on any other detective."

Duncan raised his hand. "I think this is a good time to remind you that Hallie Netter confessed to killing her husband. Snow didn't do it. That's a fact."

Lansing nodded. "Yes, it is. Snow committed a string of shootings and a murder. Two other people copied his methods to do shootings of their own. All Hallie Netter's arrest today proves is that we are thorough. We don't rest. I think that reflects well on this department and I can argue that our diligence, and this arrest, actually makes our case against Snow stronger. Now it's irrefutably rock solid."

"I don't think it is," Eve said.

Biddle groaned. "Of course you don't."

"If your case against Snow is rock solid," Eve said, "then Duncan and me giving it a second look shouldn't make a difference. But if it's *not* solid, it's going to be better for you, and for the department, if we find the holes and not Snow's lawyer, because you can bet your ass he's looking for them now, too."

Lansing stopped his pacing and considered what she'd said. "You make a good point. You and Duncan go ahead and give the case a close examination. But quietly. I don't want the press finding out."

"We can do that." Eve reached for her crutches and started to get up.

"Hold it. I'm not done," Lansing said. "The captain is right. So are Biddle and Garvey. You have no respect for authority or procedure and you keep getting away with it."

Duncan said, "She's not getting away with anything."

Biddle looked at Duncan. "I've never seen her get her hand slapped."

"She's suffered much worse than that," Duncan said. "Take a good, hard look at her." All heads turned to Eve. "She's only twenty-six years old. She's bruised, scarred, and filled with bird shot. How many times has she been in the hospital in the last five months? How many of her bones has she broken? She's paying a steep price for her bad decisions and is too arrogant and self-destructive to realize it."

Eve turned to Duncan. "Gee, thanks. I thought you were on my side."

"I am. If you go on like this, they won't need to punish you. You'll be dead in a year. I don't want that to happen."

She'd heard him say this before, too, a hundred times. She didn't buy it before or now. In fact, this time it made her angry. But she kept her mouth shut, at least for the moment.

Lansing said, "You share the blame, Duncan. You've been enabling her."

"Yes, I have, but in a few days, that won't be an issue anymore, will it?"

"If you two find anything wrong with the case against Snow, or discover any new leads, you will share them with Biddle and Garvey immediately, and you'll brief Captain Dubois before you take any action," Lansing said. "Is that clear?"

Eve said, "Yes, sir."

"Garvey and Biddle will handle the paperwork on the Netter case. You two are dismissed," Lansing said, then offered Eve his hand. She took it and let him pull her to her feet. "Try to work from bed, Eve. I don't want your leg getting amputated because you didn't rest."

She reached for her crutches and left the office with Duncan. Lansing closed the door behind them.

Eve faced Duncan. "You are such a hypocrite. You were totally behind the Vegas trip and were as into it as I was. But you stabbed me in the back in there."

"You're right, I encouraged you. I let my desire to stick it to Lansing for covering up the shootings, and suspending me when I called him on it, overcome my good judgment. It was a mistake and I own it. I'm sorry you see that as a betrayal. The truth is, I am scared for you, Eve."

"I wasn't in any physical danger today," she said and kept going toward the detectives' squad room.

"You're missing the whole point of what I said in there. You were shot and fell off a cliff. Any sane person would have stayed in bed until she got well."

"And Hallie Netter would have gone unpunished for murder."

They entered the room and Duncan slammed the door behind him. "That's a bullshit argument. You could have waited until you were healed and back on duty, then told Crockett, Tubbs, and the captain about your problems with the case."

"What if they didn't listen? What if the captain refused to let me go to Las Vegas? We would never have known about the casino surveillance footage, the bribes, Banning's involvement, or that Netter was an FBI informant."

"You don't know that," he said, "and it certainly doesn't mean Hallie Netter would've walked."

"How do you know?"

"Because you weren't going to give up on the GPS tracker lead. That would have been the first thing you jumped on when you got back. You would have found out that Hallie bought it and she still would have been hospitalized for the severe reaction to the tick bites," Duncan said. "So yes, I'm sure you would have nailed her for murder. The rest, including the bribes and the FBI involvement, would have followed. You'd be exactly where you are right now without the sheriff, the captain, and two good detectives resenting the hell out of you."

He had a strong argument, she had to admit. Besides, she could never be mad at Duncan for long for caring about her well-being.

"Okay, I'll give you that. From now on, I'll try not to be such a loner."

"It's more than that. Respect command. Follow the rules."

"I've never broken the law," she said.

"You know what I mean," he said. "Slow down, don't be in such a hurry. Give yourself time to think and, especially, to heal."

"Oh, spare me. I'm tired of your rant about my injuries. It's totally wrong and insulting."

"I've been a cop for thirty years, I've put dozens of killers in prison, and I didn't get anything more than minor scrapes and bruises until you came along."

"So you keep saying. Good for you. You're blessed. I'm not so lucky. Except for my broken wrist, which I got saving a child's life, all of my injuries were inflicted on me by some very bad people who didn't want to be arrested. They weren't caused by any rogue actions or rash decisions of mine. Do you think I want all these injuries? Really? What the hell is the matter with you?

She threw her crutches at him and took a seat in a chair. "I feel the pain and see what it's doing to my body and it scares me, too. Believe me."

Duncan picked up her crutches and propped them against her desk. "I'm sorry. I really am. I just hate seeing you hurt."

"I hate it more than anybody. But for me, injuries just come with the job," Eve said. "I wish they didn't, but I'm done letting you or anybody else criticize me for something I'm powerless to stop."

"You could move into parking enforcement," he said. "Those guys rarely get hurt."

"I know a parking enforcement officer who got stabbed six times for giving a guy a parking ticket. She transferred to a safer department."

"Which one?"

"The gang unit," Eve said.

"How do you want to tackle the case?"

"I don't. I overdid it today. Tomorrow I'll be a good patient, work from bed, and keep my knee on ice."

"Good idea. I'll join you."

"In bed?"

"A chair beside the bed," Duncan said. "Don't be a smart-ass."

"That's something I don't think I can change."

Eve had Duncan take her to the Hyatt in Woodland Hills, because they had room service, and she got a room with two double beds, one for her and one for Duncan to use as a workstation the following day.

Duncan went up with her to her room, loaded up her ice machine with ice, and headed home.

Eve got into bed, took a Vicodin, and, before going to sleep, texted Nan and asked for all the DNA reports on the body fluids recovered from the rock pond.

She woke up at 2:00 a.m., starving, her knee aching, the ice in her machine melted. She limped to the bathroom, gave herself a sponge bath, plucked a couple of shotgun pellets from her left buttock, and dropped them in the trash, the pellets pinging on the bottom of the can.

She put on a bathrobe, called the front desk, and ordered a cheese-burger, a chocolate shake, and a bucket of ice for her machine.

Once her dinner and ice were delivered, she settled into bed again but couldn't get back to sleep. So she checked her email on her phone. There were hundreds of texts and inquiries from reporters, including several from Zena Faust.

Amid it all, Eve found the DNA reports from Nan. She opened up the report on the urine on the tree and saw it was a 100 percent match for Jasper Snow, who was already in CODIS from his prior arrests and a short stint in the marines. She thought Snow, according to his DNA, had an interesting ethnic makeup—70 percent European (of which he was 28 percent Northwestern European, 23 percent British Isles, and 19 percent Iberian) and 30 percent Indigenous American (primarily from Brazil, Mexico, and Peru).

The vomit at the scene was from a woman, but there were no DNA matches on it in CODIS. She was 51.3 percent Ashkenazi Jewish, 31.2 percent Northwestern European (26 percent North Rhine-Westphalia), 14.2 percent Southern European (mostly from Calabria, Italy), and 3.3 percent Native American, specifically Chumash and Tongva.

Eve fired off a text to Burnside, requesting that she obtain a search warrant to serve on the top commercial genealogical/ancestry sites to find any matches for the unidentified profile from the vomit.

But she was just being thorough.

Eve already knew who the Malibu Sniper was and that she wouldn't be going back to sleep again tonight.

CHAPTER
THIRTY-ONE

Promptly at 7:00 a.m., after a night in bed spent googling on her cracked iPhone for any details she could find on all of the Malibu Sniper shooting victims, Eve called Sheriff Lansing on his private line.

"It's never good news when you call me," he said.

"This is, sir, depending on how you look at it."

"Uh-oh."

"Jasper Snow isn't the Malibu Sniper."

"You know that already?"

"Garvey and Biddle had the evidence to arrest the right person, but to be fair to them, and through no fault of their own, they didn't have the prior experience or knowledge necessary to realize it."

"But you do," the sheriff said.

"Duncan and I are going to save the department a lot of embarrassment. *Again*," she said. "I want something out of it."

"You're supposed to do your job because it *is your job*," he said angrily, "or have you forgotten that?"

"No, sir, I haven't and there's no detective who personifies that ethic, day after day, year after year, more than Duncan Pavone," she said. "So tell him he doesn't have to retire, even though he signed the papers and he took the buyout months ago. Offer him his job back. Let him break the deal."

"Is that what he wants?"

"I don't know," Eve said, "but I want to give him that option."

Eve knew how much he enjoyed detective work and how good he was at it. She wanted Duncan to be absolutely sure he wasn't doing something he'd regret simply because he'd already signed the papers. But most of all, it was for selfish reasons. She needed him and wanted to force him to reconsider his decision, if only for a moment.

"What terrible thing will happen if I don't make him that offer?"

"I'll talk to the press and the big story will be that a wounded detective, shot by a corrupt deputy and frustrated by the incompetence of her department, staggered out of her hospital room to set things right. She joined her retiring partner to prevent an innocent man from being convicted of the serial shootings that the sheriff and his command team either covered up or were too inept to recognize . . . and she and her partner did it by catching the actual killers by themselves."

"And if I do what you want? What exciting benefit do I get?"

"The story will be that the work of your handpicked task force didn't stop when they had the suspected serial shooter in custody. Their rigorous professionalism, and tireless devotion to the concept of 'innocent until proven guilty,' drove them to question every assumption, and every piece of evidence, again and again," she said. "That dedication to the truth led to Jasper Snow's release, with our profound apologies, and the arrest of the guilty party. This illustrates that your department isn't in a rush to close cases to placate the media or respond to public outcry. It's about getting it right. It's about justice."

"I made a mistake promoting you to homicide," Lansing said. "I should've put you in charge of public relations. I'm going to use all of that, word for word."

"Does that mean we have a deal?"

"I'll ask Duncan to stick around, to let me tear up our buyout deal, because we can't afford to lose him while he's still at the top of his game, not because of your attempted blackmail, which borders on a criminal offense."

"Arrest me," Eve said.

"Listen carefully, Eve. I'm done making deals with you, tacitly or otherwise. You work for me. You will follow my orders or I will fire you. And if you ever threaten me again, I will crush you. Are we clear?"

"Yes, sir," she said.

"Brief the captain, Garvey, and Biddle on what you know," he said. "And arrest the bastard."

Duncan showed up at eight, meeting Eve in the lobby so he could mooch off the Hyatt's complimentary breakfast buffet for their guests.

"It's not the Feast of Kings Buffet, but it will do," Duncan said. "I never thought of prime rib and shrimp for breakfast before visiting Côte d'Azur, but they broadened my perspective."

"It's good to know you're open to expanding your worldview."

"You're in a jolly mood."

"I know who the Malibu Sniper is," she said.

Duncan stared at her. "Who is it?"

Eve led him into the buffet, and while he ate his scrambled eggs, bacon, pancakes, and waffles, she had a bowl of cornflakes and milk, answered his questions, and explained how she came to her conclusion.

"That just proves my point," he said.

"Which one?" Eve said, disappointed that he didn't seem wowed by her work. "I have a hard time keeping track."

"You don't have to be all about the case. You can relax and have a life," he said. "You'd have made this discovery today even if you'd gone home every day last week at six, had a nice dinner, watched a movie or read a book, and had a good night's sleep."

"Actually, I would have made the discovery Sunday if Snell hadn't shot me."

"That's right, you would have," he said. "You're making my point for me."

"That I should eat dinner every night at six?"

"That most cases have their own natural, inevitable progression. All you have to do is perform the basic, tried-and-true investigative legwork, sit back, and let everything fall into place. The answer will emerge organically, you don't have to beat it out. It often feels to me like my cases solve themselves."

"I've never had that feeling," Eve said.

"You're having it now."

"No I'm not."

"I am," he said.

"Because *I* just solved the case for you."

"That's my point."

"You have too many points," she said. "You're giving me a headache."

"Eat something," he said. "You'll feel much better."

She had an apple, he had another stack of pancakes, and then they got in his car and drove to Lost Hills station to brief the captain.

◆ ◆ ◆

An hour later, Duncan and Eve arrived at Raylene Bradley's mobile home in a plain-wrap Explorer. Eve got out with her crutches and shuffled to the front door with Duncan. Raylene was waiting for them naked in the open doorway.

"I'm surprised to see you, Detective Ronin, after what you've been through," she said, "and the sour, unpleasant end to our last conversation."

"I've thought about that while I've been recuperating," Eve said. "It's why we're here. We couldn't close the Malibu Sniper case without seeing you again."

"To apologize?" she said.

"To thank you for your invaluable help," Eve said. "And, to be honest, to have another smoothie. I remember Chase saying they reduce inflammation and these painkillers I'm taking are tearing up my stomach."

Raylene stepped aside to let them in. "Then it's perfect timing. He was just starting to make breakfast."

They went in. Chase Orkett stood naked in the kitchen, chopping up vegetables for the smoothies. This time, Eve was glad to see them both naked and she was sure Duncan was, too.

Raylene closed the door. "Two more smoothies for the detectives, Chase."

Orkett looked up from his cutting board. "It depends if they've come to offend us again."

"Actually, they say our help was invaluable to them," Raylene said.

"Well hell, glad to be of service to our community," Orkett said and smiled at Eve. "Is it true a crooked deputy shot you, threw you off a cliff, and you climbed back out and shot him?"

"Basically, yes." Eve took a seat at the kitchen table.

"That's hard-core. You really are Deathfist."

Raylene took the seat beside her. "Some good came out of all of this tragedy and violence."

Duncan sat down, too. "What's that?"

"With Councilman Netter dead, so is New Positano," Raylene said, "which would have been an obscene blight on these hills."

"I've been thinking a lot about your devotion to this land," Eve said, "and especially your tribal sunburst tattoo."

Raylene looked down at her left nipple and the rays of the sun around it. "Do you want one?"

"I'm not 1/30th Chumash."

Orkett dumped some veggies in the blender. "You don't have to be. I'm not and I got one."

Duncan said, "You know who else is 1/30th Chumash?"

"Scarlett Johansson?" Orkett said. They all looked at him. He shrugged. "She would be a surprise, that's all I'm saying."

"Here's a surprise," Eve said. "So is the Malibu Sniper."

"How do you know?" Orkett asked.

"The sniper puked after shooting Kim and Zena," Eve said.

"I can understand getting sick," Duncan said. "It was a horrible sight, especially if you knew the victims."

Raylene seemed confused. "I don't understand. How do you know the sniper is 1/30th Chumash?"

"You told us," Eve said. "And so did the DNA in your vomit."

"I didn't shoot Kim and Zena," Raylene said.

Duncan said, "Sure you did. Vomit doesn't lie."

Eve had never heard that truism before. "This vomit also had the ingredients from your smoothies in it. Not only that, we know why you're drinking them. Chase mentioned how good they are for dealing with inflammation. You definitely need the smoothies for that, because all those Advils you're taking are eating away your stomach, giving you an ulcer. That's why you've been wolfing down antacids."

Raylene stared at her in astonishment.

Duncan took a folded paper out of his jacket and set it on the table. "This is a search warrant. You ditched the shotgun, but I'm guessing you didn't think to toss the ammo. We'd also like a look at your shoes. Did you know that worn shoe treads are as unique as fingerprints? We found plenty of impressions at the crime scene. For instance, does anybody here happen to own a pair of Adidas, size eleven?"

Now it was Orkett's turn to look astonished.

Eve faced Raylene. "The warrant also allows us to take a DNA sample from you, but that's just a formality. We've already matched the

DNA from the vomit to the sample you submitted to the genealogy website you used to discover your Chumash ancestry."

That was a lie, but there was no law saying Eve had to be truthful.

"I was in the park, I'm always in the park, and I got sick," Raylene said. "So what? I didn't shoot Kim and Zena."

"Yes, you did. You're under arrest," Eve said. "You have the right to remain silent. Anything you say can and will be used against you in a court of law . . ."

"She told you she didn't do it," Orkett shouted and turned on the gas burners on the stove, which struck Eve as a very odd thing for him to do. Was he going to fry some eggs?

"We can prove she did," Eve said.

"You're wrong. *I* shot them," Orkett said.

Eve didn't see that coming, but it didn't change anything. Even if what Orkett said was true, Raylene was an accomplice to the killings and he was likely doing her bidding anyway. Raylene could also have pulled the trigger in some or all of the earlier shootings.

Orkett stepped away from the flames on the stove and brandished a bright-yellow little butane lighter shaped like a gun that was used for lighting candles, barbecues, campfires, and the like. "Now get the fuck out of here and take Raylene with you if you want to live."

The situation was getting more bizarre by the minute, Eve thought.

Duncan was unmoved and frowned at Orkett. "You're naked and holding a lighter. I'm dressed and have a Glock. I win."

"I turned on the gas burners, dumb shit," Orkett said. "If you don't get your asses out now, this flame will ignite the gas, and boom, you'll all be blown up with me."

Raylene stood up. "Chase, please don't do this."

"I'm a free spirit, you know that," he said. "I can't be a caged bird. I have to be able to soar. I'd rather die than be locked in a cell."

It may have been a heartfelt sentiment on Orkett's part, but Eve was confused. Perhaps it was the meds she was on, but she couldn't understand what he was thinking and she didn't feel the least bit threatened. She glanced at Duncan, and apparently he felt the same way she did.

Duncan casually gestured to the stove. "You see the flames on your burners, sport?"

"Yeah," Orkett said, waving his lighter in the general direction of the burners. "It means the gas is on and the clock is ticking, asshole."

"It means the gas is already burning," Duncan said. "You can stand there all day with that lighter and nothing is going to happen."

The look on Orkett's face said *Oh shit.*

Orkett's desperate gaze shifted to the knife on the counter. Duncan drew his Glock and leveled it at Orkett's groin.

"If you twitch in the direction of that knife, or even a spatula, I'll shoot you," Duncan said wearily. "Drop the lighter, put your hands behind your head, get down on your knees, then lie flat on the floor."

Orkett did as he was told.

Raylene sat down slowly and began to cry.

Eve finished reading them both their rights. She and Duncan could sort out exactly who did what when they got back to the station, separated Raylene and Orkett, and placed them in different interrogation rooms for questioning. Maybe Eve and Duncan could even get one of them to crack and agree to testify against the other in exchange for a plea deal that was less than life behind bars. Regardless, Eve knew these two were going down for a very, very long time.

Duncan got up, went over to Orkett, and restrained him with handcuffs, then stood over him, shaking his head.

"What a doofus," Duncan said.

That was true, Eve thought, but a deadly one.

She looked at Raylene. "Turn around and put your hands behind your back."

Raylene did. Eve placed her in handcuffs and decided to underscore to Raylene just how bad her situation was to soften her up a bit for questioning.

"We've got more on you than DNA and shoes, Raylene. You had a motive to shoot them all. Each victim, in some way, violated one of your causes or opposed you. Paul Banning razed a hilltop for his house. The Truccos shot at a mountain lion who attacked their animals. Stony Jarrett gave the Truccos their predation permit. Derek Hayes wouldn't let people on a public beach. Harriet Winstead cut down heritage oaks to create a view. Jay and Joy Dube picked native plants from the park to bring home. Marco Fitch was one of the construction workers building a hotel that would deface the hillside. Chloe Stark desecrated the park with her masturbation video. Do I need to go on?"

"We didn't hurt any of them," Raylene said. "We only wanted to scare them off. It was the same with Zena."

"No, it wasn't," Eve said. "With her, it was personal. She insulted you. She betrayed you. So she had to die."

Orkett lifted his face from the floor. "It was an accident. I meant to shoot above their heads, not blow them off."

"Don't be so crass, Chase," Raylene said. "I loved Kim . . . and to see her like that . . ." She started to cry again.

"It made you sick," Eve said.

Duncan looked down at Orkett. "You wiped the shotgun and tossed it in a ravine."

Raylene said, "I couldn't let him bring it back in the house after that."

"Because it was incriminating," Duncan said.

"Because it was a tool of death," she said, "and this is a place of purity, peace, and harmony."

"Oh, yes," Duncan said. "I can see that."

He stepped outside and waved to the two patrol cars that were parked on the street, inviting in the deputies to come take the two killers away.

CHAPTER
THIRTY-TWO

The news of the arrests played out that day pretty much as Eve had envisioned it during her call with Lansing. Duncan spoke briefly to the press, basically following a script Lansing had given him, portraying the arrests as the result of a team effort, led by the sheriff and the captain, and that included Garvey, Biddle, and Eve.

The charges against Jasper Snow, including those for breaking and entering, were dropped in exchange for his confidential written promise not to sue the department.

Snow's lawyer wanted to have a press conference, too, but Snow refused to participate, insisting on remaining in his unlocked cell until he was good and ready to leave. It was unusual, but the captain ordered everyone to give the man his space.

So the lawyer did his press conference alone, getting his cherished moment on TV, and went back to his Century City office.

Jasper Snow walked out of the Lost Hills station late that night, after eating a take-out dinner from Taco Bell, courtesy of the captain, and shortly after all the reporters were finally gone. But Eve Ronin was lingering outside on her crutches, waiting for him.

He nodded at her. "I remember you. You gave me a breakfast biscuit last week."

"That's right," she said.

"My lawyer says you're the one who believed me and got me out."

"I'm sorry this happened to you," Eve said. "It was wrong."

"Now you know why I hate people. Nothing good ever comes from being around them."

"It can be good and bad."

He motioned to her crutches. "What happened to you?"

"The bad," she said. "Where will you go?"

"Somewhere nobody else is . . . where I can be alone . . . and find food without breaking into places. The pioneers of the Old West did it. So I suppose I can."

"Those were different times."

"Better times," he said.

"If you ever need any help, give me a call." Eve handed him her card.

"Why are you doing this for me?"

"So I can feel good about myself," she said.

He nodded and walked away, up into the hills behind the station. Eve watched him until he disappeared into the darkness.

Duncan came out of the station and stood beside her. "I just did an Eve Ronin."

"What does that mean?"

"I leveraged the overwhelming positive press I've been getting since Saturday to convince the sheriff that it would be good PR for the department if he gave me a medal and allowed me to change my mind about accepting the department's buyout offer to retire, even though I signed the papers months ago and it's way, way past the cancellation deadline. This whole experience has shown me that I can still do some good."

"He must have loved that," she said.

"He tried to make it seem like it was his idea and not mine to tear up the buyout deal and pretend it never happened."

"Of course he did," Eve said. "So does that mean you're going to be staying on the job?"

"In an advisory capacity. More of a consultant than a full-time detective. The details are still being worked out."

"That's wonderful. How is your wife going to take the news?"

"Those are the details I still have to work out," he said. "She had her heart set on moving to Palm Springs."

"I am so happy for you, but mostly for me," Eve said. "Now you will be here for both real me and fake me."

"Fake you?"

"The TV character," she said. "We both need you watching our backs and keeping us honest."

"That's one of the reasons I decided to put off my retirement. Real you needs me more than fake you does right now. I mean, just look at you."

"Thanks," she said.

"I'm still going on vacation and you're on medical leave for a few more weeks. I'm sure Gracie will keep me busy furnishing the Palm Springs condo. What are you going to do with your free time? Find Jimmy Hoffa's body?"

"I'll try to relax," she said. "My mind and body need the rest."

"I'm glad to hear that, but your place is in ashes. Where are you going to stay? At the Hyatt? Or with your mother?"

"Tarawa," she said. "A remote, little island in the South Pacific."

"Isn't that where Indiana Jones is?"

"Yes. Daniel has finished his work there but he can stay as long as he wants," she said. "He's invited me to join him. We'll have the beach to ourselves. We can live like castaways."

"Sounds romantic. You may not want to come back."

She looked at the station, and beyond it to the Santa Monica Mountains in the moonlight. It was her land as much as it was Raylene Bradley's. Eve's scars were her tattoos of devotion, not to the dirt and trees, but to the people who lived there. Someone had to protect them. Someone had to restore order. Someone had to right the wrongs.

"I'll be back," Eve Ronin said. "That's a promise."

Author's Note and

Acknowledgments

This book is entirely a work of fiction, but it was inspired by a series of actual shootings in and around Malibu Creek State Park that culminated in the murder of a man camping in a tent with his two young children.

I attended the August 19, 2018, community meeting at King Gillette Ranch, where local politicians, state park officials, and detectives from the Los Angeles County Sheriff's Department briefed residents about the shootings. The authorities stated that the killing and the various shootings reported in the area over the years were totally unrelated, which nobody in the audience seemed to believe, including me. I took copious notes. When the meeting was over, I knew that I had another case for Eve Ronin.

I continued to follow the real-life investigation, which was rife with controversy and, in a bizarre and troubling twist, led to lawsuits being filed against the LASD by some of the detectives involved in the case and who spoke at the meeting. I won't go into the details here. You can google them for yourself, but it makes for some very interesting reading.

My fictional resolution to the mystery is very different from how the real case turned out, though as I write this in the final days of 2021, there are still many unanswered questions about the investigation, which have sparked numerous conspiracy theories and this book, too.

In October 2018, a homeless man living in the park was arrested for the deadly shootings, which the LASD conceded *were* all related, a belated admission that surprised no one. The alleged shooter was only recently declared mentally competent to stand trial and is awaiting his day in court. Perhaps that day will have come—or will have already passed—by the time you read this.

This all happened against the backdrop of a huge, and ever-widening, corruption scandal involving Los Angeles city and county politicians that is still playing out with new, shocking revelations, seemingly every day. I was inspired by some aspects of those bribery scandals for this story.

I should mention that the Calabasas City Council has not been implicated in, or accused of, corruption of any kind and that the integrity of the council members has not been doubted, certainly not by me, nor do I intend to imply otherwise with my story. I've known many of our city council members and sincerely admire the work they do for our community. Not only that, but they have been enthusiastic supporters of the Eve Ronin series, so they must be terrific people.

I am indebted to Danielle R. Galien, associate professor of criminal justice at Des Moines Area Community College; Pamela Sokolik-Putnam, supervising deputy coroner investigator for the San Bernardino County Sheriff-Coroner Department; Alyssa Moser, deputy coroner investigator for the San Bernardino County Sheriff-Coroner Department; Kelsey Parsons, deputy sheriff, San Bernardino County Sheriff's Department; Judge David Ellis, Illinois Appellate Court, First District; Daniel Winterich, professor of criminal justice, Lakeland Community College; Jason Weber, public safety coordinator at Northeast Wisconsin Technical College; Karen Dinino, attorney-at-law; former law enforcement officers–turned-authors Paul Bishop, Robin Burcell, and David Putnam; and doctors-turned-authors D. P.

Lyle and Melissa Yi for sharing their invaluable experience and knowledge with me.

In my research, I also drew upon the excellent reporting of journalists Dana Goodyear (for the *New Yorker*), Ian Bradley (for the *Acorn*), Devon O'Neil (for *Outside*), Scott Johnson and Peter Kiefer (for the *Hollywood Reporter*), Libby Denkmann (for the *Laist*), Cece Woods (for the *Local Malibu*), and Al Seib, Emily Albert Reyes, David Zahniser, and Joel Rubin (for the *Los Angeles Times*). Brian Rooney's wonderful book *Three Magical Miles: L.A.'s Amazing Historical Neighborhood* was also very helpful to me.

Eve Ronin is back again thanks to the enthusiastic support of my editors Gracie Doyle, Megha Parekh, and Charlotte Herscher, the marketing skills of Dennelle Catlett, and the negotiating powers of Amy Tannenbaum.

Finally, the city of Calabasas, Malibu Creek State Park, the Lost Hills station, West Hills Hospital, and many other places mentioned in this book actually exist. But I've taken broad creative liberties with geography, police procedure, and other inconvenient aspects of reality for the sake of telling my story. I hope you didn't mind.

About the Author

Photo © 2013 Roland Scarpa

Lee Goldberg is a two-time Edgar Award and two-time Shamus Award nominee and the #1 *New York Times* bestselling author of more than forty novels, including the Eve Ronin series and the Ian Ludlow series. He has also written and/or produced many TV shows, including *Diagnosis Murder, SeaQuest,* and *Monk,* and he is the cocreator of the *Mystery 101* series of Hallmark movies. As an international television consultant, he has advised networks and studios in Canada, France, Germany, Spain, China, Sweden, and the Netherlands on the creation, writing, and production of episodic television series. You can find more information about Lee and his work at www.leegoldberg.com.